P9-CAO-353

# STARFIRE

**ALSO BY CHARLES SHEFFIELD**

Tomorrow and Tomorrow
Aftermath

# STAR FIRE

# CHARLES SHEFFIELD

SPECTRA ™

BANTAM BOOKS
NEW YORK   TORONTO   LONDON   SYDNEY   AUCKLAND

STARFIRE
A Bantam Spectra Book / October 1999

SPECTRA and the portrayal of a boxed "s" are trademarks of Bantam Books, a division of Random House, Inc.

ISBN 0-7394-0791-0

*Published simultaneously in the United States and Canada*

Bantam Books are published by Bantam Books, a division of Random House, Inc. Its trademark, consisting of the words "Bantam Books" and the portrayal of a rooster, is Registered in U.S. Patent and Trademark Office and in other countries. Marca Registrada. Bantam Books, 1540 Broadway, New York, New York 10036.

PRINTED IN THE UNITED STATES OF AMERICA

TO NANCY, AGAIN.

Thanks to the hardworking and demanding readers of my first draft, who helped to shape the finished product: Anne Groell, Bill Groome, Sharon Keir, and Nancy Kress.

# STARFIRE

# 1

**From the private diary of Oliver Guest.
Entry date: June 25, 2053**

When you have died once, you become most reluctant to do so again.

I had been watching the man since early afternoon, ever since my Alert system detected his presence five and a half miles to the south. He came on foot, much closer to the sea edge than I would ever go. On his back he wore a light knapsack, and in his right hand he held what looked like a solid walking stick. Ten steps to his left the three-hundred-foot cliff dropped sheer to the crawling waters of the Atlantic.

He was in no hurry, pausing from time to time to turn and stare seaward. He might be a solitary and contemplative hiker, wandering the wild west coast of Ireland from Donegal Bay to Tory Sound, admiring the scenery and enjoying his own company. He might; but that hope vanished when at the point of closest approach to the castle he made a sharp right turn and headed straight for it.

I studied him under maximum magnification as he came nearer. He was of middle height and medium build. A strong west wind blew his long hair over his forehead, and that, together with the dark beard and moustache, hid most of his features. There was, surely, nothing about him to make me nervous. Wasn't it reasonable that a walker might ask for a drink of water, or even inquire about accommodation for the night?

It was long years of caution and a determination never again to be captured that speeded my pulse and tingled along my spine.

*Above all, do no harm.*

Therefore, assume that the man is an innocent stranger, and he will come and go peacefully.

He ignored the scullery entrance, closest to his direction of approach. Instead he walked around the building to the leeward side and found the solid oak door of the main entrance. I am sensitive to loud noises, and I had covered the massive iron door knocker with felt. The triple knock was soft and muffled, as though he knew he was observed and had no need of a loud announcement of his presence.

I opened the door and confirmed my first impressions. Outside the threshold stood a stranger, a man of uncertain age and nondescript clothing, long-haired and full-bearded, four or five inches shorter than me. He was not smiling, but there was an expectant look in his brown eyes.

"Good afternoon," I said. "Can I help you?"

"I don't know about that." He raised dark eyebrows and took a step closer. "But I sure as hell hope so, Doc. Because if you can't, I'm beat to say who can."

The voice and West Virginia accent provided the link, far more strongly than the casual "Doc." It had been twenty-seven years, but I knew who he was—and I knew that he knew me. My instincts shouted, "Kill him!" but instincts are highly unreliable. Moreover, I lack a talent for unpremeditated murder.

Instead I said, "Seth Parsigian. Would you like to come in?"

I did not offer my hand. He nodded, grinned—I would have recognized that smile, after much longer than twenty-seven years—and stepped through into the hallway of gray slate. He stared around him.

"I wondered if you'd recognize me," he said. "Where are the kids?"

"They are away in Sligo, and they will be gone for two days. Furthermore, I cannot believe that you are unaware of that fact."

He winked. "Could be. Not very smart of me, eh? Coming here alone, nobody else around. Might be dangerous. But I don't think it will be. You an' me, we got too much to offer each other."

That short exchange told me several things. He knew about my darlings, and I must assume that he had possessed the information for some time. And he could not be the only one with knowledge of my whereabouts. Seth Parsigian merited several unpleasant adjectives, but *stupid* was not one of them. His best insurance was that I would realize others knew where he was and would pursue me implacably if he failed to return. He was also telling me, very clearly, that the reason for his presence was not to recapture the infamous child murderer Dr. Oliver Guest, and return him to the blind cave of centuries of judicial sleep. He was here because he needed something from me.

Otranto Castle is, as castles go, of mean proportions. The short entrance hallway leads to the long dining room, and off to one side of it lies my private study. "Come in," I said, and led the way there. "Come in and sit down."

As I poured whiskey and put the pitcher of peat water beside it, I studied my visitor. My first thought, that he was here because the telomod therapy was failing, did not bear up under examination. Seth Parsigian appeared no older now than when I had last seen him, over a quarter of a century ago. If anything, he was healthier.

But if it were not the telomods, what could I possibly have to offer that might guarantee my continued freedom and safety?

He was examining me as closely as I scrutinized him.

"Looking good." He raised his glass. "Here's to the Oliver Guest telomod protocol. Been taking it yourself, haven't you?"

It was not a question that required an answer. I also appeared no older than at our last meeting. The mystery was that everyone did not employ the protocol. The teratomorphic potential, I suppose, frightened many. Speaking for myself, it interests me little what I may resemble at my death.

"How did you know that I was still alive?" I asked.

"I was pretty sure you weren't killed in the fire. The body we found had dentures. But I didn't have evidence that you weren't dead an' rotting until eleven years ago."

A most comforting statement. He had known of my existence for eleven full years, and I was still a free man.

"How did you learn that I was living, and where I could be found?"

"Oh, through the kids," he said casually. So much for all my precautions. "I figured you'd find a hiding place an' lie low for as long as you could stand, but eventually you'd not be able to resist. You'd get around to cloning 'em. I knew that if you did it one at a time, I'd never find you. But you did all eighteen too close together. I had a long-term screen on the data net for that type of anomaly, and it popped right up with the first six."

"Starting eleven years ago."

"Right." Seth picked up on my unasked question. "So why haven't I turned you in? You can answer that as well as I can."

"Because I am a specialist in telomod therapy, and if I were to be placed again into long-term judicial sleep, you would have no access to my knowledge."

I knew what Seth apparently did not. Although a pioneer—hubris tempts me to say *the* pioneer—in the techniques of telomod therapy, I left that field many years ago. I have since gone on to new researches, and others have developed protocols less risky and more routine than mine.

"A bit of that, at first." Seth, disdaining peat water, refilled his glass with neat whiskey. "But it's really a lot simpler. Try again, an' let's put it the other way round. Why *should* I turn you in?"

I considered. With Seth Parsigian there was no need for pretense. "Because I am Oliver Guest, a murderer and monster. Because I killed eighteen teenage children. Because I was sentenced after due process in a court of law to spend six centuries in judicial sleep, and most of that sentence has yet to be served."

"Not my department. Justice wants you, let Justice find you. If they can't, screw 'em. I told you, it's simpler than you think." He leaned forward. "I get you locked up an' iced down, you're gone. History. No way you can ever help me. But I leave you free, you owe me—bigtime. If I need help, you can give it to me. An' I'm telling you, Doc, I need help now."

I had been living in western Ireland for twenty-seven years, far from the scientific mainstream. True, I had indulged my own interests and followed progress in related fields through the web, but that did not add up to an ability to serve Seth Parsigian's needs.

However, it would be unwise to suggest that. Instead I said, "I'll be glad to help you. But how?"

"First, you can answer a couple of questions. I'm pretty sure I know the answers, but let's get 'em out of the way. You were a world expert on cloning—don't go modest on me an' deny it. Did you ever clone yourself?"

The idea was so ludicrous that in spite of my internal tensions I snorted with laughter. "Clone myself? Certainly not. Do you think the world is ready for a second Oliver Guest?"

"Not ready for the first one, if you ask me. But I wanted to be sure. You see, I knew you were living here and had been for ages, so cloning was a natural thought."

Not to me. But before I could comment he went on. "All right, tell me this. How much do you know about Sky City and the shield? And have you ever been out there?"

More easy questions, although disquieting ones because of their possible implications. We were moving to an area of expertise where my chances of helping Seth Parsigian were negligibly small. "I know very little about Sky City, and even less about the space shield. Far less, I suspect, than the average interested ten-year-old. I have never been into space, and furthermore I never intend to go there."

"Don't be too sure on that last one. How much have you heard about the deaths in Sky City over the past six months?"

"I have heard not one word. Don't deaths happen all the time during space construction work?"

"Not these deaths. Twelve of 'em. All teenagers. All girls. All beauties. Your personal specialty, an' you've not heard a word? Jeez." Seth stood up and walked through to stare at the dining hall, with its long, solid oak table that we used only when all my darlings were home. "I hope you got some way of feeding me tonight, Doc, because we gotta talk about those deaths on Sky City, an' we gotta figure out what's goin' on out there. An' I can tell you, from a standing start that might take us quite a while."

# interlude 1

## interlude: Sniffer, Model A.

The Sniffer had been built to serve a single purpose, but in their eagerness to achieve that goal its human creators had overengineered their product. They had intended no more than a robust machine, a versatile and long-lived sensing mechanism able to protect itself in the interstellar environment. Instead they had built an entity that inhabited the hazy boundary between sentience and nonsentience.

Certainly Sniffer-A lacked emotion and a true sense of its own place in the universe. Equally certainly it was self-aware, knowing of and concerned with the protection of its multiple parts. And certainly the Sniffer knew its own history, even if that history consisted only of the catalog of experiences since the probe was launched from Earth orbit.

The internal clock placed pointers at the key events:

The origin, before which there was nothing, not even the markers of time itself.

A few thousand seconds after the origin marked the moment of first acceleration. The Sniffer measured the Doppler frequency shift of Earth's beacon signal and approved it. As planned, the increase in speed was a uniform ten meters per second squared.

One and a half million seconds after first acceleration, Sniffer-A came to the end of the heliosphere, the great bubble of gas controlled by Sol's influence. The Sniffer was more than eleven billion kilometers from the Sun, twice as far out as the orbit of Pluto. The event came a little sooner than predicted. The Sniffer added that information to the data stream sent back to Earth and hurtled on its way, still adding to its speed.

Two million seconds after first acceleration, the mirror-matter engine ran out of fuel. The Sniffer had reached the end of acceleration and the beginning of coast phase. Terminal velocity was measured as almost twenty thousand kilometers a second, matching the mission profile to better than one part in a million.

Nothing built by humans had ever traveled so fast. The Sniffer registered small reductions in its speed as the fading gravity field of the distant Sun slowed its progress. The deceleration was in the flight profile, and it called for no remedial action.

The Sniffer checked that the guide star of Alpha Centauri lay directly ahead. Then it banked down into power-conserving mode, with the internal clock speed slowed by a factor of four million. Almost dormant, the spidery structure glided through the void between the stars. The main functions of the mission still lay far in the future.

At four hundred and eighty million seconds, almost fifteen years after launch, the incident particle flux rose above a preset threshold. The Sniffer activated all sensors and began a fine profiling of the medium through which it was now moving. At once it found differences from the projected situation.

The supercooled central brain of Sniffer-A had no circuits that might be described as worriers, but it was built to register, record, and transmit anomalies. The great bow wave of charged particles generated by the Alpha Centauri supernova had been reached ahead of time. Also, the particle mixture was grossly different from that in the mission profile.

The Sniffer began its comparisons. The particle flux was more energetic than anticipated, but that was consistent with a greater overall velocity and early arrival. A more significant oddity lay in the unexpected abundance of nuclei heavier than the protons of bare hydrogen. Everything was too plentiful, from deuterium—too weakly bound to have survived the fires of the supernova—to uranium. Odder yet, the data suggested patterns within the particles, as though the ions were somehow maintaining their exact relative separations over large distances.

Sniffer-A's analytical powers were confined to a comparison between the observations and the predictions loaded into it before launch. It contained no physical models or programs to perform correlations, and it lacked the concept of a *structure* that ions or other units might follow as they moved through space.

The data went to the communications channels, for return to Earth and to entities with the power to speculate. The Sniffer flew on. In another year, thirty million seconds on the steady internal clock, the main wave had passed. The flux of particles steadily became less.

The reduction was consistent with the onboard math models. Sniffer-A's closest equivalent to human contentment came when observations matched a preloaded profile. The Sniffer's activity level gradually decreased.

One more year, and the power levels were down to preencounter values. Sniffer-A cruised quietly on.

It would coast for another half a century. Then it would rouse itself for one final frantic spell of recording and transmission before plunging to its immolation in the turbulent supernova remnant of Alpha Centauri.

# 2

If you average seven meetings a day and there is a fifty-fifty chance that any given meeting will be a stinker, then about one day in every four months *all* your meetings will be stinkers.

President Celine Tanaka reviewed her list of appointments and decided that today was the day. In five meetings through mid-afternoon, all held outside the White House, she had heard nothing but bad news, complaints, attempted money grabs, and self-serving excuses.

In space, the mirror-matter thrustors on one whole segment of the shield were below par. But instead of correcting the problem, the manufacturer's and integrator's representatives were busy pointing fingers at each other. In other space activities, half a dozen congressional groups were pushing to have another Sniffer built and launched. Celine detected a distinct whiff of pork barrel. She made a note: *Check position and status of Sniffers.* A dozen of the high-acceleration probes were already racing to sample the particle wave front on its way from Alpha Centauri. How would another one help?

More likely, lobbyists for the Sniffers' manufacturer were behind the political moves. The game never ended. If Sol were guaranteed to go nova tomorrow, today she would hear from lobbyists for sunscreen.

Meanwhile, closer to home, the Cabinet officer in charge of energy allocation did not seem to know the differences between fossil fuel, nuclear, and solar power plants, or be able to estimate the country's base load capacity of each. The head of the United States census had just informed Celine that "sampling errors" were responsible for the obvious and grotesque inaccuracies in the population count of the West Coast states. The chief of health services offered no explanation for the rise in the infant mortality rate in the rural South, except to suggest "unusual weather." They didn't know it yet, but all three men were out of a job. Incompetence was something you might be able to tolerate in easy times. These were not easy times. There had been no easy times in the twenty-seven years since Alpha Centauri improbably went supernova.

The good news was that Celine had only two more meetings on her schedule. Returning to the White House through the overcast heat of a July afternoon, she reflected on the bad news: that her two final encounters were likely to be the worst of all. She went straight to the Oval Office, sat down in her specially designed orthopedic chair, and told the autocom: "All right, send Mr. Glover in."

The armored door slid silently open and Milton Glover marched into the office. He stood before her and inclined his head. "Ma'am."

He was a great one for offering every respect due to the presidency. His inner feelings were another matter. "Sit down, Milton. It's good to see you."

The smile he gave her was that of a man without a care in the world. He remained standing and took a long look around the sparsely decorated office. His eyes lingered on the side table with its vase of Oceanus roses. He nodded appreciatively and sat down. "I've been here many times over many years, Madam President. And I must say, I've never known this place to look so good."

Beneath the compliment lay the second message: *Presidents come and Presidents go. I was here long before your time, ma'am, and I'll be here long after you leave.*

Milton Glover was of medium height and build, with blond hair, a fair moustache, and innocent eyes of pale blue. He was in his late seventies, but the telomod treatment gave him the appearance and bearing of a man in his forties. He laughed loudly, frequently, and in Celine's opinion wholly insincerely. He was also not nearly so smart as he thought he was.

"Thank you, Milton." *Take all compliments at face value.* "How can I help you?"

She had learned the quickest way to bring a meeting to the point. Nothing could be more polite than the simple question "How can I help you?" but it cut through all flowery courtesies. Of course, it was based on a cynical assumption: No one requested a meeting with the President who *didn't* want something. So far that premise had seldom been wrong.

"I won't take much of your time, Madam President." Glover spread his hands wide. "For myself, I want absolutely nothing. I am here on behalf of a group of concerned citizens."

"How can I help *them*?"

"The Trust In Government coalition is unhappy with this nation's most recent policy statements and budget proposals. It is not too strong to say that many of them—of us—feel betrayed."

"How so?" Advice from her political mentor: *Let the visitor do the talking.*

Glover pulled an envelope from an inside pocket. "Last year, an unprecedented thirty percent of our national resources went to the global protection project. That was already far more than can be justified. Now we see from this—your budget, signed with your own hand—that you propose to increase our contribution to the World Protection Federation to almost thirty-four percent. More than a third of the country's expenditures will vanish into space."

"Where it will be used to protect our citizens. *All* our citizens—including the members of the Trust In Government coalition."

Celine could see nothing remotely humorous in her statement, but Glover laughed heartily. "Madam President, you know as well as I do that there are less expensive ways of protecting our people. Particularly when you recognize that the bulk of the funds you are proposing to give away is drawn from the members of the TIG coalition. And our members will not be the primary beneficiaries of such gross expenditures."

Their meeting was being recorded. Milton Glover knew it. His statement was as close as he would come to what he really meant: *Lots of foreigners don't contribute a dime, so screw 'em. Why should my friends and I build a space shield to protect a bunch of gooks? And why pay here at home, either, to save no-hope welfare trash and idlers who don't pull their weight?*

TIG. Trust In Government. An old political principle, to give your organization a name that's the opposite of what you mean. As Vice President Auden Travis had said to Celine, "TIG doesn't really stand for Trust In Government. It stands for Troglodytes In the

Ground. They want to dig holes to hide away from the particle storm, and to hell with everybody who has to stay outside."

Celine agreed with Travis, but Milton Glover and his friends controlled too much wealth and had too much influence to be ignored. They insisted that the mockery of language was with the World Protection Federation. WPF, their literature said, stood for Wasters, Paupers, and Foreigners.

"Milton, you give me credit for power I don't have. Even if I wanted to, I couldn't pull us out of the WPF. Remember, this country *started* the organization."

"Yes. Twenty-seven years ago, when you were still an astronaut. I know it was nothing to do with you. I don't even blame President Steinmetz." He saw her expression. Saul Steinmetz had brought her into politics, and he was her idol. Hale and hearty, though long retired, he was rich and powerful enough to be a TIG member. In fact, he was the one who had first warned Celine that the TIG consisted of a bunch of self-serving hogs.

Glover knew that Celine and Steinmetz were friends. He hurried on. "Old Saul did what seemed right at the time, starting a global effort to make the space shield. But now it looks dumber and dumber. The project is way behind schedule." (How did he know that? It was supposed to be secret information.) "A shield that's only half built when the particle storm hits is like a paper umbrella in a thunderstorm. Worse than nothing, because you don't know you have to run for cover."

"Milton, this year's budget is signed and sealed. I ask again, how can I help you?"

"I'll tell you, Madam President. It's something simple, and something you have the authority to do. The Nevada federal properties have been deserted and ignored for more than a quarter of a century. You could make them available for leasing by private interests."

Celine had been expecting another plea for reduced international support by the United States. Glover's request threw her completely. He was right; the Alpha Centauri supernova and the resulting population dip had emptied the Nevada federal lands. She had seen no mention of those lands in official reports during her five years in office. A proposal to open them to private leases would surely sail through without opposition.

But why was the TIG coalition—or anyone else—interested in Nevada? The whole state was barren desert.

Glover was not about to tell her. He was smiling smugly, waiting.

"I'll see what I can do, Milton. On the face of it, I see no reason why a request like that couldn't be granted."

"Quickly? If it would help, TIG can offer technical assistance in drafting an agreement."

"I'll see what I can do."

"Thank you, ma'am. And let me mention one other thing. If the federal lands in Nevada do get opened up for leasing, I guarantee there will be no further TIG opposition to this year's budget. In fact, we will support it." He was on his feet. "Madam President." He inclined his head politely, then turned and walked out.

Celine glanced at the clock. Four thirty-eight. Eight minutes since he walked through the door. Glover had certainly come through on his promise not to take much time. All she needed now were his motives. What did he know that she didn't?

She jotted another note to herself, *Nevada?,* and braced herself for the final appointment. She had never emerged from a meeting with her next visitor without feeling that she had been bested or manipulated—even in cases, like this one, where the meeting was held at her request. "Is Ms. Wheatstone here?"

"Not yet," the autocom said. "Her appointment is scheduled for five o'clock, nineteen minutes from now."

"Ask her to come in as soon as she arrives."

She and Maddy Wheatstone had much in common. They were bright, ambitious, overachieving women, successful in what were still largely male pursuits. Celine was farther up the ladder, but she was quite a bit older. Maddy Wheatstone had plenty of time to go anywhere she chose, and she seemed to know exactly where she wanted to go.

Celine checked the crib sheets prepared by her staff for each meeting. Maddy had just celebrated her thirty-first birthday. At that age Celine had been a member of the first Mars expedition, with never a thought of politics. Space had filled her whole life. When she first heard of the space shield it had seemed like the project of her dreams.

Celine tilted back her padded chair and stared up at the ceiling.

Far above her head, Sky City moved in its high-inclination synchronous orbit. She could visualize the looping figure-eight pattern that it followed relative to the surface of the Earth, and she knew exactly where to look in the sky to find it. Twenty years ago, when Sky City was no more than a skeleton frame and a set of ambitious plans, her own role had seemed clear. She would work on completing Sky City, then construct the space shield that would save the Earth.

The yearning was still there. So why was she down here on Earth? Even when you were President, it was no more than a desk job. She could offer only one answer: People change. What Celine needed and wanted at thirty and at sixty were not the same.

Would Maddy Wheatstone change, as Celine had? Was she, too, plagued by worries and self-doubts?

If so, she disguised it well. The Argos Group had a reputation. It took the brightest young people in the world and rewarded them generously, but it worked them so hard that they burned out fast. After an average of two years, the new recruits had taken all they could stand. They left the organization and took their pick of jobs elsewhere—often with Argos clients.

Maddy Wheatstone had worked inside that crucible for nine years. Celine had observed her through five of them. In Maddy's case, heat and pressure had not destroyed. They seemed only to strengthen and harden.

Celine heard the sound of the door sliding open and tilted her chair back to its upright position. Maddy Wheatstone stood on the threshold.

Argos representatives all had certain things in common. Politeness was observed, even in such small matters as waiting to be invited into a room. Manners were deferential, even in cases where the Argos representative was offered rudeness in return. Dress was formal, stylish, and restrained. This afternoon Maddy wore a business suit of dark green and a white blouse, secured at the neck with a single cameo brooch. The design on the brooch was the Argos Group emblem, a blue-green globe gripped by a scarlet talon. Maddy's hair was piled high on her head, with not a strand out of place. Its shining blackness contrasted with the pale and flawless complexion.

"Please, come in. Sit down." Celine wondered about her own appearance. It had been a packed day of meetings, with minimal breaks to freshen up. She waved a hand toward the side table. "Can I get you something?"

That was more a polite formality than anything else. In five years of visits, Maddy Wheatstone had never accepted any form of stimulant. Perhaps public abstinence was another part of Argos policy. But today Maddy hesitated, then shrugged.

"A fizz, maybe? I think I could use one. Our bus from Sky City was grabbed for inspection—we had a mass anomaly—so it was a long trip back."

Human weakness. It was nice to know that even Maddy admitted to it. Celine pushed a small, bulbous flask toward the other woman and watched as she filled a tiny liqueur glass.

"Aren't you going to join me?" Maddy was smiling. Celine felt the intensity of personality shining through those sparkling blue eyes—more personality than she herself had ever had.

She shook her head. "Not this late in the day. If I did, I'd never get to sleep without a downer."

"Me too. I'll worry about that later. A *lot* later. I still have a meeting with Gordy Rolfe today after we get through. Gordy was always difficult; now I think he's getting worse. Anyway." Maddy Wheatstone raised the little glass. "Here's to successful enterprises."

She drained the glass, blinked a couple of times as the fizz hit, and sat staring at Celine.

Celine wondered. Was that what was eating at Maddy? Gordy Rolfe was Maddy Wheatstone's boss, an electronics wizard of legendary reputation who was also the founder and head of the Argos Group. Since Maddy's promotion to vice president of development, Gordy was her *only* boss. Celine had met him only twice, but he seemed a person likely to bring an edge of uncertainty to any employee's voice.

Maddy was calmer now, quietly waiting. This wasn't a supplicant asking favors, where Celine's "How can I help you?" might be applied. Celine wanted something out of this meeting, and Maddy knew it.

The place to start was with the simple mechanics. "Were you able to arrange for a meeting with Bruno Colombo when you go up to Sky City again?"

"It's all set. I can't claim credit, though. Gordy Rolfe fixed it for me through Nick Lopez. He says that's the only sure way."

"And the engineer who works for Colombo?" Celine glanced at her crib sheet. "John Hyslop?"

"That's where I'll earn my pay. I have to persuade Bruno Colombo that he can spare Hyslop, then I have to make him assign him to us. I just hope we have the right man."

"You haven't met Hyslop yet?"

"No. Next time."

"But he was your group's suggestion for the person to bring the asteroid work back on schedule."

"Based on what our staff on Sky City told us. Didn't you check him out?"

Celine nodded. Of course she had. The Argos Group had suggested Hyslop, but that wasn't enough. Her checks had all come back positive: Hyslop's reputation as an engineer was superb. But that didn't stop Celine from worrying. She wanted to meet John Hyslop *herself*, to take the gauge of the man. But she couldn't hold things up waiting for that meeting.

"When are you going back to Sky City?"

"Within forty-eight hours." Fatigue showed for a moment in Maddy's eyes, and the pale skin seemed a little too pale. "As soon as I've met with Gordy and we've put out a few fires locally."

"The sooner the better. We really need that third Aten asteroid to supply us with raw materials. *You* really need it. Without the asteroid, the shield schedule is a mess and Argos carries part of the blame for delay. But if we solve the schedule problem, then I may be in a position to help you."

That was as far as Celine was willing to go in a recorded conversation. It ought to be enough. More than six months ago the Argos Group had requested a license to construct a launch facility off the southern tip of Florida. Political pressure to veto the application came from World Protection Federation, but it was assumed that on this issue they acted on behalf of someone else. Argos had its eye—one of its many eyes—on a big new station in geostationary orbit. That would provide a jumping-off point into deep space that did not depend on Sky City. And Bruno Colombo, director of Sky City, had the backing of Nick Lopez, head of the WPF and a man with more power than most heads of nations.

The real battle was the Argos Group versus Sky City, and Celine had just taken sides. She was promising that Argos would get their license—as soon as the space shield project was back on schedule.

Maddy had picked up that commitment, and its conditions. She said nothing, but her tiny nod of the head was enough. They had a deal.

"How's it going on the Sky City murders?" The change of subject was Celine's way of telling Maddy Wheatstone that the main meeting was over. "If you can get results there, then everybody will owe Argos. Are you getting anywhere?"

Celine wasn't expecting an answer, but Maddy said, "We have someone assigned to it. I gather it's someone good, but as far as progress is concerned, I have no idea."

When the wind unexpectedly blows your way, hoist a sail. Celine kept her eyes away from Maddy and fixed on the round bottles of fizzes. "Your man doesn't keep you posted?"

"I don't think he keeps anyone posted—not even Gordy. It makes more sense than you might think. That investigation runs under Special Projects, so it includes special methods. Some of their stuff can get pretty ripe."

"Ripe how?"

But Maddy finally caught herself. "I couldn't tell you if I wanted to, because I don't know. I'd better be going. I've had my time and more."

"That's all right. This is my last meeting for today."

"So early?"

"Last *official* meeting. I still have to see who's waiting out there. When do you hope to bring Hyslop down from Sky City?"

"Three or four days, if I can. You think you'll be free?"

"I'll be free. I'll make room on my calendar even if I have to cancel an appointment with—" Celine paused. She had been about to say "God," but she didn't know Maddy Wheatstone's religious beliefs. She remembered the history of the Argos Group, and she finished weakly, "—my entire Cabinet."

As Maddy left, Celine made another note. *MW's religion?* It was not on her crib sheet. Her prep team was getting sloppy. She added a note about that, then turned on her autocom and spoke into it. "Maddy Wheatstone was the last of my scheduled meetings. Who's waiting?"

There would be someone. There was always someone.

The autocom answered, "You have nine individuals or groups of individuals requesting meetings."

She could ask for a ranking of priorities, but for such judgment calls the autocom was still unreliable. A more sophisticated piece of equipment was promised "soon," whatever that meant.

Meanwhile. "Put Claudette Schwinger on, if you please."

"One moment." There was a five-second silence, then the steady voice of the human appointments secretary. "Yes, Madam President?"

"Claudette, what do you have out there? Anyone we can offload to the VP or a Cabinet member?"

"Yes. Three of them should not be here at all. I suggest a meeting for the Surinam minister with the Secretary of State, followed by attendance at a White House dinner next week. All she really wants is to be able to say that she met with you, and it does not have to be one-on-one. The head of DNAture arrived early from Zurich, but his samples are still in transit. He has an appointment tomorrow, so I suggest we stay with that and arrange for accommodation tonight in the White House. That will please him. Dennis Larksbury of ConCern is here again, although we told him on his last visit that the thinning of the ozone layer is an inevitable consequence of the frequency of space shipments and the building of the shield. He wants us to stop building the space shield."

"He's a lunatic. Send him to Milton Glover and the Trust In Government coalition, with a note from me. They deserve each other. What about the others?"

"Everyone has legitimate reasons for meeting with you, except for two that I can't comment on because I have never heard of them. A Mr. Jahangir Hekmat represents the Society of Socinists, whatever that is. He was referred here by Secretary Branksome. The note from Mr. Branksome says, 'This may be important.' But it doesn't explain why."

"It can wait. What about the other one?"

"I do not know." Claudette's voice betrayed her irritation. She was a first-rate appointments secretary, with endless patience and tact, but she took any lack of information about White House visitors as a personal failing. "He says he was not referred here by anyone. He does not have an appointment. He refuses to tell me what he wants. I don't even know how he got into the building. All he says is that his name is Wilmer, and he insists that it's urgent—*most* urgent—that you meet with him right away."

Celine felt a tingle all through her. "What does he look like?"

"He's tall and broad, and a bit pudgy."

"Balding?"

"More like bald. With a high, lined forehead."

"Claudette, Wilmer is his *first* name. It's Wilmer Oldfield." She waited, and when no gasp of recognition came from the other end of the line, she went on, "Dr. Wilmer Oldfield was with me on the first Mars expedition. Tell everyone but him to come back tomorrow, say there's no chance that I can meet with them tonight. Then give me ten minutes alone before you show him in."

"Yes, Madam President. Ma'am, he insists that when he meets with you he must bring someone else."

"Who?"

"He says you don't know her and you have never heard of her. She's waiting in one of the outer offices."

"Security cleared her?"

"Apparently so, Madam President."

"Very well." Celine thought for a moment. Unless Wilmer had changed beyond belief, this was going to be a long session. "Arrange for us to have dinner here. Three of us."

She stood up, went through into the washroom off her office, and laved first hot and then cold water onto her face. She noticed that her cupped hands were trembling slightly.

Wilmer Oldfield.

Claudette Schwinger was what, twenty-six or twenty-seven? So much for fame. The appointments secretary was reasonably well-educated, and she could surely rattle off the names of the three Mars expedition members who had died. Zoe Nash, Ludwig Holter, and Alta McIntosh-Mohammad had monuments, separately and together, all over the country and all over the world. Celine's own name was also famous, because she was President. But Wilmer Oldfield, the brightest of them all, had quietly gone back to research in what was left of Australia, and the new generation didn't even recognize his name. Somewhere in the annals of the Mars expedition was surely recorded the fact that during the journey and for a year after the return, crew members Celine Tanaka and Wilmer Oldfield had been lovers. But that, to the post-supernova generations, was ancient history.

Since then there had been a quarter century of casual contact, without even a face-to-face meeting during the last ten years. When she had been elected President, Celine had informed Wilmer of her new position. His congratulations were sincere, but puzzled. Anything resembling politics was far over his horizon.

Wilmer never was flustered, never overreacted, never became overexcited. So why had he arrived unannounced for a "most urgent" meeting, bringing with him a total stranger?

Unlike Wilmer, Celine was a world-class worrier. Part of her internal jitters was at the thought of seeing him again after so many years; but a larger part was her conviction that he brought bad news. The final meeting of the day, she was sure, was going to be more disturbing than all the others combined.

# 3

The call came in to Will Davis's suit. He at once turned to John Hyslop, just a few feet away from him.

"This is for you, boyo."

"Cusp Station local? If it is, it can wait until we're finished."

"Not this one. Urgent, from Sky City. They called me because they say your suit doesn't answer."

"Of course it doesn't. I switched off so we could get some work done. But I can't ignore it if it's Sky City and urgent. Damnation. What do they say?"

"I don't know. It's personal, and it's scrambled. We can't go direct link. I'll have to relay through Cusp Station control to your suit, so you can decode."

It seemed ridiculous. The two men floated side by side, less than four feet from each other. They could have put their helmets together and talked without any radio link at all, but a scrambled message could not be transferred and interpreted that way. Also, from John Hyslop's point of view the communication could hardly have come at a worse time. Sky City maintained mid-Atlantic, a clock zone convenient for workdays in America and Europe. So far as city workers were concerned, the call to John was made at eight in the morning—a reasonable time.

But the few humans and innumerable machines working on the space shield enjoyed no regular hours and no fixed clock. Schedules were defined by need, with always the same underlying message: *Do this as fast as you can, and remember that it may not be fast enough.*

The cat-sized rolfes, robotic brainchildren of Gordy Rolfe and his great contribution to the building of the space shield, could work twenty-four hours a day. But humans could not. So the call arrived when John Hyslop, Amanda Corrigan, Will Davis, Lauren Stansfield, Rico Ruggiero, and Jessie Kahn were at the tail end of a thirty-hour troubleshooting stint. John and Lauren were also at the tail end of their stamina. They had been up for seven hours before this effort began, tying up a meeting at Sky City before heading for Cusp Station. For the final ten work hours their awareness had been Neirling-boosted, so they would have to boost again soon, or crash. And when you crashed, you stayed out for a full sleep period. John had hoped to see this meeting to its end, then fade at once.

He switched to internal mode and listened to the message as it was unscrambled by his suit. "Dr. Colombo needs your presence as soon as possible on Sky City. We have a new problem."

The voice was that of Goldy Jensen, Bruno Colombo's personal assistant. Her tone—like her message—revealed nothing more with repeated hearings.

*A new problem.*

That might, please God, mean a technical difficulty. The John Hyslop job description, if anyone ever bothered to pull it up and read it, said he was chief engineer for the shield. In practice, he seemed to do whatever Bruno Colombo needed him to do, on Sky City and off it.

John switched back to external mode. Will Davis and Lauren Stansfield were uploading the proposed revision for the construction profile of one section of the space shield into the subsidiary computation network at Cusp Station while Jessie, Rico, and Amanda transferred the group recommendations to Torrance Harbish and the main network back on Sky City, where the real computing power resided. But they all had one eye on him. As soon as he clicked back to local circuits they stared at him expectantly.

"Everything all right?" Lauren asked. She was John's number one assistant, a short, soft-spoken woman with auburn hair and big eyes. She dressed well and expensively, which together with her careful attention to her appearance made some of the engineers regard her as a lightweight. John knew better. He had learned to rely on Lauren in any emergency. She knew more about the interior layout of Sky City than anyone—John included—and her only hobby seemed to be roaming the space city's thousands of corridors, checking the various life-support systems.

Now she was asking a question within a question. They had two more decisions to make before the meeting ended, and Lauren wanted to know if that would be possible.

There was no point in waiting, and no way to pull out gracefully. "I'm sorry." John spoke on open circuit. "Everything here is going well, and I think we're pulling things back toward schedule. But I have to leave. I must return to Sky City."

Jessie Kahn was young, new, naturally shy, and up from Earth only four months. She also had an intensity and an honesty that outweighed her natural reticence and, in John Hyslop's view, pointed to a very bright future.

She said at once, "The questions of reduced shield efficiency and probable sensor losses *must* be addressed today. They can't wait. And those issues require your personal involvement and approval."

"I know." John realized that he was going to shock her, but she had to learn sometime about the world of impossible deadlines. "I'll fly back. You get in touch with me when your meeting finishes. Whatever you decide, I'll approve it."

He saw her face. He was feeling the pressure himself, and he was tempted to add, *Don't give me a hard time, Jessie. I'd hate to spoil your idealism, but I don't have time for polite discussion. I have to boost again, because when I reach Sky City I have to be awake for whatever shit Bruno Colombo throws at me. And the thought of that second boost doesn't thrill me at all.*

His warning wasn't necessary. Will Davis was a seasoned shield engineer who had spent only three days on Sky City in the past year—the opposite of Amanda, Lauren, and Rico, who left Sky City only when dragged out for emergency efforts like today's. But Will was Jessie Kahn's unofficial mentor, and he knew enough to step in and ask in his lilting Welsh, "What is it then, John Hyslop? A direct command? Might it be you've received marching orders from His Lordship?"

"You've got it."

"What's he want with you this time?"

"Do you think he's going to tell me before I get there?"

"No, man. Not if he's half the pain in the ass he used to be. I'm glad it's you off to see him and not me."

Everyone but Jessie laughed. They had suffered their own unpleasant experiences with Bruno Colombo. She, not sure how the conversation had suddenly veered away from her concerns, looked from one person to the other but said nothing.

John decided that there was no point in further discussion. The others could give whatever additional explanations they liked. "I'm going to do a second boost, Lauren," he said. "Right now. You don't need to do that, so make sure you get somewhere safe before you crash. Will, you'll have to wrap it up here in an hour or two. Make sure the rolfes are reassigned to the shield when you're done with them."

Their meeting was taking place in hard vacuum. John headed straight for the station exit, switched to suit channel as soon as he was outside, and said, "Take me to Sky City. Use a continuous one-gee thrust trajectory, and provide a zero relative velocity on arrival."

It was a routine command. The return trip along the extended spine of the space shield and the transfer trajectory to Sky City would require none of John's attention. His personal suit informed him that a one-gee boost with midpoint turnover would carry him the hundred-thousand-plus kilometers from Cusp Station, at the outermost limit of the shield, to his usual docking port on Sky City in one hundred and sixteen minutes.

One hundred and sixteen minutes, in extended boost mode and with little to do but indulge in worried speculation. Couldn't Bruno Colombo have offered a word or two to indicate the nature of the difficulty? Something like, they had a different problem and not just *another* problem? Or had there been another death, another disappearance, another frightful episode in a lengthening sequence?

Probably not. But the murders were getting to him, as they were to everyone living on Sky City.

The suit was accelerating him smoothly along the axis of the space shield. The shield was eighty-five percent complete, but for that you had to take the word of the computers. There was nothing to be seen.

John looked out to the side anyway, at right angles to his direction of motion. Of course, he saw nothing. The three-billion-ton mass of the shield was there, but it spread out to form a narrow cone almost a hundred thousand kilometers long and eighteen thousand kilometers across at the base. The matter in the shield, about a gram of it per square meter, formed a delicate spiderweb of superconducting fibers, load filaments, node sensors, thrustors, and computing tubules. It could stand considerable tension forces, but an ounce of compression anywhere would make it buckle. The structure made small but constant adjustments in relative geometry and overall position to prevent that. The computational problem was continuous and complex. The shield had to maintain a fixed shape and position in the presence of time-varying forces: Earth attraction, lunar, solar, and planetary perturbations; solar wind and radiation pressure. And, of course, it must deal with the variable but steadily increasing sleet of charged particles that provided the shield's whole reason for existing.

John looked down past his feet. For reasons of personal comfort, suits usually accelerated you headfirst. Until turnover time that meant Cusp Station lay directly below him, at the apex of the cone, while Sky City was above his head.

Sky City, which for the past seven months had been prowled by an insane—

*No. Not that.* Those thoughts were the effects of the second Neirling boost on his nervous system. He had to get his attention fixed on something tangible.

Cusp Station was still visible below, a bright cluster of green and orange lights. No word from Will and the others. Presumably they were still chewing on the technical problems.

But Cusp Station was not what he wanted to see. He added an apodizing disk to the suit's optical sensor, removing the unwanted glare of the station, and scanned the area close to it. After a few seconds he located his target and locked on.

And there it was. An undistinguished second-magnitude star, one of hundreds of that brightness in the sky. Yet a star like no other.

For all of recorded history Alpha Centauri had been the third brightest star in the heavens: Rigel Kentaurus, a splendid visual binary with a third and faint companion, Proxima Centauri.

Thirty-one years ago, the Alpha Centauri system had exploded as a mighty supernova. But because Alpha Centauri was about four and a third light-years from the Sun, no one on Earth knew what had happened until twenty-seven years ago, when early in 2026 a torrent of light reached the solar system. For several months Alpha Centauri blazed down on Earth like a second Sun.

The cascade of light had created freak weather and global devastation. The flux of high-energy gamma rays, a few weeks later, knocked out all microcircuits and everything that depended on them. Civilization shuddered, gasped, staggered—and thought it had survived.

Until it realized that the Alpha Centauri supernova, unpredicted by all scientists and proclaimed impossible by most, had not finished with the Earth. The star had waned, until the faint remnant provided a poor object for visual observation. But most of the energy of a supernova is not given off as light or gamma rays. It resides in the sleet of electrically charged subatomic particles thrown out during the stellar explosion. That particle storm, fast-moving as it is, travels much more slowly than light. In the case of Alpha Centauri, the densest cloud was calculated to move at about nine percent of light speed. Travel time from Alpha Centauri: about forty-eight years. Arrival date for the storm center: forty-four years after the first blaze. Say, in 2070.

Earth would need protection. But there were further complications, introduced by the particle velocity distribution. To find when a particle storm has its biggest effect, you must look not at simple particle density but at the *product* of particle flux density and particle kinetic energy. The most energetic and destructive particles are the ones that travel fastest. Hence the worst time would be earlier than 2070. It was predicted as 2061.

*No. The worst time is here and now, with murder most foul on Sky City* . . .

The suit's acceleration ended abruptly. The skyscape swirled dizzily, bringing John shuddering back to reality.

Turnover time. Halfway to Sky City. Still an hour to go. An awful situation. The Neirling boost was designed for when you were desperately busy with more work than you could handle. Employ it when you had nothing to do, you were like a motor running against zero load. Your brain spun faster and faster until it burned out its bearings. And in this case John knew exactly where his brain would run until it blew: on the subject that he was trying to keep out of his mind, the awful deaths.

He had to find something to do.

He transmitted to Cusp Station. "Will? It's been an hour and I've not heard a word from you. What's going on?"

It was a few seconds before he heard a reply. The delay wasn't travel time; that was negligible over such a short distance. He must be interrupting something.

"We've been solving problems, what do you think?" Will Davis's voice held a touch of surprise and perhaps reproach. "Not like some people. We're done with what we were working on when you left, it's on the way to your office for you to approve. Lauren's down and out; she crashed a few minutes ago. What's wrong, John? Feeling lonely?"

"Not lonely. *Insane* would be better. I had to give myself that second boost, otherwise I'd be sleeping when I get to Headquarters. But now I'm going crazy out here with only the stars for company. I need something to *do*. Link me in for your visuals, will you?"

"I could, but you won't get much from seeing me and the others just sitting here. I can give you something a lot better to chew on. It's what we're stewing on ourselves, when we'd all be better off sleeping. Yesterday the deep space network received a new Sniffer profile, and nobody likes the looks of it. The flux profile for uncharged particles from Alpha Centauri has changed. Increased."

"Bad news." John didn't need to say more. The electromagnetic field created by the finished shield would change the trajectory of *charged* particles. They would be diverted, passing around Earth and leaving it untouched. But neutral, uncharged particles were not affected by the field. They would get through and smash into the shield. Too much of that, and the fragile barrier would be destroyed. Then *everything* would get through, charged and uncharged, to hit an unprotected Earth.

"Also, we just received a new simulation," Will went on. "It came in from the analysis team back on Earth after you left. We assume that they incorporated the new Sniffer data, though it's hard to see how they could have done it so fast. Either way, they've worked out what will happen from now to the time of maximum particle flux if we don't make changes to the construction schedule. Remember the protocol for changing display time rates?"

"I do."

"Then here goes. Standard color codes."

John's personal suit switched to remote visual mode. The real external world remained visible as a faint superimposed star field. Fatalities early in the construction of Sky City had led to a decision that the immediate environment must never be completely excluded in favor of remote image data.

The simulation employed a standard vantage point for shield display, a position in space a million kilometers from Earth and fixed in the plane of the ecliptic. The planet sat at the middle of the field of view, a blue sphere almost twice the size of the full Moon as seen from Earth. The space shield formed a long, narrow cone, slightly flared at the end like a trumpet. Invisible to human eyes, it had been stylized in the simulation to show as a web of light blue against a black background. The cone was widest closest to Earth, with the central axis pointed directly away from the planet at about forty-five degrees to the ecliptic. In that direction lay Alpha Centauri, impossibly remote yet dictating every human priority.

The effectiveness of the shield at a given time depended on the balance of two factors: the shield's stage of completion, and the energy and composition of incident particle flux. "Hot spots," locations where the shield was inadequate to redirect the charged particles, were delineated in vivid hot pink. Trouble locations where the situation was improving sat as green islands within the hot spots. Places where things were getting worse showed as stigmata of flaring orange.

The default time rate for the simulation was forty-two thousand to one. At that setting the Moon provided the observer with a natural feel for the pulse of events. Once a minute the sunlit white marble made its four-hundred-thousand-kilometer sweep around Earth, oscillating four or five degrees above and below the plane of the ecliptic.

At that rate, the display of the period from the present to the time of maximum flux energy would take a hundred minutes; long before that John would be at Sky City. He called for a tripling of simulation display rate and settled back to watch. Already he was having premonitions. Will Davis would never suggest such a viewing unless the implications were severe.

In any case, John would have caught the problem even without prior warning. He remembered the results of the simulation from four months ago. Superimposed on the blue web you would always see a scattering of pink patches, within which the flecks of green and orange came and went apparently at random.

Today was different. Eight minutes into the display—less than two years ahead in real time—the pattern began to change. Pink patches spread. Within them he saw few flecks of green. The orange glow of worsening problems dominated.

Something had changed, rapidly and for the worse. It surely had to be something more than the number of uncharged particles, which John still judged acceptably low. He kept watching until the simulation reached the time of maximum flux. By then the space shield had become a sieve. In such a future, Earth would suffer far more than during the initial wave of twenty-seven years ago.

His imagination, heightened by the boost, flashed to scenes of disaster made vivid by early childhood. The first effects of the Alpha Centauri supernova had been calving of the Antarctic ice shelf, blizzards at the equator, tidal waves, and nested sets of tornadoes. When the gamma pulse hit, planes dropped from the sky, telephones and television and radio became useless, and mayhem, starvation, and disease took over.

That surprise would not happen again—the gamma pulse would not be repeated. But there was scope for new and worse disasters. His boosted consciousness threw images at him with awful clarity.

The upper atmosphere had shielded Earth from the direct effects of the gamma-ray pulse. It would not do the same for the particle storm now on its way. The charged nuclei, predicted to be mostly bare protons, would come like a hail of tiny bullets, smashing into the air at relativistic speed. Most would be absorbed on the way down, producing a cascade of forward-scattered mesons, electrons, and gamma rays. Some of those would in turn be absorbed and scattered, some would continue. The atmosphere would turn into a cloud of charged nitrogen and oxygen ions, opaque at every wavelength from hard ultraviolet to short-wave infrared. In the darkness below, a deadly blend of radiation and particles would hit the surface. That final mixture would depend on the type and energy spectrum of the incident particles.

Marine organisms would be lucky, at least at first. Water was a fine absorber, and within a few feet of the surface it would quench the main radiation storm. Troubles would begin at the bottom of the food chain, when plankton and algae lacked solar radiation for photosynthesis. Starvation would work its way steadily up, to the krill, to the vertebrate fishes and crustaceans, finally to the seals and dolphins and whales.

Long before that, all land forms would be in trouble. Water was a good absorber for the torrent of high-energy radiation and particles, but unfortunately most plants and animals were at least seventy percent water. Microscopic explosions would happen in a billion cells at once, disrupting protein synthesis and demolishing the delicate nucleotide sequences in the germ plasm. Old organisms would sicken and die, embryos would form with mutation levels high enough to kill, and all under a smoking sky of reactive ions and toxic rains.

Things would improve—slowly. In perhaps a year, when the main storm was over, sunlight would bleed back in and the air would turn clear and clean. Before that, the species die-off might be worse than anything seen during the Permian or Cretaceous/Triassic mass extinctions. Humans ought to survive, but there could be another halving in population, matching that of twenty-seven years ago. Said that way, it didn't sound too bad. Say it as two billion people dying in awful ways, and it became unthinkable.

John's head and stomach were churning. The shield team's job was to make sure that the worst you could imagine *didn't* happen. But was the team up to the task, even without the new problems?

He turned off the visual feed from Cusp Station. Into the foreground sprang the sunlit upper face of the "space pill," the thin disk of Sky City, a kilometer across and a hundred and ninety meters deep. He was closing on the nerve center for space operations, and he must prepare himself for arrival.

The trouble was, his brain refused to cooperate. The images of Earth's once and future woes distracted him, boiling and bubbling through his mind. John glanced at the condition monitor and understood what was happening. These were Neirling boost side effects, annoying but not unusual. He squeezed his eyes shut and concentrated. After a few minutes the disturbing mind pictures began to fade.

A law of diminishing returns applied to the Neirling boosts. Boost once, and you gained a clean twelve hours of wakefulness and heightened attention. Boost again, before you crashed, and you had maybe eight more hours, with some loss of judgment at the end of it and a danger of making decisions you would later regret. If you tried to stay awake too long in second boost, your consciousness turned off without warning like a failed light bulb.

And third boosts?

They were done only in life-or-death circumstances. The user had at most five good hours, followed by an unavoidable twelve-hour crash. You woke feeling fine. However, observers insisted that the person who came out of a three-in-a-row Neirling boost was not the person who went in. Psychological tests were inconclusive.

John did not intend to add to the body of available evidence. He would go to Bruno Colombo's office and listen to what the Sky City director had to say about the "new problem"—presumably the simulations. After that he would find a place where he could hide away.

Then he would sleep, as soundly as Henry Neirling himself, dead for the past six years.

# 4

Bruno Colombo's office sat in the half-gee environment of the outer perimeter of Sky City. It was the choicest real estate on the space arcology, a place where Coriolis effects of rotation were at a minimum and you were far away from the noisy zero-gee workshops of the central axis.

Maddy Wheatstone didn't begrudge the director his palatial surroundings. So far as she was concerned, Bruno Colombo had the worst job in the universe. Judging from all that she had heard of the man, he loved it. He was *Homo bureaucratiensis,* the pure product, happy juggling the mishmash of everyday affairs needed to run an eighty-thousand-person flying city. His worries were budget and construction priorities, plus international politics both Earthside and spaceside.

Different strokes for different folks.

The shuttle craft had docked smoothly on the zero-gee central axis of the rotating cylinder of Sky City. Maddy was late, she was exhausted, and she was hungry. She kept her suit on and hurried toward the perimeter. When she reached a quarter-gee chamber she operated the airlock, and at her command the suit removed itself from her body. Receiving her approval to leave, it headed back toward the axis. It would seek out the service facilities to take on new supplies and exhaust waste products. In half an hour it would be ready for reuse, by Maddy or anyone else.

Maddy didn't intend to be that next user. She appreciated the suit's devotion, but she had spent the past fifteen hours inside it, nine of them trying to catch up on lost sleep while the acceleration of her space environment ranged between the two and a half gees of takeoff and the easy float of free fall. The shuttle, for the fourth consecutive time that she had taken it, had been delayed at both ends. Enough was enough.

And in some ways it was too much. Her travel case would not be unloaded and taken to her room on Sky City for another two hours, but her appointment with Colombo was *now*. Maddy checked her appearance as she drifted down the incline of a spiraling outward corridor. The personal suit did a good job of removing waste products, and it tried to keep body and clothing free of perspiration; but it didn't quite succeed. Late or not, she had to do something.

Just before she came to Bruno Colombo's office she slipped into a washroom and did what she could in the way of repairs. Water and a quick brush and comb took care of her hair and skin. Makeup hid the signs of weariness around her eyes and mouth. Clothing was a more difficult problem. Her outfit was reasonably clean, but rumpled. It looked as though she had slept in it—exactly what she had been unable to do.

A woman occupied Bruno Colombo's outer office. She was, according to Maddy's information, the notorious Goldy Jensen. She was barely forty, but she had been Dr. Bruno Colombo's personal assistant for twenty years. She was also, according to the Argos Group information services, his longtime mistress. But beyond all that, she was his guardian. No one made it in to see Colombo without being subjected to Goldy's scrutiny. Maddy had heard that even Bruno's wife had to be cleared for access.

Goldy let her off easily. She gave Maddy's clothes a disdainful stare, but she said, "Go on in. You are late. Your meeting was scheduled to begin seven minutes ago. The others are already here."

Others? Maddy had assumed that Gordy Rolfe had arranged for a one-on-one. "Who is in the meeting?"

Goldy Jensen stared at her stonily. "I feel sure that Dr. Colombo will introduce you as he thinks fit."

*And screw you, too.* But Maddy didn't say it. The briefing documents also noted that Goldy held grudges and forgot nothing.

Maddy slid the door open and walked through into Bruno Colombo's office.

The view, if you felt comfortable in space, was spectacular. On the perimeter of Sky City "down" meant "outward." The whole floor of the room was transparent. As Sky City turned on its axis you looked past your feet and watched the panorama of the heavens sweeping by. Once a minute the same view returned, except that Sky City was itself in synchronous orbit about Earth. Sometimes the benign face of the planet intervened, blocking out a full fifteen degrees of the sky.

Maddy knew that the transparent floor could turn opaque with the flip of a switch, but Bruno Colombo apparently had a habit of showing the wheeling starscape whenever he had visitors from Earth—particularly first-time visitors with weak nerves and little space experience.

If he hoped that was true in Maddy's case, he had missed his target. She walked forward, stared down and out, and said, "Magnificent. I'd pawn my soul for an office view like this." She held out her hand to the tall man standing with feet planted in the middle of the floor/window, and said, "Dr. Colombo, I'm delighted to meet you. And . . ." She stared pointedly at the other man in the room.

He was lounging at the low table. He had been speaking, but broke off in midsentence as she entered. Then he scrambled to his feet and held out his hand. "John Hyslop."

Something was wrong already. According to her plans, John Hyslop should not be here. Her meeting was with Bruno Colombo alone, and her main task was to persuade the director that Hyslop should be made available to assist the Argos Group in the asteroid capture program.

She needed time to think. Colombo already looked grumpy and ill at ease. Was Gordy Rolfe the cause, playing power games behind her back?

John Hyslop was still holding out his hand. She took it, held on for a fraction longer than custom demanded, and used the time to study him. He was short and stocky, only a few inches taller than her own five-four. Steady gray eyes, dark-smudged with fatigue or illness, stared into hers. He wore a dark two-day stubble of beard. The beginnings of male pattern baldness, easily treated with follicle protozoans, sent a different message: He didn't much care what he looked like.

Her peripheral vision made a lightning scan of his clothes. She concluded that she had worried too much about her own appearance. Compared to him she was well groomed and elegant. Her clothes looked as if she had slept in them. His looked like he had died in them.

Bruno Colombo moved between the two, forcing her to take a step backward. "Hyslop, this is Madeline Wheatstone. She lives in the United States. However, as I told you, she is not visiting us in any official government capacity."

Hyslop's gray eyes had been gazing at her with a curiosity that matched Maddy's own. She felt a sudden conviction that he did not know why he was here. And he did not know why Maddy was here, either. Her background data said that he was all engineer, as much the pure product as Bruno Colombo was the pure bureaucrat. His expression asked, *Why have I been dragged here from my work?* The director, Maddy knew, was the last person on Earth—or off it—to waste time with casual visitors.

Colombo had somehow glided forward again so that her view was mainly of the director's back. Bruno was enormously tall and broad-shouldered. He must seldom be in a setting where that groomed halo of silvery hair did not tower above the crowd.

Maddy took a quick step sideways, so that she and John Hyslop faced each other again. She said, "Actually, I prefer Maddy to Madeline. Why don't we all sit down? I don't think we've ever met, Mr. Hyslop, but I've heard a lot of good things about you."

Judging by the look on Bruno Colombo's face, none of those had come from the director. They all sat down, and now she and Hyslop were eye to eye. She was long-waisted, so a lot of her height was in her torso. John Hyslop was probably self-conscious about his own short stature. He would have been just the wrong age, all set to be given a series of growth hormone shots, when the supernova hit.

He leaned forward. "Ms. Wheatstone—"

"Maddy."

"—I feel sure that you and I have never met. Actually, I don't even know why I'm meeting with you now."

It was a cue, and not a very subtle one. But Bruno Colombo picked up on it before Maddy could. "I did send you a message, Hyslop, when you were out on the shield."

"If this concerns the new simulations of shield performance and shield failure, then I agree that the problem—"

Maddy wanted to hear his next words, but Colombo broke into

Hyslop's reply as though an impending shield failure and the consequent collapse of civilization were of no great interest.

"This has nothing to do with simulations. It concerns the unfortunate—" Colombo paused, considering his next words. "—the unfortunate series of events that has occurred here over the past few months. More to the point, it concerns the consequences of those events as they are apparently being perceived on Earth. Hence the presence of Ms. Wheatstone."

*Hence.* Hence what? What in the name of heaven had Gordy Rolfe told Bruno Colombo? And why had no one bothered to inform Maddy?

An old axiom: When you are totally confused, don't make things worse by talking. Maddy kept her mouth firmly closed, and after a few moments Colombo went on, "I should explain to you, Ms. Wheatstone, that although I have followed the problems at a general administrative level, my duties as director of Sky City and chief implementor of the space shield program prevent the day-to-day detailed involvement that Hyslop, as my assistant, has been able to enjoy. We admit that progress has been slow."

Buck passing was nothing new to Maddy. She had watched it happen many times during her nine years with the Argos Group, as that organization burgeoned from its original role as a provider of unique electronics to a worldwide deal broker and powerhouse. But John Hyslop seemed decidedly unhappy. Presumably he knew where he had failed to make progress, even if Maddy didn't.

The problem was Colombo's habit of talking in language designed to stifle any transmission of information. What *events* was Colombo talking about? The deaths?

That might be it. Through all the desperate years of space and shield development there had been deaths on Sky City and on the shield, hundreds and hundreds of them. They were inevitable in any construction program in a new operating environment where speed was more important than safety. No one back on Earth had ever offered criticism, or done anything but cheer the space workers on to greater efforts. But there had been nothing like this.

"The murders?" Maddy began, and paused when John Hyslop raised one eyebrow at her.

It was that, it had to be. And she was paid to make things happen, not to watch them happen. She gave Hyslop the hint of a smile and turned to the director.

"If I may, Dr. Colombo, I would like to express our concerns in my own words." She swiveled to face John Hyslop directly, making it clear that her question was addressed to him alone. "You alluded to the new simulations, and I assume that you have had a chance to review them. What do you think of them?"

He paused for a long time before he answered. If Colombo had done that, Maddy would have assumed that he was posturing, but John Hyslop actually appeared to be thinking. "The simulations are terrifying," he said at last. "But I need to know what new data the Earthside team put into the analysis before I can give you a real assessment. For example, were the latest Sniffer data included?"

"No. The main new information was the rate of progress on shield construction and the efficiency of general in-space operations for the past seven months. You know the schedules better than I do. And you know how poorly things have been going."

Bruno Colombo was sitting to Maddy's right. She saw the director's lips tighten, but he said nothing. That was odd. His reputation said that normally he wouldn't sit quietly in a meeting, no matter who was present. What *had* Gordy Rolfe been up to?

"You are right, Ms. Wheatstone," John Hyslop said. "Things have slowed down. One reason is the uncertainty and fear here on Sky City. We are more than eighty thousand people, and we grow in numbers every month. We have more technical training per head than anywhere since the first atomic bomb was developed at Los Alamos, more than a century ago. But in many ways we are like a small town. Risk of death in adult work is one thing. Risk to the children is quite another."

Not his own kids, Maddy knew that. Her briefing documents said that Hyslop was unmarried, without children or current partners. But he was continuing, "It's likely that the teenage murders are affecting everyone. I know they've had an effect on me, because I was forced to move one of the bodies from her place of death to where her parents could view the remains. And my assistant, Lauren Stansfield, had a cousin who was one of the victims."

Bruno Colombo was glaring. Maddy had seen his official statements to the Earth authorities. He insisted that Sky City security was close to capturing the killer, but also that the Sky City murders were having no more than a trifling effect on work schedules.

Clearly, John Hyslop didn't believe that, though what he said stayed close to the official line. *He* was affected, since he personally had been forced to view the bodies. Lauren Stansfield was affected, because she had lost a relative. But workers without families could see the murders as little more than a nasty news item. And so far as capturing the killer was concerned, no one had a clue.

John Hyslop seemed paler. His left eye was developing a tic and his voice was strained. When neither Maddy nor Bruno Colombo responded, he said, "We are looking for any help that we can get. If you yourself are with any kind of investigative group . . ."

It was open fishing, but Maddy approved of that. She smiled and shook her head. "Far from it. As Director Colombo mentioned, I do not work for any particular government. I also know less than nothing about criminal investigation methods. I am vice president for development of the Argos Group. I assume that you know of us?"

It was a rhetorical question. The Argos Group wasn't government, but Gordy Rolfe claimed, at least internally, that it was more powerful than any government; the Argos Group provided the technology that allowed governments to run. Maddy wondered about a new connection, one that she had never heard about. Could that be what was making Bruno Colombo so subdued?

She saw an easy way to find out. At John Hyslop's nod, she added, "We had early advance warning of the simulation results, and we have been able to study them more than you have. The deaths here have had an effect on morale and efficiency, but they are not the main reason that the project has fallen behind.

"The Argos Group has done its own simulations. The critical path for finishing the shield on time is the availability of construction materials in space. The Aten class of asteroids all have orbits that cross the orbit of Earth, and the Argos Group has during the past eight years contracted with Sky City for the transfer of two of them from their original paths to stable near-Earth orbits. We have also led the mining of those asteroids for metals and volatiles needed in shield construction. The transfer and material extraction went without difficulties, but deadlines were missed. We learned of problems only after the fact.

"If we are to make up for schedule slippage, then the third Aten-class asteroid must be brought to Earth orbit and processed more quickly than proposed. Certainly, the deaths on Sky City must end and the murderer must be caught, but we regard that as a subsidiary problem, one that we are already taking steps to deal with. The central question for the Argos Group remains: Can we rely on Sky City to deliver the third asteroid as required, or will we be forced to examine other alternatives?"

There it was, the first part of the story that she was here to tell. It contained its own veiled warning. For the past decade, Sky City had dominated all space activities connected with the shield. Colombo's position and influence depended upon keeping it that way. Competition to Sky City's monopoly would hit Bruno Colombo in his most vulnerable place.

As Maddy prepared to deliver the second part of her message she felt doubts of her own. Would any single individual, John Hyslop or anyone else, be able to make a difference to the whole schedule? Gordy Rolfe insisted that Hyslop could and would, but Maddy was not so sure.

She had been keeping one eye on Colombo for a possible outburst. When he remained totally calm, Maddy's suspicions grew. Colombo was so unruffled because he had known of the whole agenda for this meeting in advance. All her instincts said *setup*.

"I feel sure it will not be necessary to look anywhere but Sky City," Bruno Colombo said quietly. "We will cooperate with you in every way and respond to your every request. If there is ever a shred of difficulty, you will have direct personal access to me. I can promise our maximum effort in returning the whole program to schedule. As for the project to bring a third asteroid to suitable Earth orbit, I propose that the program manager for that work be John Hyslop. There is no better person to lead such a project in the whole solar system."

Setup, sure and certain. The whole thing smacked of Gordy Rolfe's fine Italian hand. Maddy was listening to Colombo, but she had been watching John Hyslop's face. Colombo's sudden proposal for Hyslop's reassignment had clearly come as a shock. The engineer was sitting speechless, eyebrows raised and mouth open like a startled frog.

"I know nothing of Mr. Hyslop's background," Maddy said. *See, Dr. Colombo, I can lie as well as you.* "However, I have every confidence in your judgment of him. When would the transfer take place?"

"I assume that time is of the essence." Bruno Colombo frowned. "Therefore, I see no reason for delay. Reassignment can happen immediately."

"No!" Hyslop came back to life. "Director, that's totally impossible."

"Why?"

"Because things can't just be dropped when I'm right in the middle of them."

John Hyslop's rush of words and incredulous look told Maddy a lot. Bruno Colombo might think he was the god of Sky City, but there was an awful lot going on here that he didn't know about.

"I'm deep into a dozen projects," Hyslop continued, "here and out on the shield. We must have continuity—at the very least, I have to summarize the things that only I know about."

"Hyslop, you have filed numerous reports attesting to the competence of your chief assistant. Are you denying the truth of those?"

"You mean Lauren Stansfield? Of course not. She's exceptionally able and knowledgeable. She understands all the systems of Sky City as well as anyone. But she's mainly an *inside* worker, not an open-space specialist."

"Where is she now?"

"At the moment she happens to be out on the shield. But that's unusual. She doesn't have nearly as good a grasp of shield engineering as, say Will Davis."

"So we will divide your old responsibilities. Lauren Stansfield will handle problems of Sky City engineering, and Will Davis will deal with outside activities relating to the shield. I assume that you are confident of Davis's abilities?"

"Certainly. He's first-rate. But—well—it's not really that easy."

Maddy could see how the argument was going. John Hyslop didn't have a chance against Bruno Colombo. It had little to do with seniority, and nothing to do with who was right. She would bet that John never won an argument with Colombo. The director had a more assertive personality.

And Maddy? Maybe. It was just as well that there had been no argument. But Maddy was increasingly sure she deserved no credit for that. Everything had been greased before she ever set foot on Sky City.

"I agree, you need to tie up what you've been doing." She interrupted Colombo, who was now demanding to know why the full status of each project had not been given in weekly progress reports. "We are hoping for fast action, too, but we don't want to jeopardize ongoing work. We don't want to make anyone have to admit he acted too quickly, and without adequate thought." *Yes, Director, that could mean you.* "How long will you need, Mr. Hyslop, before you are ready to make the transfer?"

"I can coordinate everything with Lauren Stansfield and Will Davis and be ready to go in a week."

"A whole week!" Bruno Colombo spoke to John Hyslop, but he was looking at Maddy. "Really, that sounds ridiculously long."

"It's acceptable." Maddy was sure of it, someone had been applying heat to Bruno Colombo. She turned to the director. "So we agree. One week it is, then the official transfer. But I need Mr. Hyslop to make a brief trip to Earth beforehand, for general introductions. That should be done as soon as possible." Maddy winced inside, knowing that she had just committed herself to another shuttle trip and no sleep. "We also need a planning session here to discuss overall schedules. Where can we hold such a meeting?"

The director waved a hand around the office. "Right here. We can continue where we are."

"Not unless you are ready to give up your office." Maddy was pushing deliberately, curious to see just how much ground Colombo was willing to give. "I need a *private* session, just me and John Hyslop. We have to get to know each other, and there are sensitive matters of Argos Group activities that cannot involve you."

Bruno Colombo's face reddened, and for a moment Maddy thought that she had gone too far. Finally he nodded. She saw the set of his mouth, and decided that she had probably made a mistake. He would not fight now—apparently she still, for no reason that she understood, was in a controlling position. But Colombo's assistant, Goldy Jensen, must have learned her own grudge holding from a master. It was going to be tough on Maddy if she ever had to depend on the director of Sky City for charity.

"You may use my office if you so wish." Colombo had himself

under control. "Also, there are several rooms available on this level. Whichever you prefer."

"We don't want to disturb you. We'll move."

She gestured to John. He followed her out. As soon as they were through the outer office and beyond the hearing of Goldy Jensen, he said, "Ms. Wheatstone, I've heard of the Argos Group, but I don't know anybody in it. How come you picked me?"

It was an excellent question. Unfortunately, Maddy didn't have a good idea of the answer. She stalled, saying, "I'd rather you called me Maddy. After all, we're going to be working together."

"Fine. But why me?"

"Let me answer your question with a question. Do you think you are the best engineer on Sky City?"

He hesitated. "I don't know."

"Well, do you know of a better one?"

"No." He seemed highly uncomfortable, refusing to meet her eye. It could mean that he was lying, but Maddy didn't think so. More likely, he was the kind of person made thoroughly uncomfortable by compliments. She found that rather sweet.

"What you say matches what we've heard," she said, "that you're the very best. That's why we want you."

It didn't answer his question, but he didn't ask again. Instead he scowled at her in a puzzled way and said, "If you think I'm the best, it seems strange to switch me from what I'm doing to the Aten asteroid work."

"You don't think you can handle that?"

"No! I know I can. It's more like—well, this is going to sound like boasting, and I hate boasting. But the Aten asteroid transfer and mining aren't all that difficult. I'd be willing to trust the job to any of my senior assistants. What I'm doing here is far harder, and far more urgent."

He was raising a question that Maddy was not equipped to handle. Was he right—was there more going on than she knew about? Gordy Rolfe might again be playing his own game.

Fortunately, John Hyslop didn't press the point. He went on, "You know, Dr. Colombo isn't the way you think he is."

It was an odd non sequitur. Maddy asked, "And what way do I think he is?"

"You think he's all empty talk. But he used to be an engineer, and a good one."

"He doesn't seem to care for that sort of thing now."

"No. But sometimes, when you think he's not been listening and has no idea what you are talking about, he comes up with a key insight for an engineering problem or he puts his finger on a fatal design flaw. It's a terrible waste, doing what he does all day long."

Maddy had the urge to tell him that it took a good man to defend a boss who would surely never defend him. She wanted to see if a compliment would again produce that boyish look of discomfort. However, before she could speak he put out a hand to steady himself against the wall of the corridor, grunted, and gave a prodigious yawn. Then he blinked at her and said, "I'm sorry, Ms. Wheatstone. We can't have our meeting now."

"Call me Maddy." She frowned. "Are you all right?"

"No." His words became breathless. "Not all right. I've been awake and at work for over forty hours. I either have to lie down or throw up. I'm approaching the end of a second Neirling boost, and I'm going to crash. Soon. Give me twelve hours. Then we can talk."

Maddy took his arm in hers. "You should have told me sooner. Of course you must have sleep. If you're on a second boost, you absolutely need sleep." *And not only you.* The prospect of twelve hours of rest rose ahead of her like a prospect of paradise. "Come on, let's get you to where you can lie down in peace. We'll have plenty of time for our meeting when you wake up."

The look in his weary gray eyes surprised her. It was gratitude. You didn't see much of that when you worked for the Argos Group.

She led him away along the corridor. John Hyslop promised to be intriguing to work with—even though he insisted that they didn't really need him for the Aten asteroid work.

And did they? What other reason could there be for his transfer? She could ask Gordy Rolfe, but he'd take that as a sign of weakness. Better to file the question away in Maddy's box of minor mysteries, and try to find the answer for herself.

# 5

**From the private diary of Oliver Guest.**

A peat fire is like no other: silent, sullen, and slow-burning, red in its hidden heart. Not unlike, to one of morbid imagination, the man seated in front of it.

Seth Parsigian fitted well into an ancient castle of western Ireland; better, perhaps, than I did. Burly, primitive, cross-legged by my broad stone hearth, he made a rather formidable leprechaun. His skimpy black singlet revealed long-healed scars on his chest and neck. His eyes, glittering in the light of fire and wall lamps, were like a snake's.

"A dozen of 'em, and countin'," he said. "We can do this any way you like. I have a ton of stuff with me, pictures, descriptions, video reconstructions, locations and murder method, plus ages and background for each girl. What foxes me—an' not only me, half the security forces an' probably all the amateur sleuths in the world—is the *pattern*. There isn't one. I mean, so far as normal people are concerned, there ain't. Mebbe you, with your special talent, can make sense of it."

Of course. Maybe you, Dr. Guest, with your perverse, sick, disgusting, psychotic mind, will realize at once who did it.

"Spare me the doubtful compliments," I said. "I will certainly read, and I will look, and I will think. I will do all these things—at my leisure. For the moment, I prefer to have your impressions. You were surely engaged on this effort for some time before you decided to seek me out. Tell me what you know, what you deem can be ignored, and what you conjecture. When I feel a need for information, I will interrupt. Surely you have observed some pattern, however faint."

"Yeah. The pattern is, never the same thing twice. It started on December twenty-fifth, 2052. Myra Skelton went to a Christmas party at a friend's place on level eighty-eight."

"Level eighty-eight?"

"Locations on Sky City are named from the central axis. The axis is level zero. The outer edge of the cylinder is level one hundred. Myra Skelton lived with her parents on the eighty-second level, so she didn't have far to go to her friend's. Down six levels, and a hundred-meter walk around. She left there at nine at night. But she never made it home. They found her body the next mornin', stuck in an empty storage room on level eighty-seven."

"What was her age?" I sat back in my chair with my eyes closed. For the moment I was not attempting logical analysis. I sought only a sensation, a certain feeling, the stir of the small worms creeping up from the base of the brain.

"She was fourteen an' a half. Actually, more like fourteen years and eight months. She died from a blow to the back of her head. No murder weapon, no suspect, no motive. I got full medical reports. Want to see 'em?"

"Later. Continue."

"No rape, and no sexual molestation. Of course, I know that don't prove a thing. In your own case, from all I've heard, you never even touched them, before or after—"

I opened my eyes. "At your peril, Seth Parsigian. This truce is fragile enough, without unnecessary provocation."

"Yeah. Sorry." He did not look it. "Anyway, she hadn't been touched. Big mystery, an' no clues, even though her family's well connected an' pulled strings to get high-powered investigators on it. They come up from Earth an' talked a lot, but they found out zilch. They said, we got us an unknown killer—brilliant—and January seventh, they left.

"January tenth, Tanya Bishop played a game of three-ball on a court up near the axis, where it's close to zero gee. She pulled a muscle and had to drop out before the game was over. Instead of waiting for the others, she said she was goin' home to shower and rest her leg. Home was level sixty-six. She never made it. They found her in an airtight tank on level five. Thought at first it was an accidental death—gone in there, fallen asleep, asphyxiated. I know, that sounded like a bunch of crap to me, too. When they took a closer look at her body it turned out she was strangled. Fourteen years and one month old. This time she was naked. There was no intercourse, but there was mutilation after death. Sexual mutilation. Everybody said, we got us a crazy sex killer."

I nodded. Once again I sat with eyes closed. Fourteen years and eight months, fourteen years and one month; the ages were right.

"On January twenty-sixth," Seth went on, "Doris Wu disappeared. Age: fifteen years and four months. They never found a body, but everybody assumed she'd been murdered and dropped out into space. Wouldn't be hard to do—earlier that day she had been on level hundred, right at Sky City perimeter. Dump her outside, and centrifugal force would carry her out and away. Pretty risky if you left any evidence on her, because the outside of Sky City is packed with meteorite sensors and the body should have been seen. It wasn't. Soon as the disappearance was reported, people made the connection. Sixteen days between Myra Skelton and Tanya Bishop, sixteen days between Tanya Bishop and Doris Wu. Hey, we got us a killer who's regular as clockwork. We better watch real close come February tenth.

"Except that Cissy Muller was found stabbed to death on January twenty-ninth, only three days after Doris Wu. No sexual interference, though Cissy was more mature-looking than the others. Mature-acting, too. Only fourteen years and three months old, but a real hot number. Experienced. If the killer had just wanted sex, best guess on Sky City is all he'd've had to do was ask.

"April Jarrow was murdered February sixth, eight days later. No intercourse or sexual interference, but maybe that's not too surprising, because April was only eight." Seth paused. "What's up? You havin' ideas?"

One might say that Seth Parsigian was brutish, vicious, uncouth, and self-serving; I certainly approve all those descriptors. But he was not without observational powers. He had seen my eyes open.

I shook my head. "Far from it. I have nothing close to a productive notion."

That was the exact truth. I had been sitting, absorbing and sifting the information flow, and *waiting*. For what? It is hard to describe, although I am normally blessed with an adequate vocabulary. Let us say that I awaited the burgeoning within me of a strange desire, the joy of an old wound waking. The methods of murder described by Seth Parsigian were barbaric, and those I could not relate to. But the hunger, gusting through the cold arches of the mind, unpredictable and variable and irresistible—that should have resonated between the murderer's brain and my own. April Jarrow's death provided a jarring sense of dislocation. "Eight years old? You are sure she was so young?"

"Eight years and six months and one day. She looked a lot older, big and mature for her age. Might have passed for eleven or even twelve." He waited, and when I closed my eyes again he went on. "Death was from a single wound, the severing of the jugular vein. It was up on level nine, only a twentieth of a gee environment. Must have been a devil of a mess, blood everywhere. Don't see how the murderer didn't get covered with it."

If Seth were distressed at the picture that he was painting, it did not show in his voice.

"Suppose that the murderer had worn a space suit." I opened my eyes again. "Would any blood boil away if he went—" I paused, then forced myself to continue. "—if he went outside? Into space?"

"Dunno. I can check that. Think it's important?"

"I suspect that it is not. Continue."

"Right. Myra Skelton, Tanya Bishop, Doris Wu, Cissy Muller, April Jarrow." Seth counted them off on his fingers. If he had notes, I did not see him referring to them. "All right, we're up to number six. There was a gap here, an' people must have wondered for a while if the killer was done or died or shipped away from Sky City. Until March second, more than three weeks later, when they found Brenda Cleve with her throat cut."

"Her age?" I wondered if the eight-year-old had been an anomaly.

"Thirteen years and three months. No signs of mutilation, but in her case there had been recent sexual intercourse. They found a se-men sample, an' over the next few days they did a DNA match for ev-ery blessed male on Sky City. They thought for a while they had the killer, a fourteen-year-old by the name of Donovan Summers. But it turned out that he and Brenda had been humpin' for months, and they'd had sex early the evening she died. He'd been home with his family on the other side of Sky City at the time when Brenda was murdered, and he had alibis for most of the others. The reason he didn't come forward as soon as he heard about Brenda was because he didn't want his parents to know he'd been having sex." Seth shook his head. "Boy, can I relate to that. If my old dad had known what I was up to when I was fourteen, he'd have tanned my ass."

The thought of a fourteen-year-old Seth Parsigian was too incongruous to sanction. And yet such a person had existed, just as there had once been a fourteen-year-old Oliver Guest. Unlike Seth, I had been a paragon of pious virtue, then, and for many years after, my father's greatest source of pride. He never contacted me after my arrest. I suspect that my filial image at that point became somewhat tarnished.

"Number seven was another disappearance," Seth continued. "An' this was different for a lot of reasons. First off, the girl who was killed wasn't a Sky City kid at all. Her name was Lucille DeNorville, an' she was up from Earth for a sight-seein' vacation. You may have heard about it because the media made a bigger noise over her than all the others put together."

He glanced at me expectantly, and I shook my head. "I have little time to spare for the worries of others. My own problems are quite sufficient."

"That right?" Seth's face showed not the slightest hint of interest or sympathy. "Well, Lucille vanished on March tenth, one week shy of her thirteenth birthday. Her granny an' granpappy back on Earth—she was an orphan—made a gigantic fuss about it. The DeNorvilles are loaded, so they could pay whatever it took to explore every last avenue. Not only that, they're from a really old and well-connected family—claim their line goes back over a thousand years—an' they have political and social clout. They had investigators talkin' to every single human on Sky City, an' as many robots and rolfes as could answer. The family offered a big reward, too—still waitin' for a taker—an' they made it pretty clear they didn't care if they saw the murderer dead or alive. So there were bounty hunters all over, clogging up the works. Didn't do a bit of good, because they all come up blank. Never found a body, never had a suspect.

"But the DeNorville family paid for reconstructions of all the murders, takin' everything anyone knew or could guess about what happened." Seth glanced around the long, stone-walled room, filled with smoky shadows cast by the dying peat fire. "Got a playback unit here, or did you go caveman all the way?"

Twenty-seven years had done nothing to improve his manners. "Over in the corner," I said, "you will find the best playback equipment in Ireland. I will show you how to use it should your mechanical aptitude match your tact and diplomacy."

It was wasted on him. He grinned, stood up, and headed for the far corner of the room. It was past midnight and the wall lights were already dimmed.

"You'll be gettin' full sensories," Seth called from over in the corner. "I'll do an override when I think I ought to. Tell me when you're ready."

"You may proceed."

"All right. This one is for Lucille DeNorville. Hold your hat."

Darkness dropped around me like a shroud. The air that filled my nostrils had an unfamiliar smell of machine oil and some kind of disinfectant. I heard a soft, steady pumping, so regular and soothing that after a few moments it began to fade into the background.

Light bled in slowly, building a scene around me. Ahead lay a long corridor, maybe four meters wide and three high. Occasional branching passages ran off it, and every few meters a white overhead strip provided lighting. I saw a couple of rolfes carrying a curved wall section between them. The little eight-legged machines scuttled along efficiently in the low gravity and were soon out of sight in a side passage. It was the interior of Sky City, as that space habitat had been portrayed a thousand hackneyed times in every visual medium.

The corridor ahead stood empty for half a minute. At last, from one of the side passages, appeared a woman dressed in yellow. Her hair was held back from her face by a matching yellow headband. She floated more than walked, and when she came to one of the overhead strips I could see that she was not a full-grown woman but a girl in the first bloom of youth. She advanced easily and gracefully, with all the dawning beauty of a thirteen-year-old.

For the first time in many years I felt the spider's touch inside my head. It was ruined by Seth's voice, hissing in my ear, "That's Lucille DeNorville."

Did the man think I was an imbecile? "I know who she is. Shut up."

A second figure had appeared from another side passage. He was holding some kind of long bar and he moved fast, silently closing in on Lucille from behind. She apparently had no idea he was there, even at the final moment when he raised the bar and brought it around with sickening force to the left side of her head. I heard a crunch as the metal smashed the bone of the cranium.

She fell forward without a sound. Her attacker pulled a black square from inside his coat, opened it up to form a bag, and slid it around her. The metal bar went in next. Then he was lifting her—easy in the light gravity—and hurrying away with the bag in his arms. He did not enter a side passage, but traveled along the corridor until he was finally hidden from sight by its curve. The whole thing, from the appearance of Lucille DeNorville to the vanishing of her attacker, had occupied perhaps thirty seconds.

"Replay?" Seth asked, and reality came drifting back.

"Perhaps later. That's it, the whole thing?"

"That's it, squire. I agree, not much for three million bucks. Think we should ask for our money back?"

"How much of this was derived from established fact, and how much was conjecture?"

"We're sure of a few things. How she was dressed, the fact that she died at that particular place. Like her, the weapon was never found. But that's gotta be the way he killed her."

"Got to be? Why?"

"Splashes of blood and scraps of brain tissue on the wall. The DNA tests confirm that they came from Lucille DeNorville. And they were *splashes,* not smears. No blood or body tissue anywhere else in that corridor, and I mean *anywhere.* The people DeNorville hired went over the corridor with every gadget ever made. The body must have gone into a bag or a box and been carted away."

"Carried away by the murderer?"

"I guess so. Are you suggesting that there could have been two of 'em?"

"No. I merely wish to emphasize the boundary between knowledge and conjecture. Do you assume that she never saw or heard her murderer?"

Seth stared at me dubiously. He was, perhaps, wondering if his transatlantic journey was worthwhile. "Well, she couldn't have, could she? The brain tissue came from the occipital lobe, they reckon from the left rear of her head. If she'd've heard him, she'd have turned and tried to defend herself."

"That is plausible conjecture, but it is not fact. Suppose that she knew the murderer and was walking with him?" I was perhaps being deliberately perverse, since I could in truth see no reason to disagree with Seth's conclusion.

He snorted. "What about the others, then? Did he know *all* of 'em?"

"That seems improbable."

"Damn right it does. Even if he did know her, after six deaths wouldn't you think that a young girl would get pretty damn careful who she'd walk with alone on Sky City?"

That thought had already occurred to me. I nodded, and Seth stared at me intently. "We're up to number seven. Want to hear about the other five, or do you need to take a break?"

He *was* observant. He looked as fresh as when we had started, but I doubt that was true of me. Even though I felt no kinship with the murderer, too many sea wraiths had been swirling up from the subterranean ocean of my past.

"Go ahead," I said. "I am tired, but let us briefly review the other cases. Then I have to rest. I must inform you, however, that to this point I am utterly without ideas."

It was rather worse than that. I could find no mental point of contact with the murderer, despite the fact that his victims interested me greatly.

Seth was not at all put out. "Fair enough," he said. "I've worked this for weeks, an' still got nowhere. I'll go quick with number eight. Denise Braidley was twelve and a half years old. We think she was killed March twenty-second; at least that's when she disappeared. But she's another case where the body was never found, an' it's even possible it wasn't a murder at all. Denise had a bit of a screw loose— three or four times in the past she'd grabbed a suit an' took off into space by herself. Once she was gone for three days an' rode way out past Cusp Station. Said when she got back she'd have liked to keep going all the way to Alpha Centauri. Fat chance. She couldn't have gone farther than she did in the suit she had, an' she was lucky one of the big scopes spotted her. If no one had seen her an' stopped her, she'd not have made it home. She'd never bothered to make sure her suit was fully charged or the com unit was workin'. Maybe that's what happened this time, she drifted off an' died in open space."

I shuddered, for reasons that Seth was unlikely to comprehend. He was continuing. "Number nine is more interesting. Julia Vansittart was killed April third, an' her case is the closest anybody's ever come to gettin' a peek at the murderer. In fact, except for a bit of bad luck we'd have at least a low-definition picture of him. It's pretty certain—I know what you're thinkin': facts, not conjectures—that Julia was murdered *outside* Sky City, an' we know to within ten minutes when it happened.

"She an' a bunch of other students had gone off in a science class to take a look at the power-generating equipment, out along the axis beyond the main structure. Routine hop in suits, some class does the same sort of thing every few weeks. There were ten kids in the bunch, an' when they were done at the power-generation plant they were allowed to go back by themselves to a city entry port on level zero. Julia was in her suit when they left the power plant. All the others swear that. A quarter of an hour later, the rest of 'em were inside an' ready to get out of their suits. One of her friends, Walt Christie, noticed that Julia wasn't with 'em, so he popped back outside to see what was keepin' her. He found her body floating in space, communication unit smashed and suit ruptured. Somebody had skewered a line extender right through the suit, through her heart, an' out the other side. Normally, the meteor detection systems would have caught a picture of what happened, but they were out of action for scheduled maintenance. A bit of luck for the killer.

"We have a reconstruction of what happened, but it come out lousy. I don't think you should bother with it. You'll get a much better idea when you see everythin' for yourself."

I had to concentrate hard to keep my self-control. My mind had filled with an image of the body of Julia Vansittart. It floated in the great void, lost in a cavernous emptiness without end.

*You'll get a much better idea when you see everythin' for yourself.*

Those words raised the level of my discomfort to the point where my record of the next five minutes is based on despised conjecture, rather than the hard evidence of accurate recall.

"What do you mean, see for myself?" I croaked, terrified by the implications of his statement.

"Up on Sky City." Seth stared at me. "We gotta go there. Even the best reconstructions are nothin' like the real thing. I was thinkin', you get your head around the facts, then in a day or two the pair of us make a little trip."

"No! Absolutely not." The room was spinning around me. "A visit on my part to Sky City is totally impossible."

"It is? Look, if you're worried about gettin' caught, you don't have to. I got the system greased. I can make sure that nobody even suspects—"

"Did you not hear me?" I cried. "I cannot go to Sky City—or anywhere else in space." And, when he stared at me, "Did you not check my background before you came here? Since childhood I have suffered from extreme forms of acrophobia and agoraphobia. I cannot, to save my life, tolerate heights or open spaces." I pointed toward the invisible cliffs, half a mile to our west. "I can go no closer to the sea than we are now. As for outer space"—the very words caught in my throat—"in that intolerable environment I would be unable to think, to work, even to breathe."

He did not, to his credit, argue or rage or deny the reality of the problem. Instead he stood up and went to stare into the dying fire. "I didn't know that," he said at last. "I should have. There's nothin' you can do about it? I mean, like with drugs and fizzes?"

"Nothing. I have tried. Anything that damps my reaction sufficiently to tolerate an open environment leaves me unable to think."

"Which ain't too good, since your brain is what I need an' it's no use when it's mush." Seth turned to me, and to my astonishment he had a little smile on his face. "Dumb of me not to check everythin', wasn't it? But I guess I was in too much of a hurry to get here."

He went to sit once more by the fireside. "Well, now we got us a problem. You can't go to Sky City, an' Sky City sure as hell can't come to you. But it's real important for me to catch our murderer, an' I still think you're my best bet for that. So let's you an' me sit down, talk slow and easy, an' see what we come up with as a solution."

The man, mirabile dictu, was *humoring* me. For possibly the first time in my life I did not object.

# 6

Celine was used to kisses. She had spent her teenage years in the Philippines and traveled widely in Europe and the Middle East. In many nations of the world she knew that an embrace or a kiss on the cheek was as natural as a handshake.

Less common—unique, in fact, in Celine's experience—was the visitor who strode across the Oval Office, grabbed you in a bear hug, and gave you a great smacking kiss on the lips.

But that was Wilmer. He had acknowledged few of the rules of polite society when he and Celine were partners on the Mars expedition, and in the twenty-seven years since, he had apparently changed not at all.

Celine kissed him back, just as heartily. Lovers, even long-ago and faraway lovers, possess privileges denied to others. After a couple of seconds she pushed him away and held him at arm's length. "Wilmer Oldfield, you're as handsome and debonair as ever." His head, close to bald, wore its remaining hair close-cropped, and his idea of suitable White House dress was a faded brown shirt and pants short enough to show two inches of white socks.

"Now you must introduce me," Celine went on.

She had glimpsed the woman walking in behind Wilmer in the moment before she was grabbed and hugged. She made a more detailed survey now. The other visitor was short and broad and very black, with clear, shiny skin. She wore a tiny skirt of bright lime green and a yellow sleeveless top that showed off muscular limbs. Her hair was shaped into an array of jutting black spikes that suggested to Celine's eye an electrocuted cartoon character.

Wilmer's companion was in her mid-twenties. She appeared subdued and upset at the same time. "Celine," Wilmer said, "this

here's my friend Star Vjansander. Star, this here's Celine Tanaka."
He added, as an afterthought, "The President of the United States."

The woman bobbed her head. "Pleased t' meet yer, mam. I'm actually Astarte Vjansander; but if you want ter call me Star, like Wilmer does, that's all right."

The accent was unfamiliar. A broadness to the vowels, plus the occasional *ter* for *to,* and *yer* for *you.* Celine wondered if that was typical North Australian, and decided that she rather liked it. More familiar was the look that Astarte Vjansander gave Wilmer. Celine recognized it at once as adoration, though it was unlikely that Wilmer did. But it accounted for Astarte's discomfort when she saw the other two kissing. Had Wilmer bothered to mention that he and Celine had been an intimate item in the remote past, although there had been nothing more than platonic friendship for many years?

Probably not. It wasn't the sort of thing that would occur to him.

And was it a sexual relationship between Wilmer and Astarte? Probably, in spite of the big age difference. Wilmer might collect his female partners in a bemused and abstracted way, but he certainly collected them. Celine sensed her own objection to the idea that Wilmer and Astarte were lovers, at the same time as she was astonished by her reaction. If she didn't like to share Wilmer when he had not been part of her love life for a full quarter of a century, then no wonder Astarte was jealous. Humans were inexplicable only if you assumed that they were logical.

She smiled at the young woman, offering nonverbal reassurance that she had no territorial claims on Wilmer. But it was a waste of time, because before she could get onto Astarte's wavelength Wilmer was off and running.

"We probably sounded a bit mysterious to your lady in the outside office, insisting we had to see you in person and not telling her why. But you see, I didn't want to put her in a panic or have her spreading bad rumors."

"Given some of the things that Claudette has heard in the past few years, I don't think you need to worry. It would take news of the end of the world to shake her."

As a light remark, it fell flat. Astarte gasped and turned to Wilmer.

"She knows."

"No, she don't. Go on, Star, you tell it. It's your story. I mostly came to get you in to meet Celine."

Astarte nodded, but she didn't say a word. Celine had seen the same thing often enough in the past. People entered the office with their story carefully prepared, and promptly became tongue-tied in her presence. After the first few times she realized that it had nothing to do with her. It was the office of the presidency, carrying a weight unrelated to the personality and character of its current occupant. The surprise was that Astarte Vjansander felt it.

Celine said, "Let's all sit down and make ourselves comfortable. And Wilmer, why don't you start instead of Star? You've briefed me often enough, you know how to keep it down to my level."

She was making a trade-off. Wilmer must certainly know whatever it was that Astarte Vjansander wanted to say, otherwise he would never have brought her to meet Celine.

On the other hand, Wilmer's briefings had their own problems. Clarity, yes. Brevity, never. Celine sat back and prepared for a long evening.

"Is that all right with you, Star?" Wilmer said. And, at her nod, "You take over whenever you feel like it." He put his hand to the top of his bald head and rubbed at it for inspiration. "I think I'd better go a fair way back. Celine, you know how I told you there was something odd about the Alpha Centauri supernova, right from the beginning?"

"Told me once, told me twice, told me a hundred times. You may not remember this, but when we had our first look at the supernova, back on the *Schiaparelli,* you said that Alpha Centauri was a double star system, and double stars can become Type Ia supernovas only if one of the pair is a white dwarf. And Alpha Centauri didn't qualify."

"Still doesn't," Wilmer said placidly. "Bit of a nuisance, really, since the thing *did* go supernova. Zoe Nash told me then that if that's what the astrophysicists' theories said, we damn well better get new theories. She was right, of course. Poor old Zoe." He stared off at nothing for a few seconds, then shook his head. "Anyway, I worked and worked trying to explain the Alpha C supernova. And I got nowhere."

Celine could imagine what lay behind those simple words. When Wilmer latched on to a question he was a bulldog, worrying at the problem endlessly. He had picked up and solved many other problems during the past quarter of a century, but she suspected that there had never been a waking moment when the mystery of the supernova was fully out of his mind.

Wilmer wouldn't have had much help, either. Since the supernova, human survival and planetary rebuilding had been the sole priorities. There had been no spare money or resources for pure research, and you met few young physicists.

"You had no theory?" she asked, when neither Wilmer nor Astarte seemed ready to speak.

"Worse than that. I had a dozen." Wilmer blinked at Celine. He was almost sixty, yet his eyes still had the clear innocence of a young child. "A few of the ideas were beauts, too. You could go to bed with 'em at night, and still be in love when you woke up in the morning. But you know what they say, a beautiful theory gets destroyed by one ugly fact. I could make up all sorts of mechanisms that might let Alpha C go supernova. I could even make my models match bits and pieces of the data. Sometimes I fitted the recorded light curves, or maybe the neutrino arrival pattern, and a few times I got the gamma pulse profile. What I couldn't do was find a theory that would match all the data at once. Which means, when you get right down to it, that I didn't have a theory at all. That's where it stood for all those years. And that's where it stood four months ago, when Star came to see me."

He beamed at his young companion. She smiled back, a quick flash of crooked white teeth, but she ducked her head when she saw Celine was watching.

"Would you like something?" Celine asked. What she had in mind was a low-level fizz, something to calm Astarte and make her feel more at ease. All the while that Wilmer had been speaking, the young visitor had fidgeted on the edge of her chair.

"Yes, mam." Astarte gave another wriggle, but still she didn't look at Celine. "Mam, I'd like ter go ter the bathroom. In fact, I have ter, right this minute, or I'll pee on the chair."

"Last person to do that was probably Calvin Coolidge," Celine said. She wondered if Astarte heard her, because as soon as she added, "Private facility through that door, help yourself," Star was off, vanishing into the bathroom.

"Ta, mam," she said as the door closed.

"Nerves," Wilmer said. "She'll get over it. If it's all right with you, we'll wait 'til she comes back so she can hear everything and join in when she feels ready. Star's not normally like this. You'll see, she'll perk up."

"We'll wait for her. I've got nothing to do."

Wilmer nodded. Irony was wasted on him, or possibly he found it reasonable that the President of the United States had lots of free time. Celine looked for a tactful way to phrase her next remark—though tact, like irony, was alien to Wilmer.

"Astarte doesn't seem like one of your usual colleagues."

"She's not. She's a damn sight smarter. Smarter than them, smarter than me."

At Celine's skeptical glance, he added, "She is, you know. I'm sure of it, but most people can't recognize that because the way she does things is so off the wall. You'll see it when she's at ease and can relax a bit. It's her first time north of the line, too, so she's nervous. When she feels at home she can get a bit crude. Some of the people at the New Sydney institute say she needs to be housebroken."

"I can understand anyone's feeling strange the first time they're in this office. I know I was." It seemed to Celine that Astarte Vjansander was already quite as crude as she needed to be. As for her talents, Celine would reserve judgment—although Wilmer was not one to underrate his abilities. "How did you find her?"

"I didn't. She found me. Star thinks she's twenty-four, but she's not sure. She's had a hell of a life. She was born in what used to be the Northern Territory, a few years after Alpha C, when the whole of Australia was still a wreck. She doesn't know who her parents were, but she reckons they have to be dead. She was about seven years old, living in the middle of nowhere, when the Vjansander party found her during the first post-supernova survey. She ate bugs and little lizards and crocodile eggs and anything else she could find. She could speak some, which is pretty much a miracle, considering there was nobody else around. She didn't know her name."

"So where did she learn science?"

"Beats me. Breathed it in through her skin, I guess. Things in science that the average twelve-year-old would know, she's never heard of. But she finds other ways. I don't believe she works in words at all; it's pictures and equations. After she arrived at the institute, at the first seminar that I took her to—"

"Later," Celine said quietly. She hoped that the housebroken remark was not to be taken literally, because the bathroom door was opening. "Everything all right, Star?"

"Real good." Astarte gave Celine her first full smile, and she seemed like a different person. "There's nothing beats a pee, is there, when yer really have ter go? I feel loads better."

"Like to take over, then?" Wilmer asked. "It's your theory."

"That's all right." Star went to her chair, staring at it before she sat down. "Did that Coolidge fella yer talked about really sit here and unload?"

"I doubt it." Celine laughed. "But who knows? Silent Cal, they called him. He'd never have admitted it." The meeting was taking a downward turn. "Wilmer? Where were we when you stopped?"

"I said I was churning out supernova theories by the cartload, and all of them crashed when I compared them with experiment. I showed 'em to Star in the first month after she came to New Sydney. She agreed they were all junk. *Data rules.* Theories have to fit observations, not the other way round. So I thought that was the end of it."

Wilmer paused again, looking right past Celine and frowning at the wall of the office.

"But it wasn't?" she prompted.

"For a long time I wasn't sure. Star came to me with something new, but it made me real uncomfortable. Right, Star?"

She nodded. "He told me that I knew bugger-all about how to prove things, an' all I was doing was making wild-arse guesses. And he told me if I kept dropping monkey-nut shells on the floor where he stepped on 'em in his bare feet, I'd get a boot up the wazoo and be out of there so quick I wouldn't know where I was 'til I landed."

Celine decided that she might as well relax. This meeting would go at its own pace, regardless of her preferences. "Still works barefoot, does he?" she said. "I used to tell him he only did it in case he ever needed to count to more than ten."

Astarte hooted, and Wilmer said mildly, "Star still doesn't know how to prove things, and she's a bugger to have around the house because she never cleans up. But she's infernal good at guessing.

And there are great ideas that just can't be proved until long after they're discovered. Remember Max Planck."

"The physicist?" Celine did remember Max Planck, but Wilmer had lost her. "Planck, like in Planck's constant and the Planck length?"

"That's him. A hundred and fifty years ago, there was a problem in physics that had everybody baffled. When you worked out the formula for how much energy should radiate from a closed box, you found that at short wavelengths the calculated value went to infinity. In the real world that obviously wasn't the case. And data rules, theory only serves. But people who looked at the analysis all agreed with the results, and they were some of the best minds of the time— men like Rayleigh and Jeans and Boltzmann.

"So there was a big problem, and no solution. Then in 1900 Max Planck showed that if you used a *trick,* you could get a curve that fitted the experiments for all wavelengths. It was a really odd trick, because to get the right answer you had to use a formula that would apply only if the energy radiating out of the box came in little discrete packages. Planck gave the package a name, a *quantum,* and he could calculate how big each quantum had to be. He found that it involved a new constant. Planck's constant."

"Wilmer, I heard all this thirty-odd years ago, and then I forgot it. Do I really need to hear it again?"

His high forehead furrowed. "Yeah. Of course you do. Otherwise I wouldn't be saying it, would I?"

"Go on, then." Celine had forgotten how impervious Wilmer was to distractions. "Just keep in mind that we can go to dinner as soon as we feel ready to eat it."

"I'm ready now. I'll speed up a bit. Everybody thought that what Planck did in 1900 was a *mathematical* trick, that it didn't mean squat in the real world. Energy couldn't really come in little bundles. Even if the method worked for some reason when you were dealing with radiation from a closed box, that wasn't the way the rest of the world operated.

"But then Einstein took what Max Planck had done at face value. He explained the photoelectric effect by saying that light, and all radiation, interacted with matter as though the light was made up of quanta. If a quantum had enough energy, it would jar an electron loose from a surface that the light hit. If it didn't have enough energy—if the wavelength of the light was too long—then no matter how intense the beam of light, there would be no release of electrons."

"I've heard that before, too, and I'm getting hungry. Wilmer, what's your point?"

"It's this. Star made an assumption. We can go into details about what it is later; all I need to say at the moment is that it's the same order of assumption that Planck made in 1900. Radical, and simple, and enough to make you drop your back teeth. Star can't give you a justification for it, and neither can I, any more than Max Planck could. But with that assumption, and with nothing else that I didn't already have in my theories, Star matched the recorded light curves from Alpha C, *and* the neutrino arrival pattern, *and* the gamma pulse profile. The lot, all at once, which was something I had never been able to do. And it's something I would never have been able to do, nor would anyone else, if Star hadn't made that leap of intuition."

"That's great." Celine looked from Wilmer to Astarte, who was now basking in Wilmer's praise. "I believe you, and I think it's wonderful for both of you. And I'm glad to see you, Wilmer, anytime. But I don't see why you had to come running over here to tell me this when you could just as easily have called."

But did she know, or at least suspect? Celine recalled Astarte's gasp when she mentioned the imminent end of the world. The bad thing about being a world-class worrier was that being right was worse than being wrong.

"No," Wilmer said. "We absolutely had to come, as soon as we finished checking the calculations. Star's theory says that one component of the particle flux released at the time of the supernova ought to be traveling a lot faster than the old theories predicted. So we have less time than we expected."

Celine's mind ran ahead, wondering about the rest of it. "When?"

"We're not absolutely sure. We need the latest Sniffer data to determine accurate dates, and we don't have it. Can you get that for us?"

"Yes. When will all this happen?"

"A big slug of particles could be here soon."

"*When?*"

"Real soon. Months, maybe even weeks." Wilmer leaned back and told Celine something she already knew better than he did. "Trouble is, the space shield you're building can't possibly be ready."

Wilmer and Astarte added to Celine's problems during dinner.

Meals were not optional events for Celine, even if the sky was falling. She had learned something during the disastrous return of the Mars expedition to Earth: Even when you were worried sick, even when you had zero appetite, even when you were so depressed that food felt like it stuck in your gullet, you had to eat.

First, though, Nick Lopez needed to know that the World Protection Federation—and the world—was in for bad news. Celine tried a quick call while Star went out to collect her and Wilmer's luggage. The call turned out to be a wasted effort. On a planet where everyone could supposedly be reached at any time, Lopez did not answer. His whereabouts were stated as "unknown" by the staff of the World Protection Federation.

Celine didn't believe that for a moment. They knew, but they weren't telling. She left a message saying that she and Nick needed to talk on an urgent matter. After a moment she added the words *highly sensitive.* That ought to tickle Nick's political curiosity.

As soon as Astarte had their luggage she would be conducted by the White House staff to the private dining room, where their meal should be waiting. As Celine and Wilmer headed that way she asked him how he had first heard of Astarte Vjansander.

"Out of the blue," he said. "One day, five months ago, I got this package from the convent at Weipa, way up north on Albatross Bay."

"You mean Star is a *nun?*"

"Gawdelpus, no. If Star's a nun, Madame Curie ran a whorehouse. Star lived in the wild; she just used the convent as a mailing address and a place to beg free meals. Anyway, the envelope I received was full of pages of equations and drawings, all handwritten. I recognized the name Vjansander, it's common in the territory, but I drew a blank with the name Astarte. At first I thought it had to be a man, because if a woman was given a name that sounded like *ass* and *tarty* put together, she'd change it soon as she could. Then during the tea break I found that Maria Greene and old Herbert Westerly had received copies of the same thing I had—all hand-written, must have taken ages. They'd looked at a few pages and found no sign of a proof for anything, so they'd chucked out the whole mess. I went back to my room, ready to follow their example, because there's more nuts in the world than you can believe. It's always the same old story: Einstein was wrong, Dirac didn't understand what he was doing, Feynman was too simpleminded, Gottlieb missed the point. See, they always go after the big game in physics, and their own alternative ideas are always gibberish. It's like Pauli says, most of the theories are so bad they're not even wrong."

They had reached the dining room and Astarte was not yet there. Celine walked over to the window and stared out at the night sky, looking to where Sky City would be, as Wilmer went on: "So I was all set to dump the papers into the trash. But I riffled through as I was ready to drop 'em, and I saw equations that I recognized at the bottom of a couple of the pages. One was the Klein-Nishina scattering formula, and the other was an old equation for something called an Emden polytrope, in an odd notation. That said we were in Eddington country. But the thing that struck me about what I was looking at wasn't that those were *new* results—they were old, both of 'em—but that they were *detailed*. People with half-assed ideas always go grandiose, and they start by throwing overboard things like relativity or the conservation of energy. No sign of that here.

"So I glanced at a couple more pages and I saw variations on more things I recognized, like nucleosynthesis and stellar structure and stability. That's when I cleared my desk, put my head down, and took a real good look."

Celine could imagine what that meant. Wilmer had more *sitzfleisch* than a tired camel, more stamina than anyone in the world to sit in one place and worry at a problem while the seasons changed around him. He would remain at his desk forever, his high forehead with its heavy brow ridges scowling at nothing while his mind bludgeoned Nature into revealing its secrets.

"And I decided that whoever sent me the stuff wasn't a nutcase at all," Wilmer concluded. "Some of the ideas still seemed crazy, some I felt sure were dead wrong, a few I could see ways maybe to improve. But I knew I'd have to talk to the feller first and make sure I was reading him right. So I headed up-country to look for him. And I found Star. And I brought her back to the institute. I got her a staff position."

A staff position, when there was precious little money for anything and none for theoretical physicists. Of course. As simple as that—if you were Wilmer Oldfield and you paid no attention to obstacles.

"She didn't really live in the wild, did she?"

"She said she didn't. I think she did, though, and I bet you would, too." Wilmer turned away from the window and went to help himself to the stuffed celery sticks. "They do you well here," he said with his mouth full. "Maybe it's not all that bad being President. Anyway, Star had a little one-roomer at the edge of a wet-weather creek. Outside fireplace. No plumbing. No crapper. You want to take a dump, you do it out in the bush like the animals, and hope there's no saltwater croc around to take a bite out of your arse. No electronics, of course, so no reference service or webwalks. Star had a couple dozen physics and astronomy books, all pre-Alpha C. She wouldn't tell me where she got 'em—pinched 'em, for a guess—and a big slate board for writing down results. Not much used. She does analysis mostly in her head, like me. Saves on chalk."

"So what was the big new idea she had?" Celine asked. "Even if it's hard to understand, you have to be able to explain it to me. If I don't get it, I guarantee that not many others around here will."

"Best you ask Star about that." Wilmer paused in his steady munching. "You give her a drink or two, get her loosened up, and she'll talk. Do I hear her clogs out there? What's she doing?"

The footsteps on the hard polished floor of the corridor had an odd cadence. They clopped forward half a dozen paces, paused for five seconds, advanced, and paused again.

"I think she's looking at the pictures," Celine said. "It's a portrait gallery of the Presidents." She suspected from Wilmer's expression that he had walked along the same corridor three minutes earlier and never noticed the walls at all. She moved across to the side table and said as Star came in, "Here you are. How about a drink, then?"

"Yer better believe it." Astarte was carrying a single bag. Like Wilmer, she apparently believed in traveling light—the travel bag was for both of them. She walked forward to the table, picked up a bottle of vodka, and sniffed at it. As she poured two tumblersful she said, "Lot of ugly old buggers out there in the hall. Yer the only woman, and the only one of the whole lot who looks halfway human."

If you tried really hard, you could take that as a compliment. Celine pointed to the ice bucket as Astarte handed one of the tumblers to Wilmer. Star shook her head. "Dilutes the goodness out." She raised her glass, took a big gulp, and breathed in deeply through her nose. "Not bad. Better than at the convent. Tastes a bit turpid, though. D'yer make it yerself?"

"In the basement," Celine said, and saw Star's accepting nod. Another joke fallen down dead. She made a decision and poured herself a glass of chilled white wine. In politics it often helped to be the only one sober, but tonight was not politics.

Though what it was, Celine was not sure. Not the end of the world, but perhaps the beginning of the end?

"Come and sit down." She nodded at the server, and it began to rotate the loaded tureens slowly to each place.

Astarte brought her tumbler and the bottle with her, set them down in front of her, and watched the action of the server. "Smart little bugger," she said after a while. The server was pausing only at places where someone was sitting. "How's it know where we are?"

"Thermal sensor. Help yourself."

"Yeah. We do it that way at the convent in Weipa. Only they got *people* to serve food for yer at Wilmer's institute, so yer feel yer can't take too much. How come yer don't get served by people? Yer the President."

"People talk more freely if there's no one else listening." Which was a totally bogus explanation, since Celine knew that the whole meeting was being recorded. "Just take what you want from any dish."

"And you use a knife and fork, Star," Wilmer added. "Same as at the institute. Or you'll be in trouble."

Astarte glared at him, but she nodded. She piled her plate high with meat and shrimp, ignoring all forms of vegetable. Wilmer took his turn and helped himself to a ton of everything. As he was doing so Astarte drained her glass and refilled it to the brim from the bottle of vodka.

"No worries." Wilmer noticed Celine's dubious look. "Star's got a hollow leg. She'll drink you and me under the table and then go back to work on her physics. How about a bit of chat from you, Star? I bring you all this way, and we don't get a peep out of you. What's Celine here going to think?"

"All right." In spite of Wilmer's warning Astarte was holding three large shrimp in her left hand and a juicy veal chop in her right. "What yer want me ter say?"

"It's your theory, girl. Talk about it."

"What about my food?"

"It can wait. We're not going to pinch it."

Celine added, "If you like, we can warm it for you later."

"Oh, all right." Astarte reluctantly put down the veal chop and the shrimp and wiped her hands on the sides of her sleeveless top. "A supernova's—mmm—just one form of stellar—mmm—instability."

"Chew and swallow first." Wilmer turned to Celine. "I can't take her anywhere. She does that all the time. You'd think she was a pelican the way she packs food into her mouth."

Star grinned at Celine, a round-cheeked chipmunk smile, chewed, swallowed, and finally said, "He's always on at me, but he's all right otherwise. Let's start with a question: When is a star unstable? Wilmer proved that yer can't make Alpha Centauri go supernova if you work with the usual theories and continuous variables. But it did. Once you accept that, then yer have ter ask, can yer do it with *discontinuous* variables? Things that act like an impulse. You know what an impulse is, do you?"

"Assume I do." Once, in the distant past, Celine had possessed a first-rate technical training. The question was, how much of it remained?

"There's a few different ways to drive a star toward instability," Astarte went on. "One is, you load on mass from outside until all of a sudden you have a collapse and an explosion. Another is you run out of raw material for fusion, an' again you get a collapse an' explosion. But those don't work for Alpha Centauri; Wilmer proved that. So I asked myself, is there another way to cause instability, using some kind of impulsive events?

"Well, there is. Yer take a star—an' it don't have ter be the usual sort of star for a supernova. I mean, it don't have to be a binary with one dwarf component, or a star many times as massive as the Sun. It can be any old star, could even be Sol. There's something for yer to think about. So you take this star, an' you apply a compressive pulse. A bit of a squeeze, and it don't have to be a big squeeze, either. Yer can do it asymmetric, like on opposite poles, or you can make it work with radial squeezes, too, toward the center. Either way, yer can calculate the modes of oscillation."

"You mean *you* can."

"Yeah. Me and Wilmer." Astarte picked up a shrimp, stared at it longingly, then put it down. "A star is stable because there's a balance everywhere inside it between gravitational force inward and radiation pressure outward. So the star reacts ter the squeeze by contracting a bit, then the radiation pressure takes hold and pushes it back out. It overshoots a little bit, comes out a bit farther than it was ter start with, and oscillates. For some stars, like Cepheid variables, the wobble occurs naturally. But for most stars the oscillation will damp out—unless, just at the right moment, yer hit it again with another compressive pulse. And then you hit it again, and again, doing it each time at just the right moment. Then the oscillations don't damp out at all. Yer get resonance."

"Like soldiers," Celine said, "marching over a bridge. They're supposed to break step and not march together, otherwise the regular rhythm of their marching could hit the resonant frequency of the bridge and make it collapse."

"I didn't hear about that!" Star's eyes widened with pleasure. "I love it. Have yer seen it happen?"

"No. Actually, I'm not sure it ever has. But people talk about it all the time as if it's true."

"Yer could do it. You're the President, you're in charge of the Army. Yer could take a whole bunch of troops, and a bridge, and tell 'em ter march over and not break step and see what happens."

"Not if I want to stay President I couldn't," Celine said, and

Wilmer added, "Star, unless I hear more astrophysics I'll take that bottle away."

"First yer tell me ter talk, and then when I'm talking you complain." Astarte turned to Celine. "Anyway, an oscillating star's not quite like troops walking over a bridge. It's more like a pendulum, where if yer give it a bit of a nudge on each swing, the size of the swing gets bigger and bigger each time. But all of a sudden, instead of swinging back, the pendulum changes the way it moves." Star made a complete revolution with her arm. "It goes right over the top and comes down on the other side. That's what it does if it's a pendulum. If it's a star, it goes supernova. Like Alpha Centauri went supernova. Got it?"

"I think so." Celine had been expecting something far more complicated, and this seemed remarkably clear and simple. "The star experiences a small impulsive force, applied regularly."

"No." Star scowled. "Maybe I shouldn't have used the pendulum idea. Yer can't hit a star with a *regular* squeeze, you have ter do it at intervals that vary with time, or it won't work —and calculating the times gave us no end of trouble."

"But the principle's the same, isn't it?" Celine was reluctant to abandon her nice mental picture. "I mean, instead of coming regularly, the squeezes come at certain calculated times. And if that goes on long enough, the whole star becomes unstable."

"It does indeed," Wilmer said, and Star added, "Becomes unstable, and explodes like a son of a bitch."

"That makes perfect sense." But Celine suspected that she was still missing something. "Why did you think I would find it hard to accept?"

"Not that part," said Wilmer. "I felt sure you'd accept everything so far."

"So what else is there?" Celine looked from Wilmer to Astarte, who had bent low over her plate, grabbed her veal chop in both hands, and was tearing a big piece off it with those crooked white teeth. "What haven't you told me?"

Astarte stared at her silently over the lump of bloody meat and went on chewing steadily.

"We haven't told you the part that's hard to accept," Wilmer said. "The oscillatory squeeze process that Star describes works perfectly. It allows us to reproduce every measurement that we've made since the beginning of the Alpha C supernova. But there's something we've not discussed."

He deliberately waited, until Celine said, "What?" She had a hollow feeling in the pit of her stomach, as if her worry button had just been pressed.

"The *agent*. What is it that can impose such a systematic, exactly timed compressive pulse on a whole star?"

"You mean, what physical process can produce that effect?"

"I wish I meant that, but I don't." Wilmer seemed upset, and to Celine that was a bad sign. Wilmer *never* became uncomfortable when physics was the subject. "We've racked our brains, Star and me, trying to come up with a natural explanation for what happened. And we can't. The timing sequence of the impulses needed to make Alpha C go pop is so peculiar and improbable, I don't see how it could possibly arise naturally. Something or somebody produced that sequence *by design*. Something *made* that star system go supernova."

While Celine stared in disbelief, Astarte said, "Tell her the rest. About the gamma pulse and the particle storm."

"Oh, yes." Wilmer rubbed the bald patch on the top of his head—already red and inflamed from his previous attentions. "It turns out that the right sequence of impulsive compressions needed to provide a supernova is not radially symmetrical. Certain modes of oscillation must be excited, and that in turn gives preferred directions of emission for gamma rays and for the charged particle beam. Everyone always assumed that the fact that the gamma-ray beam was aimed to hit Earth, twenty-seven years ago, was a piece of pure bad luck."

"Wasn't it?" Celine was wondering if she could ever explain to anyone else what Wilmer and Astarte had been saying. Not one of her colleagues had any previous experience with Wilmer, or understood his brilliance and intellectual honesty.

"It wasn't bad luck," Wilmer said, and Astarte nodded firmly.

"Calculations show that it can't be an accident," she added. "Yer see, the Sun moves at thirty-two kilometers a second relative ter Alpha Centauri. Ter have a narrow gamma-ray beam intersect the position of Sol, twenty-seven years ago, and then ter have the main front of the particle storm hit Sol *again,* in its new position tens of billions of kilometers away—that's off the scale on the probability charts.

"Something *made* Alpha Centauri go supernova. And that same something *arranged* for the gamma pulse and the particle storm ter run right smack bang into our solar system."

# 7

**From the private diary of Oliver Guest.**

A Proustian obsession with one's own past is, to my mind, an indicator of mental illness.

And yet, sometimes, it is necessary.

Seth Parsigian had departed at midday telling me that he was going to "check out ideas" that might solve the problem of my inability to face a trip to Sky City. He did not tell me what those ideas were. I did not ask. Nor did he mention an intention to return. I knew the man. He would be back.

Meanwhile, there were the records. Parsigian left with me a mountain of data and conjectures relating to the twelve murders, together with the less-than-helpful advice "See what you can sift out of it, Doc."

Sifting, however, was not what I had in mind when I sat down, early the same afternoon, to begin my review of the material that he had left with me. What I sought was that intangible sense of *contact*, the ineffable touch of another's mind.

Murders, particularly murders of compulsion, represent consequence rather than cause. They occur as the result of some particular motivation. In my own case, it was—and is—a desire to match mental to physical perfection. What, then, motivated the murderer of teenage girls in Sky City? What had been in his mind *before* he killed?

I examined once more the known facts of the murders, and found thin gruel. I had the dates, the circumstances and places of death, the physical descriptions, and the names: Myra Skelton, Tanya Bishop, Doris Wu, Cissy Muller, April Jarrow, Brenda Cleve, Lucille DeNorville, Denise Braidley, Julia Vansittart, Elke Edson, Georgina Yang, and Kate Ulrey. What did they have in common?

They were young, they were female, and they were dead.

More informative, perhaps: What did they *not* have in common? They were of widely variable wealth and social class, from the dirt-poor welders' daughters Brenda Cleve and Cissy Muller to the rich Myra Skelton and the even richer and royally connected Lucille De-Norville. They were not, as Seth had suggested, all beautiful, at least to my tastes. But who could say how the murderer had seen them? Before I knew that I would have to learn to see through his eyes.

The most significant fact was the wide range in the victims' ages. April Jarrow had been eight, Doris Wu close to fifteen and a half. Although Seth had remarked that April was big for her age, he'd missed the point. I had studied the photographs and medical reports, and April and Doris lay on opposite sides of the great divide of puberty. This, in turn, seemed to place the murderer's mind beyond reach of my own, since I would never have thought to approach a prepubescent girl.

Would I?

I have an excellent memory for facts. But how to summon to mind bygone emotional states, sensations past? That must also come from the study of cold, hard facts. Alexander Pope puts it as well as anyone: "*Remembrance and reflection, how allied. What thin partitions sense from thought divide.*"

As afternoon wore on into long summer evening I put all records to one side, abandoned myself to recollection, and sought the depths of my own past.

The initiating event was clear in my mind. I was in my first year of postdoctoral study, bubbling with the ferment of ideas on the causes of apoptosis that led, five years later and via a circuitous route that I could never have imagined in advance, to a full understanding of cell death and thence to telomod therapy.

The research facility where I worked occupied a full block in the center of Atlanta. And here, for the unseen reader who is presumed to hover at the shoulder of every diarist, I must note that I am talking of a time close to forty years ago. The blooming of postapocalyptic Atlanta lay far in the future, while Atlanta's first golden age was far vanished in the past. When first created, the Institute for Probatory Therapies sat on choice real estate; by the time I moved there it was totally surrounded by the dark metallic heart of the city. The Scantlings had taken over, and that sect's insistence on uniformity of dress, diet, appearance, possessions, beliefs, and behavior had created the peculiar form of urban paralysis so characteristic of the second decade of this century.

I do not remember being much aware of this at the time. In fact, I feel sure that I was oblivious to details of my surroundings that did not relate directly to my work. The lab still possessed first-rate equipment. My own living quarters, a mile and a half away, consisted of two rooms in a four-story walk-up with a shared bathroom and inadequate hot water, but it satisfied my needs. Had I been asked, I would surely have said that I was perfectly happy.

How much of human happiness stems from an ignorance of what we are missing? I had tried sex with women in four brief affairs since the age of twenty, and found it fairly enjoyable but inferior in excitement to the intoxicating pleasures of research. I felt no urge toward sex with members of my own gender. Thus I had no partner or companion, and with no one else to set the pattern of my days it was my habit to rise late and work until I felt ready to stop. Usually that was after midnight, and often far beyond.

Sometimes, as on this day, dawn was touching the horizon as I left the institute and headed home. The Scantlings' rigidity had one beneficial effect: The hours between eleven at night and six in the morning were the decreed Scantling time for sleeping, and the streets during that interval were deserted except for the machine security patrols.

It was a half-hour walk, a fine opportunity for the solitary thoughts that summarize today's work and make plans for tomorrow. I expected to see and hear no one and nothing, except the occasional blinking and electric hum of a mobile monitor camera. With the rising sun in my eyes I did not notice the girl sitting on the stone steps of one of the buildings six blocks from mine, until she moved as I passed.

Objects came rattling down to the sidewalk and rolled under my feet. I, startled out of my reverie, trod on one of them and almost fell. I was still recovering my balance when a dark figure hurried past me and swooped on the rolling sphere.

"Got it," said a girl's husky voice. "Did you see where the other one went? Don't want to lose it."

In the morning light I saw a gleam of dull red retreating down the slight incline. I took four quick steps forward and picked it up just before it vanished into the open grille of a storm drain.

I looked at what I was holding. It was a glass marble, its swirls of white shot through with blood-red streaks. Before I could do anything else the girl was next to me and had grabbed it from my hand.

"Thanks," she said. "I wouldn't have minded losing a glaury or a spumy, but this is an alley-taw blood-orange and I got nothing else like it."

She spoke with the flat vowels and swallowed consonants of the streets. Her words were gibberish, though I realized that she must be referring to the glass marbles and some children's game. She went on talking about the little spheres, holding them out to me for inspection. I replied, but I was hardly listening. She was slim and short, no more than an inch or two above five feet. I saw a tangle of black ringlets above a pale, smooth forehead, dark, wide eyes below, a mobile mouth, a clear complexion, and the slender, budding figure of a girl on the brink of adolescence. Her clothes were ugly, too big and too adult for her.

"What are you doing outside at this time of night?" I asked. "You ought to be home in bed."

My words were, I swear it, spoken in all innocence, and with nothing but the girl's safety and welfare in mind.

" 'Tisn't night," she said. The deep, husky voice belied her age, but she couldn't have been more than fourteen. "It's light now."

"You know what I mean. Where do you live?"

"Right here." She raised one arm to point to the building behind her. The overlarge sleeve of her black blouse hung down like a bat's wing. "Third floor."

I had entered the building briefly eight months earlier when searching for a place to live. It was, like the tenement where my apartment was located, one of the few structures of central Atlanta not controlled and occupied by Scantlings. Even though it was closer to the institute, I had rejected the place because it seemed populated entirely by transients and small-time criminals.

"What are you doing out here so early?" I asked.

"That's my business, not yours." She stared up at me. "What are *you* doing out?"

"I'm on my way from work. At the institute." I pointed west, away from the rising sun.

She nodded, but her mind must have been still on my question to her, because she said, "I come outside because she brought somebody home with her."

"She?"

I knew the answer, even before she said, "My mother. She brought him last night, about eleven."

"You had to leave?"

" 'Course not." She frowned at me, as though I had asked a nonsense question. "I live there, don't I? I could have stayed, even though he was an all-nighter." She cocked one dark eyebrow at me. "There'd be nothing new, you know. I've seen it all before."

In conventional tests of knowledge and speed of comprehension, I am not boasting when I say that I score well outside the range where such measurements are deemed useful. If I seemed slow to understand what she was saying, it is only that we were beyond my parameters not only of experience but of acceptance.

"Your mother brought a man home to sleep with her last night?" I said.

"Right. Flush, by the sound of him."

"And you've been out here ever since?"

"Oh, no." She rubbed the blood-orange glass marble against her blouse and peered at it anxiously for damage. "I only come out here a couple of hours ago, when they woke me up. My bed's right up against the wall and they was making too much noise." She stared at me and added, apparently in defense of her mother, "They was both pretty high, I could tell soon as they come in."

"So when will you go back?"

She pulled a face. "Can go in anytime I want. But I don't want. Where you going now?"

It was chilly, with a brisk wind swirling around the street corner. I became aware of how hungry I felt. I had eaten nothing since the previous afternoon.

"I'm heading home, for a hot breakfast," I said. "It's not far from here. If you don't want to go home and you would like to eat, you can come with me."

She took a step closer and looked up at me with eyes too knowing for her age. "Breakfast. That all?"

"It's all I'm offering."

"Yeah. Well, okay. Breakfast."

"Don't you need to tell your mother?"

"Tell her what? She isn't invited, is she?"

"No."

"Anyway, she never eats when she's working." She stuffed the marbles into a pocket of the long brown skirt. "Ready when you are."

"What's your name?" I asked.

"Paula. Paula Searle."

"I'm Oliver. Oliver Guest."

"Pleased to meet you," she said calmly. The scream or gasp of horror that invariably followed the mention of my name would not occur until five years later. She reached out, her small hand swallowed up in mine for a formal handshake. "You must have a rotten job if it keeps you up all night. What do you do?"

We began to walk side by side, I deliberately shortening my step to fit hers. There seemed little chance that she would comprehend any element of my work, but we had six long blocks to walk. I told her of my own background in biology. I started to explain the nature and causes of apoptosis, the preprogrammed death that comes to most (but not all) cells of an organism. I spoke more for my benefit than hers—my mental review of the previous night's work had been interrupted by our chance meeting—and I made no attempt to talk down to her or to simplify the intrinsically complex biochemistry.

She said nothing, and after a couple of minutes brought a couple of marbles from her pocket and began to chink them together. I assumed that she had stopped listening, until suddenly she said, "It all happens from inside, don't it, like the cell's wearing out? I mean, it's not like a virus or something gets in and kills it."

Paula Searle, in thirty seconds, made real and tangible a truth that I had previously known only intellectually: Just as mental slowness occurs no less frequently in those of royal descent (more frequently, some would say, with an argument based on sound genetic principles), so intelligence and talent and quickness of wit may surface in the deepest despairing depths of society.

Paula was *bright*.

We walked, we talked, we came to my building and went up. I cooked while Paula explored the small apartment and made derogatory comments concerning my inadequate wardrobe and rickety table and total lack of entertainment facilities. She had removed the dark blouse and dowdy wraparound skirt that mimicked Scantling attire, and was now revealed in brief shorts and a T-shirt of pale yellow. With her coltish limbs and liquid dark eyes, she danced and skipped between the two rooms of my apartment and brightened any spot upon which she lighted.

At one point she sang a Scantling hymn, "The Narrow Gate of Heaven." She had a small, true voice, and I listened with pleasure until I realized that the song was a parody, the same tune but with words of sexual innuendo and details of illegal surgery to make you shudder.

"Don't sing that," I said.

She paused in her wandering and stared at me in surprise. "Sorry. I know somebody had it done to her, just like in the song. But if it makes you too hot, I'll stop."

"Please." But I wondered, could she be right? I was in truth oddly excited, although not in any way that I could relate to my previous sexual experiences.

Even with distractions, I am a good cook. When we ate—her reaction to my food and my cooking were positive—I asked more about her background. How old was she, how long had they been living where they were now, where had she been before that, did she have other relatives in Atlanta, where was her father?

I was making conversation, easily and naturally. Just as when we had finished eating, she, easily and naturally, went through to sprawl across my bed while I cleaned up.

It took me no more than five minutes. When I came through to ask if she now was ready to go back home, she was sound asleep.

It seemed wrong to wake her. I moved a soft chair in from the other room and sat down. She had in her answers to my questions revealed an appallingly adult knowledge of the world. Her mother had moved from Norfolk four months ago. They had become afraid when Paula's "father" was killed in an argument over stolen goods from a warehouse raid. Paula and her mother were not registered, so she had not been able to go to school for over a year. When she was older— not much older, though she was not sure how much—she would help earn her keep. Not with men like her mother brought home, Mother promised her that, but with ones young and nice. But—her red-rose mouth stretched wide in a grimace—you'd be a fool to believe that, wouldn't you?

I looked down at her. In sleep, all her cynicism vanished and only innocence remained. Here was a beautiful and intelligent child, on the brink of becoming a woman. The world ought to be opening out before her in all its glory and diversity, but that would never happen. Not to little Paula. The narrow gate of heaven had for her already closed. She was the loveliest thing I had ever seen, with grace and brains and talent far beyond the women with whom I had made love, but already she was tainted and blighted. *"That which is marred at birth, time will not mend."*

I did not intend to sleep, nor did I make plans before I slept. Nor, while I slept, did I dream. And yet, when I awoke soon after noon, the idea—the resolve, the compulsion—was already formed in my mind, to the smallest detail of planning and execution. (Yes, yes, I know; let us not trivialize a life with a sniggering and obvious play on words.)

She would be missed, maybe in hours but possibly not for days. Her mother, as an unregistered resident of Atlanta wary of authority, might never report the disappearance; and if she did, what would any rational investigator conclude? Surely that Paula had chosen the unknown future of a runaway's life over the sordid certainties of the present.

I waited two hours more, until Paula stirred and sat up and smiled at me. "Oliver Guest," she said. *"Doctor* Oliver Guest. Do you really work with all those animals and things like you said, or were you making it up?"

"I really do. And I must go back to work this afternoon. And you ought to go home to your mother."

I am sure that I said those words. They sound as though I was faint-hearted, or suffering second thoughts. The reality was more complex. I wanted to believe, at some level, that Paula was my accomplice in what I planned to do, that it was her desire as well as mine. It would be, after all, to her ultimate benefit.

"She won't care where I am," she said. "Big Maury Wellstone comes around Sunday nights, and she always needs her sleep before him."

"Is it Sunday?" I said. "I didn't realize. When I'm working hard I lose track of the days."

I was well aware that it was Sunday; in fact, I was counting on it.

The bright weather of the September morning had turned nasty. The early breeze had strengthened and scudding low clouds threatened rain. No Scantling performs any kind of work on the Sabbath, so the streets were almost empty as I and Paula—she with a short coat of mine over her blouse and skirt and a scarf wrapped around her head—made our way to the Institute for Probatory Therapies. When we passed Paula's apartment building she gave it hardly a glance.

The side door of the institute was locked, but I had a key. We entered the long ground-floor corridor. We then had to walk the full length of it, because the elevators and stairs were both at the other end. This was a critical moment. Occasionally others would work on Sundays, but even then it was a day for catching up on experiments and data analysis. People stuck closely to their own labs and had no interest in socializing or wandering the corridors. Paula and I met not a soul in the corridor, or on the way to my lab on the sixth floor.

She was delighted with the cages of cloned mice and rats and gerbils and rabbits, as any fourteen-year-old might be. Less usual was her fascination with the microtome lasers and scanning probe microscope; and downright unusual to the point of implausibility were her sharp questions about the similarities and differences between human and animal subjects. I wondered, briefly, if I might be wrong. Was she young enough to change, to become what her intelligence permitted? But then she said, with no change of tone, "I could get good street money for those gerbils. Do you know what people use them for?"

I did not know. She told me. I realized that redemption in this life was impossible for Paula Searle.

It had to be quick and painless. I went to the locked cupboard and took out the vapor spray. It was calibrated to deliver dosage based on body mass. I was about to make an estimate when it occurred to me that in this case I didn't need to.

"Paula, how much do you weigh?"

"Weigh?" She was leaning over the scanning probe microscope, which showed an image of a cell mitochondrion and the two conformational states of its inner membrane. "Oh, I dunno. Maybe a hundred and ten?"

Fifty kilos, which was just what I would have guessed. It was time for action, not thought. I set the delivery level, stepped up quickly behind Paula, and in the same moment applied the vapor nozzle to the back of her graceful young neck.

The combination of neurotoxin and DMSO skin diffuser acts in milliseconds. When Paula swayed and I caught her, she was already dead.

I lowered her to the floor and crouched beside her. Death added a new calm beauty to her face. I fought back the urge to take a picture of her as a permanent record. I reminded myself that I would have much more than that. I would have Paula herself, a better Paula than she had ever been in this life; and I would have her forever.

I have no idea how long I looked at her before I was able to force myself to stand up and take the next step.

The odd thing is that there were no decisions to be made. It was as though, unconsciously, I had established a research facility ideally suited to my present needs. I took the DNA sample at once and placed it into a sequencer and segmenter. While sequencing proceeded I lifted Paula's body, complete with clothing, and carried it to the organic disposal unit.

Full dissociation at the cell level would take at least twenty-four hours. The DNA sequencing and segmenting would be completed long before that. I wondered where I would store Paula's genome, but again it seemed as though the necessary arrangements had been made ahead of time. I had been experimenting with the storage and later reconstitution of DNA segments in the chromosomal introns of an old box tortoise that I had inherited from a previous research worker. Although the tortoise's age seemed indeterminate, its gender was not, and the name *Matilda,* painted in pink block letters on his back, was highly inappropriate.

I had cleaned his shell and renamed him Methuselah. Now Methuselah's introns would safely contain Paula until the time, perhaps years ahead, when I had a facility big enough to clone a human. Then I would bring her once more into the world, and to the perfection that was hers by rights.

When all was done that had to be done I went to my desk and sat down. I wanted to work, but I could not. I was quite calm and at the same time enormously excited. Sex had never produced sensations remotely like this. In my giddy joy I knew, even then, that what had happened with Paula would happen again. This time it had been a chance combination of circumstances. Next time, and on all later occasions, everything would be planned to the smallest detail. It had to be that way, because I would not stop and I did not intend to be caught. Ever.

Ah, the hubris of youth. I was caught, of course I was. Just as, forty years on, the murderer on Sky City would be caught. There would be a fatal moment of carelessness or indecision, or a too-long pause for savoring or pleasure. At the moment of dispatch, as I well knew, time stretches. Interval becomes meaningless. How long had I sat, suspended outside of time, and stared at Paula's calm and lifeless face?

A hand shook my arm. I opened my eyes. It was evening, and a shaft of late sunlight struck through the low western window of the castle and lit the face in front of me.

It was Paula's face, Paula changed to an eleven-year-old. She was bending over me, panting, dark hair wild and liquid eyes aglow.

"We're back!" she cried. "I won, I got here first!"

I blinked, and the present came crashing in on me. Here they were, filling the rooms, all my darlings. There was chatter, there was laughter that rang from the stone walls and the high rafters and ceiling, there was the brimming energy of eighteen stampeding girls between the ages of seven and eleven.

Behind them came a woman in her forties. She was breathing heavily and shaking her head.

"Honestly, Mr. Baxter, I don't know how you do it. They wear me out, and that's a fact."

I glanced down at my lap, making sure that the gruesome records from Sky City were safely closed.

"They'll do the same for me, Mrs. O'Keefe, before this night is over. They still have to have their lessons, and after a couple of days in Londonderry it's always the devil to get them settled in again."

"Well, they're all fed, sir, so you need have no worries on that score. And they all bought outfits for autumn. Not that *that* was easy, if you'd seen some of the things they wanted to be buying and wearing before I put my foot down."

"I'm sure that I'll approve of whatever you chose."

"I hope so." She glanced through to the dining room, where the girls now had the long table covered with clothes. Almost without thinking, I ran the count. It was not that I didn't trust Mrs. O'Keefe completely, but . . .

Paula, Amity, Katherine, Rose, Gloria, and Bridget, all age eleven. Darlene, Charity, Beth, Dawn, Trixie, and Willa, age nine. Crystal, Maxine, Dolores, Lucy-Mary, Alyson, and Victoria, age seven. Originally I had wanted them all the same age, but limitations on cloning equipment made it impossible. There had also been a temptation to give each of them a new name drawn from classical sources. Finally I decided that would not work—for me, rather than for them. I could think of their names only as they had been when first we met.

"So I'll be on my way," Mrs. O'Keefe was saying. "And I'll see you in two weeks. Oh, but I was asked to give a message to you. It was sent in to the Dunglow center and I said I was on the way here and could save them a delivery."

Her tone was a little chiding. It said, *Come on, Mr. Baxter, why don't you put a communication center here in the castle and get in line with the rest of the world? It wouldn't be as much trouble as you seem to think.*

She had no idea that in the basement I had access to all the global nets and services. Passive receive-only, of course, because I would do nothing to draw outside attention.

I held out my hand for the message, but she shook her head. "It's too simple to be worth writing. Just a man who says he's figured out how to do it without you going anywhere. He didn't leave a name."

Any more than I would. I wondered about Seth's penchant for secrecy. Was it natural, or did he have good reason? It would be nice to know, and maybe have another lever to use on him.

Mrs. O'Keefe was leaving. On the way out she stared again into the long dining hall, where my darlings were now squabbling as they compared their purchases from Londonderry.

"Look at them," she said as she headed for the front door. "Like a bunch of magpies they are, chattering and chuntering away. You never complain, but running an orphanage like this has to be harder than anyone knows. I'll say it again, Mr. Baxter. You're a saint."

A saint. Indeed.

Given the suspect hagiography of Ireland, which includes such stalwarts as Saint Terence the Wastrel and Saint Brendan the Fornicator, her statement was not as improbable as it sounded.

Before I went through to coerce the girls to evening studies, I sat for a moment reviewing my efforts of the day. What had I learned, in my attempt to summon up remembrance of things past?

One thing, but an important one. The Sky City murderer and I had no commonality of motive or feeling. The deaths of my darlings had been clean and painless, leaving them as beautiful in death as in life. The notion of stabbing, bludgeoning, and sexual mutilation sickened me.

But that left a mystery. If serial killings represent consequence rather than cause, what driving need was compelling the murderer on Sky City?

It was not, I felt sure, passion as I knew it. Was it, indeed, passion of any kind? And yet there had been mutilation—evidence, surely, of a killing frenzy.

I thought once more of the dates of death, from number one, Myra Skelton, to number twelve, Kate Ulrey.

Almost three weeks had passed since Kate had died, her brains bashed out on a well-traveled and well-lit corridor close to the central axis of Sky City. Another murder was overdue. Would it happen?

If it did not, that would be a clue. A clue as to what, I could not say. But murder, especially murder of this type, keeps its own schedule and imposes on the killer its own imperatives.

# 8

Celine had been half right. Nick Lopez's staff on the World Protection Federation did not know where he was, but they could certainly exchange messages. Celine's request for an "urgent and highly sensitive" meeting had been forwarded to Nick as soon as it came in. Normally he would have answered at once, but for the moment something more urgent was on his mind.

What was happening to the aircraft?

He was on his way from Washington to a private meeting with Gordy Rolfe, and all their previous sessions had taken place either at the World Protection Federation offices in New Rio or at The Flaunt, the corporate headquarters of the Argos Group. The steel-and-glass splinter of The Flaunt towered four thousand feet above the Palladian architecture of Houston, and Gordy's summit suite overlooked the rebuilt city. Nick had assumed that they would use the same rendezvous site today. That would give him a comfortable and productive flight of at least an hour and a half, during which he could attend to other business. But his craft was beginning its descent less than twenty minutes after takeoff.

He glanced at the telltales and saw that all mechanical and electronic conditions were normal. The weather was clear and fine. Still the vehicle went on descending. He checked the Automatic Vehicle Control. The AVC's destination coordinates had been provided from Gordy Rolfe's office, and Nick had never thought to question them. But instead of the glitter of The Flaunt ahead there was only a peaceful landscape of rural Virginia.

The craft went into a gentle bank, and as it leveled off Nick caught sight of a runway. The black strip was short, and it was narrow, but from the way that the vehicle was behaving, a full electronic landing system was in operation.

Nick could see no sign of any other aircraft. He waited through the gentle touchdown and taxi to the end of the runway. Then he slid open the hatch and allowed the glide stair to carry him from plane to ground.

He found himself standing in a shallow valley, with low grassy hills to the east and more substantial wooded mountains to the west. A solitary building hugged the ground two hundred yards past the end of the runway. Beside it rose strange shapes, red and green and yellow, oddly angular and complex in the late afternoon light. He began to walk toward them.

At the moment when he recognized both the building and its neighboring structures—it was an old schoolhouse, its playground still filled with brightly painted seesaws and monkey bars—a figure emerged from the schoolhouse door.

Gordy Rolfe was easy to identify. He was diminutive, with a head too big for the slender body. A great sculptured upsweep of snow-white hair exaggerated the disproportion. It was styled for effect, as were the big steel-rimmed glasses. A black jumpsuit, Rolfe's standard attire, emphasized rather than disguised the crooked back and uneven shoulders.

Rolfe did not walk toward Nick. He waited, leaning against the schoolhouse wall. When the two were within earshot, he said, "Don't judge this place by appearances, Senator. I learned to read and write in there."

"I guessed as much." Lopez peered in through one of the windows. "Been a while since the school was used, though."

"You knew where we were going to meet?"

"Not until we landed. I thought I was headed for Houston. But I've seen pictures of this place before. I was Senate Majority Leader in Washington when the headquarters of the Legion of Argos was raided and the Eye of God was taken prisoner. The old headquarters is directly beneath us, isn't it? We had pictures of the whole attack plastered all over the place."

"So did we." Rolfe grimaced, increasing his likeness to a sinister elf. "Of course, the Legion members had a rather different view of events."

Nick Lopez nodded. He was round-faced and brown-complexioned, and the hair above his broad brow was set in a high, old-fashioned pompadour. Despite Rolfe's extravagant coiffure, Lopez towered a foot and a half above the other man. "Did you know her well?"

"Pearl Lazenby—the Eye of God?" The gray eyes behind their big lenses glittered, and Gordy laughed harshly. "Fucking right I knew her. From the time I was six until I was seventeen she was more important than my own parents. Of course, for a lot of that time she was serving a sentence in judicial sleep. But there was morning-noon-and-night talk of her, and I was *raised* with her rules."

Raised by the members of the Legion of Argos, Nick thought, with their rigid attitudes. Lots of prayer, lots of dogma, lots of discipline and harsh punishment. But no medical treatment to make Gordy Rolfe of normal height, even though that had been a standard procedure long before the supernova. No simple corrective changes to his vision, to make those anachronistic eyeglasses unnecessary. No protocol to adjust the spinal curvature that threw the right shoulder a little lower than the left. It was no wonder that the head of the Argos Group now had his own rigidity and strangeness.

Nick said only, "I'm surprised that you can stand to come back here, with all those memories."

"*Stand to* come here?" Gordy Rolfe twisted his head to look sideways up at Nick, even though Lopez had stooped slightly to see in through the classroom window. "Senator, you're so-o wrong." He moved into the schoolroom, gesturing to Lopez to follow. "When the Eye of God was recaptured and taken away to be put back into judicial sleep, my mother and father and the other Legion members wailed and moaned and acted like it was the end of the world. Me, I did the same—in public. But in private I danced. Pearl Lazenby scared me shitless. When I heard that she had died after three more months in judicial sleep it was the happiest day of my life."

"Were you still here then, with the Legion?"

"Yeah. But it was already starting to fall apart. See, the Eye had prophesied that she'd wake up at a time of great disaster and lead the Legion members to take over the whole world. The supernova happened, and they hauled her out of judicial sleep. The prophecy was validated. Everyone said, this is it. They were primed and ready to go. Pearl assured them that the great victory of the Legion of Argos was only days away. Then the boys from Washington came in here and grabbed her, and suddenly the holy cleansing was over before it started."

"Not just the boys. Did you know that Tanaka led them here?"

Gordy Rolfe stood in front of a bank of three old elevators, ready to enter the middle one. He swung around sharply at Lopez's question. "President Tanaka? I thought she was off on the Mars expedition when the gamma pulse hit. That's what her bio said when she ran for President."

"She was. She got back just in time to help Special Forces capture Pearl Lazenby."

"Then I owe her one. Hell, if I'd known that, I might have voted for her. Anyway, when Pearl was taken away, nobody in the Legion could believe it. Her prophesy had been wrong, see, and when she prophesied as the Eye of God she was supposed to be infallible. Some of the old-timers tried to weasel round that, but the newer members weren't buying. People started leaving."

"Not you, though." Lopez followed Rolfe into the elevator.

"No." Gordy Rolfe pressed the bottom button, which bore an icon like a flaming torch, and they began to descend. "Once *she* was out of the way, why leave? There were opportunities for a genius at headquarters."

"A genius like you?"

"Who else? I knew I had talent. And I didn't know a damn thing about the world outside. I stayed behind, looked at what the Legion was ready to walk away from, and started work. That was the beginning of the Argos Group. Houston is the official headquarters, but I prefer this. I come here more and more often."

The elevator was descending, slowly and noisily. Nick wondered what would happen if it broke and they became stuck a thousand feet underground. He decided that anyone able to design and build robots as complex and capable as the rolfes would certainly have allowed for elevator maintenance. Gordy was just doing what Nick had so often done, choosing a meeting place where he had the psychological advantage. Probably there were other surprises ahead.

But not, perhaps, at once. The elevator creaked to a stop and the door opened on a long chamber painted in gunmetal gray. Every few feet along the walls, Nick saw a lurid and unvarying design: the scarlet talons of a bird enclosing a green globe.

He stopped by one of the painted symbols. "The original symbol of the Eye of God."

"Yeah. I didn't change the paintings down here; they're all over most of the walls. Don't you think it makes a nice official emblem for the Argos Group?"

Rolfe's voice burned with a nervous energy that Nick Lopez encountered only in his meetings with Gordy. Even with the aid of telomod therapy, how long could a man operate at that level of intensity? Rolfe was forty-three years old and he looked over sixty.

Nick made his own reply deliberately casual. "It all seems pretty run-down. I assume we'll have a shielded environment where we can talk?"

"Right here. We can start anytime. I doubt there's another human within five miles, and we'll be under a thousand feet of rock and earth. That's good against most taps—unless one of us is recording."

*Which, as it happens, I'm not. But we would both deny it if we were.* Nick ignored the patronizing tone and the implied question and ducked his head to follow Gordy Rolfe up a tight spiral staircase of gray metal designed for someone a foot shorter than Nick Lopez. At the top Rolfe paused to operate a circular hatch, locked from below. Nick wondered about that. Wouldn't a private hideaway be more logically locked from the other side? He had seen nothing to stop anyone from wandering into the old schoolroom and taking the elevator down.

Nick followed Gordy through the hatch, straightened, and glanced around him. "I don't remember talk of anything like this when the Legion of Argos was in the media. Is it new?"

"Depends what you mean by 'new.'" Gordy Rolfe closed the hatch. He stood with his hands on his hips and watched Nick's examination of their surroundings. For a change, he seemed genuinely pleased. "None of this was here in Pearl Lazenby's time. I've been developing it for twenty years."

The spiral staircase and entry hatch led to the center of an enormous room that was at first glance a conventional combination of living space, engineering laboratory, and office. A compact kitchen, complete with generous storage cabinets, sat behind a waist-high partition on the left. On the other side of the partition was a bedroom and a small closed-off area that Nick assumed must be a bathroom. The office was well equipped with desks, chairs, files, communications equipment, and three-dimensional display volumes. Next to it sat the work area, its long lab bench covered with tools and a mass of electronic test equipment. Half a dozen rolfes in various stages of disassembly stood along the wall.

That wall was the most unusual feature of the room. It formed one continuous circular barrier about twenty meters across, rising vertically to a white ceiling far above their heads. A single bulbous door, set in the wall close to ground level, provided an entrance big enough for a man to walk through. The door, like the wall, was transparent. Beyond lay a jungle of dense vegetation, stretching away for an indeterminate distance.

Nick Lopez craned his head back, seeking the source of light. It came from the ceiling, not as a discrete source but as a continuous glow.

"Matches the solar spectrum," Gordy Rolfe said, "and it follows the surface diurnal rhythm. It's late afternoon there, so it's late afternoon here. If we want light later we'll have to turn on separate units in my office. I don't often do that, because I want the habitat to mimic natural conditions."

"You mean out there, where the plants are?" Nick had walked forward to take a closer look at the wall and door. Beyond the barrier the plants grew dense and to shoulder height. The vegetation had an odd blue tinge to it. Nick rubbed the smooth wall, then rapped on it with his fist.

"Not just plants. Animals too." Gordy Rolfe came to his side. "Go ahead, hit as hard as you like. You won't make a dent in it. It's hardened plastic, half an inch thick and stronger than steel. It runs all the way to the ceiling. The door has mechanical as well as electronic locks, and it can only be opened from this side."

Nick Lopez backed away from the wall. He was not a nervous man, but this didn't feel like one of Gordy Rolfe's mind games. He saw the tops of a group of dark green ferny plants swaying, as though animals were moving below or behind them. "You have something dangerous out there?"

"Let's say middling dangerous if you went in there bare-handed. Years ago I had things that you wouldn't want to get within a mile of, but now I have other reasons for keeping the habitat sealed off. It took twenty years to create two thousand acres of controlled environment—three square miles of land and water—where I can run well-designed and controlled experiments. If visitors found their way in and meddled with what I'm doing, they would ruin everything."

"But there's nothing dangerous in there *now*?" Nick found himself reluctant to turn his back on the door.

"I told you, there's nothing dangerous to an armed man. But I've got some fascinating work going on in the habitat. When it gets darker we'll take a look." Gordy smiled at Nick's expression. "No, I don't mean that we'll go in. See the rovers? We'll send one of them."

Now that they were pointed out, Nick saw two of them. They were squat vehicles about three feet long, with eight thin jointed legs along their sides. At their front end a long, segmented neck rose to a round head circled with ruby sensors. They sat facing the wall of the chamber, not far from the door.

Nick said, "They look like the rolfes that Colombo and his group use in shield work."

"Yeah." Rolfe nodded. "Similar technology, though these are a bit smarter. Colombo paid top price, but I keep the best for myself. These rover rolfes are intelligent enough to wander the habitat—it's tricky in places—without getting stuck. I just tell them where I want them to go, and they figure out the rest. What they see will be displayed there."

Rolfe pointed to a set of screens in the communications center. "That will be our entertainment later. I think you'll find it interesting. But first things first." He gestured to a seat by a worktable in the central chamber. When Nick sat down, Rolfe perched on the table itself so that his head was higher than Lopez's. He stared down at Nick. "Are you ready for business?"

"That's why I'm here."

"So let's do the status review, see where we stand." Gordy Rolfe waved to the assortment of food and drink beside him on the table. Nick knew from experience that Rolfe himself would touch nothing. The word from Nick's information network was that drugs and alcohol disagreed with Rolfe's metabolism. In fact, Nick realized that he had never seen Gordy eat. The same information sources said that he was also celibate.

What were Gordy Rolfe's pleasures? Nick had his own operating philosophy: If you want to see inside a man, you find out what he does for recreation.

Nick filed that question away for future reference. He had enough hedonistic tastes for both of them. He declined the offer of refreshment with a shake of the head.

Rolfe went on, "Let's start with John Hyslop. Are you sure you didn't screw up with him?"

Nick Lopez knew Gordy's style. Deference and politeness were for the representatives of the Argos Group, not for its leader. Rolfe played rough, and he hated you to know what he would say next. This time Nick had no idea. *Be casual.* He said, "I'm sure I didn't screw up. Hyslop's an even better engineer than we thought. Leave him up there on Sky City, he'll have the shield back on schedule before you know it. Neither of us wants that."

"Okay, okay. Just want to be sure you're not backing off. I did my part. I sent one of my top people, Maddy Wheatstone, up to talk Bruno Colombo into releasing Hyslop from all shield work. I told her to get Hyslop reassigned to the asteroid capture project."

Now it was harder for Nick to be casual. "You mean it didn't work? I thought Hyslop was taken care of. No one gave me any negative feedback."

"I mean it worked too damn well. Maddy came to see me a few hours ago and asked me what game I was playing. She said that I had told her it would be tricky to make Colombo agree, but that I relied on her to carry out a difficult job. Now she says Colombo served Hyslop up to her on a plate almost before she could ask. I knew that had to be your doing, but of course I didn't tell her."

"You never met Colombo?" When Rolfe shook his head, Nick went on, "If you had, you'd understand. Bruno Colombo is big— bigger than me—and impressive. The first time you see him you think he's really somebody. The second or third time, you see right through him. It's not a man inside that beautiful suit; it's a dog waiting to be kicked. I got him his job as head of Sky City, and he'd do anything to keep it. If I say, 'Shit,' Bruno's down there squatting before I finish speaking. All I did was hint that I'd be pleased if John

Hyslop could be reassigned to help on an Argos Group project. He did the rest."

"He doesn't know how important Hyslop is to shield development?"

"It would make no difference. I'm telling you, Colombo's my man."

"I won't stand people like that working for me. I pay for self-starters. If they don't show independence, they're gone."

"You're lucky, Gordy. The Argos Group is privately owned—"

"More than privately. It's *mine.*"

"So it's yours to do what you like with. It's different when you're in my position and you run a public institution like the WPF, with a hundred countries arguing about what your priorities should be. I *have* to have people like Bruno Colombo, men who'll scramble to do absolutely anything I tell them. One worry I still have about John Hyslop is that he may be too independent."

"Could be. Hyslop's an engineer. Engineers are dangerous because they're obsessed by facts and you can't divert them or buy them off. But Hyslop's working for us now, or he will be as soon as he's wrapped up what he was doing on the shield. What about the man who'll be taking his place on Sky City? That's who I'm worried about."

"It's a woman. Stansfield; Lauren Stansfield."

"Woman, then. What do we know about her? How do we know she won't be as likely as Hyslop to get the shield back on schedule, or put facts and trends together and come to conclusions that we can't tolerate? How do we know it's a change for the better?"

"Gordy, *somebody* has to run engineering; it won't run itself. And I'm not a fool. I already looked to see who Hyslop was likely to offer as his replacement. I'll send you every Sky City background report on Lauren Stansfield. If you like, I can give you a summary right now."

"Do it. I need to be sure you know what you're doing."

It wasn't a request. It was an order, rudely delivered. Nick Lopez bit back his irritation. Gordy Rolfe had an absolute need to prove that he was the boss. That might be all very well within the Argos Group, where he had total control; but Nick had held senior government positions when Gordy Rolfe was still in diapers. Nick told himself for the hundredth time, *Steady. He's a power-mad dwarf, but we're in this thing together. Someday, though* . . .

"How much do you want to know? Lauren Stansfield is thirty-one years old. She's from a very rich family back on Earth, but she wasn't in line to inherit so she took technical training and became a systems engineer. Five years ago a power system installation took her out to Sky City. She stayed there, worked her way up to become top specialist on Sky City life-support systems: energy, air, water, food, she knows them better than anyone."

"So she's as bad as Hyslop."

"No. She's not as creative, and she doesn't have the whole shield construction program in her head the way that Hyslop does. Also, she doesn't know the inventory procedures. Remember, what we have to avoid is a single person who knows procurement for both Sky City and the shield. Hyslop does, and he might easily have compared orders and started counting. Lauren Stansfield won't."

"Are you sure she's not close to somebody who works on shield construction? Someone she sleeps with, some shield specialist who might start comparing notes with her?"

"No. She has no sexual partner at the moment, either gender, and if she ever had one, it was at least four years ago."

"Nothing wrong with that," Rolfe said mildly. Nick saw the gleam in the other's eyes. For a man who went out of his way to emphasize oddities in his appearance, Gordy Rolfe took offense easily.

"Of course that isn't peculiar." Nick knew the right answer, and his voice was as casual as Rolfe's. "It's very convenient from our point of view that she's a loner. She's quiet and competent, so she won't screw up the schedules worse than they are already. But she's not *too* smart, either. She won't make the shield a hundred and ten percent efficient, so that when the particle storm hits, nothing at all gets through to Earth. And she has never shown Hyslop's flair for putting two and two together and making seven."

"All right." Rolfe turned away, as though the whole subject was suddenly no longer of interest. "For the time being we'll go with Lauren Stansfield. If we have to make a change later, we will. Don't bother to send me your reports on her. It's time to talk about the *other* delays in shield construction. We have to find the cause of those, and we have to stop it."

Nick followed the direction of Gordy's glance. The level of light in the room was slowly fading and the vegetation beyond the barrier showed dark and dense. Again there was movement in ten-foot-high grasses, far out from the wall. It took a real effort to focus on Rolfe's question.

"Gordy, I thought we agreed that the Sky City murders are just that—the act of an individual, sexually motivated. They're causing additional schedule slippage, but that's beyond our control."

Rolfe's eyes left the gathering gloom beyond the wall and came back to bore into Nick's. "Bullshit. I used to think we were looking at a solo effort; now I wonder. Either way, we have to make sure we're the only players in the game."

"How can we? Suppose some other group has the same idea as ours? We can't be the only two people on Earth who realize there's lots of money and power to be had when the planet gets slammed."

"And plenty being spent right now, if you can get your hands on a little of it. Enough to buy . . . anything."

Rolfe made a little horizontal circling motion with his hand, palm down. The meaning was clear to Nick. The space shield consumed a third of the world's industrial production. One percent of that, or even one-tenth of a percent, paid for the development of an Argos Group sanctuary like this a thousand times over. It was less clear who would be invited to share a sanctuary with Gordy Rolfe when the particle storm hit Earth. None of that was Nick's business. He had his own if-all-else-fails plan.

"I won't have anyone else cutting in," Rolfe continued. "Our actions are not the only cause of the slippage. Which leaves the question, what else is there?"

"Does it matter?"

"It damn well does. Don't be a dumb ox, Nick. If other people are playing games with the schedule, the chance goes way up that what we're doing will be found out."

"I don't know who or what is responsible for the Sky City murders. But I do know this: They're a definite distraction, and they certainly contribute to unplanned schedule delays. You and I need to be the only people pulling the strings out there."

"Good." Rolfe tilted his head and peered knowingly at Lopez. "So you will approve if I take steps in that area?"

"Of course." Nick saw a glint of something—triumph? lunacy?—in the other man's eyes. Rolfe the gnome, Gordy the evil goblin. Childhood memories of Rumpelstiltskin. "Why wouldn't I approve?"

"I just want to be sure that the murders aren't something you have—well, let's say a direct and personal interest in."

Nick had in his time been accused of everything from rape to incest, but the serial murder of teenage girls was a new one.

"I'm not doing anything on Sky City that you don't know about. I haven't been there for years. And I'm not having anything done on my behalf. I doubt if I could, and I doubt if you can."

"You're wrong. I'm going to find whoever or whatever is responsible for the killings."

"Gordy, the WPF had a team looking into the killings for months. We got nowhere. If you try the same thing, your team will get nowhere, too."

"No team. I have only one man at work on the problem."

"What can he do that others can't?"

"He has a knack for seeing things that no one else notices, and he's efficient. He gets the job done. He also tells me that he has access to special expertise on the subject of similar killings. I'll leave it at that." Gordy's smile was not a thing of beauty. "He'll be going up to Sky City in the near future. I didn't want your people and mine falling over each other. I'm reassured."

"And I'm not. Does your man know that we've been playing games with shield schedules and delivery of goods to Sky City?"

"Of course not. Doesn't know, and won't know. That's not his assignment."

"Maybe, but I'll quote your words. 'He has a knack for seeing things that no one else notices.' Gordy, if this man is as good as you say, suppose that he also starts to see too much?"

"Then it will be my job to make sure that he stops seeing."

"By then it may be too late."

"Not for me. I'll take care of it. I have methods."

Was Rolfe suggesting what it sounded like? "Gordy, suppose the murders are the action of one person, the way it seems?"

"That's fine. We're not in law enforcement. We'll know we don't have business competition, and that's all that matters. Are you going to argue with that?"

"You know my philosophy. As one of my fellow Senators said long ago, I'm opposed to any conspiracy of which I am not a part."

"So we're agreeing. There's just one indispensable person in the Argos Group, and you're looking at him. And you deliver whatever we need from the WPF. We tolerate no other players, anywhere." Rolfe stared calmly at Nick. "End of discussion. What else is on your agenda?"

"Well, there's Milton Glover and his Trust In Government group."

"Old Numb Nuts. What about him?"

"That information we sold him. Are you sure it's accurate?"

"Better than that. I'm sure it isn't. The test-drilling reports he's buying aren't from anywhere on this continent. He thinks they're of Nevada, but they came from South Africa."

"Gordy, I talked him into paying a bundle for that data. You might have mentioned this to me."

"So you could have done what?" Rolfe peered at Nick Lopez. "Suppose he does find out before they start digging—which I don't think he will, because he and his millionaire buddies are all as thick as treacle. What's he going to do, complain that the information he bought illegally was wrong?"

"He bought it on my recommendation."

"Tell him you got tricked, too. Cry on each other's shoulder. Remember, he gave us money when we most needed it. And their digging takes attention away from all *your* digging. You should be delighted with what he's doing."

"If they dig where we said, they'll be lucky if they don't drown."

"Yeah." Gordy laughed. "Big tragedy, eh? Death of rich idiots. End of discussion. What else?"

Nick shook his head. "Nothing." He had a strong urge to get away from Gordy Rolfe and his underground lair. "Nothing that can't wait until we have a better handle on John Hyslop. Will we be able to control him in his new job?"

"Yes. Maddy Wheatstone will take care of that."

"I don't know her. What will she do?"

"Maddy will do whatever she has to do. I handpicked her and

I've watched her grow for nine years. When you meet her, remember that she's tougher than she looks. Tougher than you, Lopez. If she had to take you down, she could do it." Rolfe stood up from the table, grunting as he tried to level his twisted shoulders. His big head tilted back to stare at the ceiling, where the light was noticeably dimmer. When he spoke his voice was far-off and dreamy. "Take you down, Lopez, all the way. End of discussion. It's getting dark in there, Lopez. Dark. So let's have a little excitement, shall we? Let's explore the habitat."

# 9

Gordy Rolfe went over to the transparent door, and for an unpleasant moment Nick thought that he was going to open it. The plant life on the other side was dark, lush, and somehow ominous in the fading light. But Gordy sidled along the wall, looking through and beyond it until he had reached the rolfe rovers.

"How do you get them into the habitat without animals in the habitat getting back in here?" Nick asked.

"You'll see." Rolfe pressed a rover's back simultaneously in three marked places, and the rolfe came alive. It stood, rotated the blunt vertical column of its neck, and clicked along on jointed legs to stand in front of the door.

"Same principle as an air lock," Rolfe said. "You can't have both sides open at the same time unless you take special steps to neutralize the controls. Which we're not going to do."

He went to the communications console and changed a setting, then came back to the wall and operated two mechanical switches. Nick realized that the thick door, apparently solid, was built in two parts with a sizeable space between. When the nearer side swung open there was space within for a rover or a small animal.

But not big enough, thank God, for a tall human or a dangerously large animal. Nick watched as the rover stepped forward into the opening. The nearer side of the door closed, and the far side opened to allow the rover into the interior. The door closed again to a seamless whole. The machine stood for a moment, as though making up its mind, then pushed its way into the green gloom beyond.

"Where is it heading?" In spite of himself, Nick was intrigued. He was seeing a new side of Gordy Rolfe.

"Nowhere special. Questing." Rolfe walked back to the middle of the room, where the displays were located, and sat down. "Come join me. I have no idea how long this will take."

"Questing for what?" Nick sat down also and stared at the display.

"Particular life forms. Animals. The rovers rely on olfactory signatures as well as visual ones, but it's still not easy to track because the vegetation was designed to be dense. In most places the visibility is only a few yards. That makes the thermal infrared sensor useless most of the time."

The field of view on the display changed constantly as the rover advanced and shifted and sometimes backtracked. Twice Nick saw animals, once a possum and once something, maybe a fox, that ran so fast into the undergrowth he couldn't be sure. Those were apparently not what the rover was after, because the machine made no attempt to follow.

The binaural sensors were active, too, reporting soft clicks from the rover's articulated limbs along with the crackle of branches and the rustle of dry leaves. Nick was becoming used to those sounds when they were interrupted by a coughing grunt, right in front of the rover.

"What's that?"

"Homing in. We're getting close to the targets." Gordy Rolfe was perched on the edge of his seat. "Here we go."

The rover had tracked around a stand of broad-leaved bushes. It halted, showing a view of a small clearing bordered by towering ferns. Three creatures tore at a bloodied corpse on the ground.

Nick took one look at the gray scaly heads with their sword teeth, at the thick tails and the massive hind legs, "Gordy, you're crazy! If they broke through here . . ."

Rolfe cackled. "Not a problem! Try again, Nick. See the plants around them—and see what the three are eating."

Nick looked again. The eyes were large, but black and expressionless as a fish's eye. The hide was gray and thick, scaly except for a softer patch on the front of the neck where the skin formed a pouch like a heavy dewlap. The color there heightened to a warm beige. The forelimbs, in contrast to the heavy hind limbs, appeared weak and useless and too short to grasp or hold a prey. The animals, squatting back on their haunches, were clearly and comfortably bipedal, certainly meat-eaters, and definitely dinosaurs.

The shock of recognition was so great that Nick had been oblivious to everything else. Now he could recognize the scale of what he saw. The dead animal they were eating was a fat rabbit, fully half as big as the beasts around it. And as Rolfe said, the plants were the key to sizing other objects. The ferns in the background loomed over the rover, but the rover rolfes were only a couple of feet high, designed to wriggle their way easily through the jungle.

The minidinosaurs gave the new arrival one quick inspection, growled, and went back to their feeding.

"*T. rex* stock, of course," Gordy said. "But I mixed in a fair amount of DNA from their own ancestors. You know, the early dinosaurs and most of the late ones weren't particularly big. The ones we're looking at are less than three feet tall."

"You don't build—full-sized ones. Do you?"

"Not anymore. Of course, I did it years ago. Everybody wants to do a *T. rex* for starters. I mean, it's so famous you more or less have to try."

"You failed?"

"Oh, no. The genoforming was no problem—it's actually more difficult to create dwarf variations, like these, because you have to change the proportions from the original."

Nick examined the animals in the holographic display more closely. The midget dinosaurs had massive hind limbs and a thick tail, slightly out of proportion to their size. They also moved a little clumsily—but each of those needle teeth was close to an inch long.

"They look pretty dangerous to me."

"No more so than a dog of the same size, and not nearly as intelligent. Each one of these weighs about thirty-five pounds, though there are a few larger sizes in the habitat—up to a hundred pounds. Mind you, I'm not saying they aren't dangerous at all. Even with these minisaurs, you wouldn't want to go alone into the habitat without a weapon. They're not pack animals, and they don't hunt in groups, but they'll gang up to make a kill. Two or three might easily bring down a human."

"What do they eat?" The rabbit had been dismembered and little of it remained.

"Ah, now that's a curious fact. They'll eat most things if they have to, amphibians and reptiles and other dinosaurs. But given a choice, they seem to prefer mammals. It makes you wonder if that reflects some ancient struggle. You know, we usually think of the mammals as coming after the dinosaurs had died off, but there were mammals—small ones—long before that. One old theory was that early mammals did in the dinosaurs, by eating their eggs. And maybe a preference for mammalian meat is an evolutionary survival mechanism for the dinosaurs."

"Would a dinosaur eat a human?"

"I don't know, but I don't see why not. We'd make a good meal for a pack of minisaurs. Of course, for a full-sized allosaur or tyrannosaur a human wouldn't be more than an appetizer. Do you realize how much it takes to feed a full-grown *T. rex*? Or a big herbivore, like a titanosaur? I tried it. This whole habitat can support only a handful of large plant-eaters—and they crap like you wouldn't believe. The tyrannosaurs were even worse; I had to keep importing meat from outside. That screws up the whole idea of a self-supporting habitat. It just wasn't worth it, and I went to the miniature forms. I found that I can do the experiments I'm interested in just as well with them."

"Which are?" Nick could imagine some pretty unpleasant possibilities, none of which seemed beyond Gordy's limits.

"Answering what-if questions. Nature was unkind to the dinosaurs. They existed in the same era as the mammals, but I don't think the two forms ever had a real head-to-head competition. All the mammals were small when the asteroid hit Chicxulub and the dinosaurs became extinct. Flying reptiles went away at the same time, but I've not done any work with them yet. What I have done, though, is absolutely fascinating. It's getting too dark to track in the habitat with visible light. Later we'll watch the nocturnal forms, but meanwhile let me show you some of my results."

Rolfe stood up and did something invisible at the console, then moved back to stand directly in front of the ten-foot holograph. The natural light had faded to a deeper gloom, and Gordy Rolfe became a small, dark figure, hopping about against the background of the three-dimensional display. When he spoke again, his voice matched the animation of his manner.

"Fourteen years ago I set up my first full-scale simulation. The habitat was self-contained and isolated except for the water supply and simulated solar radiation. I put in a mixture of plants from today and those found in this region a hundred million years ago—see, I didn't want to tilt the odds one way or the other. I put in floor and ceiling sensors that can identify, track, and inventory every animal species, so there would be a continuous census of habitat contents. And I seeded the habitat like this."

A big group of animals stood frozen in holographic relief. Nick recognized four large meat-eating dinosaurs, which he thought from their size were *Allosaurus*. They, together with four lumbering specimens of *Diplodocus,* dwarfed everything else in the holo frame.

Gordy moved around on the edge of the holograph. "This is shown at one-quarter scale, but everything I put into the habitat was full-sized. See, here are the big modern predators—I chose tigers, because they function better than lions in a jungle environment. I didn't want to use zoo specimens, they might be bred for docility, so I went to the Indian genome bank for original DNA templates. And here are hypsilophodons—small, fast herbivores, according to the books, but these seem more like omnivores, they'll eat anything. And here's a bunch of little saurischian plant-eaters, and these are wolves—no, I'm wrong, they're hyenas—and if you look at the bottom, we have the smallest forms, shrews and mice and some of the saurornithoids that are not much bigger."

Nick was listening, but with only half his attention. While Gordy Rolfe spoke with such enthusiasm about his simulation, the rover rolfe was still out in the real habitat. So were the meat-eating minisaurs. It was too dark to see anything, but the rover's audio system was working. Unpleasant crunching sounds were interrupted by grunts and snorts and once by a startled, high-pitched squeal.

"Release them into the habitat all at once," Rolfe went on. He waved his short arms. With a little imagination, the stooped, big-headed form silhouetted against the display could itself be one of the dwarf meat-eaters. "Provide water and light in realistic weather patterns, stay away, and see what happens. I did that, not once, but many times, and I let nature take its course. Do you know what happened, every single time?"

Nick was thinking of other things. He and Gordy Rolfe had

formed their alliance because they needed each other to achieve a common goal: a world crippled by a space shield that would be only partially effective in deflecting the coming particle storm. The weak and the foolish would die, but Nick had his own personal hideaways dug deep beneath New Rio and the mountains of the Canadian Rockies. He did not begrudge Gordy Rolfe his secret headquarters. And beyond the particle storm lay the real goal, of ultimate personal power unimagined by most humans.

But the alliance carried its own price. Rolfe now held the stronger position. It was in part the power of a man indifferent to public opinion and support, versus one like Nick, who occupied a public and highly visible position.

There was also another, more important, difference between them. *If you want to understand a man, find out what he does for recreation.* Nick pursued men and women as well as power. Gordy was above—or below—the passions of the flesh. Gordy played God, and he was, in Nick's opinion, becoming steadily more deranged. The lack of personal ties decreased his vulnerability and increased his megalomania.

"Did you hear me, Lopez?" Rolfe came closer, into the more brightly lit area beyond the holograph display. "Do you know what happens when I seed the habitat with a variety of forms, dinosaurs and mammals, and let it run?"

"No. What happens?" Nick's skin prickled with apprehension. The circular wall of the room seemed closer. He imagined he could smell a rank odor from the jungle beyond.

"The end mix of species in the habitat is different each time, depending on starting conditions and on random variations in food supply and weather." Rolfe moved to stand next to where Nick was sitting. His head was level with Nick's and he leaned close, gray eyes glittering with excitement behind the big lenses. "Sometimes the dinosaurs seem to have the upper hand, sometimes the mammals win out. But in every case, the small mammals do well. They *never* become extinct, and they always increase in numbers. Do you hear me, Lopez? Not *big* mammals. *Small* mammals win out, every time."

Nick was six feet five inches tall. Presumably he did not qualify as a small mammal. Rolfe, stretched up to his full height in elevator shoes, was perhaps five feet two. Yet he was talking down to Nick—and loving it.

Nick nodded. "I take your point. That's very interesting."

There was one particular small mammal that he would like to see extinct. Not yet, though. This was a necessary partnership. He and Gordy Rolfe needed what only the other could provide: technological wizardry and industrial power from Gordy and the Argos Group, political savvy and clout from Nick and the WPF. The world's greatest inventor and entrepreneur, teamed with the world's savviest politician: a marriage made in heaven.

But in the long run? That was different. Nick knew very well that he and Gordy were two people as different as you could get, drawn together only by a shared desire for power and wealth. Somewhere in the undefined future, on an Earth ravaged by the particle storm, only one of the two would survive.

The competition between small and large mammals had yet to be decided.

# 10

**From the private diary of Oliver Guest.**

I am not one to derogate the efforts of others, but Seth Parsigian's "solution" to my problems of acrophobia and agoraphobia was at first sight absurd beyond words.

"You imagine," I said to him, "that I will sit here in the castle, while you and your associates wander Sky City and send me such facts and scenes as your Baker Street Irregulars deem important; and that I will then, like some improbable Mycroft, sit in my armchair and deduce from those rags and tatters of information the identity of the killer. Your faith in my powers would be touching, were it not so improbable."

He scowled at me out of the screen; one-way video, of course, since I permit no outgoing images from Otranto Castle. Seth was annoyed with me, and not without reason. If it be true that there is an appropriate era and place for every person, then Seth Parsigian would have fitted well into the Victorian London of Sherlock Holmes to which I had just made reference. He was not, of course, a model for the most famous midnight wanderer of those fog-shrouded streets. I myself, in many people's minds, form a far better match for Whitechapel Jack. Seth, however, had well-developed powers of observation and self-preservation that made him far more than a casual onlooker. What he would see and report from Sky City would doubtless be useful and probably necessary.

It would not, however, be sufficient. Three days of hard effort on my part had brought me no closer to our murderer. The crucial touching of like minds that Seth had hoped for when he came to see me had not occurred, and it seemed clear that progress through that avenue was unlikely.

I had no other suggestions; Seth, however, did.

"You got it wrong," he said. "Nobody but me's gonna be involved with you in this. An' I'm not gonna do all the work wanderin' round Sky City while you sit there laughin' an' scratchin'. You'll be right there with me."

"Impossible. I thought I had made it abundantly clear—"

"Be there as much as you want, an' as much as you can stand. An' still be safe at home if it gets too sticky. See this?" He held up a shapeless bundle of mauve and pink. "I'll wear it. Opens up to look like an ordinary jacket, but it's an RV jacket—for remote viewin', it's got sensors all over it. I send you the receivin' equipment, audio and video feeds in an RV helmet; then anythin' I see, you see. Anythin' I hear, you hear. Realistic, just like bein' there in person."

"If realism is your goal, I suspect that I will be unable to function. Full telepresence is no more tolerable to me than physical presence."

Seth offered a grin of irritating condescension. "You'll be fine, Doc. I'll arrange it so you get your place overlaid on the Sky City scene. You control the mix, how much you see of what I'm seein', how much you get of where you are. If things are tough for you to take, no problem. You just tone it down for a while."

"But where you go is as important as what you see. Suppose you visit locations in Sky City that I believe to be of no more value than random wanderings?"

"Won't happen. You'll have contact with me. Don't sit there scowlin'." How did he know my expression when I was feeding to him a voice-only signal? "We do it the same way we're doin' it now. I don't need to see your mug—in fact, I'd just as soon not—but you can talk to me and steer me anyplace you think I need to go."

The probability that the scheme would succeed seemed vanishingly small. The chance that Seth would drop his idea without trying it was, unfortunately, even less.

As James Russell Lowell remarks, it is no good arguing with the inevitable. The only argument available with an east wind is to put on your overcoat.

"Very well," I said. "If you think the matter is worth the effort, send me the receiving equipment. Before we try it in practice there must be a test to see if the idea is workable."

I broke the connection, and pondered the problem of metaphorical outer garments.

• • •

The round-trip signal travel time from Earth to Sky City in its geosynchronous orbit is about one-fourth of a second. Seth proposed to accommodate this in Earthbound tests of our communication system via a built-in electronic delay. It was similar to that employed when the question was first raised of customer acceptance of signals sent through geosynchronous satellites, and although I had not seen details of those century-old experiments I had little doubt that we would rapidly make the necessary mental adjustment.

Far more difficult was the question of my environment. Unlike Seth, who would operate wholly in Sky City, I would perforce be obliged to function in Otranto Castle, while at the same time following events several tens of thousands of kilometers away. I needed to provide a test under difficult local circumstances.

The children inadvertently cooperated in providing this. They had been unusually lively for the past few days, perhaps a consequence of my own distraction and decreased attention.

The receiving equipment compounded rather than eased the problem. The controller was small and fitted easily into my right hand, but the RV helmet, large and black with prominent silver eyes, felt heavy and looked uncomfortable. With a little juggling and much more misgivings I fitted it on over my head.

That action did not pass unobserved. I rarely regret my decision to perform minor genetic modification of my darlings, giving each of them increased stamina, better health, higher intelligence, abundant energy, and lessened need for sleep. Notice, however, the adverb *rarely.*

When I was ready to test the helmet it was early evening for Seth, but past midnight for us in Ireland. Crystal and Lucy-Mary were perhaps the liveliest and most inquisitive, not to say troublesome, of the seven-year-olds, and they should have been in bed hours ago. But they entered my study just as I donned the helmet and moved the controller to a midrange setting. I saw Seth's offices, located at the Argos Group headquarters in Houston, Texas. I also saw, overlaid on that image, two gray ghostlike outlines. When I adjusted to receive a heavier component of the local scene, the gray figures turned into Crystal and Lucy-Mary. They walked over to me and stood giggling and nudging each other.

"Can you see me?" said Seth's voice.

"Yes. But wait one moment. I must attend to something here." I turned off the audio feed. "Girls, you are not a part of this activity. Please leave."

"What activity?" Lucy-Mary said. Crystal added, "If there is any activity, we must be part of it because there's no one else here. Do you know what you look like? You look like a human being with a fly's head."

"That particular conceit lost its novelty long before you or even I was born. This helmet provides a communication capability, and I am in fact engaged in a meeting. Or I will be, as soon as you leave."

"Can't we stay and listen?" asked Crystal.

"You may not. Please leave—now."

They did so, reluctantly. I saw Lucy-Mary's curious final glance at the RV helmet, and I made a mental note to hide it safely away when it was not in use. I could imagine Seth receiving a call from one of my darlings, and enthusiasm was not on the candidate list of his reactions.

"What was all that about?" he asked as soon as we were once more in contact.

"A little local interference. We can anticipate such things from time to time."

"You really got eighteen of 'em in that castle?" Seth's ability to infer what he could neither see nor hear was uncanny. "All them young girls. I don't know how you stand it. They'd drive me dotty in a week. But I guess it don't matter for you, you were crazy before."

"Far be it from me to interrupt your valuable insights into my past and present mental condition, but may we return to the subject of the equipment test? I am restoring a full visual feed to you and minimizing my local inputs."

"All right. What do you see?"

I was rapidly adapting to the quarter-second delay between each statement that we made. However, illogical as it sounds, it had not occurred to me that the visual feeds would be subject to the same hiatus. I found myself waiting impatiently for the field of view to change.

"I see an office wall," I said.

"So do I. I'm standin' right in front of it."

"It's light green."

"It sure is. So far so good. Tell me where to go and what to do next, an' if it won't kill me, I'll try an' do it."

"Turn around, slowly."

I felt as though I myself were turning. The green wall vanished, to be replaced by a mural of some kind of jungle scene framed by real potted plants. That gave way in turn to a wall-wide picture window, seven or eight meters away, that showed a blue sky beyond.

"Walk over toward the window," I said.

There was a silence—rather longer, it seemed, than the planned electronic delay. "All right. If you say so." Seth had an odd tone in his voice. For the first time I wished that I could see the expression on his face.

My field of view moved steadily across the room, and I counted the paces. The window came closer. I was looking up and out, to a high layer of scattered cloud. And then I was looking down.

Down, down, down. Far below lay dwarfed fields, towers, and highways, and beyond them the dull, distant glint of water.

I stepped back convulsively. My legs moved, but I did not move. I stepped again, and again. Nothing. I was rooted to the spot, running backward in a nightmare. Finally I realized what I had to do and squeezed the hand controller. The video field switched at once to full local.

"You all right?" Seth must have heard my panting.

I stared at the familiar fixtures of my study: the old elephant-foot umbrella stand, the carved bone flute on the wall, the delicate glass globe on my desk that had survived a hundred close encounters with my darlings. Slowly they soothed me. "I am . . . all right. You should have warned me."

"Wrong." Seth was cheerfully unrepentant. "This was a practical test, right? You think when I'm wandering Sky City I'll be able to give you a running commentary about where we're goin'? If you think that, you're blowin' bubbles. I'll be wearin' what looks like a normal jacket, an' people who talk to their clothes get put away. You have to figure out for yourself how much input you can take."

He was, of course, absolutely right, but that made his casual callousness no easier to take. Slowly I allowed the remote scene to bleed back into my visual feed. Superimposed on the furnishings of my study appeared a faint black-and-white outline of the window. Seth must still have been standing in front of it.

"How high is the place where you are standing?" I asked.

"Don't know exactly. I'm up near the top of The Flaunt, so I'd guess over thirty-five hundred feet."

"Don't move. I wish to try an experiment."

As long as my sense of presence was firmly rooted in the castle, the fact that the other view emanated near the vertiginously high summit of The Flaunt had no more effect on me than a photograph taken from a mountaintop. The question was, at what point was the remote scene mistaken for reality?

Gradually I strengthened the feed. The sky beyond the window turned from pale gray to blue. Dark lines lower down in the image strengthened and changed. Once again I saw roads and buildings.

I had reached the point where the image was drawn equally from my own and Seth's perspective. Still I felt no discomfort.

"You havin' fun there?" Seth, I realized, had little idea what I was doing. His only input was the sound of my breathing.

I told him of my actions, and added, "Wait a little longer. I propose to see how far I can go with this."

"Take your time. Don't worry about me, I can stand around here all day." Sarcasm should not be confused with wit, and Seth's use of it suggested more tension than he would admit.

I continued to change the balance of images presented to me, gradually increasing the contribution from Houston. All went well until the scenes of my study began to lose color and appear only as a set of gray edges. At that point I felt a prickling in the palms of my hands and a sweaty clamminess on my forehead and cheeks.

Others might tell themselves that they were still in control, that they could handle the fear seeping like iced water up the spinal column and into the brain. I held no such delusions. I have known, for far too many years, that I am not in control of myself.

I decreased slightly the contribution from Seth. As the image of my study strengthened, once more I could breathe easy. I locked the setting of my controller and studied the scene presented by the RV helmet.

"I think this will be satisfactory," I said. "My surroundings are enough to anchor me in this reality, and I can see yours well enough to make my own observations. Select some feature below you."

"The ship canal. Over on the left."

"I see it. Four vessels are visible. I am not able to make out their types."

"Me neither. Four ships is right. But you can do somethin' I won't be able to do once I'm up at Sky City. Watch this."

I took no action, but the canal expanded suddenly in my field of view. One of the ships at the center of the scene sprang into vivid detail. I could see individual funnels and masts and hatches, even individual human figures standing on the deck.

"How are you able to do that?"

"Beats me, but I'll tell you what I was told. This jacket I'm wearin' has sensors all over it. They can work together, an' when they do it's like having a telescope with a mirror two feet across. You got a control for it on the side of your hand unit. When you turn it on you'll see a lot more detail of what I'm lookin' at than I can. Try it for yourself."

"I will. But not now." As Seth was speaking I had become aware that the gray image representing my own local scene was changing. The clean-edged outline of the walls had become broken and uneven. "I must go. You can call me later."

"I'll do that—from Sky City."

It was, I suspect, intended to keep me from breaking contact. If that was Seth's objective, it failed. I decreased the remotely viewed component to zero, and at once saw what I already suspected. My study was crowded. Every one of the girls was there.

I spoke to Paula, whom the others through some unidentifiable instinct recognized as their senior. "Would you care to explain your presence?" I said. "This is not some form of entertainment, devised for your pleasure. As I told Crystal and Lucy-Mary, I am engaged in an important meeting."

"I'm very sorry." Paula's face said she was no such thing. "It's just that Lucy-Mary and Crystal told us you were—well, we all wanted to see you."

"Indeed?" I stood up and walked into their midst. As always, their beauty rendered me breathless—but not speechless. "You see me. Here I am. Have I, then, become so much an object of ridicule that the very sight of me—"

I stopped. I had caught sight of myself in the long mirror next to the mantelpiece. The bottom of the RV helmet formed a seamless match to my own dark shirt. Tall, forbidding, with a swollen, goggle-eyed, hideous head, I had become a chimera, a *lusus naturae*, enough to strike terror into any heart. But not, apparently, those of my darlings. They stared at me with interest.

I pulled off the RV helmet. At the sight of my frowning face every girl, from tall and mature Bridget to little golden-haired Victoria, shrieked, turned, and ran out of the room.

It was done on purpose, planned long before they ever entered. I went back to sit at my desk. It was nice to know that my young wards were developing that most important of all senses, the sense of humor; but at the moment I had serious issues to ponder.

Seth Parsigian was relying on me to perform miracles. He would head off for Sky City, move around at my bidding, return images to Earth, and blithely wait for me to do—what?

To integrate new material from Sky City with the existing evidence, apply my own unique understanding of the mind of a serial killer, point a spectral finger at some individual, and say, "That's the one."

It would not happen. The pattern of deaths remained totally baffling, the brain behind the killings unseen and alien. There was no hint of compulsion, no suggestion of the recurring need that enforced its schedule for murder.

As I have already remarked, the savage mutilation of the Sky City bodies disgusted me. I had not touched sexually, nor would I ever touch, my victims. I had *saved* them, from poverty and misery, from hunger and dirt, from abusive parents, from sexual assault, from the degradation and drugs and dark despair that would otherwise have been their lot. They were rising again to a place where each could fulfill her own high potential.

The Sky City murderer and I had nothing in common.

As I sat alone in my darkened study, that thought led me to another. In my discussions with Seth I had already alluded to the famous resident of 221B Baker Street, London. Now I recalled one of his most celebrated cases, in which Sherlock Holmes remarked on the curious behavior of the dog in the night. When asked what the dog had done in the night, he answered that it had done nothing. He therefore deduced that the midnight visitor must be someone already known to the dog, otherwise the animal would have barked. Absence of evidence became evidence.

Could I use what I knew—what I alone knew—to guide me to a similar insight?

Question: What did the Sky City killer and I have in common? Answer: We seemed to have nothing in common. That had implications. My task was to deduce what they were.

It took a long time. When the idea finally came, it took the form of another question. The Sky City murders were savage, brutal, random, committed in fits of insane rage. What could possibly be worse than the slaughter of a dozen innocents by a sex-crazed, blood-obsessed lunatic?

It may be argued that my own flawed makeup leads me to see the dark side of humanity. But I can think of something worse.

# 11

Gordy Rolfe gave the order to Maddy Wheatstone with his usual brutal simplicity: "John Hyslop isn't your main priority, he's your *only* priority. Until I say different, where he goes, you go."

Maddy sat with Gordy at the top of The Flaunt in Rolfe's office, a three-dimensional labyrinth of glass, staircases, and mirrors that gave a visitor the sensation of inhabiting one of Maurits Escher's gravity-disdaining lithographs. The trompe l'oeil interior and vertiginous outside view were part of Rolfe's techniques for maintaining psychological dominance, and Maddy was careful to exhibit a slight edginess. In fact, she preferred visits here to their occasional meetings in the green underground gloom of the Virginia habitat.

"If he's in a technical session, you're in it, too." Rolfe drove the point in farther. "You eat with him, you drink with him, and you travel everywhere with him. If he tells you he has to take a leak, you're right there in the toilet watching him do it. If he takes somebody to bed, you squeeze in between the two of 'em. You do whatever you have to do, without limits. *Compris?*"

Not for the first time, Maddy wanted to tell Gordy he could shove it. He loved to challenge people, to see just how far they could be pushed. So far Maddy had given as good as she got. Thereby proving that she was as tough as he was? Or proving that she was a dumb masochist who didn't have the sense to come in out of the thunderstorm?

"Don't worry, Gordy. I'll be on him tighter than your tiny ass."

It was the right answer, the answer of an ambitious and confident woman. He grinned and said, "Never." But he added, "You got my point, so get out of here. And don't tell anybody outside this room you speak to me like that, or it's *your* ass that'll be in the shop for repairs."

That had been yesterday, at the tip of the four-thousand-foot needle The Flaunt. Now, following instructions, Maddy was leaving Earth again. If John Hyslop felt surprise when she said she wanted to come with him to one of his wrap-up sessions with the people who would be taking over his duties, he didn't show it. He leaned back in his seat as the shuttle completed its ascent phase, and he sat silent. He was frowning slightly.

Maddy made her inventory of the other nine passengers. She recognized four of them. The head of LMB Industries—that made sense, they had one of the three big construction contracts. The shield could not really be said to have a skeleton, but the thin cables produced and installed by LMB, and running from Cusp Station all the way to Cone End, were the closest thing to it.

In the row in front sat Mulligan Johnson, the top mirror-matter specialist for Photonics. John Hyslop had spoken of problems with the latest group of mirror-matter thrustors, and those were Photonics's responsibility. Mulligan was here to troubleshoot, stir the Photonics's staff to greater efforts, and smooth ruffled client feathers.

The other two faces presented more of a mystery. Candy Wentzel, sitting next to Mulligan Johnson, was a top media reporter. She might be doing some kind of feature article on the shield and its schedule problems, but that wasn't her usual line. She was a muckraker, chasing scandals at the highest levels of government and industry. A schedule delay might lead to a world-crippling disaster, but it still wasn't a scandal. To justify Candy's highly expensive and decorative presence, Bruno Colombo himself would have to turn out to be the Sky City murderer.

Maddy smiled inwardly at the idea—Goldy Jensen would have to be in on it, too, because Colombo's personal assistant tracked his movements every waking (and sleeping) second. And there was the question of motive. Bruno had none. He might kill, but only for promotion or political preferment.

Maddy turned her attention to the fourth figure. Familiar, yes, but in what context? She couldn't be absolutely sure, but she thought she had seen him around the offices of the Argos Group. He was of medium height and strong build, with a sallow complexion and dark, short-cut hair; it was the sort of nondescript face and figure you would never notice in a crowd, unless those eyes fixed on you as they had fixed on Maddy before takeoff.

They were a tawny brown in color, too light for that dark face, and they moved constantly to scan everything around him. If she suspected that she thought she knew him, she felt quite certain that he knew her. For the past half hour he had been holding on his knees a black cylindrical bag about eighteen inches long and eight inches across. She could see a piece of pink and mauve cloth sticking out of the end of it. The bag had been stowed away during takeoff, so why was he nursing it now? You did that only when you were carrying something precious, something that you were afraid you might lose.

She glanced again to John Hyslop, still sitting in silence at her side. Was she going to have to work with a zombie? He hadn't taken out anything to read, he didn't have a headset, he hadn't said a word. He was holding a tiny notepad in his hand, and now and again he scribbled a couple of digits. He seemed totally unaware of her presence, and she wasn't used to being ignored. She expected male attention. He wasn't gay; her own instincts told her that as well as the background briefing documents. But he seemed lost in another world, one where Maddy Wheatstone did not exist.

Her musings ended when the docking phase began and the usual string of visuals appeared on the seat displays. They showed dozens of locations on Sky City and told what the visitor might do at each one. They amounted to commercials that could not be turned off, and they were boring even the first time you heard them. When you had been shuttle-hopping as Maddy had for the past week and a half, in a constant dizzy veering between Earth and Sky, you wanted to find the owner of that soft, persuasive voice and strangle him.

That led to another thought: The person who had taken those shots had been everywhere in Sky City and must know it in detail. Wouldn't he be in a perfect position to travel around and kill without being noticed?

Maddy dismissed the thought as soon as she had it. It was an idea that security had surely explored and dismissed. Other people's jobs always seemed easier than yours until you actually had to do them.

The visuals ended as a vibration along the shuttle's outer hull indicated that an umbilical was being clamped into position. The shuttle docking was taking place at an air-match port, and the air pressure and gas mix inside the shuttle had slowly been adjusted after takeoff from Earth standard to Sky City normal. The passengers would be able to leave without the use of suits or masks.

John Hyslop showed no sign of moving. He was still writing numbers on his notepad. Maddy watched as the shuttle hatch opened and the LMB executive at once hurried away. His every movement said *Time is money!* Mulligan Johnson and Candy Wentzel were next. He was talking animatedly and Candy was smiling and nodding.

Some scandal involving Photonics?

Hard to imagine. Much more likely, Candy was a newcomer and needed somebody who knew his way around Sky City. In media races, an hour's delay could be fatal. Maddy knew what she would have done, and Candy had probably followed the same line of logic: examined the passenger list, decided in real time that Mulligan Johnson was her best bet, and collected him as effortlessly as a child picking a daisy. Maddy didn't disapprove of that. Candy, like Maddy, took her job seriously. You did what you had to do.

Next, the familiar-but-unfamiliar dark-faced stranger vanished through the hatch, still clutching his black cylindrical bag. The only passengers left were two who had arrived on the shuttle in wheelchairs and who were now waiting for nursing assistance. Both men had the puffy complexion and purplish lips suggesting congestive heart disease. The low-gee environment of Sky City might help—if they survived the shock of the launch and the strain of vomiting in the first few days. Space was the last resort for those individuals who, incomprehensibly to Maddy, refused a simple heart-lung replacement.

Still John Hyslop was sitting and staring at nothing. Maddy reached the end of her patience and nudged him. "Don't we have meetings to attend?"

He turned to look at her with those steady gray eyes. "We'll be there on time."

She knew now that his jumpiness at their first meeting had been the result of a Neirling boost. Usually he was the calmest man she had ever met—calm enough to drive her crazy.

"Not if we hang around here, we won't." Maddy stood up. "Let's go."

He nodded, stood up also, and started toward the hatch. But when he came to it he didn't go through. Instead he continued forward.

"Where—" Maddy began, and paused. A strange sensation of dizziness hit her as she left her seat. It passed as quickly as it had come, but by that time John had drifted all the way to the end of the main compartment and through the door into the pilot's cabin. Passengers were not supposed to go in there.

"Quite a difference," he was saying as Maddy came up behind him. "Fifteen percent?"

"At least." The woman in the pilot's seat was lean and blond and hollow-cheeked. She turned to survey Maddy with eyes of arctic blue, then nodded to indicate that she, too, was included in the conversation. "The end spec is supposed to be a twenty-one percent increase for the new engines, but we've not quite reached that yet."

"That will be great. What's the change in final mass ratio?"

"A factor of two with present performance. Over three if we ever hit spec." -

"I have a thought about that. How long will you be here?"

"Nine hours. Then we head back down."

"Good. Plenty of time." Hyslop again had the little notebook in his hand. "I was listening closely right through the powered ascent phase, and it sounded to me as though one cluster wasn't firing as cleanly as the others."

"Exactly right."

"L-8?"

"That's the way I feel it, and it's the way the gyros measure it. But we've been through ground maintenance twice, and they insist that everything is nominal."

"I bet your tests were done at constant external pressure. Downside maintenance sometimes cuts corners that way and uses ambient. I think the aerospike for the L-8 cluster may be following a recorded pressure that's trailing the actual pressure by a few seconds. Don't ask me why, because I don't know. But if you call Dan Iverson at the Flight Test Facility here on Sky City, the FTF can run you a dynamic test with variable ambient air pressures. You'll be able to find out if that's the reason the L-8 cluster is off."

"Great." The woman raised blond eyebrows, plucked to a thin line. "I assume you can authorize that?"

"Sure. No, wait a minute." Hyslop paused, with an expression of surprise and irritation that Maddy found comical. "Damn it, I could have last week, but I'm not sure I can anymore. Look, go to Dan anyway, and tell him that John Hyslop told you that Dan is to get authorization from Bruno Colombo to have the test performed."

"Dan Iverson. John Hyslop. Bruno Colombo." The curved eyebrows went up farther. "I hope I can remember all the names. One of them is you?"

"I'm John Hyslop."

"I've heard that name." She reached out a long, slender hand. "Kirsten Lindstrom."

"Will you do it?"

"Sure. Why not?" She shrugged. "We have lots of time before we leave, and I'd love to have that twenty-one percent increase in EJV. If it works out, I'll let you know."

"I don't know where I'll be. Go through Dan."

"It's a promise."

Maddy, at last, was able to drag him away and off the shuttle. As soon as they were out of the pilot's hearing she said, "Didn't you even *know* her before?"

"No. You heard us introduce ourselves."

"But you went right into the cabin, which passengers are not allowed to do, and you started telling her what was wrong with the way she did things."

"I did?" He was frowning at Maddy. "I don't think so."

"I heard you. All that about the way the engines were firing, and what she ought to do about it."

"But that wasn't criticism of *her*. We were talking about the engines."

"If you came into my project, and I didn't even know you, and you started telling me you understood it better than I did, and how I ought to be running it, I'd—I'd—well—" It occurred to Maddy that at the moment John Hyslop *was* her project, and he understood himself far better than she did. She finished weakly, "Well, I don't know what I'd do."

She had left herself open for a major put-down, but all he did was stare at her, very seriously, and say, "I hope she didn't feel that way. I was trying to do her a favor, because her bonus depends on the performance of her shuttle. I said a fifteen percent improvement in EJV was great, but that was only so she wouldn't feel bad. The ratio of final payload to initial mass depends exponentially on the EJV. When the spec promises a twenty-one-percent increase, fifteen percent is terrible. Kirsten Lindstrom and I both knew it, but neither of us said it."

It was a correction rather than a put-down. Not in the least like Gordy Rolfe's cut-you-off-at-the-knees mockery and open sneer. Maddy decided that she preferred John Hyslop's way of doing things, particularly when he added, "I suppose we have a different style of operations out here. But I feel sure you'll get used to it. Have you ever been out at the shield before?"

"Never."

"Then the more you know about it ahead of time, the better. Let's go and get something to eat and we'll talk about it."

It was a genuine offer, well intended. Maddy had not eaten since morning and should have been starved. Instead, the thought of food produced a swirl of nausea. Her head was suddenly aching and the dizziness was back, worse than before.

It couldn't be that she was sick. She was *never* sick; hadn't been sick since she was seventeen. But the room in which they stood was rocking about her, and the straight line of Sky City's central axle seemed to bend and twist as she stared along its length.

"Are you all right?" John Hyslop's face was close to hers. She wondered why he was asking, then realized that she was clutching his forearm in both hands. She tried to shake her head. Nausea gripped her. She wanted to swallow, and couldn't.

It had happened impossibly fast. When the shuttle docked she had been fine. Now she couldn't speak and she dared not move. She wanted to lie down and die.

"Come on." John was pulling her along in the low-gravity environment. "Just hang on for two minutes. Keep your eyes closed if it helps; I'll make sure you don't bang into anything."

She wanted to say, *What's happening? Leave me alone. Oh my God. Help me, please.* All she could manage was an anguished groan. Dizziness made speech impossible. Eyes open, eyes closed, it made no difference.

"One more minute," John said. He had her around the waist and was hurrying them along a broad, twisting tunnel. Maddy felt weight coming back. It made her feel sicker than ever, if that was possible. She realized that he was carrying her rather than steering her. They must be heading away from the central axis of Sky City. They passed two other people, who made way for them and called something to John that Maddy didn't quite catch.

Lab something, they said—was he taking her to a lab? For tests? She couldn't stand the idea of tests.

She was going to throw up.

She must not throw up.

Anytime she moved her head, even a millimeter, the nausea became worse. She closed her eyes and concentrated on holding her head perfectly still. One more minute, he said. Surely she could hang on for one minute. But how long did a minute last when you felt like this?

The icy spray on her left temple made her gasp. She opened her eyes and involuntarily jerked her head. The universe rolled sickeningly about her.

"That should do it," said a voice. "But you're moving, making things worse." Not John's voice, but a stranger's. He was standing in front of her, a fat man in a green uniform.

John was next to him, holding her at the waist. "Don't move," he said. "Give it another half minute. Stay there."

*Stay here, as opposed to what?* With that thought—with the very fact that she could think it—Maddy was suddenly enormously better. Her stomach no longer pushed up into her throat and the room was slowing and steadying.

"What?" she said. It wasn't much of a sentence, but the word came out all right.

"Labyrinthitis," the stranger said. "Have you been pogoing?"

Maddy didn't dare open her mouth, and anyway the stranger's words made no sense. He turned to John Hyslop. "Has she?"

"Yes. She's been down to Earth and back half a dozen times in the past week or two, and I don't think she had any training and preparation."

"There's your explanation, then. If you pogo between zero gee and multiple gees, it's just asking for inner-ear trouble. It's amazing she didn't get it sooner. Some people are hit the first time they come to Sky City." He turned again to Maddy. "You were lucky to be with somebody who recognized that you had labyrinthitis and brought you right here."

Maddy said weakly, "Labyr . . ."

"Labyrinthitis. Infection of the inner ear. Don't worry, it's never fatal."

Maddy wanted to protest that no one had warned her of anything like this, and why had it happened to her, who never got sick? She was not up to saying anything so complicated. Instead she said, "I feel awful."

"Soon you'll feel fine. Actually, you'll probably feel better than you are. We've got rid of the nausea and dizziness, but you still have an inner-ear disturbance. It will be a while before the shot completes the repair. And you're going to feel dopey and high and loose as a goose for the next few hours." The fat man in the green medical outfit turned to John. "Feed her, Hyslop, if she can eat. That will help. Sleep would be even better. No alcohol or fizzes; they are chemically similar to the Asfanil shot and they'll interact with it. Caffeine is all right, but no strenuous exercise. And there might be an Aphrodite effect, so no sex, and don't take her dancing tonight."

"I don't dance," John said seriously. "Thanks, Weinstein."

"Hey, unless you guys find something useful for me to do now and again, they'll stop paying me." Weinstein reached out, took Maddy's hand, and gave it a little formal shake. It seemed like pure courtesy, but she noticed that he watched her eyes and face closely while he did it.

"You'll do," he said. "Don't worry if you think and say strange things. That's standard drug side effects."

Maddy risked a tiny nod of her head. No spinning of the room, no convulsive gag reflex. "I can manage. You don't have to worry."

You *don't have to worry. The person who needs to worry is me. I'm supposed to stick tight to John Hyslop, and he's going off for a meeting out on the shield. Am I well enough to go with him? I don't think so. But that isn't even an issue. I* have *to be well enough. Or I must prevent him from going until I feel better.*

"*You do whatever you have to do." Thanks, Gordy. I know the Argos Group rules.*

The rules, the sacred rules. The rules were wonderful. They told you exactly what to do at all times.

Of course, the rules made no allowance for sickness or weariness. You probably had to die to get off the hook, and even that wouldn't satisfy Gordy Rolfe. Worst of all, though the rules said *what* you had to do, they offered no advice at all on how to do it.

# 12

John had relinquished his hold on her waist, but he still guided her with a hand on one forearm. He could not have been more proper, yet she could feel goose bumps rising under his fingers. As he led her out of Weinstein's office—a neat, pink-walled room packed with medical equipment that she had no recollection of entering—Maddy felt spectacularly strange and light-headed. She struggled for self-control. *You have a job to do. You've got to stick with John Hyslop, or make him stick with you.*

She halted, so that John was forced to turn and face her. "Five minutes ago I didn't think I'd ever feel like eating again. Now I'm all of a sudden starving. Your doctor friend said you could feed me. Will you do it?"

"Of course."

"Soon?"

"Right away. Can you move by yourself, or do you need my help?"

"I don't know. If you could . . ."

She held out her hand, letting it flop limply at the wrist. *Isn't that what poor weak women are supposed to do? Just as well there's no one from the Argos Group to see this. Maddy Wheatstone—rising star, hard as diamond, cold as Charon, never sick, never dependent—clinging for support like a delicate flower.*

*You do whatever you have to do.* John Hyslop didn't even seem suspicious. He took her by the elbow and carefully walked her to a drop chute. He halted at the edge.

"We'll be in free fall in the chute, but only for a few seconds. Can you stand that?"

Maddy nodded. The head movement was another informal test of her balance centers, and it went fine. All sense of vertigo had gone. In its place she felt a delicious, sensual languor. Was it low gravity that produced the sense of moving deep in warm water, or was it Weinstein's drug?

She stepped forward into the open space of the drop chute. The free-fall ride down added a new sensation. She felt hot and tingling in the pit of her belly, a warmth as good as the afterglow of the best sex ever.

Len Strahlig had been—how long ago? More than six months. And he had definitely *not* been the best sex ever, as well as being an empty-headed scumball liar. But he had talked a great line, just as a salesman was supposed to. The very opposite of John Hyslop. John was so serious and awkward and tongue-tied except about his work. *How would he be if he could relax for once and obey his emotions instead of his inhibitions?*

The return of weight brought Maddy out of her budding fantasy. She realized that her eyes were closed, and reluctantly opened them. When you began to have erotic thoughts about a hard-line engineer who was also your primary job assignment, something was long overdue.

Maddy felt heavier, which meant that they had dropped a long way from the central axis. And yet—she took a couple of steps—the floating sensation was still there.

The drug. It had to be the drug.

A voice at the base of her brain whispered, *Be careful!* Argos Group training forbade the use of drugs, not for any moral reasons but because they warped business judgment. The warning was intended to apply mainly to dope and fizzes, but Weinstein had mentioned that the Asfanil shot might produce the same effects.

Damned if you do, damned if you don't. She had been told that it would be good if she could sleep, except that she had to stay with John Hyslop. Both of those were possible only if she slept with him. Maddy took a deep breath. She had to get herself under control. She ought not have been thinking of sex at all at a time like this. You were permitted, even encouraged, to have sex with your assignment when that came as a necessary part of the job. But you never, under any circumstances, became emotionally involved. Thanks to the Asfanil, she felt more than involved; in her present mood she was likely to say or do anything.

Fortunately, she was no longer the focus of John Hyslop's attention. The drop chute had delivered them into the middle of the biggest room that she had ever seen on Sky City. Looking forward, along what had to be the main city axis, she saw thirty meters of floor before it reached a flat blue vertical surface. The wall behind was the same distance away. On the other two sides the floor curved up through ninety degrees to become the walls.

This had to be one of the big communal halls of Sky City, a combined social meeting place and restaurant. Scores of tables were scattered randomly on the smooth white floor. They and the one-piece chairs were all light and moveable. Small groups, mostly between two and six people, sat eating and chatting around the tables. Low-level rolfes scuttled unobtrusively between the tables, clearing and cleaning.

Everyone, it seemed, knew John Hyslop. Every few steps he paused to exchange a few words with a person or a group. Sometimes it was a question, such as how a repaired life-support subsystem on Sky City was performing. Sometimes the exchange concerned the airy web of the space shield. Never, Maddy noticed, did anyone ask or offer anything personal. No wife or kid talk, no flirting, no social chat. It was all microprocessors, monofilament strengths, q-bit rates, rolfe performance, and shield capabilities.

Geeks, she decided. Sober, serious engineers, dedicated and hardworking, the purest geek form in the universe.

And what did they think of her? Hard to tell. She was eyed with a good deal of curiosity, but no one asked who she was or hinted to John that he might provide an introduction.

So to hell with them. Except for John. He was a major challenge. There was real passion in him—you heard it when he spoke of aerospikes and dynamic tests. How could you transfer that to the human domain? Most interesting of all, how could you transfer that to *you*?

She examined the set of his shoulders and the straight line of his back. She was listening, but hardly listening, to a discussion of the installation of smart strain gauges on extended fullerene members under extreme stress, when the thin, moon-faced man talking to John brought her awake by saying, "You know, you ought to talk to Lauren. She was around here just a while back, asking if anyone had seen you. She says she really has to meet with you."

At last, a personal remark! Maddy's muddled brain was asking, *Who's Lauren? Old girlfriend, present girlfriend?* Then she remembered where she had heard the name before. It was nothing personal at all. Lauren was Lauren Stansfield, the woman who would take over John Hyslop's duties.

*No, get it right.* Half *his duties, the ones connected with Sky City. Someone else, a man—name? Don't recall—would be responsible for engineering work on the shield itself.*

The voice inside Maddy's head was busy. *If people will just go on talking to John, so I don't have to talk anymore at all, maybe I can avoid making a total fool of myself* . . .

"This will do." They had reached an empty table at last, and John guided Maddy to a seat. "What would you like to eat?"

"Mmm." She had professed to be starving, but in fact she was sure that any solid food would stick in her gullet. "Could I have soup? And a hot drink. But look, I'm fine, I can go with you and help myself. And I have a job to do. I'm supposed to—"

She managed to choke back the rest of the sentence. She said, "I'm supposed to rest, so thank you. I'll wait here." She had been about to say, "I'm supposed to stick to you tighter than Gordy Rolfe's tiny ass."

Maddy leaned her elbows on the table and rested her face in her hands, covering her eyes. The only thing she could do was sit tight, bite her tongue, and pray for the Asfanil to wear off before she said or did something awful. She felt amazingly horny. Loose as a goose, the doctor had said. How would John Hyslop react to a quiet hand sneaking up his thigh under the table? Stare down his nose at her, probably. Explain to her that she was not a certified engineer and therefore not qualified to handle extended members under extreme stress. But he was wrong about that. She was Maddy Wheatstone, and she could handle anything.

"Here we are. I hope this is all right."

Maddy took her hands away from her eyes. John was back, heavily laden. "Got you soup and a drink. But I thought you might be able to manage something a bit more substantial once you started." He pointed to the contents of the tray. "So I brought you a Sky City special. It's easily confused with real food."

He was staring at her uncertainly. Bless him, could it be a joke?

And he didn't know how she was going to react. *Look at the worry lines on his forehead, and see the concern in those lovely gray eyes. Smile at him, at the very least, show you appreciate what he's doing for you.*

"Thank you, John." Maddy gave him her top-quality seductive smile. "That's very sweet of you." She patted the chair next to her. "Come on. You sit down right here."

He ignored the invitation and sat down opposite. "Look, Maddy, I did something else when I was ordering the food. I hope you don't mind."

*I don't think I'd mind anything you do.* Not the right answer. "I don't know. Why don't you tell me what you did?"

"I put out a general message. For Lauren Stansfield, asking her to come to table forty-seven. That's us. I know you're not feeling well, and I should have asked you first. But Lauren has been telling people that she really needs to talk to me, and if she's still here, I didn't want to miss the chance."

*I hate Lauren Stansfield, and I don't want her here. On the other hand, I think I may* need *her here.* "Of course I don't mind. Where is she?"

"For all I know, she left. But if she gets my message, she'll join us."

Maddy squeezed the plastic bowl and took a mouthful of soup. It had a gritty consistency but no flavor whatsoever. He was watching as she forced it down. He watched as she swallowed another mouthful. If she didn't find something to distract him, he was going to monitor every blessed milliliter she drank and every movement that she made. And if he looked a few inches lower, he couldn't miss the fact that her nipples were erect and pushing against her green silk blouse.

She met his eyes and cleared her throat. "You know, when we were coming up on the shuttle I thought you were sitting there doing nothing."

"That's all right. I thought the same about you."

"But you weren't doing nothing, were you? You were monitoring the flight performance."

"That's right. Monitoring, and estimating. That's my job, though it doesn't usually apply to shuttle flights. But you really *were* doing nothing."

"No." Maddy reached out for the drink that he had brought her. It was, thank God, coffee, hot and even drinkable. "I was watching the passengers. That's *my* job."

It was the wrong thing to say, and she knew it at once. He was leaning forward, palms flat on the table and eyes fixed on hers. "It's odd you should say that. I've been wondering since our first meeting, just what *is* your job? In fact, I don't really know what anyone does who works for the Argos Group."

You *are my job, you strange, sweet man. I'm assigned to you.* Maddy leaned forward also, and by an act of will kept her hands away from his. He, she noticed, had not eaten a bite. "There's a joke about that in the Argos Group. We say it's our goal to have a piece of everything, and do nothing. Maybe it's like your job. You're a top engineer, but you don't actually *make* anything, do you?"

"Not for a dozen years." He had a broad, full-lipped mouth, and it twisted downward. He didn't like giving her that answer.

"So what do you do?"

"You saw it today. I look and listen and analyze, then I tell other people to do things."

"Right. So would you say you're an engineer, one level removed?"

"Two, really. The people I tell then tell other people, or they instruct the machines. The rolfes do most of the real work."

"Well, it's the same with the Argos Group. We're managers, not engineers, but we bid contracts for major space projects, like the Aten asteroid capture and mining that you'll—that *we'll* be involved in." Maddy was puzzled. Gordy Rolfe had not told her that she would be involved beyond the initial phase. That *we* had pushed its way in from nowhere. She added, "But we don't perform the contracts. We farm them out, to companies who do the actual work."

"And what do *you* do?"

"I suppose that I'm like you. I'm a troubleshooter. I keep an eye on things that might go wrong, and I make sure that they don't. But I don't mean technical things. You listen to engines. I listen to people. And I watch them, and I steer them. Do you know what I've been thinking?"

Maddy was talking more than her share—more than she should—and he wasn't talking enough. She had seen the file on his background, he was a Scots-Irish mixture, but apparently the taciturn Scottishness came more easily to him than Irish blarney. She, on the other hand, didn't seem able to shut up. When he shook his head in answer to her question, she went on, "I was thinking that you and I live in two different worlds. Even when we are on the same shuttle flight, even when we sit in seats right next to each other, what we notice is totally different. Your world is mostly engines and numbers and performance levels, mine is mostly people and their interactions and their motives. It makes you wonder, could two people like us live happily together?"

Maddy was far out of her depth. She should not be talking this way, especially to her assignment. She felt one tongue-slip away from inviting him to bed. Gordy Rolfe would skin her if he ever found out, but John was looking intrigued and decidedly puzzled.

*Change the subject.*

*What to?*

*Anything. Get* him *talking.*

"How long have you been working on Sky City?"

Maddy knew the answer: He had come eleven years ago.

"Eleven years."

*Bad question, if he could get away with two words.* "What made you decide to come here, instead of taking a job down on Earth?"

"Well . . ." *One-word answer. Come on, sweetie, you can do better than that.* "Well, you know what they say, the fool of the family goes to space. But down on Earth I trained as an engineer under Giorgio Hamman." He raised his eyebrows at her, waiting for a nod of recognition.

Maddy had never heard of Giorgio Hamman, but John was talking at last. She nodded and repeated, "Giorgio Hamman."

"Right. Old Giorgio was over eighty when I met him, but he was still the best engineer in the world. I worked with him restoring the big suspension bridges that had been damaged after the supernova, and if I'd been left to myself, I would probably still be doing bridge work. But Giorgio wouldn't let me. He said, 'Bridge repairs are a good job for an old man, they bring back happy memories. The Messina Strait bridge, now, what that means to me. Hard days and hard nights, sunshine and wine and beautiful girls. But *you,* young fellow'—I was young, but I didn't feel it—'you, young fellow, you don't have those memories. You ought to be *building* memories, to keep you warm in your old age. You must go where the action is. The space shield is the toughest engineering job in the history of the world, and it presents problems and opportunities that no one has ever dreamed of. With the talent that you have, you ought to be out there. So I'm going to do you a big favor.' "

John smiled at Maddy. "You know what his 'big favor' was? Giorgio fired me. It didn't feel like much of a favor at the time. But he gave me a farewell party that lasted two days, and sent me off with a terrific recommendation to the space shield council. And here I am."

*Building memories, to keep you warm in your old age—I like the sound of that. But I'm not building anything, and I wonder if you are, now that you're not working on the shield.*

*You love that old man, don't you? I bet the thought has never occurred to you. And did you know that when you smile like that, your eyes crinkle at the corners? I bet that has never occurred to you, either.*

*And I bet you don't realize there's not a dry seat in the house when you look at women like that.*

*Down, Maddy. But keep him talking, so you don't have to. He'll do it; you just have to push the right button.*

"Is Giorgio Hamman still alive?"

"He's not only alive, he's out here in Sky City. He came four years ago, when he hit ninety. Not for the engineering, though—I've tried to get him involved in that, but he won't listen. He says he made a mistake. What we're doing with the shield isn't *real* engineering, the way that the big suspension bridges are engineering. Instead of the cables and girders and caissons that he's used to, we're piddling about with robots and computers and strands of gossamer. He says we're building a spiderweb. The fact that it's a hundred thousand kilometers long doesn't change things."

"If he doesn't like it, why does he stay on Sky City? Because it's easier on his heart?"

"Giorgio isn't worried about his heart. He says a good engineer doesn't have one. He stays here because he's sour on Earth. Maybe it's just an old man's memories, but the way he tells it, people on Earth before the supernova were different. More easygoing. I pointed out that there were twice as many people back then, but he says that's not what he means. Half the world died, but it doesn't explain why the ones who are left are so much tougher and more selfish."

*You're describing Gordy Rolfe perfectly. Actually, you're describing the whole Argos Group. And I'm part of it. I'm the hotshot VP, the fastest gun in the place except for Gordy himself. And he's a disgusting, paranoid little shit.*

Maddy had just enough self-control to say none of that. She was helped by something else that caught her attention. A woman had appeared at one of the hall entry staircases. She stood about fifteen meters away, regarding Maddy with a puzzled expression on her face.

Now she was walking toward them. Maddy did an instinctive point-by-point comparison. *About my height. Great carriage, sexy and regal at the same time—can't compete with that. Good figure, too, far as I can tell in those clothes—bet the men go ape over those breasts. Big, serious eyes. But they're sort of lifeless, I'll take mine any day. Nice auburn hair. Color looks natural. An odd style. And that's a strange hair comb, sort of tiara-shaped—looks like it's a real antique—*

The woman halted at their table while Maddy was still busy with her inventory.

"Lauren. You got my message." John Hyslop finally saw the newcomer and gestured to her to sit down. "Come and join us."

John didn't notice as he made the introductions—of course he didn't, a geek engineer wasn't designed to pick up undertones—but some things are obvious even when you are drugged up to the eyes. Maddy could see that, so far as Lauren Stansfield was concerned, this meeting had one person too many.

Lauren immediately provided confirmation. She said, "I was hoping that this would be a private meeting." She looked at Maddy but spoke as though she did not exist.

*Not a chance, sweetheart. I stay.* Maddy nodded to Lauren, smiled at John, and sipped coffee.

"I think Maddy has to remain where I can keep an eye on her." John spoke right on cue, as if Maddy had scripted it. "She's up from Earth, and Weinstein just gave her a shot of Asfanil. We have to watch for side effects. On the other hand, if you want to talk about personal things . . ."

*Did I have it right the first time? Are they lovers?*

Maddy took another look at the woman sitting on her left. Lauren Stansfield was beautifully dressed in a custom-made plum-colored pantsuit that conformed to engineer dress code while managing to seem nothing like it. She was also impeccably made up, as though for a date. But the body language said no such thing. She sat well back from John Hyslop, knees together, back straight, hands folded at her midriff.

"I have no personal matters to discuss," she said. "My choice of words was perhaps confusing. When I said that I wished for a private meeting I meant only that I want to talk about matters concerning Aten asteroid materials, inappropriate for discussion in public."

"Oh, that's all right." John was clearly relieved. "You can talk about that in front of Maddy. In fact, it's good if you do—Maddy's with the Argos Group, and their contract includes material delivery from the Aten asteroids."

"Very well." Lauren Stansfield leaned toward Maddy, providing a close-up of the retroussé nose and the small, prim mouth. For the first time, that mouth took on the shadow of a smile. It was not reflected in the cold, wide eyes. "Ms. Wheatstone, you must excuse me if I am as blunt as if you were not present."

Lauren turned to John Hyslop, making it clear that so far as she was concerned Maddy was not part of the meeting. "As you know, John, our procedure calls for an inventory of materials every three months. We are six weeks away from the end of the quarter, but since I am taking over from you in certain areas I decided to make an inventory at once. It seems that there are major discrepancies between recorded and actual quantities. I see signs of substantial theft of materials derived from the Aten asteroid stores—"

"Hold on." John held up his hand. "Lauren, I wish you had let me know that you were going to do this."

It was not at all a reprimand, but it seemed to Maddy that Lauren Stansfield took it as such. Her back stiffened and she said, "I thought it best to proceed without telling anyone. After all, if there has been theft, as appears to be the case, I did not wish to give the thieves an opportunity to cover up their actions."

"Sure. But it's not theft, Lauren. It's only sloppiness—*my* sloppiness." John pulled out the little notebook that Maddy had seen him using on the shuttle. "When we were making fixes on the shield last week, the crew needed a bunch of chrome bars and smart sensors and carbon filament microlattices. It was a rush job, so I told them to pull straight out of inventory and I would take care of the record keeping. I did, too." He waved the notebook. "In here. But I never got round to transferring it into the data bases."

Lauren Stansfield's face was inscrutable. Even Maddy, who specialized in such things, could not read it. Was that a look of relief, that the problem had gone away? Was it annoyance, at having her theory of theft disposed of so quickly? Or was it disdain, for the primitive way that John Hyslop recorded information?

Listen and learn. Maddy had too little experience with women engineers.

Lauren was taking a small entry terminal from her own jacket. "I see. Then I suggest that we update the inventory at once. If you will read me the industry codes, and then the quantities . . ."

Maddy sat back as the conversation descended into a boring exchange of meaningless numbers. She listened with half an ear and watched much more closely. She wanted to understand, not so much what these engineers talked about as what moved and motivated them.

Her first take on John Hyslop, as a calculating and unemotional man, had been wrong. You only had to hear him talk about Giorgio Hamman to realize that his enthusiasm for the man went beyond admiration to adoration.

Lauren Stansfield was a tougher challenge. The woman presented herself as the very model of Ms. Cool, but occasionally, as when John had interrupted her assertion of theft, you sensed a spark of fire inside the ice.

Since Lauren was taking over John Hyslop's duties, she must be highly competent. That came across in her demeanor. Otherwise, she was an invisible woman. Maddy had the feeling that if she turned her back on Lauren, the woman would fade from view within seconds.

*No one is calm, no one is logical. Inside, everybody is a volcano.* That was Gordy Rolfe's guiding principle, the one he had used to build the Argos Group.

It worked fine down on Earth—brawling, selfish, tormented Earth. But what about here, in the quiet sanctuary of Sky City, with its abundance of calm and logical engineers? Maybe Gordy's principle didn't work at all.

Maddy turned away from John and Lauren, still deep in their number swapping, and looked out along the great length of the communal hall.

Everything was peaceful. Calm, logic, order, rational behavior made manifest. But someone on Sky City, perhaps one of the very people she was now watching, was an insane murderer.

Underneath, even here, burned the volcano.

# interlude 2

## interlude: Sniffer, Model B.

Two years in the million-year evolution of human intelligence is nothing, less than an eyeblink. Two years in the twenty-first-century development of machine intelligence is a significant interval.

In outward appearance and even in internal hardware, Sniffer-A and Sniffer-B were almost identical, but the second model possessed a far higher degree of program flexibility. In human terms it was still no more than a low-grade moron with unique specialized talents, a silicon-based idiot savant, but it was enormously smarter than Sniffer-A. Model B could correlate predicted and observed values, decide if the difference between the two was significant, and then—a major improvement—vary the performance of its onboard sensors and analytical tools.

The Sniffer tasted the speeding front of the particle flux and decided, as Sniffer-A had done two years earlier, that the difference from expectations went far beyond statistical tolerance. That result was sent on its light-speed journey back to Earth, while at the same time a new sampling protocol was introduced. The arrival times of the anomalously heavy particle nuclei were measurable to within an attosecond. Even moving at an appreciable fraction of light speed, nucleic separation distances of less than an atomic diameter could be determined.

The Sniffer was well equipped to analyze time series data. It was clear that the arrival times of groups of nuclei of different species were tightly correlated. Those groups were also very large, usually containing trillions of separate nuclei. The time pattern was seldom repeated, but the number of a particular type of nucleus contained within a single cluster was usually the same.

Sniffer-B pondered the problem at a thousand billion cycles a second as it flew on through the incident flux. It held in its general data base enough information to realize that the external world was not composed of one-dimensional entities. The data series that it was observing was a projection onto a single dimension—time—of three-dimensional structures. The Sniffer also had information on organic chemistry, enough to infer how a complex structure, such as a molecule, would appear if projected onto any given axis in space. Varying the axis of projection would give patterns characteristic of the molecule, patterns that looked different from each other but in which the number of a particular kind of atom would always be the same.

The Sniffer struggled with the problem of reconstructing the spatial configuration of the clusters that its sensors were observing. It made the working assumption that the structure was always the same, but might be arriving at the sensors at any angle.

Sniffer-B tried, and tried, and failed. It knew that it needed a method for the inference of spatial structures applicable to the clusters of nuclei, but the closest relevant technique—the theory of molecular crystallography—had seemed to the Sniffer's makers far beyond the set of applications likely to be useful in the interstellar environment.

The Sniffer did not know how to stop trying. It continued with its ceaseless ferment of computation long after the main flux of particles had passed. Only when all systems were powered down for the long interstellar cruise did the analysis process suspend.

It would start up again one more time, when arrival at Alpha Centauri triggered a last flurry of futile activity. The Sniffer would never know that the puzzle racking its circuits had been solved, within days of its receipt on Earth, by the slow and inefficient organic computers of its makers.

# 13

Nick Lopez was waiting for Celine when Suborbital One touched down at the New Rio port. As they taxied in she saw him waiting on the tarmac. His broad, simple face and warm, welcoming smile made her think, not for the first time, *I'm the President, but he's the politician.*

How could you dislike somebody so cheerful and so positive? How could you resist that sunny smile? When you were with him, you couldn't. Only when you went away and read the thirty-year catalog of suspicions and rumors and unsuccessful charges against him did the doubts come back.

"Good flight, Madam President?" He engulfed her hand in his warm brown paw as she reached the bottom of the glide stair, and grinned down at her from his thirty-centimeter height advantage.

Celine shrugged. The plane had squeaked in under the nose of a July storm racing in from the northwest, and during the final approach a bout of turbulence had been too much for the stabilizers. "You know what they say—if you can walk away from a landing, it was a good flight. Actually, I've known better. But we had to do our final approach from the south because of the weather. And I wondered, are those new beaches that I saw?"

"Under construction." Nick fell into step beside her. "New beaches, but with the old names. Copacabana, Ipanema, Leblon, Gavea. Don't you just love them, the dreams from the past? Though of course, I don't plan to visit the new beaches; they're for the younger generation."

Celine was not so sure. Nick's file was a thick one. Long before the supernova, U.S. Senator Nick Lopez had been a frequent visitor to the Rio de Janeiro beaches. He had not been above bringing his young male pickups back to Washington and showing them off around the halls of Congress. Now he wore his trademark hairstyle, a shaped high pompadour, deliberately gray, but he was in excellent physical shape. It would be no surprise if he still followed his old habits. It was Nick, after all, who had decided that the main headquarters for the World Protection Federation would be in New Rio.

Still, no one could argue with his logic. New Rio had space available, and lots of it. The old line "And I alone lived on to tell the tale" applied literally to Joachim Salazar, an inhabitant of the old city of Rio de Janeiro. After the supernova, rain had fallen continuously and torrentially in the Serra dos Orgãos, the mountains to the west of Rio; rain from March 2 to September 5, one hundred and eighty-eight days and nights. At the end of that time the city was gone. The great bridge across the harbor had been riven from its supports and lay on the bed of Guanabara Bay. The airport on Ilha do Governador had disappeared, along with the island itself. The famous beaches south of Rio, Copacabana and Ipanema and the others, had vanished.

So had Rio's seven million residents. The post-supernova surveys found no trace of them. Only Joachim Salazar survived. Huddled inside an inverted mobile home, he had washed out to sea on a vast slurry of mud and water surging into the Atlantic between Sugarloaf Mountain and the Parrot's Beak promontory. He had floated in the open ocean for thirty-nine days and been picked up, dehydrated and demented, six hundred miles out to sea. Salazar's memories, such as they were, provided the only record of the last days of Rio.

Guanabara Bay, the splendid natural harbor north of Rio, remained in altered form after the floodwaters receded. Where better, then, to make a fresh start and build the wonderful New Rio, a fitting headquarters for the World Protection Federation?

That had been Nick Lopez's argument. Celine had not been deeply into politics at the time, but she could not remember any opposition to Nick's idea. Only recently had she come to realize that Lopez was, for all practical purposes, the final authority on everything that happened in New Rio.

"What's the population now?" It seemed to Celine that there were fewer people around than she remembered on her last trip.

"About one hundred thousand." They had reached the limo, and

Nick opened the door for her. "The road northwest is finished, and the interior is once more accessible. Lots of space to fill."

That was an understatement. Celine had seen the satellite maps, old and new. Brasília was gone; Manáos was gone. Eight million square kilometers of Brazil's heartland lay empty.

"The inland region is a big draw for young people," Nick went on. "I don't mind that at all. New Rio is close to the right size."

*The right size?* Celine thought. *He means the* controllable *size. I bet no one realized at the beginning that this was going to become Nick Lopez's private domain.*

Sometimes, struggling to serve a hundred and fifty million people in fifty-three states scattered over ten million square kilometers, Celine wondered if Nick Lopez didn't have the better idea. Find a place small enough, and manage it completely. The United States—even with its population halved by Alpha C and with an infrastructure far less than fifty percent of what it had once been—often felt unmanageable. It was an act of faith that said progress was possible, that the country could be united to rise to and surpass its past; that there would one day be another Mars expedition, a strong program in basic science, a confident populace, and faith in the future.

As the limousine rolled along the splendid avenue that led to central New Rio and the WPF headquarters, Nick Lopez noticed Celine's subdued manner. He pointed to the chauffeur beyond the sliding glass panel and said, "We tried an AVC system for a few years. But a human can do things that Automatic Vehicle Control will never do. Did you ever ask an AVC to bring you a beer and a sandwich?"

Celine came back to the present and inspected the silent chauffeur. "No, but it could be done. Why not add a rolfe to the car? That would be smart enough." Nick nodded, but Celine doubted if beer was the issue. A rolfe kept a complete log of when and where it went. So did the AVC. Unlike a human driver, they could not be paid to "forget" a midnight trip or a destination.

"Is he listening?" she asked.

Lopez shook his head. "He doesn't speak English. And in any case, you don't need to worry. He's my man. We can talk. Just how bad is the problem?"

Ten years ago Celine would have been shocked by the question.

Now she wondered if it was possible to keep anything secret, ever, in Washington. She stared north, to where a dense black thundercloud hovered over the bay. Already it was raining there. "How much do you know, Nick?"

"Rumors only. Word that shit will hit the fan sooner than we thought."

"That's all?"

"All I know. Of course, I can make guesses. When you ask for a meeting and become annoyed when my staff can't find me, it's a marker. When you tell me you'll fly down to New Rio for that meeting, that's another marker."

"You said you were willing to come to Washington."

"I did and I was. But I also said that I couldn't make the trip for three days. When you ignore that and fly here, it means you have something that can't wait so long. That's when I begin to worry."

"Join the club."

They had reached the WPF building, a tall pyramid of white limestone and glass standing out against the dark sky. Celine wondered how they would get inside without getting soaked. Rain lashed the avenue in front of them, and the building was at least fifty meters from the road. To the north, jagged spears of lightning flashed down in concert, a multilegged angular monster stalking across the bay. The storm would intensify before it blew away to the east.

Well, this year it seemed to be always raining. And there were worse places than a limousine for a private conversation. It could be bugged, but the only person likely to listen to the record was Nick Lopez himself. A bigger worry was whether the other plane, leaving Norfolk at almost the same time as Celine had left Washington, would be able to fly in and land. She ought to have checked that before she left Suborbital One.

Nick was waiting patiently. As he had implied, this was her move. "I didn't know you when you were a Senator," she began.

"Not *quite* true." His voice and relaxed manner took away any suggestion of criticism or correction. "I was a Senator when you captured the Eye of God and brought her to Washington. I also stood in line and shook your hand as one of the survivors of the first Mars expedition."

*First and only expedition,* Celine thought. *Earth has other priorities at the moment. But you have to keep the faith. We'll survive the particle storm, and someday we'll go back to Mars.*

She said, "Happy days. You know, when I was on the Mars expedition, we used to tell each other that it was really important to build a permanent base there, so that if something happened to Earth, the human species wouldn't become extinct. It never occurred to any of us that something might be so widespread that it could wipe out life on both planets."

"Me neither. While you were on the Mars expedition, I didn't give a second's thought to issues like that. If all politics is local, then I was all politics."

"I didn't work with you when you were in the Senate. I've talked to people who know you, though, and I've checked your reputation."

"Ah. Now it's coming. The old scuttlebutt." Lopez reached forward to pull out the service module in front of the seat, and waved his hand at the array of choices. "Something for you?"

Celine declined with a shake of her head. "Nick, I'm not talking about what you do with your private time. If you screw, who you screw, when you screw, that's none of my business."

"Madam President, you disappoint me."

Was he deliberately trying to distract? Even after years in politics, Celine still had doubts about her own ability to read a situation. She said, "I'm talking about your professional reputation."

Nick nodded. He said nothing more, but sat watching her with an intent expression. He had taken a bottle of Calvados and poured an ounce or two into a snifter. Now instead of drinking the apple brandy he held the balloon glass under his nose. The thunderclouds were directly overhead; there was a darkness like nightfall, and continuous thunder rolled around the limousine. Reflected lightning flickered pale on Nick's face.

"What I heard wasn't all good," Celine said. "You made enemies when you were in the Senate. I found people who said you couldn't be trusted with anything, large or small. I met people who said you always looked out for yourself, first and last. I found someone who would have stuck a knife in you if they could have got away with it."

"If you'd looked harder, you'd have found more than one." Still Lopez only sniffed at the brandy. "And yet you flew here?"

Celine nodded. She was oddly reluctant to get to the point. "You told me once that you learned a lot from President Steinmetz."

"A great deal. I sometimes think I was frightened of Saul Steinmetz. No insult, Madam President, but he was the master of us all."

"I agree completely. He told me something many years ago, when he first suggested that I ought to enter politics. You've got the fame already, he said, and that's half the battle. Leader of the survivors of the Mars expedition, no one has to ask who you are. You ought to take advantage of it. President Eisenhower had it, Saul said, and damn little else except a famous bald head, and he rode it all the way to victory and a two-term presidency. You can probably win the election already, but if you're to stay the course you need something more. You have to be able to work with your enemies as well as your friends. You have to be able to work with *anyone.*"

"Ah." The dark heart of the storm hovered overhead, lightning-free. Nick Lopez had become a dark bulk with an invisible face. Celine could see him slowly nodding. Rain rattled on the roof and half obliterated his words. "That's the authentic Steinmetz. He said the same to me when I took over the World Protection Federation. For some reason he thought I was prejudiced against foreigners."

"And you're not?"

She saw his teeth flash in the gloom. "Only Koreans. I hate those fuckers—but don't quote me. Madam President, are you saying we have to work together? If so, I thought we already were."

"I won't quote you. I'm going to quote President Steinmetz instead. He said that Nick Lopez pretends to be straightforward and simple, but he has the most complex mind in the U.S. Senate. He never works with a single agenda."

"That used to be true, but my Senate years were a long time ago. I don't know if that's the case anymore. I'm getting old, Celine. At my age people worry about their monuments, how they'll be remembered."

"Nick, if you don't mind my saying so, that is one hundred percent pure bullshit."

He laughed so hard that the car shook. Then he was silent for a long time. The rain was ending, and when at last he spoke his quiet words were hardly audible against the background grumble of departing thunder. "I have no children of my own, Celine. That makes my personal survival very important to me, because I'm the last of the line. I hate the idea of leaving this old world, and I take precautions to minimize my own chances of dying. But I also love the planet, and even when I'm gone I don't want anything bad to happen to it. If I'm still around when the particle storm has passed, I hope Earth won't have changed too much. I want it to be a place I will recognize and can enjoy. Things and people I know, familiar sights and sounds and smells, not some alien landscape. If that's multiple-agenda, then I'm multiple-agenda."

"If you want the Earth that you know, Nick, you have to listen to the scientists I'm bringing in. You have to understand what they say, and see if you agree with me that it is correct and important."

"Why me?"

"Because you're smart—everyone agrees on that, even your enemies."

"You want me to listen and give you a second opinion?"

"No. I've had a second opinion, and a third. My senior Cabinet members were all briefed, and they didn't buy what they heard. I want some assurance that I'm not off my head."

"Celine, I'm no scientist."

"You are more than you pretend to be. You cultivate a simple public image, but it's bogus. You speak several languages, and you quote romantic poetry in all of them—but only when you think no one is there to record your words."

"Now you've been listening to Auden Travis. Never have an affair with the Vice President. Of course, he wasn't VP at the time. He was just an aide." Lopez sighed and shook his head. "What a beauty he was, back when I first met him. That curling brown hair, the sensitive mouth, that lovely straight Greek nose. And eyes to die for."

"Auden says nice things about you, too." Celine knew that a second conversation was going on below the surface. She and Nick Lopez were feeling each other out, testing the chemistry. His presence was oddly relaxing. You had to remind yourself constantly that Lopez had a dark side to him. She went on, "The Vice President also confirmed my other impression of you. Publicly you claim suspicion of technology, but actually you respect science and scientists."

"Let's say I believe, generally speaking, that scientists know what they don't know better than most people. But they're often wrong in what they *do* know. Or think they do."

The rain had stopped. The storm was speeding away to the east, and the soaked walkway leading from the car to the white pyramid reflected prismatic colors. Celine glanced back toward the airport. No planes seemed to be taking off or landing.

"Wilmer Oldfield is a scientist, and a good one," she said.

"I believe you." Nick was opening the door of the limousine. He had drunk not a single drop of the Calvados, and placed the glass on a shelf in front of the seats. "But I don't know him."

"You do, from a long time ago. Wilmer was with me on the Mars expedition."

"Hm." Lopez frowned. "Mars expedition."

"Nick, we're alone. You don't have to act dumb for me; I know you remember."

"Ah." The head shaking changed to a nod. "Big, balding, sort of sloppy-looking? Sure."

"What did you think of him?"

The analytical flash in the brown eyes came and went like the departed lightning. "He struck me as lucky in his choice of work. That much uncompromising concentration and focus is dangerous. If he'd picked religion as his business, by now he'd be a saint or a martyr. What became of him?"

"He's here. At least I hope he's here. I want you to listen to what he has to say. I need help on this more than I want to admit." Celine glanced again toward the airport. "Assuming his flight made it on time. It was supposed to land right behind us. But we sneaked in just under the storm."

"You should have said so. I can easily check." Lopez left the car door open and queried the telcom set on the arm of his seat. After a few seconds he nodded. "They had a twenty-five-minute hold at the airport because of the storm, but now planes are landing again. I'll make sure your friend is brought to us at once. We can go inside and wait." He climbed out of the car, then turned back to Celine as she followed. "What makes you so sure that I'll be willing to listen?"

"You do. You say you love this world, and you don't want anything to kill it."

They set off side by side along the paved rainbow walkway. After a few seconds Lopez gave Celine a wry sideways glance. "I also said I'd hate to leave the world. And you were the one accusing *me* of multiple agendas."

The ground floor of the building that they entered seemed even bigger from the inside. It was one huge, open plaza, with a floor of intricate marble mosaics and an inner atrium that became suddenly sunlit as they walked in. Curved escalators, of a design unknown to Celine, wound their sinuous way to higher floors. Nick Lopez nodded at the uniformed men and women who stood around without apparent function on the plaza floor and bowed as he passed. He ushered Celine onto one of the gleaming metal escalators, stood close behind her, and said softly, "I'm not keen on pomp and ritual, but it's expected for someone in my position. I blame it on the South American tradition. Come down here sometime for Carnaval."

Celine wondered: *If you were the boss, couldn't you control the amount of bowing and scraping?* Then she reflected. *She* had not been able to stop people fawning and groveling, or installing extra features in her office that she neither needed nor wanted. Why should Nick Lopez be able to do any better?

The office that they came to on the third floor at first suggested that Nick was no different. His name and title were embossed in gold on the outer door. The room beyond was vast and sumptuously furnished. Its floor was covered with a deep-piled Persian rug, and every wall held paintings that looked both genuine and old.

Farther on, however, deep in the interior of the suite, they entered Nick's private office. There was no name on the door. The furniture was simple, almost spartan, with one terminal, one desk, and two chairs. The four walls held one picture each, three of them watercolors and one a black-and-white photograph. On the desk sat one telcom, with a red, single-purpose handset with no video unit next to it. The set was beeping as Nick ushered Celine into the room.

"Damnation." Nick walked across and picked up the handset. "I told my people to hold all calls, but this one bypasses the general circuits and comes straight to my office. Excuse me for a moment."

He spoke into the unit. "Yes? . . . Yes, it's just the way I told you it would be. It rings only here, in my private office. If I'm not here, no one else will answer. And it makes no recording."

He paused for a few seconds, then said, "Well, that's true, if you call and I'm not here, you'll have no way to get a message to me. But that's the way we agreed to do it. I hope it's the same at your end. I don't want to be making broadcasts when I talk to you. Are you underground or at your other place?"

Lopez shot Celine a quick glance as he spoke the final sentence. She walked across to the wall and made a big show of studying one of the watercolors. She was no artist, but she had seen the picture somewhere before. It was famous—and this looked very like the original.

She moved to the wall on her left and examined the black-and-white picture. The man in it was familiar, though this shot seemed different from any photograph that she had ever seen. Was this maybe Lopez's brother? The man was young, very tall, big-nosed, grinning, and wearing a Stetson hat.

Behind her, Nick Lopez was saying, "I'll call you back, and we'll make sure this is two-way. But I can't do it now—I have visitors." He winked at Celine as she turned around, and spoke again into the set. "Well, as a matter of fact, it's *one* visitor, if you know what I mean. So this isn't a good time for you and me to talk . . . Sure. We can do that. Later."

He dropped the handset back into its cradle. "There. That's how a man's reputation gets ruined. Take my advice, Celine, and never put in a scrambled private line."

"I never will. I don't believe there is any such thing as an unbreakable ciphered message."

"I'm inclined to agree. But an associate insisted on a direct line between us, person to person. So now we have one." Lopez nodded to the photograph on the wall behind Celine. "I saw you studying him. You know who he is, don't you?"

"I think so, but he looks so young. It's Lyndon Baines Johnson, isn't it? President Johnson."

"No. It's LBJ all right, but that's *Senator* Johnson, before he became President. The person you are looking at was a much greater and wiser man than President Johnson."

"I didn't know you were an admirer of LBJ." Celine was genuinely astonished. Nick Lopez was not the person to have pictures of personal idols on the office wall.

"I'm not his admirer." Nick came to stand beside her and studied the picture. "He's there to remind me of something important. LBJ knew how to run the U.S. Senate better than anybody, ever. He could squeeze and coax and reward and punish, and he got just about anything he wanted. Then he became President, and he was a disaster. His ego was too big. He wouldn't admit when he was wrong. He got stuck in a war that he couldn't control, and now people look back on him as one of the worst U.S. Presidents. I keep him there because I believe that you can learn more from failure than you can from success. LBJ sent my grandfather off to war, and killed him. So I hate the son of a bitch. But I also know that he was once a great, great Senator. Past success doesn't guarantee future success, and you can do one thing very well and another very badly." Lopez stared at Celine, who was smiling. "Which part do you think is funny?"

"None of it. I smile because I'm like you. I keep a holo display just for me in the corner of the Oval Office."

"The way that Saul Steinmetz had one of Disraeli? But I've never seen yours."

"You never will. I only turn it on when I'm alone, and I don't show it to anyone. I daren't. Want to make a guess as to who it is?"

"Well, with those rules it can't be Saul, though I know he's your hero." Nick puffed out his cheeks and frowned in thought. "I'll skip the obvious guesses, because you wouldn't hide any of the Presidents. I'll bite. Who?"

"I have a hologram of Adolf Hitler."

"Hitler! Why not Pontius Pilate? That's heavy stuff." Lopez wandered over to the desk and sat at the chair behind it. He placed his elbows on the uncluttered top and cupped his chin in his hands. "Not my guess as to your first choice—or your second, third, or fiftieth."

"Want to know why he's there?"

"No. Not yet. Let me think. Isn't that what you want me to do?" He sat silent, staring straight ahead. Celine caught a glimpse of another Nick Lopez, a man as concentrated and tightly focused as Wilmer Oldfield.

"Obviously it's not because you admire him," he said after a few seconds. The telcom unit on the desk was beeping again, but he ignored it. "And my picture of Lyndon Johnson must have something to do with it. He's there to remind you that you must never forget something. But what? All right. I give up."

"It's not as direct a reminder as yours. Hitler's my symbol for the analogy between today and the state of the world a hundred and twenty years ago. In the 1920s, everyone knew that they had been through a terrible disaster. The world war had been frightful, but they had survived and it was over and everything was peaceful. The 'war to end wars,' they called it, and it seemed part of the past. Only a few people recognized that there was trouble ahead. *Hitler* was ahead, just a few years away. But most people took no notice of the danger signals. They didn't prepare for trouble until it was too late."

Lopez had walked across to stand by the desk. He had his hand poised over the telcom unit, but he did not touch it. He said, "The supernova was our First World War. We survived it. Now we're between disasters, but most people don't understand how much trouble we're in. Half of them don't even believe in the particle storm. We have the equivalent of a Second World War in our future. Right?"

"We do. We have to learn from history."

" 'Ancestral voices prophesying war.' " Lopez nodded and pressed the telcom switch. "Yes?"

"The other visitors from the United States are here."

"Bring them in." Lopez raised an eyebrow at Celine. "Visitors? More than one?"

"I don't know." Celine stared blankly at Lopez, then toward the half-open door. "It should just be Wilmer. Unless—he'd better not, I told him—"

She was speechless. The open doorway was empty no longer. A black hand had appeared around the edge of the door. It was followed a moment later by a black, grinning face.

Celine realized again what she had first learned thirty-odd years ago: What you told Wilmer to do and what Wilmer did were not always the same.

# 14

Nick Lopez had a reputation of being a bad listener, someone who in the middle of a meeting would fiddle with papers, start reading an unrelated document, or even leave and not return. Celine found it hard to match that to Saul Steinmetz's comment that Nick had possessed the most subtle and complex mind in Washington. Now, half an hour into the meeting, she thought she could reconcile the two.

Nick had received Wilmer Oldfield and Astarte Vjansander politely. He seemed secretly pleased by Celine's irritation at Astarte's presence. When the introductions were over he sat down at once, nodded to the newcomers, and said, "Your ball. Talk."

Apparently Wilmer and Astarte had agreed in advance that Wilmer would be the spokesman. Being Wilmer, he of course favored completeness over brevity. Celine watched and listened as he carefully explained two different types of supernova, and how the Alpha Centauri binary system, according to long-established theories, could not possibly belong to either class. He pointed out, as though it were news to Nick Lopez, that Alpha Centauri had in fact become a supernova; then that no one had been able to explain how this might happen until recently; but now a new theory, based on original work by Astarte as modified by Wilmer, provided a full explanation.

Wilmer outlined the new ideas and defined the pattern of compressions that must have been applied to Alpha Centauri A, the larger star of the system, to induce a supernova explosion. He spoke clearly, but certainly not simply. Celine had to concentrate to follow, and she had heard it several times before. While he spoke Astarte sat cross-legged on the floor, grinned up at Nick Lopez, and unselfconsciously scratched her belly and bare thighs.

Nick did not seem upset at that. He listened closely to Wilmer's every word, and when Wilmer talked of stellar resonance Nick nodded as though that idea was no more than common sense. He did not fidget, and he ignored the occasional beeping of the telcom unit. Twice he asked for additional details. Once he asked that a subtle point be repeated.

Celine decided that Saul was right. Nick Lopez was very smart. But in nine meetings out of ten he was *bored,* and that was when he wandered off to do other things.

Wilmer had reached the most controversial point in the presentation, the one that the Cabinet officers and government research heads had rejected out of hand. "So the compressive pulses couldn't have occurred naturally," he said. "They were induced by some other agent. That, and the fact that the directions of both the gamma-ray beam and the particle storm precisely intersect the solar system, indicate that the geometry for this event was *arranged*."

"Arranged?" Lopez was frowning.

"Deliberately contrived. It didn't just happen."

This was the point where Wilmer was supposed to end the presentation, as he had ended it before. Celine was ready to defend his heretical suggestion of supernova *intention* when Wilmer nodded to Astarte and said, "That's me done. Your turn up the gum tree."

"Right." Astarte came to her feet with a grace, fluidity, and energy that Celine envied. She glanced at Celine. "Hey, this'll be new ter you as well. We just come up with it yes'day."

Celine directed a lethal glare at Wilmer. Hadn't he learned at his age that surprises in presentations were anathema?

But he remained oblivious, and Astarte went on, "We didn't have the latest Sniffer results 'til two days ago. They agree with everything me and Wilmer calculated, and it's the way we worried it might be. There's one mode of the particle flux traveling a lot faster than the rest. It's going to hit real early—mebbe as soon as a month. But there's something else in the Sniffer data, and this one's a real bugger." Her chubby black face glowed with excitement, and she paused for effect before she exclaimed, "The particle charge-termass mix is all fucked up!"

She stood up straight, as though waiting for applause.

"You'll have to tell 'em more than that, Star," Wilmer said. "Don't assume they know the predicted energy spectra."

"Or much else," Lopez said. "What's a particle charge-to-mass mix?"

"It's like a—like a—" Astarte placed her fists together and rolled them around each other in a churning motion. "All right. Yer got yer supernova, right? The star blows up, and it's hotter than hell."

Lopez nodded. "Got that much."

"Well, that's when all the different element nuclei get made, everything from protons—hydrogen nuclei, they was there to start with—up to the nuclei of the transuranics, with hundreds of protons and neutrons in each of 'em. Most of the unstable ones and all the superheavy ones split down to something lighter real quick, so after that you've only got stable ones left. D'yer get that, too?"

She spoke to Nick Lopez slowly, as though to a rather backward child. He nodded gravely. "I get that, too."

"All right. Now let's take a few of them nuclei. Say helium, carbon, tin, and lead. Helium has two protons and two neutrons, carbon has six protons and six neutrons, tin has fifty protons and seventy neutrons, lead has eighty-two protons and a hundred and twenty-six neutrons. I'm simplifying because there's isotopes, too, but that's all right, in't it?"

"Perfectly all right. The simpler, the better."

"Now, there's a different amount of each type of nucleus formed in the explosion, so naturally yer'd expect different proportions in what comes out of the supernova. But that's only part of the story. The stuff don't just fly out, bang, it's gone. It gets accelerated, real hard, by electromagnetic fields. But the field can't get a hold on the neutrons 'cause they got no charge. The field only pushes on protons. So the two protons in helium get grabbed by the field and slung away, and the two neutrons in the nucleus hang on tight and get a free ride. The helium nucleus shoots off just half as fast as a single proton would without a neutron. With carbon, it's six protons get grabbed and flung, an' they got six neutrons as freeloaders. So the carbon nucleus goes off same rate as the helium nucleus, neck and neck. But when you get to tin, there's only fifty protons to boost and they have to carry seventy neutrons along. So they only finish up five-twelfths as fast as a proton, which means five-sixths as fast as helium or carbon. An' when you get to poor old lead, eighty-two protons lumbered with a hundred and twenty-six neutrons, it can only go eighty-two two-hundred-and-eighths as fast as a proton. That's slower yet, only seventy-nine percent as fast as helium or carbon. So you see, different nuclei come out from the supernova with different speeds. That means they fly different distances in the same time, which means they'll arrive in the solar system at different times. And it all depends on the charge-ter-mass ratio of the particular nuclei. See?"

Astarte had uttered this in one great breathless spate of words. Celine understood, but she felt sure that Nick Lopez didn't. He sat staring at Astarte with an unreadable expression on his face.

Finally he smiled, shook his head, and said, "I don't see. But I don't have to, do I? Because you started out telling me that this charge-to-mass-to-particle thing is wrong, which must mean it doesn't come out the way you calculated it."

"Too bloody true." Astarte came close to Lopez and peered at him curiously. "Yer really listen, don't yer?"

"Sometimes. I know what isn't happening, but I still don't know what is."

"That's because I haven't told you yet. Hold your water, and we'll explain." Astarte looked to Wilmer. "You wanna do it, or you want me ter?"

"You keep going, girl. It's your show."

Astarte scowled at Wilmer and turned back to Lopez. "He's a lazy bugger for everything bar physics, but I s'pose I ought to be used ter that by now. What we found in the Sniffer data wasn't what we expected. We got something a lot more interesting. See, you can work out what the supernova chucked out, the proportions of different nuclei. And you can calculate how fast they should be going, and how they ought to have spread over time. What we found, the thing that's real terrific, is that the Sniffer data shows *groups* of nucleus types, with some elements moving along together when according ter us they shouldn't have been because they had different charge-to-mass ratios. And it turns out that the speed they're moving is exactly as though they're tied together physically. We found carbon linked with oxygen and iron and mercury."

"They've formed molecules," said Celine.

That earned the President of the United States, the most powerful woman in the world, a reproving look.

"We're not dealing with *atoms,* you know," Astarte said sternly. She turned to Lopez. "D'you see why that makes a difference?"

"I have no idea."

"Well, you oughta be ashamed of yerself. A man in your position, building the shield an' all, yer ought ter know some science. So I'll tell yer some. Atoms are electrically neutral, they have the same number of electrons as the number of protons in the nucleus. But the particle flux isn't electrically neutral—if it was, the shield wouldn't be a damn bit of good, would it? The particles would go right on through without the EM field of the shield touching 'em. The particles in the storm are bare nuclei, charged, no electrons attached. Molecules are atoms with shared electrons. So how can you have molecules if you don't have atoms with electrons?" Astarte shook an admonishing finger in Nick Lopez's face. "Stands to reason you can't."

Seated, he was taller than she was standing up. In his brown eyes was a curious expression. Celine felt that at any moment he might call for his imperial guards—or whatever their equivalent was in New Rio—to come and drag Astarte Vjansander away to the dungeons.

"Star," she said. "Keep quiet for a minute. And you, Wilmer, I'm sick of hearing what the particle flux *isn't;* that kind of talk could go on forever. In two sentences, what's your new theory?"

Celine was aware of passing time—Lopez had promised an hour, and that was long past—but with Wilmer she should have known better. He didn't speak often, but when he did it took him two minutes to tell you the time. Now he scowled and frowned and rubbed the top of his head, and finally muttered, "Do you know what Einstein said? An explanation should be as simple as possible, but no simpler. I can't describe a new theory in two sentences. Nobody could."

"Two for the President, then, and two for me," Nick Lopez said mildly. His telcom was beeping. Once again he ignored it. "Go ahead, Dr. Oldfield. I'm supposed to be somewhere else, but when we're talking about the way the world ends I'll find an extra ten minutes."

Wilmer nodded. "That should be enough. Star already pointed out the important fact: The particles rushing toward the solar system are bare nuclei and they're electrically charged. More than that, they're all *positively* charged—nuclei are just protons and neutrons, no electrons. That means they repel each other, and certainly they have no tendency to travel in groups. But that is precisely what the Sniffer data says they *do*.

"Now, that gives us a few possibilities. The thing you think of first is that the groups of nuclei might contain equal amounts of matter and antimatter. Antimatter might be created in a supernova explosion. The antiproton has a negative charge equal to the charge of the electron, so a nucleus made up of antiprotons and antineutrons will be *attracted* to a nucleus of ordinary matter. We looked at that idea, me and Star, and chucked it out in two minutes. For one thing, it's hard to make stable matter-antimatter constellations. Worse still, any antimatter would annihilate itself when it met the Sniffer—and it wouldn't do the Sniffer much good, either. So forget that idea, and what's left?

"Well, we looked at other possibilities—a fifth force, which has been speculated on lots of times. Associated toroidal EM fields, binding clusters together. Phase change condensations. You can do calculations for all of them, and nothing comes close to reasonable answers. But we finally found something that works. Suppose that the strong force—that's the glue that holds nuclei together, in spite of the electrical repulsion of the protons inside them—has been modified. Sounds wild, because we're used to thinking of the strong force as something in nature that can't be touched. Like people thought about magnetism three hundred years ago. But Gottlieb, before he went off his head, had an alternative form of unification theory, and if he was right, there are ways of locally modifying the strong force so that it's longer-range and nonmonotonic—it will permit regions of attraction and repulsion at different distances. Of course, we have no idea how to make that happen."

Celine had listened long enough. She began to stand up, and for a change Wilmer noticed it. "I'm nearly there," he said, "don't get steamed. We did the calculations. A local modification of the strong force can allow *stable assemblies of nuclei,* just like the Sniffers are finding. Extremely stable, as a matter of fact, with trillions of nuclei in each group. Matter clumps. That's what I'm getting at."

"Wilmer, you blithering ditz, so what?" Celine was amazed at

Nick Lopez's patience. He was still listening, and still smiling. "A particle storm is going to reach the solar system years earlier than anyone planned. It will smash Earth back to the dark ages because the shield's not finished. We're in trouble, and you're wasting our time telling us about some new half-assed theory?"

"Yer still don't get it, do yer?" Astarte stepped in front of Wilmer. "We got good news, not bad news. It's like Wilmer says, we don't know *how* to modify the strong force. But we don't need to. Thing is, if the particle flux is coming at us in big, stable particle groups, you want a different shield design. You've been buildin' an umbrella net with a mesh close enough to keep off a fine rain of single nuclei, but that won't do you a bit of good. What's going to hit isn't a drizzle, it's matter clumps. Bloody great hailstones, trillions of nuclei at a go. Sounds at first as though you're a lot worse off, but you're not. 'Cause with big clusters you can detect, catch, and divert 'em one at a time. Only you can't do that with your present shield design. You hafta make big changes, and you hafta go at it arse-over-teakettle to finish in time. But we think it can be done."

She turned to Nick Lopez. "Get it? We brought you good news."

"I get it, Star. Dumb as I am, I really get it." He stood, and the top of Astarte's head reached only to the middle of his chest. "Now, you and Wilmer will have to excuse us."

"Yer can't leave. I don't care what your other bleeding meeting is, this is more important than anything."

"I agree. It is." Nick met Celine's eye.

She nodded. "As Senator Lopez said, you must excuse us. He and I have to discuss this in private."

"Hmph." Astarte reluctantly allowed Wilmer to usher her to the door. On the threshold she turned. "Yer all right, Senator. Not full of shit, like I expected."

"Don't mind her ways," Celine said as soon as the door was firmly closed. "She was raised in the North Australian wilderness."

"And I was raised in an eighties LA ghetto." Lopez sat down. "Until I was fifteen I thought that *fucking* was a necessary adjective in every sentence. I don't mind the way Star speaks. I think she's terrific. She paid me the most sincere compliment I ever had."

"I heard it. 'Yer all right, Senator.'" Celine imitated Astarte's broad accent and delivery. "So what do you think?"

She was not referring to Astarte's comment. Lopez sat motionless, his brown eyes staring far beyond the walls of the room. At last he spoke.

"It's easy to be distracted by the wrong thing. In this case, the wrong thing is Wilmer's insistence that the supernova was somehow *arranged*. Because if it was or if it wasn't, that's not our current problem. The supernova happened. A lethal particle flux is on the way, and it will get here a lot sooner than we expected. The shield we're building won't be ready in time. That's what's important. Do you believe it?"

"I've known Wilmer Oldfield for thirty years. I believe him without reservations."

"So, oddly enough, do I. So we're in deep trouble with the present shield. It won't be ready in time, nor will I."

Celine did not ask for an explanation of that last sentence. Nick Lopez had already indicated that he would be taking precautions to ensure his own survival.

She said, "The other important thing is that the particles arrive in big clumps, rather than solo and uncorrelated. We're building the wrong shield. Do you believe they are right about that, too?"

"I don't think it makes much difference. Look at where we stand." Lopez began to tick off points on his long, carefully manicured fingers. "Fact: The particle flux will be arriving sooner than expected. Fact: The shield can't be ready in time with its present design. Conclusion: Even if Wilmer and Star are wrong, we're screwed with the shield the way it is. Therefore: Our best shot is to assume that they are right, and modify the shield so it can deal one at a time with large clusters of particles. That leaves only one question: Can we make the changes fast enough?"

"Wilmer says we can."

"Right. Notice I'm not asking if we want to try."

"You're missing a couple of other questions, though. Can we persuade other people that we *need* to try?"

"I'll work on that. So will you."

"And what sort of staff changes will we need? Just yesterday I saw a paper from Bruno Colombo approving the transfer of the shield's chief engineer to the asteroid capture problem. Now that looks like a terrible idea."

"Ah." Lopez turned away so that Celine could not see his face.

"I agree with you, I see possible problems there. Let me look into it."

She read worry in his tone. "Do you want me to get involved?"

"Thank you, but no." He turned to Celine, and his face was impassive and unreadable. "I will speak with Bruno Colombo, and anyone else who seems appropriate. If I need help, I will call you. How long do we have?"

"Astarte said the wave could hit as soon as a month from now. Let's hope she's wrong."

"If she's right, that's no time at all." For the first time, Lopez's amiable face bore signs of weariness and worry. "Excuse me, Madam President, but we must stop this meeting right now. I have calls to make."


The private line rang and rang. Lopez was ready to give up calling the Virginia underground location and try The Flaunt when at last he heard a waspish voice at the other end.

"Yes, what the hell do you want?"

"Gordy, this is Nick Lopez."

"I know it's Nick Lopez, you stupid asshole. Didn't we agree that we were the only people who would have access to this line? What do you want? I'm busy."

"We have a problem. A big one. We need to get Hyslop assigned back to Sky City, and we need to do it as soon as possible."

"No fucking way. Hold it, I'm switching to a general circuit visual." There was a fifteen-second pause, during which Nick wondered where in his hideaway Gordy Rolfe kept his private line. It was certainly well hidden, because Gordy would not permit visuals when he was using it. There seemed little point to the line, however, if Gordy was willing to put discussions like this onto general circuits.

At last the miniature screen in front of Nick Lopez shimmered with color. Gordy Rolfe appeared, a tiny scowling gnome. The green of the habitat was visible in the background. Rolfe was holding a wire cage containing half a dozen guinea pigs and the same number of white mice.

"Now, what's this crap you're giving me?" he began. "You

agreed just a few days ago that we had to get Hyslop out of Sky City before he put the shield back on schedule and picture-perfect."

"I just sat through a presentation that changes everything. Listen to this." Nick ran through what he had heard an hour earlier, while Rolfe sat with barely controlled impatience.

"Yeah, yeah," he said when Lopez finished. "So you like the little black one. Fine, screw her if you get the chance. But even if you believe those two weirdos, so what? The blast gets here sooner than anybody thought. Earth gets crisped a few years early. Big deal."

"The wave will hit before the shield is ready. We're talking billions of deaths."

"Don't say that, Lopez, you'll make me weep." Rolfe put down the cage that he was holding and glared out of the screen. "Look, I don't give a damn about who gets offed. The way they've treated me, I'll be glad to get rid of most of the fuckers. I'll be snug down here, let 'em go. And good riddance."

His expression suddenly changed, and his eyes glittered behind the big lenses. "Oh, but I get it. I see what you're really worried about. You don't give a shit about people getting fried, any more than I do. You're afraid that the place the Argos Group is building for you won't be ready in time. Well, don't sweat it. I'll put in triple shifts and quadruple the workforce. You'll be all set in your private pleasure palace before the first protons hit."

Nick had learned to control his feelings before Gordy Rolfe was born. He grinned and said, "That easy to read, am I? But Gordy, finishing my place isn't the real problem. We both know there's no payoff for either of us if Earth gets clobbered too badly. You need customers, and I need an infrastructure. If these scientists are right, we'll not have either after the storm. Hell, we may not even be alive to worry about it. We have to get Hyslop back up there and let him try to finish the shield, at least until we have a better take on this new thing."

"And suppose he gets the shield back on schedule, and the storm's not as bad as your pinhead scientists are saying?"

"Then we'll find some other way of slowing down the project. Look, Gordy, there's another factor here. I'm a public figure. I can't say, 'Pull up the ladder, Jack, I'm on board.' You see how it will go—everybody will cry out to finish the shield as soon as possible, and the first thing that Bruno Colombo will do is assign Hyslop back to his old job anyway."

"You told me that you had Colombo in your pocket. You say 'shit' and he squats."

"True. But Gordy, I can't make him into what he isn't. Bruno comes across impressive, but inside he's cream cheese. If people like Celine Tanaka start leaning on him, he'll cave. And I daren't try to stop it. Remember, I have to act like I'm on the same side as they are."

"So you want Hyslop to have his old job back, and go charging all over Sky City poking into anything he likes? No fucking way, José. Lopez, you've lost your mind."

"Don't give me no shit about losing my mind. You listen to me for a minute." Nick hadn't been in a street fight for half a century, but it was amazing how easily you dropped back into it. He lowered his voice to a growl. "We've got no choice on this one. We're talking a crash project, balls out, shield modification in a month or less. Hyslop, he'll be too busy to worry about anything else going on. And just to make sure, we keep somebody close to him with one hand on his dick—your woman Wheatstone. You say she's ambitious, does whatever it takes. Well, tell her to prove it. Control Hyslop. If the shield changes get made and there's no particle storm, we can still switch him back to the Aten asteroid work. Okay?"

"Might be easier to off him and have done with it."

"No. Suppose we need him again? Reason we're worried is the same reason he's useful. He's smart, does things nobody else can."

Rolfe nodded grudgingly. "All right, all right. Would have been easier to off him in the first place. Except everybody was telling me how useful he'd be on the Aten asteroid work. Okay. Do it." He picked up the wire cage and peered in at the contents.

"More experiments?" Nick asked. If the fight was over, he was more than ready to change the subject.

"Continuation of one in progress. I pulled these from one section of the habitat a few weeks ago. Now the newborn dino count is way up. So I'm putting mice and guineas back in, along with more food for all of 'em. Want to bet that the dino count doesn't start down within two weeks, food or no food? And the mammals thrive?"

"I'm not a betting man, Gordy. But I want to be sure we're agreed. Hyslop can be reassigned to his old job on Sky City?"

"I guess. Go ahead and do it." Rolfe seemed to have lost interest in the subject. He was crouched down on his haunches. His attention was on the guinea pigs and mice, nosing about their wire cage as he placed it into the hollow middle section of the transparent door leading through to the habitat.

Suddenly he stood up and walked forward to the camera, so that his image stared out of the display at close range. Nick could see each individual dark whisker on Rolfe's upper lip, and the pore-filled skin around the gray eyes.

"Just one thing I don't want you to forget, Lopez." Rolfe was smiling. "I'm going along with you on reassigning Hyslop to the shield because it doesn't make much difference to me. I plan ahead in ways you don't even dream. But I want you to know that so far as I'm concerned, it's your ass on the line, not Hyslop's. Fuck this up some way, so word gets out that the Argos Group has been playing games with the shield deliverables and also skimming a little off the top, and I will become very upset. I don't think you want me very upset."

"Of course I don't." *You ignorant birdbrained weeny-dick byblow of a syphilitic whore.* Once you dropped back into the old way of thinking, it was remarkably easy to stay there. The danger was that you'd talk that way.

Nick blamed himself more than Gordy Rolfe. What had ever led him to become dependent on such a savage? He knew the answer to that. No one else had the Argos Group's capability to manage and if necessary mismanage so large a project. No one else had Gordy Rolfe's genius for electronics. And no one else was as willing to damage the Earth in order to control it.

Of course, Nick had also cultivated Gordy Rolfe to be assured of his own survival. But was that guaranteed? How long would Gordy feel that he needed Nick Lopez?

"Don't worry, Gordy." Nick's smile was broad and easy. "I'll stay on this twenty-four hours a day. How about Maddy Wheatstone, though? Can you make her available to keep close to Hyslop?"

"Lopez, you don't give me enough credit." Rolfe cut the video link to slow fade and went back to fussing over the wire cage. He sounded pleased for the first time in the conversation. "I've had Maddy riding Hyslop's ass for days, and she'll keep right on doing it. Talk to her anytime you feel like it, but just remember one thing. She can tell you how Hyslop is spending his time—but overall she reports only to me."

"What about your man looking into the Sky City murders? Is he making progress?"

Nick's question came too late. Gordy did not hear him, and the image on the display was slowly losing color. The final, graying scene showed a crouching Gordy Rolfe. Beyond him a group of small shadowy forms scuttled nervously away into the dark interior of the habitat.

Nick Lopez watched until the picture vanished completely. He felt sympathy for all but one of the mammals pictured in the display.

# 15

**From the private diary of Oliver Guest.**

Seth Parsigian is amoral and self-serving, but he is not in any sense unintelligent. That he would fail to anticipate a major problem with his presence on Sky City is surprising. That I would make the same mistake is unforgivable; yet make it I did.

Let me place certain important events in proper chronological order.

With the successful test of the remote-viewing jacket and helmet, Seth had announced that he would proceed at once to Sky City. Given my psychological problem with heights and open spaces, not to mention my other responsibilities, I of course had never considered the possibility of such a trip. And humans being what we are, I had previously taken little interest in a place that seemed forever inaccessible to me.

Now that had changed. I would experience Sky City, albeit vicariously, as Seth wandered where I directed and examined whatever seemed of interest to me.

He had warned me that the flight up from Earth would not permit him to wear the RV jacket. I would see and hear nothing until he actually reached Sky City. He had informed me, however, exactly when he expected to leave Earth, and given me the expected time of arrival at the Sky City docking facility.

It may sound strange, but ten minutes before the ship was projected to reach Sky City I was already sitting in my study, the RV helmet in position. I had no idea what I might see, but I looked forward to my "arrival" at the great flying island of Sky City with the same mixture of expectation and inbred Swiftian skepticism with which Gulliver came to the flying island of Laputa. Not knowing what the first view of Sky City might offer, I was careful to retain a generous contribution of my local scene in the helmet image.

Five minutes after projected arrival time, the picture in my helmet visor flickered with an added signal. A twisting, nauseating sequence of partial walls and corridors flashed in and out, too fast to study. Fortunately the audio link was less complex, since its encryption, transmission, receipt, and decryption depended not at all on the optical system of the RV jacket. Seth's voice sounded clear in my ear.

"We've arrived. Don't take notice of the picture yet. 'Til I have the jacket all the way on and fastened, the processors can't keep up and the image tends to go haywire."

It was a little late to warn me, but I had already taken remedial action. After one whirligig moment of partial pictures I had changed the balance of remote and local viewing. "Let me know when you are ready," I said, more to test my audio transmission circuit than from any real need to speak. Seth's inputs formed a changing gray pattern on the static and comforting background of my own study.

"That should do it," Seth said after another fifteen seconds. "You can start takin' more signal from this end. Tell me how it looks."

He had guessed that I would retreat to my local environment until the RV images were right. As I said, whatever else Seth might be, he is no fool.

I took the cue and adjusted the picture balance. I was looking at an array of circular black apertures, several dozen of them in a broad, square wall covered with a smooth iridescent layer. Scale for the whole scene was provided by a couple of human figures who came floating out from two of the holes. They wore no suits, which indicated that they and Seth were in a room with breathable air.

I briefly described what I was seeing. It was the first time, to my certain knowledge, that I had taken any interest in how a person moved in free fall. Since we were interested only in system performance I saw no reason to mention the odd balletic grace.

"Color check?" Seth's replies seemed to take longer than in the simulated tests.

I summarized the colors that I saw for each object. At first I waited each time for Seth's grunt of agreement, but the signal delays became a nuisance. Finally I ran rapidly through everything in sight, relying on Seth to demur if and where he chose.

"Spot on," he said when I was done. "You're seein' as good as me, maybe better. We're all through check-in, so let's take a little tour. What do you wanna look at?"

He was testing me; not for my physical tolerance of heights and open spaces, which so far as he was concerned had been dealt with on our first test of the RV system, but to see if I had done my homework.

I had. Days ago Seth had made available to me the architectural drawings and full operating system schematics of Sky City. I am blessed with a powerful short-term memory, and years of studying the conformational properties of protein molecules had taught me to hold within my mind complex three-dimensional structures.

"Where are we now?" I asked.

"Level one, sector eighty-two. The black circles are port entry points from vacuum docking stations."

For the first time, the signal delay was an advantage. I could take an extra fraction of a second to think before I replied, "That means we are not too far from the place on level five where Tanya Bishop's body was found. As I recall, the route from here to there has no locks and constant air pressure all the way."

This time it was Seth's turn to take appreciably longer than the signal delay. At last he said, "True. But don't expect to see anythin' new or useful. Her body's long gone, an' I doubt the tank's been used since." He did not indicate that he was impressed by my knowledge of the local geography. He would not give me the satisfaction. But at least any fears that I might be an ignorant dead weight to be towed around Sky City would be allayed.

"I don't expect to see anything new," I said. "Quite the opposite. I merely wish to compare the factual data and reconstructions that you brought to me with what I see now. And, of course, I am eager to obtain a feel for the general ambience of Sky City. I do not know how or even if that will be important, but it could be."

Seth's reply was a noncommittal snort. We began to move off along a dreary dark-walled corridor. It took us, I knew, along the fastest path to our destination at level five, sector fifty-six. The scenery as we progressed was uninspiring. If anything, it reminded me of the basement levels of a neglected hospital in a run-down area of a large city. There were the same endless corridors, leading to elevators unadorned by any touch of personality. There were rooms and cubicles and overhead pipes and ducts, all color-coded in a way that stamped out all chance of individuality. In saying that I was eager to experience the overall ambience of Sky City, I had lied. Already I had had enough of Sky City. The fact that the RV helmet could not provide olfactory experiences was probably a blessing. I am exceptionally sensitive to smells, and I felt sure that those around Seth were all unpleasant.

Neither of us chose to speak, and as we went on in total silence I considered Seth's own probable thought processes. He had come to me from desperation, when his hopes of solving the murders were at lowest ebb. He needed my help; and judging from my recent researches into the Argos Group, he was, like anyone in their senior echelons, willing to do anything to obtain an objective. He would love for me to catch the killer, but he would surely like it better were he able to discover the key clue and solve the case himself.

At the moment, neither of those eventualities appeared probable. Tanya Bishop had been killed on January 10. It was now the middle of July. We were following a trail that was more than six months old, in an environment where every scent, either literal or metaphorical, was routinely obliterated by the ever-active cleaning machines of Sky City.

I had a random and improbable thought, shocking enough to make me blurt, "The Sky City cleaning machines are fairly intelligent, aren't they? Could one be programmed to commit a murder? If it could, that would explain why the victims don't seem to have been suspicious of the murderer before they were killed."

The moving scene before me froze; Seth had stopped in his tracks. "I don't know," he said at last. "But the cleaning machines are just simple forms of rolfes. Since Gordy Rolfe's the mastermind behind all of them, an' he's a warped little bastard, I assume that the answer is yes. It would need special programs to bypass inhibitor circuits, but you could probably make a cleaning machine—or any other rolfe—kill somebody. So what?"

"So we find out who's in charge of them. That person would be in the absolute best position to arrange for the killings and still have a perfect alibi."

Even before Seth's reply reached me, I saw the fatal flaw in my idea. "Suppose a machine could kill 'em," he said. "How would it know who to kill, and where to do the killin'? If a rolfe hung around one place and splattered anybody who came by, they wouldn't all be young girls. An' if the murderer decided who he wanted to kill in advance, a machine would be noticed if it followed her around. And what about the sexual mutilation?"

I could imagine a killer, sufficiently deranged, deriving gratification from the simple knowledge that such an act was being performed; but Seth's other arguments were unanswerable. The problem was, my question still had validity. Why hadn't the victims been suspicious of their murderer, particularly after the first few deaths?

It has long been observed that any fool can ask more questions than the wisest man can answer. Seth decided, rightly, that this was one of those cases, though we might disagree as to who was the fool. The image in my visor began to change again. The subject had for the moment been dropped, and soon we were emerging to a totally different and disconcerting environment.

The chamber was gigantic, at least a hundred meters across. I cannot use the terms *high* or *wide*, since the space was so close to free fall that it lacked any indicators of preferred direction. I was saved from the possibility of acute discomfort at the sight of the great open arena ahead only by the extraordinary number of curvilinear structures that crisscrossed it in all directions. Most had obvious uses: pleated ducts, anything from a few centimeters to a full meter across, suitable for the transport of bulk materials; silver beams, from their placement employed as structural supports; thin and convoluted branching pipes, holding either optic bundles or serving as pneumatic delivery systems; and delicate-looking silver wires and cables, along which swarmed a variety of multiarmed machines.

I must pause here and seek to articulate why this chamber had an immediate effect on me. In one sense, nothing was new. I had, after all, seen every item in the great room before, albeit not in space and not combined as they were here. Why, then, did the whole induce a profound change in my overall pattern of thought?

During the twenty-seven years since the supernova event, I had known what every thinking being on the planet must recognize: A great disaster lay in the future, worse than the one in the recent past. A deadly particle storm was on the way from Alpha Centauri. It would arrive, as certainly as tomorrow's sunrise. The space shield was humanity's best answer.

I knew what was coming, and had made preparations accordingly. The tunneled shelters deep under Otranto Castle contained supplies sufficient for several lifetimes. I and my dear ones would survive, come what may. That effort had been completed years ago, before the youngest six had been born again.

I regarded my efforts as necessary, but clearly not sufficient. The prospect of a long stay in the deep shelters held no appeal, and a superior answer to the problem of survival was a shielding of the whole planet. That called for construction of the space shield, and in turn a nerve center and nucleus was needed for that effort: Sky City. The human race embarked on its first—but not, one hoped, its last—worldwide and long-term construction program.

I am, in spite of what my detractors might say, a member of that human race. I am also aware of my own abilities. Why, then, did I not, with survival at the castle ensured, apply my talents to the other and greater issue of species survival?

For three reasons. First, my expertise lies in the field of biological and medical science, which one might argue has little or no value to shield construction work. Second, the thought of flying out to space was like a clammy hand around my heart. Third, and most significant, my fingerprints, retinal prints, and DNA signature are on record. If I ever appear in a situation, anywhere in this world or off it, where a routine ID is called for, my capture and return to long-term judicial sleep are guaranteed.

Given these powerful reasons why I could not involve myself in humanity's salvation, I had pushed everything connected with the space shield to the periphery of my attention. For more than a decade, news items about Sky City were deleted or skipped by my news analyzer, and headlines on shield progress or problems ignored.

One cannot, however, fail to see what lies literally before one's eyes. Faced with the evidence presented by the RV helmet, my own shield of deliberate ignorance vanished. I was out in space, Sky City was real, the shield was real, and our disparate destinies had suddenly coalesced.

Need I add that I did not approve of the change?

Meanwhile, Seth moved slowly but confidently through the maze of the chamber and reached a tunnel on the other side. He advanced maybe forty meters, then suddenly halted. It was not because of word or action on my part. It was also, so far as I could see, not because of the intrinsic information content of the scene ahead. We were descending a long, sharp-angled spiral, an empty twisting stair that led from one level to the next.

"What is it?" I asked. Now I did miss olfactory inputs.

"Not sure." Seth spoke in a whisper. "But I think I'm bein' followed. Hold it."

He must have spun around rapidly, because after a moment of flickering confusion the scene steadied. I had a partial view of the way that we had just come. Seth was standing flattened against a wall, just where the staircase turned.

He seemed to have stopped breathing, and after a couple of seconds I heard the sound of careful footsteps. The light from around the corner cast a looming shadow on the far wall.

I heard a grunt from Seth, saw a blur of movement, and then I could see nothing.

"What the hell do you think you're doing?" said an unfamiliar voice.

"I could ask you the same thing." That was Seth. "Move, an' you're gutted. Were you followin' me?"

I could see again. A man's face was right in front of me. He and Seth had their arms locked, and I realized that a moment ago they must have been chest to chest.

"Damn right I was." The man pulled his arm free, and I saw that he was holding a metal bar. He was a huge, square-jawed brute, a foot taller than Seth. "Put that knife away unless you want your head bashed in. My money says I'll do you before you do me. You'd better explain who you are and why you're here."

"Why I'm here is none of your business." Seth was holding something out in front of him—not a knife, but a folder. "Here's my ID and my travel permit. I can go anywhere I like in Sky City."

The man stared at Seth, then at the identification. "This says you just arrived here, but it don't say why. Why you wandering around by yourself?"

"What you said. Wanderin' around the place, findin' out what's what."

It happened to be the truth, but the stranger snorted in disbelief. He had lowered the metal bar, and he no longer had an eye on Seth's knife. "Don't give me that. You were heading for level five, sector fifty-six. Want to deny it?"

"What if I was? What I do's my business. An' what makes you think that's where I'm goin'?"

"Because we've had hundreds of you buggers up here the past few months. You come for a few weeks, make a nuisance of yourselves, learn nothing, and go home. I've seen it over and over. Who's paying you? The DeNorville people, or the Skeltons? I know Tanya's family don't have a pot to piss in."

"Does it matter who's payin' me?"

"I guess it don't at that. Because I'll tell you one more thing—" The man glanced again at Seth's wallet. "—Mr. Parsigian, if that's really your name. Whoever's paying you isn't getting value for money. Not if you come here and prowl around by yourself."

"No reason I shouldn't. I'm a free agent."

"Yeah. A free agent, and a dumb shit. Wasting your time and somebody else's loot. Take my advice; go home now. You'd need a miracle to solve anything when our best people—trained professionals who've lived here for years and know this place inside out—haven't been able to learn who did it."

It was not my intention to involve myself in their argument, but I felt an obligation. Both the man and Seth were skating over a critical question.

"Why did he follow you?" I said softly. "He hasn't told you that. Ask him again."

Seth repeated my question, and the thug snorted. "You kidding me? Just shows how little you know about this place. Since the killings started, any male over the age of ten who's hanging around the axis gets watched every minute of the day or night. I didn't come after you to admire your ass or invite you home for dinner. I followed because I thought you might be the Sky City killer." He swung his metal bar, and looked like a good candidate for a murderer himself. "But you're not. You're just another asshole investigator. So the hell with you."

He turned to head back the way he had come.

"Don't let him go," I said urgently. "Ask him if it's the same all over."

My hurried remark lacked precision, but Seth caught its meaning—and its importance.

"Hey, butt-face," he called. Hardly a mode of address to encourage cooperation, but it served to halt Seth's new friend in his tracks.

He turned around, slowly. "What did you call me?" He headed back toward us, swinging his metal bar.

Seth stood his ground. "I didn't call you nothin'. You must have misheard. But I was wonderin', this business of people followin' other people all over the place. Is it the same near the perimeter as it is round the central axis?"

"You got to be kidding me. You sure you're an investigator?"

"What else could I be?"

"A shit-eating newsie. We had plenty of them, crawling all over Sky City and feeding on the dead."

"I ain't with the media."

"I believe it. No newsie could be so ignorant. What was it you were asking again?"

"Would I be followed around if I was out near the perimeter?"

"A damned sight more than here. Any man, by himself, can't take ten steps in perimeter territory without somebody demanding an ID. People round the axis don't roll in spare money; we're all volunteers when it comes to the murders. Up near the perimeter they got the wealth, and the hired help swarms over everything. But you know what?" He smirked, which did nothing for his appearance. "As many died there as here. Myra Skelton and Lucille DeNorville and April Jarrow, they had families with money pouring out of their asses. But all three of 'em died, as certain as Brenda and Cissy and poor Tanya. You going out to the perimeter?"

"Could be."

"Then if you don't get printed and ID'd and questioned ten times the first hour, come back here and I'll buy you a drink. Ask for Jesse Tarmigan, you'll find me easy enough. But I don't think you'll ever be in a position to collect." The man stood a few moments longer, apparently studying Seth's face and dress. "What's that funny faggy shirt you're wearing?"

"The jacket? It has built-in sensors. Video and audio."

"Like the scandal newsies wear. But you're not one. And you been around. You look like you seen a few wars. So why you on a job like this? Who you working for?"

"Give me volume," I said quietly to Seth. And then, assuming that he had done what I asked, I said, "He works for me."

Tarmigan recoiled a meter. "Hot damn," he said to Seth. "You a ventriloquist, or did you learn to talk through your ass?"

"Neither," I said. "He is an investigator, and I employ him. You don't need to know more than that."

"And who the hell are *you*?"

"You don't need to know that, either."

Tarmigan raised a clenched fist. "I'll decide what I need to know." After a moment he lowered his arm. "Ah, the hell with this game. I punch, I'd just be punching the dummy. Why don't you fuck off back to Earth, voice-man? Or come here where a body can take a swing at you."

"That is not a possibility."

"Sure. That's what all the rich say. Let somebody else do the dirty work." Tarmigan addressed himself to Seth. "I feel sorry for you. At least I get to do my job without some invisible joker pulling my strings and watching me every minute." He paused. "What *did* you call me a minute ago, when I was leaving?"

"Butt-face," Seth said. "Of course, you realize it wasn't *me* what said that. It was *him*."

*Him* was, of course, me. Tarmigan snorted with laughter. "You got me there, buster. He said it, eh? And I can't do him, 'cause he's not here." He started back along the tunnel, then turned and added, "Maybe you'll do something useful after all. You don't look like a weed. Good hunting. If you nail the sick bastard doing the killings, I'll hunt you down and personally kiss your ass."

"I can't wait," Seth said. But he did wait, in silence, until Jesse Tarmigan was out of sight. Then he said, "I don't deserve to have my ass kissed. By rights I ought to have that metal bar stuck up it. How could I be that dense?"

"I deserve censure far more than you. You were busy, making preparations for the trip to Sky City. I am the one who is supposedly responsible for thinking. And that I clearly failed to do."

"So think now. What next?"

"We accept the truth of what we were just told. You cannot possibly wander unencumbered and unnoticed. We need help—preferably female help. Unfortunately, such assistance appears beyond our reach."

"Mebbe. Mebbe not." Seth sounded frustrated, but also thoughtful. "The people I work for got resources. I hafta see what I can do. You want to come along?"

"For the moment, no. I wish to pursue a little cerebration." I was also, though I did not choose to mention it, stifling within the heavy RV helmet.

"Then I'm goin' to take off this pansy jacket—why's it hafta be pink and mauve?—and cut the video and audio connection for an hour or two. I got somethin' needs doin' here, but it's sort of confidential. I'll buzz you later. Okay?"

The image swirled in a dizzying flurry of colors before I could essay an answer. Seth was gone.

I removed the RV set and wiped my forehead. I was sweating monstrously, but less, I suspected, from my heated condition than from psychological factors. The period of my telepresence on Sky City had been short, less than one full hour, but that brief exposure had been enough to confirm one earlier suspicion and provide a clue as to the nature of the Sky City murderer.

Of course, I am still in some sense as far away from an answer as ever. In order to catch a murderer, it is necessary to possess two crucial items of information: first, an identity; second, the proof that links murderer to crime.

Suppose, however, that you are closing in on the first but the second element is lacking. Then one must hope to catch the killer redhanded, *in flagrante delicto*. But what if there should be no more killings?

It is far past midnight in Otranto Castle. The girls ought to be—but, in view of past experience, probably are not—asleep. They are, at least, quiet.

Think, Oliver Guest; think. Once you were good at thinking, and you have the whole night ahead of you.

As for that sly shade of a spectral reader who hovers always behind my shoulder as I write, you must do some thinking, too.

Or is that not necessary? Are you, my unseen companion, already far ahead of me, confident of motive, sure of the murderer's identity, certain of a method of capture?

I will never know; but as for me, I am like Gulliver: newly returned from the magical flying island of Laputa, happy to be home, but unsure of what strange voyages may lie in the future.

# 16

John Hyslop was showing off, but he didn't know it. Even with a knowledge of what he was doing, he would have had trouble explaining why.

He and Maddy Wheatstone stood at the entrance to the shield simulation chamber. The sight alone was enough to make most visitors gasp, even without explanation of the technological marvels hidden within.

The chamber sat far out on the central spindle of Sky City, at the opposite end from the power-generating plant. It was a structure only in the Sky City sense, of material enclosing a volume. It would not have survived for two seconds down on Earth. The wall of the chamber was a micron-thin sheet of fullerenes, held to its spherical shape by an internal pressure of a few micrograms per square meter.

At the center of the sphere floated a physical model of the shield, built at a scale of a hundred thousand to one.

"It's a little more than a kilometer lengthwise," John explained as he guided Maddy toward the wide end of the cone. "Everything is in exact proportion to the real shield. The important thing, though, is that you get an overview of where the project stands at any time, which you can never get by looking at the shield itself— for one thing, most of the shield components are too small to see, and for another, the whole thing is too big to look at all at once. The model is updated in real time to reflect progress—or problems— with the real shield. See, it's happening now. A section is going out of commission. Either it's part of a routine check, or a horde of rolfes will be heading that way on the real shield."

Maddy followed his pointing arm. A small section of the shield, no more than a meter square, was changing from green to red. Except that a one-meter square was not small at all. With a scale of a hundred thousand to one, one meter on the model represented a hundred kilometers on the shield itself.

"Let's go take a look at it," John said casually. "Hold tight, I'm switching us to VR mode."

He saw Maddy turn and stare at him inside her suit helmet. A VR session was not on their schedule. In less than an hour, John was supposed to meet with Will Davis and Lauren Stansfield for a final wrap-up before he went to his new assignment in asteroid capture.

"I know," he said. "But I've worked with the shield for a lot of years. Call it one last look."

"Hey, you're the boss. You don't have to give me explanations for what we do."

Her helmet was only a foot away from his, and she was smiling. That smile made John profoundly uncomfortable yet pleased at the same time. Will Davis had met Maddy only once, three days ago, but as soon as he and John were alone he said, "Better not get ideas, boyo—and if you have ideas already, drop 'em. That there's one heavy-duty alpha female. She eats men like me and you as appetizers before the main meal."

*Heavy-duty alpha female.* That struck John as an understatement. But he still wanted an answer to his question: Why did someone like Maddy Wheatstone trail along with him when she could be doing so many more important and interesting things?

*Don't ask, or you'll hear what you don't want to hear.* John took a quick breath and threw them into virtual reality mode.

The shield sat in front of them, exactly as before. Its apparent size had not changed, but the far-off wall of the chamber had vanished and Maddy Wheatstone no longer smiled at him inside her suit.

He heard her gasp. "What happened?"

"We're in VR. What you're seeing on your visor isn't the model of the shield anymore, it's the real thing. We're picking up radio feeds from sensors located around the shield, in the same relative position as we are to the model. Smart sensors on the shield surface send out messages describing their condition, and those are converted to light signals of the right color by the message sensors."

"Neat. But suppose I want to look at a different part of the shield?"

"You move along using your suit controls, just as if you wanted to visit a different piece of the model."

"Like this? Hey, I'm moving."

"Keep going. You can use VR all the way to Cusp Station." John did the same thing, gliding steadily toward the point of the cone that formed the terminus of the shield.

He was used to the effect, but Maddy wasn't. After a moment she said, "I don't get it. I'm moving all right, but if I travel along in my suit at ten meters a second I must be going like hell in real space."

"It's a hundred thousand to one scale. Ten meters a second converts to a thousand kilometers. You're moving along the shield at a thousand kilometers a second."

"But that's impossible. Nothing can accelerate me so fast to move at that speed."

"Quite true. Nothing at all is accelerating in real space. Observational sensors watch every part of the shield, and the VR system simply switches to provide us with signals from whichever set of sensors is appropriate. What you're seeing is a succession of frames, like in an old-time movie camera. If your eyes could handle a hundred frames a second, you'd be able to watch the individual scene change each time you were switched to a new set of observational sensors."

He wondered if he was talking down to her. Maybe Maddy already knew this; it was well-known stuff. He rapidly switched himself out of VR, leaving Maddy in it. The suits' proximity sensors and collision-avoidance systems had cut in as soon as they went to VR mode, so he and Maddy now floated ten feet apart. John overrode them and approached close enough to peer in at her face. She couldn't see him, and he was relieved to find that she appeared anything but bored or irritated. Her lips were slightly apart, her eyes were wide, and her nostrils flared. "Alpha female" didn't even begin to describe it.

"That tiny thing is Cusp Station?" Maddy's words brought John back from his private version of virtual reality. "How big is it, John? It looks small enough to reach out and hold in my hand."

"It's almost a kilometer across—as big as Sky City." John went back to VR and felt a gentle push as the proximity sensor cut in again and moved his suit away from Maddy's. Cusp Station was a cherry-sized glowing ball at the very end of the shield. As Maddy said, it seemed close enough to grab. "Of course, Cusp Station has nowhere near as many people as Sky City, and hardly any computer power."

"How many people?"

"The last time I was there we had a human staff of a hundred and forty, plus about three thousand rolfes either in Cusp Station or out on the shield. But a lot of the rolfes are early models. They can't do nearly as much as the newer ones."

"That was the day we first met, wasn't it? We dragged you back for a meeting in Bruno Colombo's office. You were so tired you looked like a walking corpse. That's the last time you were out on the shield."

"Yes." *The last time.* That could mean the time before this one, or it might mean the final time.

Could you feel nostalgia for something as vast, remote, and austere as the space shield?

John had a sudden urge to see it—not the model, not the VR presentation, but the real thing in its elusive gossamer glory. He dropped out of VR and checked the time. They had forty minutes before the meeting with Will and Lauren. He and Maddy could do it, provided they kept their suits on and used the old exit lock from the simulation chamber.

He brought Maddy out of simulation mode and watched her shocked expression when he appeared from nowhere in front of her.

He said, "Relax, you're out of VR now. The change is a bit of a surprise when you're not used to it. Come on. I'll take you outside so you can see the shield. The real thing this time."

He took over her suit controls and steered them toward the far side of the simulation chamber. Maddy protested, "But this isn't the way we came in."

"No. The usual way outside takes you back along the axis, but there's a faster route to space using an old exit lock and tunnel at this end."

"Are you sure it will be all right?" Maddy was used to the old office buildings of Earth, where many escalators and elevators knocked out by the supernova had never worked properly since.

"Sure. The maintenance machines keep everything clean and in perfect working order. The worst thing that can happen is there might be maintenance work going on, and we'd not be allowed to enter."

They passed into an exit lock hardly big enough for two people. The doors groaned and creaked as they opened and closed. "Just old," John said, though the poor lubrication surprised him. He made a mental note to check that a suitable vacuum-rated lubricant was being used, then realized that was no longer his job. Sky City maintenance was Lauren Stansfield's responsibility now.

They emerged at the entrance of the curving corridor beyond. Maddy paused to stare at John. She did not speak, and she did not need to. He could see for himself. Everything in this section might be in working order, but clean it certainly was not. He ran his glove along one dimly lit wall and wiped off a layer of gray dust. Now that he looked closely, he could see that a couple of nearby fluorescents on the tunnel wall were not lit. But all the corridor lights were supposed to come on automatically when the lock was cycled.

Maddy was standing perfectly still, taking her cues from him. "We'll be safe," he said. "Even if all the wall lights failed, our suit lights would be enough. All we have to do is go along to the end of the corridor, then another lock takes us outside to open space. One more thing before we go."

He opened a circuit to maintenance and left Maddy in the loop so that she could hear his message. He kept it short. The corridor they were in seemed to have been overlooked by the cleaning machines. From the look of the place it had been this way for months.

She watched him send the message and made no comment. After his boast about everything being in perfect working order, why should she? He already looked like a half-wit. "Along here," he muttered, and ushered her into the main body of the corridor.

A small residual field showed that they were not exactly on the central axis of Sky City, so the path they followed had an apparent floor and ceiling. The upward curve was gentle, and as they moved John could examine the walls and follow the line of the corridor. He kept track of failed lighting and looked for any signs of recent visits by cleaning machines. Possibly it was just one particular machine that needed repair.

A grunt from Maddy brought his attention back to her.

"Are you all right?"

"I'm fine." She gestured ahead of them. "But what on earth's that?"

It was a shapeless dark object on the floor about thirty meters ahead.

"Probably a cleaning bag." John moved faster, but it wasn't until he was within a few yards of the sack that he felt any sense of uneasiness. The bag was bulky, about four feet long and two feet across, and the lumpy shape was suggestive.

The sack's neck was loosely secured by a drawstring. He lifted it easily and pulled the string fully open. The bag fell away. The contents appeared as though emerging of their own volition. Two feet from John's suit helmet a human face and naked torso floated into view. The skin of the head was desiccated and freeze-dried, withered lips pulled back in a dreadful grin. The eyes showed only whites, deep in their sockets. A deep indentation in the skull on the left-hand side gave evidence of a savage blow. The delicate throat had been hacked and slashed, and dried blood blackened the ends of long, fair hair. A deep cut began just below the sternum and ran downward to the navel.

And beyond.

John swallowed hard, lifted the black plastic of the bag back into place, and pulled the drawstring tight.

He looked at Maddy. She sagged against the wall, eyes unblinking behind the visor of her suit. He wanted to speak to her, but could not.

He opened another circuit, this one direct to Bruno Colombo's office and without Maddy in the loop. "This is John Hyslop," he said. He sounded strained and unnatural, even to himself. "I am in the old extension tunnel leading from the simulation chamber to space. I will transmit exact coordinates after this message. I need security here as soon as possible. I have found . . ."

He paused. He had been about to say "a new victim of the Sky City killer," but the body showed signs of long duration in space. Such a degree of drying could not have happened in a few hours.

He shielded the bag from Maddy with his own suited body, and forced himself to open the drawstring. This time he examined the body closely, for as long as he could stand. "I believe," he said at last, "that we have found one of the missing victims of the Sky City killer. There has been mutilation. Judging from the wounds and the apparent age of the victim, I think that this must be Lucille DeNorville."

Under other circumstances the prospect of a private dinner with Maddy would have made John delighted but nervous. He had been aware of her oddly amorous look after the attack of labyrinthitis, but he had done nothing to follow up on it because he felt sure it was all the effect of her medication. Now, the discovery of Lucille DeNorville's mutilated corpse overshadowed all personal issues.

He and Maddy had been grilled for an hour by four Sky City security staff. John knew each of them personally and hoped that they saw him and Maddy as no more than the accidental discoverers of the body. But a full and careful questioning was inevitable. At what time had they entered the simulation chamber? At what time did they operate the air lock? *Why* had they chosen that particular lock, out of date and normally out of use? Had they seen anything or anyone in the tunnel before Maddy caught sight of the black plastic bag? Had either of them heard anything?

To that last question John was tempted to give a sarcastic answer. What can you possibly hear when you are floating in a vacuum?

He remained polite and cooperative. The security officers had no choice but to ask their questions, it was standard procedure. Unfortunately, neither he nor Maddy could offer a scrap of useful information. They had not touched the corpse, or moved it from where they found it, or seen anything out of the ordinary.

John knew, as Maddy did not, that the location of Lucille DeNorville's body had other implications. The killer, either before or immediately after the murder, must have tampered with the central data bank that governed the maintenance of Sky City. Otherwise, routine service by cleaning machines would have found Lucille within a few days. Without such service the discovery might have gone unnoticed for years. John could not recall the last time that he, or anyone else, had gone directly from the simulation facility to open space.

The security staff confirmed John's suspicion. The air lock maintained an electronic log of the date and time of its use, and there had been just two previous openings in the past three years. The first was four days before Lucille DeNorville vanished. The second was on the actual day of her disappearance.

That raised a question in John's mind: Why had the murderer failed to do the obvious thing and taken the body to release it in open space? Why leave Lucille DeNorville in a location where, even if it took months or years, the corpse would ultimately be found?

The security officials had no answers. They departed at last for the medical center. Their leader, Alyssa Sisk, had ordered an autopsy even though the cause of Lucille's death seemed clear. She had died when her skull was bludgeoned. The other wounds and the sexual mutilation had taken place after death.

Alyssa and John had been friends for eight years. She told John and Maddy that they were free to stay in the private security office for as long as they liked, but formally she warned him that he must remain on Sky City for the next twelve hours in case more questions came up. Alyssa was gray and drawn and tended to repeat herself. Living with the murders night and day had been hard on her.

When John and Maddy were finally alone and with their suits off, she slumped on a blue padded chair and he sat opposite. Food had been provided at the beginning of the meeting, but neither had even glanced at it. A low table between them bore a collection of cooked dishes, now all cold.

"You don't have to stay, you know," John said. "Alyssa Sisk's instructions apply only to me."

Maddy's slight nod was her only sign that she knew John was still in the room. The discovery of the corpse had turned her into a different woman. Every shred of vivacity and resolve had vanished.

"I'm sure you have other work waiting," he went on. "Down on Earth, or with the Aten asteroid capture people, or something else on Sky City. Everybody these days always has too many things to do."

Still she said nothing. John had zero confidence that he knew how to deal with distraught women. When she did not reply, not even with a nod or a look, he felt that he had to find a way to fill the dismal silence. It didn't matter if he sounded lightweight and trivial—it might even be better that way.

He told himself, *Talk! If she can't, you have to.*

He said, hardly knowing what words would come out of his mouth, "When I think you're doing nothing, like now, I bet that's not true at all. On the flight up you were sitting and evaluating people and what they do, and I had no idea what you were thinking. I didn't realize you were thinking at all." *Just as I have no idea what you are thinking now.* "Even when it's logical for people to have the same thoughts, they often don't. When I first applied for a position on Sky City, we were told that we would work on building the shield and it was presented as the only worthwhile task in the solar system. We were saving humanity from a guaranteed future disaster. I'm sure that's true, and I nodded as much as any of the others. But it wasn't the reason I wanted to come."

Maddy looked up and raised an eyebrow. It could be an expression of inquiry—or disbelief.

John went on, "I was born on the Canadian border, but I was on vacation in Washington state visiting my aunt and uncle when the supernova hit. My sister was already grown up and married and living back East, and she made it through all right, but we never heard from my parents again. I stayed on with Aunt Sue and Uncle Jake. They were too busy putting things back together after Alpha C to worry a lot about me, so I was pretty much left to myself. I spent my time backpacking in the Cascade Mountains. I just loved exploring and rock climbing. When I finally got hauled in from the mountains and had to work with the learning machines, my heroes were Columbus and Drake, Amundsen and Peary, Mallory and Whymper and Hillary. I saw myself like them, king of some new frontier—until I realized there was nothing left to explore. The blank spots on the map were recent; all the remote regions had been explored and mapped long before the supernova. Every desert had been crossed, every island had been charted and surveyed, every mountain had been climbed, solo and in groups, with and without oxygen. There was rediscovery and reconstruction to be done in South America and Africa and Australia, but that's not the same as discovery."

He was boring her to death, he just knew it. He was all ready to apologize when Maddy grabbed his hand, squeezed it, and said, "Go on. Please."

It wasn't the response he'd expected. He had nothing more to say. There were things you didn't talk about, and there were things you couldn't talk about. Maddy Wheatstone sat squarely at the intersection of the two. He wasn't much of a talker at the best of times. But Maddy was staring at him imploringly.

John took a deep breath and spoke of the things you didn't talk about. "I was in despair. I was seventeen years old and I thought I had reached a dead end. I didn't see any future for myself as an explorer, because even if there had been anywhere on Earth left to explore, nobody could afford to support luxuries like polar expeditions. Space exploration was dead. The one Mars expedition had been a disaster, and there was no chance there would ever be another. Alpha C had put an end to that.

"So I gave up and trained to be an engineer. There was more than enough work for me then; we had to rebuild the whole world. I didn't climb any mountains, and I didn't go to the poles or to Jupiter. But I did walk the high steel four thousand feet above Tokyo, and I rode the span of the ninety-kilometer arch across the Messina Strait, and I planted the deep caissons in the Mariana Trench. I told myself that was sufficient, that I didn't miss the thrill of the old dreams, of being where no one had ever been before. And for a long time, what I had was enough. Then Giorgio Hamman fired me. He pushed me into space, and I finally found what I'd been looking for. The new frontier wasn't on Earth at all. It was out here, building the shield. Not exploration. Application." He wanted to tell her of the thrill of it, hanging beyond Cusp Station a hundred and fifty thousand kilometers from Earth, with a straight fall through the insubstantial fabric of the shield if your drive system failed. But he could not summon the words. At last he said, "If Edmund Hillary were alive today, he wouldn't be struggling up the South Col of Mount Everest. He'd be out on the shield perimeter with us, living in a suit for weeks at a time, drinking recycled water, eating his own reprocessed wastes . . ."

John trailed off. He had run down, and at a most unedifying point.

"It *is* there. Inside you. I knew it." Maddy was sitting upright, her blue eyes so intense that he burned up in their gaze. She went on, incomprehensibly, "It wasn't the body, you know. I could have stood that. It was her face and hair. She looked so much like Meg."

Was she talking to him? Did she even know that he was there?

He stared at her hopelessly, until suddenly she reached out and gripped his arm.

"It was different for me." She spoke dreamily, like a woman in a trance. "My family seemed so lucky. We were living in Edmonton when the supernova happened. I was only five, but I remember my reaction. It was annoyance. We lost all the entertainment channels. That, and the electric power went off for a while. Nothing else seemed wrong."

John had heard the story before, but never from anyone who had been there. Somehow, in an area of Canada about a hundred miles across and centered on Edmonton, all the global changes and violence caused by Alpha C had canceled out. In that eye of the hurricane the puzzled residents heard reports of devastation and disaster everywhere, while their own town and countryside remained untouched.

"My sister Meg was ten years older than me." Now Maddy was talking rapidly, almost in a whisper. "She was so smart and so talented, everybody in the family said that one day she'd run the country. I thought she was a goddess; she could do absolutely anything. But she wasn't with us when the power went out. She was on a visit to Calgary. When the AVC of her car failed along with everything else, it ran into a downed power line. The line was still live. When they brought her body back home they told me I couldn't see her. I really wanted to, and when everybody was asleep I sneaked into her bedroom. I knew the car had hit a power line, and I sort of imagined that she would be all lit up and glowing, like a fairy. It wasn't like that. Meg was lying on her bed. She had beautiful long blond hair, but the ends of it were black. Burned. Her face wasn't glowing, the way it should be. It was gray and twisted and blotchy, and her eyes were white and bulging. I remember thinking, it's not possible, how could someone be burned, the way they'd told me, and have their eyes go *white*?

"What I hadn't realized was that my father had been sitting in the room with Meg. He didn't move for a few seconds when I came in, but then he stood up. I was terrified. I thought it must be Meg's ghost. When I realized who it was I thought he'd be mad at me because I'd disobeyed him, but he wasn't like that at all. He came over and put his arms around me. He said, 'I didn't want you to see Meg, not the way she is. But I was wrong. You have a right to say goodbye to her, Maddy, as much as anyone else.' He gave me a big hug. 'You're all I've got now,' he said. 'Make me proud of you. Make Meg proud of you, too.'

"I've tried. But I don't think I did, ever. I never could."

It was a sad, vulnerable Maddy, one who John hadn't known existed. When she stopped speaking she folded her hands together in her lap and sat with her eyes lowered. He knew what he ought to do. He should comfort her, put his arms around her and tell her that everything was all right, that she herself was better than all right.

But he couldn't do it. John sat silent, cursing his ineptitude and inhibitions and insecurity. Maddy Wheatstone was his superior in every way, even when she was at a personal low. Would it be taking advantage of her if he hugged her to him and offered help? And if he did try to comfort her now, how would she feel about it later?

In a strange, dreamlike separation of mind and body, John moved to Maddy's side. He put his right arm around her shoulders. He couldn't find words, but he lightly kissed the top of her head. After a moment she leaned against him and stayed there. They sat silent, bodies together, while John's mind took off in unthinkable directions. It was a moment when anything might happen.

The mood shattered when the door jerked open and Alyssa Sisk came hurrying in.

"I wondered if you'd still be here." She took no notice of the fact that John was sitting with his arm around Maddy. "You must be going deaf. Didn't you hear it? There's a call out for you, John, on the general alert system."

"About the murder?" With Alyssa's sudden appearance John's mind jumped for no reason to the image of Lucille DeNorville's ravaged corpse, drifting alone for months in that dark, unattended corridor.

"Not the murder, man." Alyssa sounded impatient. "That's my business, not yours. Bruno Colombo wants you in his office."

"Why?"

"How should I know? Whatever it is, do you think he'd announce it to everybody in Sky City? But there's lots of action everywhere. Rumors of bad news about the particle storm, changes of plans, tighter schedules—as if that were possible."

John took his arm away from Maddy. He stood up and glanced down at her.

"Don't worry." Maddy read his concern. "Go to your meeting. I'll be all right now, and I'll see you later. And—thanks, John."

"I'm sorry we didn't talk more."

"We said lots. I didn't need more talk. I needed what you gave me."

"Well, then." He paused, then said uncertainly, "If you're sure you're going to be all right . . ."

"I'm all right."

He nodded and hurried out, and Alyssa turned to Maddy.

"I know you say you don't need more talk, but there's some character hanging around outside. He says he needs to talk with you right away."

"He must have the wrong person. Nobody knows I'm here."

"You'd better tell him that yourself, because he doesn't seem to know it. He certainly knows your name. He asked for Maddy Wheatstone. He says he only needs five seconds with you. After that, he says, you'll be the one wanting to meet with him."

# 17

John Hyslop stared around Bruno Colombo's office and found himself speechless. He was losing count of the number of shocks he had received in the past couple of hours. The latest blow—the wave of the hand from Bruno Colombo, and a dismissive "Go ahead. It's all yours"—lifted the afternoon away from Sky City and moved it to the realm of the Mad Hatter.

First there had been the horrifying discovery of Lucille De-Norville's space-dried corpse. Next came the unexpected summons to Bruno Colombo's office. Third, Goldy Jensen greeted John at the outer vestibule with the savage smile of a black widow spider about to eat her mate. What had he, a mere engineer transferred away from Sky City, done to deserve such a look? Offended Bruno Colombo? But if so, how, when they had not spoken to each other since John's transfer to the Aten asteroid project? Goldy shook her head when John asked what was going on and ushered him without a word through to Bruno Colombo's inner sanctum.

If Goldy had some unknown reason to smile, Bruno Colombo apparently did not. His private office was his shrine, an organized and well-ordered perfection. His telcom was discreetly hidden away in a drawer of the long wooden desk, and the desk itself never carried more than a single folder placed in the middle of its nine-foot length. A cut-glass bowl of red roses, fresh every morning from the Sky City hydroponic gardens, always graced its polished top.

Today the roses lay scattered on the floor. The folder was there with them, and the oriental rug on which they sat was soaked with water. The bowl had found a new use. A short black woman dressed in a lurid pink blouse and yellow shorts was crouched on the floor, bending over the ornament, which sat between her legs.

A tall, bald-headed man watched her gloomily. "I warned you," he said. "But would you listen? Of course not. Are you ready for it now?"

The woman—she appeared to John hardly more than a girl—raised her head and glared up at the man. "Yer can stuff yer pills. I don't want 'em."

Bruno Colombo stood at the other side of the room, as far from the desk and the other people as possible. He gestured to John to come across to him.

"Hyslop," he said as soon as John was close. "There are going to be major changes in the shield program. You will once again occupy the position of chief engineer for shield development. I have summoned other members of your old staff, and they are on the way here." He waved a hand at the man and woman. She was now making dry-heaving sounds. "These people have come up from Earth and will be working with you. They have"—his voice turned to acid—"been given total authority to direct changes in shield construction."

"But we're already behind schedule!" John could hardly believe what he had just heard. Restoring him to his original position would have been good news, but not if he had to take orders from a pair of newcomers. No matter how talented they might be, they didn't know the job. "Why are you letting them make changes?"

"I am not." Colombo grimaced, as though swallowing something unpleasant. "That decision came from Earth. Needless to say, I do not approve of the situation. I, in fact, wash my hands of this. I'm leaving. It's all yours."

He was out of the room before John could ask *what* was all his. The bald man stared gloomily at the seated woman and said, "Listen to her. I never would have thought it. Star's got a digestion like an emu, and I've never known her to be sick."

"Her first time up from Earth?"

"That's right."

"Then it's the gravity changes." When the man stared at John blankly, he went on, "Some people take to low gravity easily, others have real problems. It doesn't seem to depend on whether a person is in good or bad physical shape, or how old you are, or how strong your stomach is. You can still get sick. But being young and strong helps. With any luck she'll feel better in a few minutes."

"I told her that. She's looking better already."

"Better? I feel like shit." The woman spoke with her head over the bowl.

John said to the man, "How about you? How do you feel?"

"Me?" He seemed surprised at the question. "Why, I'm fine."

"You've been in space before?"

"Oh, yes. But as I say, this is Star's first time. I told her to take a pill, and would she?" The man rubbed the top of his head. "Would she hell. She's pretending she's not feeling well enough to introduce herself, so I'll do it for her. The pigheaded lump of obstinacy throwing up in the bowl there is my friend Star—Astarte Vjansander, the brains behind the shield changes."

Again, references to shield changes. John couldn't understand it. Didn't people realize that the project was in deep trouble already? And you couldn't drop new players into the middle of the job, no matter how good they were, without screwing things up.

"She's an engineer, is she?" John asked. It seemed a harmless question, but the woman glared up at him, said, "Engineer! Bloody hell, no," and bent forward to spit into the bowl. John began to feel a rare sympathy for Bruno Colombo.

The man said calmly, "Star's not an engineer. Experimental equipment breaks when she walks into a room. She's a physicist. She can tell you what needs to be done with the shield, but don't for God's sake let her try and do it herself. Me neither; I'm no good when it comes to the practical stuff."

"And who are you?"

"Me?" The man reacted as though that was an odd question. "I'm Wilmer Oldfield."

John had his hand extended when the man's name and the Australian accent meshed. It had been many years, but everything fitted. He even had a vague memory of seeing pictures, a younger version of that heavy-browed face.

He froze with his hand still outstretched. "I'm sorry. You're Wilmer Oldfield? Dr. Wilmer Oldfield?"

"Yeah, that's me. But I don't see what I've done to make you sorry."

"I mean I'm sorry I didn't recognize you when I first came in. You were on the Mars expedition, with Celine Tanaka. And I asked you if you had ever been in space!"

"Well, I have." Oldfield took John's hand and shook it. "That's all right, it was ages ago. I've not been off Earth for years and years."

"When I was growing up, you were one of my idols." The words were absolutely honest, but as soon as John said them he wished he hadn't.

There was an awkward silence, broken when the woman on the floor said, "And he's still idle. Bone idle."

She laughed.

"Told you she was feeling better. And look who's talking." Wilmer Oldfield reached down and took hold of her arm. "Come on, you lazy mass of convent reject. On your feet. We've got visitors, and it's time for work."

Four more people were entering the room. John knew each of them well: Will Davis, Amanda Corrigan, Rico Ruggiero, and Torrance Harbish—all his old senior team members, with the exception of Lauren Stansfield. From the expressions on their faces, they were as puzzled by recent events as he was. And Bruno Colombo, in spite of his words, had not left completely. He was peering around the edge of the door.

John made a decision. He didn't know what was going on, but if he was ever to find out, he had to impose his own kind of order on things. He turned to the newcomers. "Do you know why you were asked to come here?"

They shook their heads. "Something about changes to the shield?" Will Davis said. "I've been hoping I misunderstood the message. We can't afford to make changes."

"I know. Where's Lauren?"

"On the axis, with the power generation maintenance team."

"Then we'll start without her. She can catch up later." John waved his hand at Wilmer. "This is Dr. Oldfield. He was on the original Mars expedition. And this young lady—"

"Young lady be buggered." Astarte finally stood up. She rocked for a moment, then planted her feet. "I'm Star Vjansander, and I'm not a lady. An' if yer don't like me now, wait 'til yer hear what me and Wilmer have ter say. 'Cause yer going ter have ter work yer buns off."

"That's enough, Star." Wilmer Oldfield turned to John. "I'd not have brought her at all, except that we absolutely can't do without her."

"Do *what* without her?"

"We'll get to that, but it may take a while." Wilmer sighed, subsided into a chair, and rubbed the red patch on the top of his head. "Let me start at the beginning. When we first had the Alpha C blowup . . ."

Later, John decided that Wilmer Oldfield had a gift for understatement. *It may take a while* translated into the longest technical briefing ever. Six and a half hours passed before the last question was asked and the last answer given.

Lauren Stansfield arrived at the end of the first hour, at the point where Wilmer paused for his first break and Star Vjansander began an explanation of the anomalous data from the Sniffers.

Lauren stared hard at Star but said not a word. She gave John one questioning glance and took her place quietly at Amanda Corrigan's side. Bruno Colombo slipped into the room a few minutes later. He had been hovering uncertainly at the door while Wilmer was speaking. He took a seat next to Lauren. Amazingly, the director also said nothing.

Finally Wilmer shrugged and said, "That's it, then. Unless you have more questions?"

John couldn't speak for the others, but he personally felt stunned. Assuming that Wilmer Oldfield and Star Vjansander were right in their analyses, the whole shield project—twenty years of frantic labor—had to be turned on its head. And changes had to be made *fast*. Instead of years, they had at most months. The only good news was that the proposed changes would make the whole engineering problem easier.

"Let me make sure I have this right," he said. "Almost all the charged particles won't arrive independently of each other. They will be grouped in stable structures, the things you call bundles, each containing a few trillion nuclei. Instead of building a continuous shield structure, we have to detect each separate group and divert it away from Earth with an electromagnetic pulse generated for just that bundle."

"Right," Wilmer said, and Star nodded and added, "You got it. All very doable. And the obvious place to put your pulse generator is on Cusp Station, out at the end of the shield."

"But if your interpretation of the Sniffer data or your supernova model is wrong—if all the particles actually arrive independently of each other—"

"Then we're up shit creek," Star said cheerfully. "Because the one thing that's for certain is the particle storm is going to hit sooner than you thought six months ago. That means the shield you got now is no damn good no matter what."

"Suppose you're right," Torrance Harbish said. He had the final word on shield balancing and stability. "All my work for the past eight years will go down the tubes, but that's not what's worrying me. You're saying we have to find and deflect every particle bundle. I don't understand how we'll know where each one is. Remember, they're flying at us at something like ten percent of light speed."

"We've looked into that." Wilmer did not sound worried. "We generate a wide-angle, low-intensity radiation beam from Cusp Station that extends out toward Alpha C. Easy, and probably best done at microwave frequencies. It won't be anywhere near strong enough to *divert* a bundle, but each bundle will interact with the field enough to produce its own weak radiation. We can detect that signal when the bundle gets near enough. It will give us enough information to determine the speed and exact trajectory of each bundle. And *that's* what we hit with a pulse strong enough to divert it safely away from Earth."

"Do we have time to do all that?" Will Davis, like Torrance Harbish, could see his efforts of many years crumbling to nothing. "It sounds like an awful lot of work. I mean, we have to detect a signal, calculate a trajectory, and generate and fire a pulse. How much time do we have between bundle detection and bundle arrival?"

Wilmer nodded. "We've studied that, too. Star?"

"No worries. Yer can't get a useful return beyond about fifteen thousand kilometers. From there the signal takes a twentieth of a second to reach Cusp Station, and the pulse needs that long ter go back. Knock that off the bundle travel time before it gets ter the shield—say half a second—and you're left with point four seconds to generate a pulse and spit it back out ter the bundle. Bags of time. 'Course, it's a monster computing problem to know just where ter fire. But I understand you've got computers up here coming out your wazoo."

She saw their faces. "Uh-oh. Did I screw up?"

John spoke first. "I think so. Let me make sure I have this right. We receive a return signal at Cusp Station. From that we compute where the bundle is. On Cusp Station we generate a powerful EM pulse and aim it at the bundle."

"That's right. Look, we assume you don't have equipment on Cusp Station to generate the signal field or the pulses. That's all right, they can be shipped there easy."

"Not the problem." Amanda Corrigan was the computer specialist. Shy and gawky, she ducked her head and made her first contribution to the meeting. "You said we had a 'monster' computing problem. How monster?"

"Yer might need to do simultaneous path computations for a few million bundles a second. I was told you could do that here, dead easy."

"We can," Amanda said. "Here on Sky City. But we don't have anything near that much power at Cusp Station."

"So yer beam the information from there—" Star paused.

"You've got it," John said quietly. "We have all sorts of computing power on Sky City. But there's not much on Cusp Station. The minimum distance between Sky City and Cusp Station is more than a hundred thousand kilometers. That's more than a third of a second for a one-way signal, two-thirds of a second round trip. Far too long."

There was a long silence, broken by Wilmer. "We've got some time, a few weeks. Ship computers out to Cusp Station, enough to do the job."

"Amanda?" John Hyslop raised his eyebrows.

She shook her head. "Sorry. The computing system here is integrated and distributed through the whole of Sky City. We have plenty of spare capacity, but it's impossible to pull part of it out without screwing up everything. Air, water, waste disposal—the systems all call on the same computing resources."

Star flopped down on the floor and sat with her legs sprawled inelegantly wide. She leaned forward like a gymnast, touched the carpet three times with her forehead, sat up, and said, "Then we *are* buggered. Any chance we can get enough computer power shipped up from Earth?"

"Possibly." Bruno Colombo had sat silent through the whole long meeting. Most of the time his eyes were closed. John had wondered if the director was even awake.

"Possibly," Colombo repeated. "But it's not an answer that I—or anyone—would be happy with. Either we'd have to ship people up from Earth who know their own systems well but are not used to working in space, or else our staff would be faced with the task of learning unfamiliar equipment and programming intricate life-or-death calculations in a very short time. Not just life-or-death for us. For everyone."

"Even so," Wilmer said, "it's our best shot. I can promise you, even if the old shield were finished and working perfectly, the particle bundles we're talking about will go through it like it's not there. We need computer power on Cusp Station, lots of it. If the only place we can find it is on Earth, that's where we take it from. I know Celine Tanaka, I'm sure she'll cooperate."

"Maybe she would." Bruno Colombo stood up. Suddenly he had gone from being a bystander to the person in control of the meeting. "But I don't think that's the best answer. Hyslop? You know Sky City as well as I do, maybe better. Can it be done?"

"I have to check. It will involve accelerations and stresses beyond any that were ever dreamed of. But my gut guess is that yes, we can do it."

"Do what?" Star was still on the floor, but now she was sitting bolt upright and scowling. "What are you two going on about?"

"If the mountain will not come to Mahomet . . ." Bruno Colombo turned to John. "Hyslop, you and the others here work out the engineering details. I'll start on resource allocation. Even if it is possible, it's not going to be easy."

He hurried out of the room. John felt an odd mixture of irritation and admiration. Just when you were convinced that Bruno Colombo was nothing but a big bag of wind dressed in an expensive suit, he did something to prove that deep inside the pomaded head sat a highly creative brain. Sure, part of it was Colombo protecting his territory—but he also happened to be proposing the only possible solution. And then he left you to "work out the details."

John found himself once more running the meeting. "It's going to be an interesting few weeks," he said. "We need loads of computers out near Cusp Station. We have all kinds of computational power here, but we can't ship it anywhere else."

"So Mahomet . . ." Will Davis said.

"That's right." In spite of the enormous size of the problem, John felt the thrill of a new technical challenge. "We're heading for the front line—all of us. We'll take this place and fly it all the way out to Cusp Station. And then, assuming that Sky City doesn't disintegrate on the way, and certain people stay out of our hair"—he stared at Star Vjansander, who was grinning at him in delight—"well, then we'll find out if certain harebrained ideas are anywhere close to reality."

# 18

The face of the man who wanted to see Maddy was familiar, even if she could not attach a name to it. He was—somehow she was not surprised—the sallow, dark-haired man she had seen on the shuttle up. He was leaning nonchalantly against the wall outside, holding under his left arm the same cylindrical black bag with its pink and mauve lining.

He greeted her casually, as though they were old acquaintances.

"I've seen you a coupla times round The Flaunt, and I recognized you on the flight up. You're Maddy Wheatstone. I'm Seth Parsigian. You an' me got the same boss."

"The same boss?" Maddy wasn't ready to give anything away.

"Mister you-know-who. The toxic midget."

In spite of herself, Maddy smiled. "I bet you don't call him that to his face. Do you have identification?"

He did not speak, but he slipped a card from his jacket and passed it to her. He waited as she placed it face-to-face with her own Argos Group card and his image flashed onto its back face.

He raised one dark eyebrow. "Satisfied?"

"Not yet. It doesn't state your division."

"It wouldn't. I'm Special Projects." He grinned at her. "And just to prove that I'm Special Projects, try this one."

He passed a second card to her. Her ID tracer showed the same picture and the same name, Seth Parsigian; but now he was identified as an undersecretary in the French armed services.

He said cheerfully, "I've got three or four more if you want to see 'em."

"Don't bother. So you're Seth Parsigian, and you work in Special Projects for you-know-who. I'm here on a special assignment, too. I don't have time for social chat."

"Good. 'Cause this ain't one." He tucked away the cards. "I need help. If you can do something for me, I'll owe you big-time."

The rules within the Argos Group were quite clear: You helped another member if you could, but not at the price of your own assignment. Another's success would not balance your failure.

There was one exception. "Did GR tell you to ask me to help?"

"Hell, no. If Gordy knew that you and I were even talking, he'd shit bricks."

"Then we shouldn't talk." But Maddy didn't turn and walk away. An ally inside the Argos Group—especially one in Special Projects—might have many uses.

He was watching her with those light, flickering eyes. She had the feeling that he had surveyed her up and down in the first second, made his assessment, and was acting on it.

"Why don't I tell you my problem?" he asked. "I'll be real quick, no more than five minutes. Then you can decide if you'll help or not."

"I'll give you two minutes."

"Fair enough. I've come up here to find the person who killed a dozen teenagers. You know about 'em?"

Maddy thought of Lucille DeNorville's ravaged body. "I know too much. I was there when we found one this afternoon. It was horrible."

"So that's what all the excitement was around security. Another one? He's killed again?"

"No. This was the body of one of the earlier victims, a girl called Lucille DeNorville."

"I remember her. Number seven. Disappeared, but evidence at the scene said she'd had her brains bashed in."

"She had. That and—other things. She'd been badly cut up." Maddy found that she couldn't add details. She went on, "Look, if I could help you, I would. But I don't know much about the murders. You need an expert."

"I've got me an expert. No, I won't say who, so don't even ask. I'm up here tryin' to do the legwork, but it's damn nigh impossible."

"Why? I've been anywhere I wanted to on Sky City. Nobody has bothered me."

"That's because you're a woman. They'll leave you alone. Try bein' an adult male. A man like me, a stranger to Sky City wanderin' round by himself, six people ask who you are and tell you to move on every time you stop to scratch your ass."

Maddy could see why. Seth Parsigian did not have the look of a man she would like to meet in a dark alley, and Sky City was full of dimly lit, empty corridors. She said, "I can't do legwork for you. I wouldn't know how."

"I'm not askin' you to. All I'm saying is, if you were with me when I was doin' walk-arounds, I'd not have amateur sherlocks trailin' me every step I take."

"So you want me to go with you. How do I know you're not the murderer yourself?"

"Trust me. No, I guess that dog won't run. Well, for starters you can check the dates of the murders. You'll find I wasn't on Sky City for any of them."

"I think I'll do that. Now you've had your two minutes, and more."

"An' you're still here."

"I want to talk payback. Suppose I decide to help you. What do I get out of it? What's in it for *me*?"

"You sound like Gordy Rolfe. What do you *want* to get out of it? Can I do somethin' for your job up here? Tit for tat?"

At the beginning of the meeting Maddy would have denied that she needed help. It took only half a second to realize how wrong that was. She had been told to stick with John Hyslop every second of every day. In practice that was impossible. She wasn't with him *now,* for instance, and she didn't know where he was or what he was doing.

She made her decision. "You may be able to help me keep an eye on someone up here—someone whose actions are of direct interest to Gordy Rolfe. Do you know John Hyslop?"

"I know who he is. He's the big-wheel engineer for Sky City and the shield. But I don't *know* him know him."

"Gordy assigned me to watch him, see what he does. I could introduce you. Tit for tat. I help you poke around Sky City, you help me keep an eye on Hyslop."

"Suppose he won't let me?"

"Let me handle that end."

"You say Gordy knows about this?"

"He'll approve. Do you have your communicator hooked into the local system so I can get in touch with you?"

"Give me ten minutes, and I will have."

"Good. I'll call you. If I decide we have a deal, I'll tell you where and when we meet Hyslop."

"You want to check me out first."

"Of course. Do you mind?"

He grinned. "I'd mind more if you didn't. You got a hell of a reputation in Argos—yeah, I've seen your file, did that after I spotted you on the shuttle up. But files can be faked, and there's too many amateurs in this game already." He turned away and said over his shoulder, "Call me, Maddy Wheatstone. Professionals need to stick together."


A tedious and interminable search of the information banks, both on Sky City and Earthside, found no sign of a Seth Parsigian. No one in the Argos Group matched his detailed description. Maddy was not too surprised. You could look at it the other way round: Anyone in Special Projects who *could* be traced was not right for the job.

When she finally headed for Bruno Colombo's office, John Hyslop was no longer there. Colombo himself was busy in a meeting and unavailable. Goldy Jensen, asked to provide information, was not cooperative.

She looked up from her immaculate desk in the outer office and frowned at Maddy's question. "I don't keep track of everybody on Sky City, you know."

"It's important that I locate John Hyslop."

"Important to whom? I suppose you might try the engineering information center. He spends a lot of time there."

"Where is that?"

"Any of the directories will tell you how to reach it." Goldy turned impatiently away and initiated another call to Earth on Bruno Colombo's behalf. Five lines were already active and two others blinked for attention.

Maddy knew she would get no farther with Goldy. And yet today's rudeness did not feel deliberate. It was more as if Goldy Jensen was working under unusual pressure and had no time for her normal discourtesy.

The feeling of pressure persisted as Maddy used a directory to find the location of the engineering information center and made her way toward it. Everyone she passed gave off an impression of urgency. Something important was going on inside Sky City. Everybody but Maddy seemed to know what it was.

As she moved upward toward the lower-numbered levels—the engineering information center, to her surprise, lay far from Bruno Colombo's office and close to the axis of Sky City—she left a message for Seth Parsigian. He was to meet her in an hour unless she called and canceled. The limited information in her Argos data base confirmed Seth's position, but it did not indicate that he knew anything about space activities. Rather the opposite. Like Maddy, he was ground-based. It added to the mystery of his presence. Why would Gordy Rolfe send his Special Projects head to look for a murderer out here?

Maddy did not consider calling Earth for answers. Gordy played his games at multiple levels, and he delighted in withholding information from his staff—even information that would help them. He also kept his projects tightly compartmentalized. Maddy might have guessed that Gordy had other operatives working on Sky City, just as he had them in every major facility and government on Earth. They were engaged in everything from bribery (certain, from Maddy's personal knowledge) to assassination (rumored, but, knowing Gordy, she was willing to believe it). She would learn of no other Argos Group members on Sky City unless, like Seth Parsigian, they broke Gordy Rolfe's rules and identified themselves.

She had almost reached level zero. The low-gee environment of Sky City's axis added physical discomfort to Maddy's mental uncertainties. Her stomach still did not approve of free fall, and she had no idea what she would say to John Hyslop. The last time they were together she had fallen apart and practically wept on his shoulder. He hadn't seemed to mind, though if Gordy Rolfe had been there he would have fired her on the spot.

The sign beside the door of the chamber ahead stated in crude block capitals: INFORMATION CONTROL. AUTHORIZED ENGINEERING

PERSONNEL ONLY. So far as Maddy could tell, no one on Sky City paid any attention to instructions like that. Security, even after all the murders, was nonexistent in this part of the city. Also nonexistent, it seemed, was any interest in decor. Out on the perimeter Bruno Colombo occupied an office where walls, furniture, and carpets were exquisitely balanced in style and tone. Here on the axis the paint and fittings had apparently been selected and installed by a color-blind monkey.

*Engineers.* What was she doing, letting herself get involved with one?

She floated through the open door and looked inside. Good. John was there. But he was not alone. Half a dozen people sat with him in reclining chairs. They were all staring at a three-dimensional hologram of Sky City. The display, ten feet across, was slowly turning around its central axis. The one-minute rotation period matched the leisurely spin of the structure itself. Maddy had a full view of the whole space city for the first time. The wide, flat pill of the disk seemed solid and substantial, in contrast to the delicate axial spikes that connected the main body of Sky City to the power-generation plant on one side and the shield simulation chamber on the other.

Maddy recognized two of the other people in the room with John: Will Davis, the lanky, skeptical Welshman whom John had introduced her to three days ago, and Lauren Stansfield, the cold-eyed woman with the antique hair comb and the queenly walk, whom Maddy had met and probably deeply shocked when she was drugged to the gills on Asfanil. Maddy's minimal self-control on that occasion must have made a disastrous first impression.

Confirmation: Lauren Stansfield greeted Maddy with a welcoming scowl. John Hyslop gave her a single puzzled glance and went on talking. "Sky City was designed as a free-orbiting structure. So naturally, nothing more than station-keeping movements to maintain the right geosynch orbit were ever anticipated. We're facing an unprecedented situation. We can attach mirror-matter boosters at any or all of these places." He did something to the panel on his lap, and dozens of flashing points of yellow appeared on the hologram. "We already have attitude control engines at each of those sites, so the new installation ought to be easy. But we're dealing with a structure that masses millions of tons, and it has to travel over a hundred thousand kilometers." He turned to a slim girl who seemed to be in her early teens. "Amanda, did you check the accelerations?"

*Amanda Corrigan. The computer specialist on John Hyslop's old team. Skinny, angular, no figure. Just a kid.* Nothing to do with the Aten asteroid project. Why was she with John now? Why were *any* of them here? Including John. Had they asked him for help? What he was talking about had nothing to do with his current assignment.

Amanda Corrigan was nodding. She, too, had given Maddy a single glance, then ignored her. "I did a worst case, then a most probable case. I've put both of them in the simulation files, so anybody who wants to can take a look. One open question is the travel time. Torrance and Will think it will need at least four weeks to install a low-intensity beam and pulse generator on Cusp Station, and until those are working there's no point in computing anything. Also, John and Lauren estimate that it will take a couple of weeks to install the thrustors here. So for purposes of analysis I assumed a three-week travel time."

The others all nodded in agreement. Maddy was bewildered. It was as though she had been transported to a foreign country where she understood not one word of the language. Move Sky City? If so, where and why? But it was a bad time to interrupt with questions. Amanda Corrigan was talking again.

"Worst case calls for Sky City to move two hundred and thirty thousand kilometers. That's if you start to accelerate when Sky City is on the opposite side of Earth from the shield. I think you'd be insane to try it that way, but I did the calculations anyway. Naturally, you'll want to finish at rest relative to Cusp Station. So you'll be accelerating for the first half of the trip, decelerating for the second half. Turning Sky City over out-of-plane to do the changeover would be a nightmare. So you put a double set of mirror-matter thrustors, one set of them on each side. When you do the arithmetic it comes out to an average acceleration of point two seven millimeters per second squared—a few hundred-thousandths of a gee. Peanuts. Acceleration stresses won't be a problem, even in the worst case."

John Hyslop was nodding. "That's what I hoped. I know I didn't ask you to consider this, but what about rotation? Will we have to stop Sky City turning on its axis when we move?"

"If you do, you will introduce all kinds of other problems." The speaker was Lauren Stansfield. "Life-support systems are calibrated to the current rotation rate. Air and water circulation pumps assume a certain level of centrifugal forces working either for or against them. I'm not saying that it's impossible to go through the whole interior and adjust the pump settings, but I am saying it would be a nuisance. If there is any way that we can avoid it, we should."

*Cold, crisp, competent.* Lauren Stansfield had sounded that way when Maddy first met her; now it looked like her normal style.

Will Davis added, "Not to mention the screams you'd get from everybody on the perimeter if you halt the rotation." He grinned at the others. "Wouldn't do, would it? Pay all that money for prime half-gee living space, then find you're sitting in free fall like the poor peasants on the axis."

The smiles and nods of agreement said *Poor like us.* To someone with Maddy's sensitivity to people, that was easy to read. How much money did a Sky City engineer make? She could ask that some other time. Her bet was that she had an income more than this whole group combined, except maybe for Lauren, who was as expensively dressed as before. The harder part was to comprehend the rest of what the others were saying. She was getting the picture very slowly, not because she was unintelligent or because what she was hearing was particularly obscure but because the idea was so alien. This small group was quietly discussing ways of moving the vast and complex Sky City out to the end of the shield and parking it next to Cusp Station. And that, in turn, had huge implications. Why would anyone ever consider such a move, unless the project to save Earth was in dreadful trouble?

Once again, the trained observer in Maddy noted another oddity of the group. Something was missing. Where was the jockeying for position? Where were the hidden agendas that you found in every meeting back on Earth? Even Celine Tanaka, whom Maddy liked, possessed secret meeting goals that she would never reveal.

And where were the egos? Maddy could see no sign of them. All that seemed to matter were technical problems. It was a different world from the one she was used to. It was also a world with its own attractions; men like John Hyslop and Will Davis, awkward and often inarticulate, without the smooth, persuasive line of talk you were so used to. You were not always fighting with them for a controlling hand, or wondering what they wanted from you. They were men who were what they seemed to be.

Not that Sky City was without its own unpleasant characters. The faceless murderer, wandering unseen through the corridors, the blood of a dozen young girls on his hands. Seth Parsigian. Not a murderer—at least, not *this* murderer—but one of Gordy Rolfe's hard-core bully boys.

John Hyslop's quiet voice brought Maddy back from her brooding. "So we know where the immediate problems are. Optimal placement of thrustors—even though the accelerations are low, we're moving an awful lot of mass. Local stresses will be fierce and local strains need checking. That's your area, Lauren. I'll worry about balancing thrust movements about the center of mass. Low-intensity beam generator and pulse generator we've already discussed—that's you, Will and Torrance. Allocation of computing resources when we need them—that will be you, Amanda."

"You say *when* we need them." Amanda Corrigan was a slim brunette. Maddy took a closer look and revised her first impression. While that undeveloped body and slender legs made her seem about thirteen years old, her eyes told a different story. She was in her mid-twenties or older. She must also be highly competent to hold a place in John Hyslop's elite engineering group. "Isn't it really *if,*" Amanda went on, "and not *when* we have to move Sky City? Do you honestly think it will be necessary to do it?"

John took the question very seriously, finger-tapping at the control panel on his lap while he was thinking. Finally he nodded. "It will be necessary. I wish I didn't feel this way, and I'm surely no physicist. Astarte Vjansander acts a bit peculiar, but she and Wilmer Oldfield have me completely convinced. The particle storm is coming sooner than we thought. And it will be nothing like we expected."

He glanced around the group. "Any other questions?"

"Materials," Will Davis said. "We're going to need lots of electronics for the broad-beam field and pulse generators, but I'm not sure yet what the requirements will be. When we do know, we'll be in a hurry. Standard procurement channels are a pain—and they're slow."

"Good point. Until we're out near Cusp Station and ready for action, I'll put a no-limits ceiling on material requests. If you're going to need anything really outlandish, you should contact me and discuss it. I'm available anytime, but don't call me unless you really have to. It's not that I'm antisocial; I just like to sleep now and again."

The group dispersed and drifted out of the room. John Hyslop stayed. So did Maddy, despite the curious glances that she received from the others.

John, at least, seemed pleased to see her. He smiled shyly, looked away, and said, "Well, I don't imagine that was very much fun for you."

"Not great. You love all this, don't you?"

"I suppose I do. It's my world, Maddy. Where I live." He hesitated.

Maddy waited.

*Could you learn to live here, too?*

He hadn't said that. Of course he hadn't. It was her own mind, producing perplexing questions. Nothing had been the same since the sight of Lucille DeNorville's body. Old memories, dredged up from Maddy's deepest levels, pushing away the present, drawing in the past. The white bulging eyes, the gray and blotchy face. *You're all I've got now . . . make me proud of you.*

She had done her best. She was Maddy Wheatstone, close to the top in the Argos Group and ready to rise farther yet. She was starbright, diamond-hard, tough as she had to be. Even Gordy Rolfe treated her with respect. Meg could have done no better.

And then in one moment it all became meaningless. Lucille DeNorville's dry, ravaged corpse floated in front of her, abandoned like trash in the dark and barren corridor. Lucille had been mourned long ago. Now there could only be second sorrow and a quiet interment.

Lucille's death, like any death—like any life—was meaningless. Everything that Maddy had done was meaningless. Nothing had significance. Nothing brought the slightest satisfaction.

She felt a hand on her arm. John Hyslop was at her side. "Are you all right?"

Maddy took a deep breath. "I will be. I'm just—a little tired."

"You ought to be taking things easier. Come on, sit down." He led her to one of the reclining chairs. "Dr. Weinstein said that you might not feel a hundred percent for quite a while."

"I'm all right now." The feeling of desolation was passing. Had that been mentioned as an aftereffect of labyrinthitis and the Asfanil injection? If so, Maddy didn't remember it—or believe it. The change was deeper and more long-lasting. It had begun on her first visit to Sky City, her first meeting with John Hyslop. *Make me proud of you.* Even if she could one day take over from Gordy Rolfe and run the whole of the Argos Group, was that something to make a father proud? What about the rest of her life?

Maddy made herself sit up straighter in the chair. She found John Hyslop staring at her. He looked worried. She forced a smile and said, "I'm feeling better. But John, I can't afford to take things easy. None of us can." She deliberately made the switch of subject. "Why does Sky City have to change its position?"

The change was immediate and obvious. As John began to speak she saw him relax. Technical discussions, no matter how complex, were easy and natural for him. Personal issues, things such as dealing with an emotionally tattered and unstable Maddy Wheatstone, came much harder.

He explained about the meeting with the two physicists who had arrived from Earth. Maddy had never heard of them, but that was not surprising. The world of science and that of the Argos Group intersected only in very specialized areas.

Halfway through John's summary of the meeting with Wilmer Oldfield and Astarte Vjansander, Maddy caught another of its implications.

She interrupted him. "Sky City has to be moved, and the old shield will be useless. If there's to be a new defense system for the particle storm, who is going to do all that?"

"Well, it will naturally be a team effort. But if you mean who will lead the engineering design, I guess that's me."

"Then the Aten asteroid project—"

"Is on the shelf. It's not needed for the new protection method."

"And you?"

He hesitated. "I'm back in my old job. Actually, it isn't much like my job used to be."

While Maddy, by the sound of it, didn't have a job on Sky City at all. She had to get in touch with Gordy Rolfe. Did he know what was happening? It would be typical of Gordy to have information and not bother to pass it on. But if John had been reassigned, where did that leave Maddy? John himself would surely see no reason to have her around.

He had fallen silent and was fingering the control panel on his lap. In the display in front of Maddy, the holograms constantly changed. First, Sky City dwindled to a bright point of silver in a steady diurnal orbit around the Earth. Then at some new command the silver dot began to move outward. The space shield appeared, a ghostly green lattice defining a long cone. Sky City veered toward the axis of the cone and started along it, beginning the long ascent away from Earth.

Maddy realized that she was seeing a new simulation, one that reflected Amanda Corrigan's recent calculations. John might be too polite to say so, but when he was trying to work it was better for Maddy to go away and leave him to it.

The display began to change again, moving to an image of the space shield—the old space shield, useless now because it was unable to deal with the problem of particle bundles. Maddy felt reassured. If John needed to work, it made no sense for him to be examining an obsolete solution. He was doing the engineering equivalent of doodling.

They sat silently until he said, "I suppose that if I'm not going to be involved in the Aten project, you'll be heading back to Earth."

Maddy tried to catch his eye. He stared resolutely away from her, focused on infinity. At last she said, "Back to Earth. Yes, I guess so."

He nodded. His fingers tapped faster at the control panel on his lap. The display changed randomly, different sections of the space shield appearing and disappearing every few seconds. Maddy glanced at her watch. It was past midnight in Houston, but Gordy Rolfe kept strange hours. If he was at The Flaunt, she had a good chance of reaching him in the next hour. The deep hideout in Virginia was another matter. He was often busy with his habitat experiments there. In either place, though, he usually kept an eye on his messages. There was a strong chance that Maddy would be on her way back to Earth in the next few hours.

"I don't suppose there's any way you could stay, is there?" John said abruptly. His eyes moved to her face for a moment, then as quickly looked away. He went on, "My group hasn't talked much about schedules, but if Oldfield and Vjansander are right, it will be touch and go. We'll need every hand that we can get. You could be very useful."

That wasn't true. Maddy would be almost useless. Also, she heard stronger come-ons almost every day of the week back on Earth. But she was learning. From a man as romantically tentative as John Hyslop, an expression of interest in her continued presence on Sky City was close to a proposal. It didn't sound like much, but it changed her mood to one of confidence and energy.

"I'd like to stay," she said. *Don't be wishy-washy.* "I'd absolutely love to stay with you. I'll have to check with my boss, make sure he doesn't have other plans for me."

"I understand."

But John didn't, because Maddy had already made her decision. Forget that check-with-my-boss stuff; she was staying. If she had to, she would fabricate a role for herself with the Sky City engineering team. She would also invent for Gordy Rolfe a reason why her continued presence here was of vital importance to the Argos Group. She would, in fact, for the first time in nine years do something that was not aimed directly at advancing her career. And it didn't worry her at all.

Maddy saw John turning in his chair. Seth Parsigian stood in the doorway.

Right on cue. She actually felt pleased to see him. She waved him forward.

"John, I want you to meet a colleague of mine, Seth Parsigian. Seth and I are working together. He has things for me to do part of the day around Sky City. The rest of the time, we'll be available to work with you."

She saw their expressions. Surprise. Logically, she had some explaining to do. In practice, she proposed to explain nothing. John wanted her to stay; she wanted to stay with John. Seth needed her to help him; she needed Seth to help her. Explanations were unnecessary when everybody wanted the same thing.

And life? Maddy sat down between the two men. Life was meaningless only when you let yourself think it was meaningless.

# 19

**From the private diary of Oliver Guest.**

Uncharacteristically, I am drawn to quote from another source. About to set down my own thoughts, I find myself unable to better another's description of a psychological phenomenon.

Here, then, is my translation and summary of the statements of the nineteenth-century French mathematician Henri Poincaré concerning the process of intellectual discovery:

For fifteen days I struggled to prove that a certain class of mathematical functions did not exist. Every day I sat down at my worktable, but despite all my efforts I arrived at no result. One evening, contrary to my custom, I took black coffee; I could not go to sleep; ideas swarmed up in clouds; I sensed them clashing until, so to speak, a pair hooked together to form a stable combination . . . By morning the main work was done, and I had only to write up the results.

Next I wished to represent the functions in a certain way. That called for a great deal of straightforward labor, which I performed without any major new insights.

I then left Caen, where I was living at the time, to participate in a geological trip sponsored by the School of Mines. The travel made me forget my mathematical efforts, until at Coutances we took a bus for an excursion. The instant I put my foot on the step a new idea came to me that integrated and illuminated all my previous work. I did not at once make the verification—I did not have the time, because once in the bus I resumed an interrupted conversation; but I felt an instant and complete certainty. On returning to Caen I verified the result at my leisure . . .

I then undertook the study of certain other mathematical questions without much apparent success. After much hard work, disgusted at my lack of progress, I went to spend a few days at the seaside and thought of something else. One day, while walking along the cliffs, the solution came to me with the same characteristics of brevity, suddenness, and immediate certainty.

Given my susceptibilities, it is highly improbable that I would experience anything other than panic if forced to walk along the edge of cliffs, as Henri Poincaré did. However, the process that he describes is familiar to me, as I imagine it is to every other creative individual.

First one engages in long hours of hard work on a problem, apparently unproductive but completely under the control of the conscious mind. One at last ceases the effort; and then, at a time and place that cannot be predicted, comes the illuminating idea.

Poincaré did not understand the process any more than I do, but he clearly believed that this semblance of "sudden illumination" is "a manifest sign of previous long subconscious work." The drudgery is a necessary precursor to the inspiration.

As others have stated it, more succinctly, "No pain, no gain."

The relevance of all this will soon become clear.

For two weeks I had pondered the problem of the murders. I had the records that Seth Parsigian delivered to me, together with my own direct observations as Seth roamed Sky City in the limited way permitted to him as an adult male. I worked hard, night and day, since so long as the killings remained unsolved, so long must my own researches be interrupted.

On July 25, I took a break from my labors. It is the day every year when we celebrate the birth of my darlings. Since it happens to be my own birthday, they accept it as theirs only by convention and custom. Each of them also has a singular day, which she believes to correspond to her own true day of birth. In truth, July 25 is the date when each of the girls reached the age of delivery as a cloned form. On this occasion they would attain ages of twelve, ten, and eight.

I do not encourage the presence of strangers in Otranto Castle, which a birthday party for nineteen people would require. Each year we therefore hire a bus and driver and travel to the nearby town of Letterkenny, where we enjoy a catered meal. The indulgent owner of the inn, a loquacious French transplant named Michel Darboux, has become used to us, and he decorates the place with flowers and crude paper streamers to add to the festive atmosphere. While we wait to eat, Monsieur Darboux and I, but not the girls despite their pleas, share a bottle of Hugel white wine from Alsace-Lorraine.

Not, I must add, that the girls seem to need such stimulants. On this occasion the weather was both warm and dry, a rarity for western Ireland. Our meal would be served outside, on crude wooden tables in the south-facing fenced courtyard that leads to a broad and level meadow of close-cropped grass.

I did not, then or ever, regret my choice of western Ireland. The selection had been made carefully. Just as the remoter regions of Ireland had been left behind in the world's twenty-first century surge of technological progress, so the living standards there had been less affected by the Alpha Centauri supernova. I judged that the same was likely to be true in the devastation caused by the coming particle storm, and I rarely felt nostalgic for the vanished amenities of my former life.

The bench where Michel Darboux and I had placed ourselves sat in the shade of an old horse chestnut. The tree was too close to the inn for safety, and should long ago have been pruned or removed. Today, however, its leafy curtain was welcome. Even where we sat, the volume of noise that the girls generated was considerable. Their enjoyment of their games served as partial compensation for the fact that we were out in the open air, and I was for that reason a little uncomfortable.

I sipped, did my best to relax, and firmly resisted Alyson and Lucy-Mary's adjurations to join them in an activity that they described as a game, but which seemed to consist mostly of a pile of girls sitting on top of each other and screaming. At the same time I had my eye on the line of village lads beyond the fence. They were watching my darlings, while pretending to be busy with other matters. The older girls were very aware of them. The gestures of Gloria and Bridget, and to a lesser extent Katherine and Darlene, possessed an exaggerated quality, with screams, tossed-back hair, and bare limbs much in evidence. They were playing to the crowd of their admirers.

Who would know, watching them at careless sport, that even the youngest of my darlings was fluent in three languages and had scientific training and knowledge beyond the average educated sixteen-year-old? Not, I felt sure, the row of pimpled teenage males at the fence.

Darboux was watching, too, over the rim of his glass. He caught my eye. "You are a brave man, *m'sieur.* Your children are very beautiful. It will not be long before older men will come knocking at your door."

The idea that this type of behavior could only become worse with adolescence was not one to bring me comfort. I noticed that when Bridget and Katherine were close to the boys they were deliberately showing off their legs.

Michel Darboux had seen the same thing. "Perhaps it will happen sooner than you think," he said. "Your girls can provide sweet nectar for many bees. The men will fly to them—especially if the girls encourage it."

The suggestion was truly alarming. I had known, as he could not, all the girls in their original incarnations. Before I rescued them, Amity and Bridget and Darlene and Katherine had been child prostitutes, as had Crystal and Alyson (eight years old today and still, thank God, far from puberty). I had saved them from that fate, bringing them anew into a world with every advantage of education and opportunity that I could provide. Only at the genetic level were they what they had once been.

But genetics might be too much. The old debates of nature versus nurture, heredity versus environment, had ended in a standoff. Neither factor could be ignored; either might dominate in an individual case.

Darboux was touching my arm. "*M'sieur,* we are ready to serve lunch. If you would summon your young ladies . . ."

I nodded. My attention was divided: the clatter of serving dishes behind me; in front of me the girls, seeing or smelling food and standing up to smooth flowered skirts over strong young limbs; off to my right the ogling audience of youths, knowing that the show was over but reluctant to leave. It was at that strange and inopportune moment, when murder, mayhem, and mystery seemed farthest from my mind, that I grasped the nature and dark motive of the Sky City killer.

I did not yet have an identity, but the information to provide that should be readily available. As soon as we returned to the castle, I would download certain Earth-based financial and genealogical data. And then, at last, I would be able, like Shakespeare's poet, to give "to airy nothing a local habitation and a name."

How sure was I of my answer? It may sound implausible if I say that I was utterly sure. Yet I was. Like Poincaré, the solution had come to me with such "characteristics of brevity, suddenness, and immediate certainty" that I had no doubts at all.

I cannot pretend that I enjoy meetings with Seth Parsigian, either in person or at a distance. His intelligence is not in question, but there is a rude directness to the man that I find hard to tolerate. Rarely, as now, did I look forward to a call from him.

Which, with the perversity of events, did not come when expected. According to our agreement I would call Seth only in an emergency, but he could call me anytime. That was not as unreasonable as it sounds. I hated to make outgoing calls from the castle, and would do so only on a voice-only line. He, however, was out on the front line of Sky City, juggling permits and people and equipment (his RV jacket was finicky and sometimes unreliable), while I was "sittin' safe at home laughin' and scratchin'."

Scratching I was not; itching I certainly was—itching to tell Seth what I knew. Half an hour's work at the general data banks after we returned from the birthday party had been enough. I knew the name of the murderer.

What I did not have was proof. Worse than that, I saw no way for Seth and me ever to obtain proof unless there was another killing, which seemed, for good and sufficient reasons, unlikely to occur.

When the call came it was past three in the morning. I was not asleep. Excitement at my discovery kept me awake, along with another growing concern arising from the events of the day. It had been my original intention for my darlings to reach the biological age of fourteen, and remain there indefinitely. I now knew that was impossible. The telomod protocols that I myself had pioneered made it a simple task to reset the telomeres of each chromosome to any length, from that of newborn babe to octogenarian. That was not the problem. At issue was the wisdom and feasibility of my plan. Even if no one else discovered the existence of eighteen girls forever in the bloom of early womanhood, my darlings themselves would certainly notice. They had the disposition to demand answers from me, plus the intelligence to dismiss evasions and falsehood.

The alternatives were equally unappealing. Oliver Guest, serial killer of young girls, might seek to do what he had done before: remove them from the world as they came to puberty, and begin with new clones. Except that was now unthinkable; the misery and degradation of their sometime existence was no longer a justification for such an action.

The other option was to allow the girls to age naturally, and thus inevitably to lose them when they became full adults. It occurred to me, as never before, that this was the plight of every parent. I pondered, I agonized, and I discovered no acceptable answer. Seth's call, when it finally came, was doubly welcome.

It was also surprising. The RV link was on, but I could see Seth's face against the background of the one-room apartment that he had rented for use on Sky City.

"Oh, yeah," he said at my question. "I keep the earpiece in all the time, but I don't wear the RV jacket at night 'cause it's too hot. It's hung on the wall over there, an' you're gettin' its picture."

It was, in fact, a rather superior picture. The suit was in a fixed position, which removed the need for image motion compensation and restoration.

"I was expecting your call much earlier," I said. "Have you been experiencing difficulties?"

I was surprised by the strength of his reaction. I was looking forward to revealing to him my own discovery, and had asked my question more to extend the moment than in anticipation of a positive answer.

He glared at me. His eyes were bloodshot and dark-rimmed. "Difficulties? You gotta be kidding. Don't you know what's goin' on up here?"

"I assume that you are seeking evidence and possible assistance on Sky City."

"Well, you're wrong. Both counts. This place is a madhouse. They're gettin' ready to move the whole shebang out to the end of the shield. Nobody knows if the stresses will make the city fall apart. An' it's worse than that. Listen."

It was clear from his manner that I was going to do so, whether I elected to or not. He spoke of the harassment and continuing suspicion he had encountered when he tried to wander the corridors and chambers of Sky City alone. He spoke of his increasing conviction that he needed help. I made sympathetic noises, waiting to reveal my own discovery.

Then he told me of his meeting with and solicitation of assistance from another Argos Group employee. All my sympathy vanished.

"You did *what*?" I said. "That is pure insanity."

"I guess you know that when you see it."

"We agreed that everything between us would be held totally secret!"

"We did. It will." Seth remained calm. "Hold your water, Doc. Your name and your role in this were never mentioned. All I asked Maddy Wheatstone to do was roll round Sky City with me for a while, so I could go places in peace. She has no idea what the RV jacket does. Even if you spoke to me, she'd never know it. The earpiece don't make enough noise for anybody but me to hear."

"That attitude is naive beyond belief. The woman could learn too much in a dozen ways."

"Name one."

"I will name three. First, suppose that you at my request suddenly follow a person, or undertake a different course of action from the one you have been engaged in."

"I'll tell her why I'm doin' it."

"Suppose you do not know the reason? Are you claiming to be privy to my innermost thoughts?"

"Not for a pension. You tryin' to give me the creeps? I'll find a reason to give her."

"Very well. Consider this situation. Both of you work for the Argos Group, and from what you say she is highly placed within it. Suppose that she goes to her superior and asks who else is involved in what you are doing."

"She'll strike out. Gordy Rolfe don't work like that. Nobody in the Argos Group knows I came to you, an' no one will. The only person who knows I'm on this job is the man who assigned it to me, an' Gordy'll let you have fifteen feet of his small intestine before he'll give up information."

If Seth was typical of the Argos Group, I readily accepted what he said regarding the paucity of information transfer. But I was not yet satisfied. "This woman, Maddy Wheatstone, will surely not assist you for no reason. There must be a *quid pro quo.* Suppose that she insists on knowing more of what you are doing, as a condition for her cooperation."

"I told her I was looking for the murderer, an' that was enough. She wants me to help her keep an eye on a guy called John Hyslop, a big-shot engineer on Sky City. And no, she didn't tell me why she's watching him. She's as tight as Gordy Rolfe." Seth lay back on his bed, so the RV jacket no longer provided me with a view of his face. "Anyway." His voice was weary. "If you had let me finish before you blew off, you'd have seen why none of this matters worth a damn. I met John Hyslop, an' I'm spendin' a helluva lot of time diggin' into the data bases, lookin' for clues an' findin' diddly-squat. An' Maddy Wheatstone an' me are traipsin' round Sky City like a couple of mad tourists. But the places where the kids were killed have been picked over fine. I'm tellin' you, chances of us comin' across anythin' like a lead to the murderer are flat-out zero."

My moment had come. "That," I said softly, "is no longer necessary."

"Say what?" He raised his head.

"You no longer need to seek evidence on Sky City. I know the name, occupation, motive, and present location of the murderer."

I exaggerated a little. My knowledge of the killer's present location was in truth a little imprecise.

Seth was on his feet again. "I don't believe it. Tell me everything."

I did, slowly, carefully, and completely. It took many minutes, but there was no danger that Seth's attention might wander. At the end I said, "Well? Are you persuaded?"

"Yeah. You got it." He was silent for a while, then repeated, "You got it. You don't even need to send the data you pulled in today. I believe you. But you know the problem?"

"Of course. A court of law is a curiously irrational place. It disdains a mosaic of collateral evidence that any rational person regards as conclusive, and asks for proof. The knife in the murderer's hand, the foot still on the victim's windpipe. Proof."

"Which we need and don't have."

"Precisely."

"And until we got it we got nothin'."

That was hardly fair. I forbore to point out to him that if we now had nothing, an hour ago he had had considerably less than nothing.

"So we still have problems," he went on. "You feel sure there'll be no more killings?"

"What would be the point? There is no need for them. And our murderer is supremely logical."

"Logical, and a monster. What do we do?"

"We think. Or, more precisely, I think. For the moment, I suggest that you remain on Sky City."

"Great. I stay up here while this crapheap flies off to nowhere or comes apart tryin'."

"Remain there for the time being. Continue to cultivate Maddy Wheatstone and, if you can, the engineer, John Hyslop."

He stared at me shrewdly. "You're holdin' out on me. You got somethin' more."

"No." I shook my head, even though there was no way that he could see me. "I have nothing close to an answer. If and when I do, you will hear from me instantly. I have no more desire than you to prolong this enterprise."

"Mmm. An' I thought you were gettin' fond of me." Seth paused for a moment, then added, "Good one, Doc. You did some fancy thinkin' after all, just when I was ready to write you off. Do it one more time, and let's nail the bastard."

He broke the connection, rather before I was ready to do so. It had been my intention to warn him to take care. The murderer would certainly be willing to kill again for one reason: to prevent discovery.

Then my rational processes gave me reassurance. Even if Seth's wanderings through Sky City had been noticed, there was no reason to believe that our search would be more fruitful than anyone else's. The evidence was old or vanished. Furthermore, Seth had in the past given ample proof that he was able to look after himself. He would not be an easy man to kill.

I reflected that Seth's final words showed, in his own bizarre way, sincere appreciation for my efforts. I *had* done "some fancy thinking," just as he said. As for "Do it one more time," I wondered if that would be possible.

I am not ready to say otherwise, although I have in truth no idea how to catch our killer. What I do have is a conviction that waiting for another murder, or seeking additional evidence of past murders, will be pointless. We are dealing with an individual who employs precise calculation before taking action. Twelve murders were enough, so there will be no more. And such material evidence as has already been found has been picked clean, over and over, by numerous investigating teams. It is old and unlikely to yield a single further shred of useful data. The killer must be feeling very comfortable.

How, then, to catch such a person?

Again I defer to you, the invisible reader of my words. You were ahead of me, perhaps, in divining the identity of the murderer. Do you also know how to ensure apprehension? Remember, the evidence must be strong, direct, and incontestable.

I do not know. Not yet. But I do know this: No passive procedure will work. Any successful approach must take the initiative.


The conversation with Seth took only half an hour, but by the time I went to my bedroom the clock on the dresser showed almost four. After a busy day—and night—I had earned, one might think, a little sleep. However, at fifty-five degrees north the late-July sunrise already lightened the sky. Long experience has taught me that I cannot sleep during daylight hours.

I went back to the kitchen, made strong coffee, and sat down at the long butcher-block table to record the events of the past twenty-four hours. I was very tired, and my mind interspersed memories of the pleasant birthday party with thoughts of the Sky City murders. Regrettably, I achieved no insights comparable with those of the great Henri Poincaré after partaking of black coffee. However, one useful conclusion did emerge.

During the next few weeks, unprecedented events would be taking place on Sky City as it flew far out from Earth to take its position close to Cusp Station. It was possible that those same events would provide an unprecedented opportunity to catch our killer.

I had been patient in restoring my darlings, waiting many years before I began their cloning. Seth and I could not wait so long, but we, too, must be patient—and always ready to act.

# 20

It took Nick Lopez three tries before Celine was persuaded.

"You don't have to *like* the son of a bitch," he said. "Hell, I don't like him myself. But he's the brains behind the rolfe designs, and all the related patents are his."

"I don't deny that." Celine felt besieged. She had tried to begin a normal day of work, but urgent messages from Lopez had popped up everywhere until finally she had agreed to meet with him in the Oval Office. It was almost ten o'clock, she had yet to make her first planned meeting, and her schedule was in tatters. "I know how valuable the rolfes are for space work, but we already have a slew of them in Sky City and on the shield. If Rolfe says he's pulling them out of there, we'll simply invoke emergency powers and say no."

"That's not the problem." Lopez pulled a sheaf of papers from his case and brandished them at Celine. "These are orders from Sky City for *additional* rolfes with special new capabilities. We know that Gordy Rolfe can provide the machines—he has advertised them, even boasted about them. We'd like to see them shipped up as soon as possible, but without Rolfe's cooperation it won't happen. He laughs and says the changes are trivial; but no one on my staff or on Sky City knows how to make them."

"Have you asked him to cooperate?"

"Of course. I told him about Wilmer Oldfield and Star Vjansander's work, and I stressed the urgency of the new schedule. He says it's all nonsense. He's heard all the panic talk from me before, and he doesn't believe there's going to be a different form of particle storm. Even if there is, he says, he'll be safe."

"Probably true. He'll hide underground. But I don't see how I'll be any better at talking Rolfe into helping us than you've been."

"He likes you." Lopez was pouring on the charm. Celine could feel the force of his personality washing over her like a relaxing tide.

"Nick, that's rubbish. I don't think Gordy Rolfe likes anyone."

"He says he's willing to meet with you. That's better than I could do."

"You tried?"

"I called him again yesterday. He told me to go away and stick my head up my ass."

"That's not very nice. On the other hand, Gordy Rolfe told one of my staff, less than a month ago, that I was a raddled old trollop who'd be more at home in the whorehouse than the White House. Likes me? Nick, you'll have to do better than that."

"Well, he did agree to meet with you."

*"Why?"*

"Because he admires you. You're probably the one woman in the world—"

"Nick! Gordy Rolfe doesn't admire *any* woman. He tolerates a few, but I'm not one of them."

He sagged back in his suit and ran a hand through his bushy gray hair. His frown of defeat was more friendly and disarming than the average smile. "All right. So he doesn't admire you. I have no idea what that twisted little runt thinks of you. My best guess, he says he'll meet with you because he thinks there's a chance he'll be able to humiliate you. Me, he's already humiliated."

"Thank you, Nick. At last. That, I can accept. Now tell me how I'm supposed to talk Gordy Rolfe into coughing up the rolfes that we need on Sky City."

"He needs your help. You've got something he wants."

"Remind me."

"Well, according to what I've heard—only rumor, of course . . ." Lopez was gazing down and sideways, as though fascinated by the old wicker wastepaper basket beside Celine's desk. "According to rumor, you promised you'd help the Argos Group with a license for a new launch facility on U.S. territory, off the coast of Florida."

"How the hell did you learn *that*? What I said was unofficial, and it wasn't to go outside this office."

"Oh, you know how it is." A shrug of massive shoulders. "Word about these things gets out . . ."

"If you see Auden Travis before I do, tell him to expect to be sent up in flames. Do you know who I said that to about the license?"

"A Miss Maddy Wheatstone. Or so I have been told. But Gordy's having doubts about her. He's having doubts about everybody these days. I think he's really losing it. But that's to our advantage. You go to see him, you tell him that you promised nothing to anybody, and you negotiate."

"A bit hard on Maddy."

"Could be. These days, times are hard all over. She's a big girl, she'll get by. I'll try to do her a favor, if that's what it takes to get you to Gordy."

"We'll put that on hold." Celine was examining her calendar. "Today, I suppose?"

"You know how urgent this is."

"Nick, *everything* is urgent. Everything has been urgent for twenty-seven years. You reach the point where crisis is so much the normal operating condition that you can't respond to it."

"If Oldfield and Vjansander are right, we have less than thirty days."

"Don't lecture me, Nick. I'm quite capable of doing that to myself." Celine was examining a list and crossing items off it. "I have to see Milton Glover."

She noticed Nick's tiny grimace at the name. "I can't stand the man, either," she went on, "but I've slipped his appointment every day for two weeks and he's outside waiting. Jahangir Hekmat, too—he's the head of the Socinists. They believe that God is a still-evolving entity. I owe them a meeting as a payback for a political favor."

"I could try my hand with Hekmat if you like. I have some sympathy with the idea of an evolving deity—certainly the gods we've had in the past haven't done too well by us. Why are they called Socinists?"

"They claim to be followers of a sixteenth-century theologian, Sozzini, who said that God wasn't omnipotent and omniscient. God is still learning and growing. But let me warn you, today's Socinists believe that the Alpha Centauri supernova is part of the evolving consciousness of the universe, and they say we ought not to defend ourselves against it."

"Hekmat should be talking to Wilmer Oldfield. If I understand correctly, he and Astarte Vjansander believe something along the same lines. The gamma pulse and the particle flux didn't come our way by accident. It all happened by *intention*."

"Don't believe everything Wilmer and Star tell you. When they get going they can be as crazy as Hekmat. Anyway, he can't talk to them. They're out on Sky City. Their work is too important for me to bring them back here." Celine stabbed her pencil at the page and viciously crossed out another line. "I sometimes wish I were out there, too. It's where the real action is."

" 'They also serve who only stand and wait.' "

"Right. Stand, and wait, and meet with power-mad crazies like Gordy Rolfe, or self-centered bags of wind like Milton Glover. Don't you ever long for the old times, when if you did just one thing well, at the end of the day you could feel satisfied with your efforts?"

"You mean your days on the Mars expedition?"

"That's what I was thinking of."

"You were young then. Look at it realistically. You spent a few years locked up in a metal can, you flew back home, and then half of your crew died."

"Nick, you've got the soul of a sausage maker." Celine stood up. "No trace of romance."

"I could give you the names of fifty people less than five miles from this room who'd tell you different. But that would be gross indiscretion and betrayal." Lopez stood up, too, towering over Celine. "I'll go tackle Mr. Hekmat and his Socinist friends. But I'd rather not meet Milton Glover if I can avoid it."

"No argument there. You go out the other door and I'll direct Hekmat around to you. First, though, I've got to call Gordy Rolfe and make a date, then tell Claudette to arrange a flight to Houston—"

"No. Gordy's not at The Flaunt today. He doesn't go there much—doesn't go anywhere."

"Then where is he?"

"At his underground facility in Virginia. I told you, he's getting stranger and stranger. Anybody who wants to see him now has to go there."

"I don't know where it is."

"You do, actually—better than most people. The Argos Group underground location is where the old Legion of Argos had its headquarters. It's the place where you were held prisoner when you returned from Mars. It's the place where the commando team captured the Eye of God, Pearl Lazenby."

"Hell and damnation." Celine flopped down again onto her padded chair with its special back support. According to the physicians, the bone loss from the long Mars trip had been completely restored, but her back had its own opinion. "That's a place I never expected to go again, and never wanted to."

"Better than standing and waiting. But I agree with you. I've been to Gordy's hideaway, and I must say I didn't like it one bit."

"What's wrong with it?"

"You'll see. I wouldn't want to spoil the surprise." Lopez gripped Celine's hand briefly and headed for the door. "Good luck with Gordy. Call me as soon as you get back. I can't wait to hear what he says. And let me know what you think of his underground habitat."

After he had gone, Celine sat for a long time and stared at the wall of her office. Had she been conned? Conned into visiting Rolfe? Maybe it was a necessary act. But Nick Lopez's voice, on his final remark, suggested that he already knew very well what she would think of Gordy's underground home.

By midday Celine was eager to leave. Gordy Rolfe had agreed to a meeting easily. In her view, too easily, but Nick Lopez was not available for questions. He had spirited Jahangir Hekmat and his Socinist contingent away—to where, Celine neither knew nor cared.

One gone. The only other unavoidable meeting was with Milton Glover of the Trust In Government coalition, and that just might turn out to be an unexpected pleasure.

Celine had hopes as soon as she picked up her briefing folder and read the two notes inside. They came in response to her own one-word question, *Nevada?*, after the last meeting with Milton Glover.

1. Trust In Government interest in leasing federal lands in Nevada stems from their stated desire to have access to old Comstock mine.

Forty years ago, the mine had underground tunnels and chambers extending for many miles.

2. A recent classified survey indicates that the Comstock mine and associated deep drillings and excavations were filled in by floods and land subsidence at the time of the Alpha Centauri supernova, and all tunnels remain inaccessible.

The Trust In Government group might be unaware of the contents of that second note. But why weren't they more cautious? Was there was some other reason for their willingness to purchase?

When the door of her office slid open and Milton Glover walked in with his old-fashioned white suit and insincere smile, Celine couldn't wait.

She cut off Glover's usual florid greeting before it could begin. "Milton, I'm delighted to tell you that your request to lease the Nevada federal properties has been approved. As soon as you sign on behalf of TIG and thereby provide legal commitment, rights to the lands will belong to your organization for the next fifty years."

"Why, Madam President, that is splendid news." But Glover's face was puzzled.

"Why don't I bring in witnesses, and we can sign the papers?" Celine buzzed her outer office. "Claudette? Would you and Frederick come in, please."

"Wonderful!" Glover laughed, but his pale blue eyes were not smiling. Instinct told him that something was not quite right. "However, I think we must let our lawyers take a look and approve before I actually sign anything."

"But they have already seen the documents, and they *have* approved. See? Their legal opinion is attached." *I guess Trust In Government lawyers and Trust In Government geologists form nonintersecting sets.* "The Secretary of the Interior has already signed also."

"So he has." Glover spoke slowly. He stared around the room, first at the two people who had just entered and then at the window.

*No escape for you that way.* Celine held out a pen. "Milton, you already know Claudette Schwinger, and this is Frederick Wollaston. They will serve as witnesses. If you would like to sign first?"

"Well, I still think—"

"I have one question for you, just out of curiosity. What led you to choose the Nevada site? Did you have private information available to you?"

Glover grabbed the pen out of her hand and pulled the first copy of the document toward him. "No, no, not at all. No special information. Just good, competent, old-fashioned analysis."

Who was it said that a man would die rather than appear to be a fool? Will Rogers, over a century ago. But Celine couldn't ask Milton Glover for assistance on that quotation; he was too busy signing.

She added her signature below his on each of the seven copies, and passed them on to the witnesses.

"I'm sure the members of the Trust In Government coalition will be as pleased as I am when they examine the Nevada lands and see the results of all your work." Celine signed the last copy and handed it to Claudette. "I'm afraid I can't stay for any kind of celebration. I have to head for southwest Virginia just as soon as I can."

Celine was out of the room before he could ask a question—or she could burst. There were moments, few and far between, when slimy bastards like Milton Glover got their comeuppance. Old Miltie was in for an exciting few hours when he and the other Trust In Government bigots took a close look at Nevada and learned what they had actually leased. Someone had sold them bad data concerning the Nevada mines.

It would be nice to meet with and personally shake the hand of the person who had sold the data to old Miltie, but that was too much to hope for. One treat a day was all that a President could reasonably expect.

# 21

Pleasure at the prospect of Milton Glover's impending shock stayed with Celine for a long time. Even the weather report did not lower her spirits. A line of afternoon thunderstorms with violent wind shears was running across Virginia, and the White House transportation team was recommending ground travel. It would be a little slower, but acceptable for a short trip and less likely to have problems with the weather.

Celine did not argue. She viewed the upcoming meeting with Gordy Rolfe with mixed feelings. The whole Mars expedition and the twenty-seven years of life after it had taught her that she could handle just about anything. It had not taught her, however, to like many of the things that were thrown at her. And it could not stop her worrying.

Accompanied by her usual four security staff, she climbed into the car.

"Take it slow." She needed time to prepare herself for the meeting with Gordy Rolfe.

The driver nodded. His presence was hardly necessary, except to set the Automatic Vehicle Control. The armored vehicle went from the underground parking lot, across the new Tidal Crossing Bridge, and on into Virginia. The heavy, brooding weather put Celine in a strange mood. Returning to a place that had so affected her in the past, she felt that she was also moving back through time. Heading south and west toward Richmond, she recognized the rolling sweep of the land. She had traveled this same path, in darkness, in another armored vehicle. She had encountered there a person who, like Gordy Rolfe, was arguably mad: Pearl Lazenby, the Eye of God. Pearl's ideas had undoubtedly influenced Gordy Rolfe, the head of the Argos Group.

The beginning of the trip seemed long; but then, before she expected it, she saw ahead a gentle slope leading down toward a children's playground and a small schoolhouse. She would have sworn that she did not remember the setting, but on first sight it became immediately familiar. The car rolled down to the foot of the hill, halted beside the schoolhouse, and switched itself off. The AVC screen went blank.

"We're arrived," Celine said. "Tell Mr. Rolfe we're here. No, better than that." She reached out for the headset clipped to the partition in front of her. "I'll do it myself. Hello, Gordy Rolfe. Are you there?"

"Of course I'm here." The gruff reply came at once. He must have been waiting for her call—probably monitoring her progress. The Argos Group possessed the world's most advanced surveillance systems. "Do you know where the elevators are?"

"I know where they used to be. In the back of the schoolhouse."

"They haven't moved. Come on down. No, I don't want the Secret Service meatheads. Just you."

He *was* observing them. The first of the security staff had climbed out of the vehicle ahead of Celine.

"They're supposed to accompany me wherever I go." Celine saw Chesley Reiter, her security chief, nodding vigorously.

"*Supposed* to." Rolfe produced a harsh sound that could be interpreted as a laugh. "That's a load of bull, and you know it. Who was with you when you went down to New Rio to see Nick Lopez? We do it my way or not at all. You want to see me? Then you come down by yourself."

Celine glanced at Chesley Reiter, shrugged, and climbed out of the car. The sky was black, even though it was only midafternoon. To the west she saw forked lightning. "Ches, take your staff and find somewhere comfortable. I'll call when I need to be picked up."

"With respect, Madam President, we'll wait for you here."

Chesley Reiter did not add, *just in case.* Nor did Celine argue. It was his job, his decision. Celine went inside the schoolhouse without another word. One thing about being President, no one's time was as important as yours. If necessary, Ches and the security detail would wait all night.

The inside of the schoolhouse had changed little in the twenty-seven years since Celine had last seen it. There had never been toys—the Legion of Argos did not permit such distractions—but the old wooden desks still sat in neat lines, and the turn-of-the-century teaching aids sat by the wall. Celine picked up an orange folder from one of the diminutive desks, blew away the dust, and opened it. The lined sheets inside, covered with a child's careful lettering, were yellowed and brittle.

She looked around. Not everything was unchanged. Gordy Rolfe's personal interests showed in the tiny red eyes set at each corner of the room. Celine had never seen anything so compact. The new surveillance system must be at the limit of today's technology. Gordy's inventions in fact defined those limits.

As she hesitated, his voice came from nowhere.

"Go to the elevators and take the left-hand one all the way down. I'll be waiting."

And watching.

Celine wondered. The Argos Group was famous for its up-to-date and detailed knowledge of what went on all around the world. Did Gordy Rolfe's remote observation systems extend to the White House—even, perhaps, into the Oval Office itself? After all, there were maintenance rolfes there, even though you rarely saw one. Could they be the source of Nick Lopez's information about the meeting with Maddy Wheatstone?

Old advice, but still good: Assume *nothing* is off the record, nothing that you ever say, do, or write.

The bottom button of the elevator panel bore an icon like a flaming torch. Celine pressed it and began a slow, uneasy descent.

He was waiting when the door finally opened. He was even smaller than she remembered, unshaven, and dressed in a black jumpsuit with a leather belt and its array of clip-on instruments. He was scruffier than usual—his hair was greasy, and his hands were smudged with oil or graphite.

"Esteemed Madam President." Gray eyes glittered behind the outsized and antiquated frames. His mirthless smile suggested that the honorific was no more than a form of sarcasm.

Celine remembered that he tolerated no form of physical contact. Just as well, since she had no desire to touch those blackened, claw-like fingers. Instead of holding out her hand she nodded and said, "Gordy Rolfe. I'm glad you were able to meet with me."

"Good. Let's see if you stay glad."

He turned and led the way up a steep spiral staircase. Celine followed. A round hatch brought her through into a broad circular chamber bounded by a thick transparent wall. Beyond the wall she saw what seemed to be a wilderness of vegetation, but she paid little attention to that or anything else because of the other contents of the room.

Just a few yards from her squatted a small bipedal dinosaur. It was, she felt sure, a carnivore; a genetically down-bred form from one of the largest meat-eaters, *T. rex,* or maybe *Gorgosaurus.* The creature was muzzled and tethered by a short chain to a heavy ring bolt in the floor of the room. The blue-black eyes turned in the oversized scaly head and fixed their dead gaze on Celine. The mouth opened as far as it could against the green muzzle, to show the tips of white needle teeth. The animal growled, deep in its throat, and the smell of rotting meat that gusted out made Celine hold her breath. The animal stood up and moved toward the newcomers until it reached the limit of its chain.

"Place is a bit of a mess." Rolfe walked, unconcerned, to within two feet of the chained carnosaur. "Come sit down."

Celine edged after him, and saw that the place was indeed a mess. Rolfe's desk and a nearby table were covered with a clutter of electronics and test units. On the floor beside the table, upside-down and eviscerated, lay a trio of eight-legged machines.

"Those look like rolfes." Celine dumped a tangle of wires and a miniaturized scanning probe microscope onto the floor and sat down. The carnosaur was a deliberate attempt to make her ill at ease, but she refused to acknowledge its presence. She wanted Gordy Rolfe to know he had failed.

If he had failed. It was hard to sit calmly with your back to the minisaur, especially when you could hear its harsh breathing and the grating of stressed chain links.

"They are rolfes—of a sort." Gordy perched on the arm of a chair, so Celine would have to look up at him. "I originally designed them to function in there." He jerked his thumb toward the wall and the jungle beyond. "Now I'm doing a bit more fiddling, adding a few special functions. The new ones have the same general organization, but they'll be smarter and more versatile. The sort of things your space dummies say they're going to need, but won't get."

Deliberate provocation, designed to start an argument. Celine delayed her response, swiveling in her chair to add to her original first impression of the chamber. The floor was dust-free and clear of small objects. Cleaning machines would remove those, also the dust and dirt and spilled liquids. These machines—rolfes of the most primitive kind—were clearly in use here. Two moved across the room as she watched, little low-end servers no more than a foot long and a couple of inches off the floor. They would ignore large objects, or at most clean, lift, and replace them exactly.

Part of the room had been partitioned off, and she could see the end of a bed through an opening in the waist-high barrier. There were no doors, beyond one that led through to the encircling area of dense vegetation. A heap of spare machine parts lay in disarray against the wall on the side opposite to the chained carnosaur. She recognized axles, gears, motors, gauges, and metal rods and pipes of many sizes. A bench nearby was a jumble of wrenches, saws, pliers, hammers, and pincers. Stacked against the wall next to that stood a stack of cages, each one the size of a large chest. Changes in light and dark behind narrow slits in the front of the cages showed something moving within, but Celine could not determine what it might be. Next to the chests, incongruously, stood an old-fashioned bicycle.

"Do you ride that?"

"Sure." Rolfe had his eyes fixed on Celine, as intent and unblinking in his gaze as the tethered carnosaur. The communications unit on his desk was buzzing with an external call, but he took no notice. "Got to stay healthy, you know. *Mens sana in corpore sano.* A healthy mind in a healthy body."

Did he ride the bike down here, somewhere out there beyond the tangle of jungle? No. The whole thing was an obscure joke. Gordy Rolfe rode nothing. His face had the gray pallor of a man who shunned all forms of exercise. Furthermore, the bicycle sat in front of a dozen other anachronisms. Celine pointed to a radio that was not of this century, and from its appearance hardly of the last. "I suppose you use that, too."

"No. Too valuable. It's a real rarity. The woman who sold it to me guaranteed that Noah used it for ship-to-shore."

"Why did you really agree to meet with me? You seem to have made up your mind that you won't make more rolfes available on Sky City."

"I did so because I owe you a favor."

"I can't think what."

"I've owed it to you for a long time. If you hadn't come here, Pearl Lazenby might not have been captured. I might never have got my start in electronics, never been able to found the Argos Group."

"But you knew that so far as I was concerned, my visit here would be a waste of time. You'd already decided that you wouldn't provide the rolfes."

"I never said that."

"Would you meet with Wilmer Oldfield and Astarte Vjansander, and hear what they have to say?"

"Waste of time. I know what they told Nick Lopez. Crazy. Somebody out at Alpha Centauri decided humans were a nuisance, so they deliberately destroyed a whole stellar system and made an impossible supernova just to zap us. That about it?"

"There's more to it than that." But it was disturbingly close to Star and Wilmer's view.

Rolfe was grinning down at her from his perch on the chair arm. "I'm sure there's more. I don't need to hear it, because the whole idea is pure bullshit. You may believe it, but on this one *you're* the person who's not rational. And I'll tell you why you're not. Fucking scrambles the brain, and you used to fuck old Wilmer."

Celine wanted to say, *How on earth do you know* that? Her second thought, *That was nearly thirty years ago!* was not much better.

She said, "What about Nick Lopez? He heard Wilmer, and he believed him. Are you telling me Lopez fucked Wilmer Oldfield, too?"

"I wouldn't put it past him. But I think he's more interested in fucking Oldfield's little black chippie Vjansander, even though she's female. Wouldn't you agree?"

Celine stood up. "I'm leaving. I have work to do. This is a stupid waste of time."

"Maybe not. Sit down. Forget who's screwing who, and what I believe and don't believe. I might be willing to provide what you say you need—if the terms are right."

"What terms? Money?"

"No—though I do run a business." Rolfe strained forward, eyes gleaming. In intensity there was little to choose between the eager man and the carnosaur heaving at its chain. "I do want something, and it's not money. Get it for me, and you'll have rolfes for Sky City. All the rolfes you want."

"Why didn't you ask Lopez? He controls more of the world's resources than I do."

"Not this particular resource. I want land—this land, here where we sit and all around us. From ground level to the center of the Earth. I'm willing to pay, but the United States has to deed it to me for my lifetime plus fifty years."

"What do you want it for?"

"That's my business. But I have to be totally outside U.S. laws and U.S. justice. I must be able to do what I like, on it and in it—and with whatever lies within it."

Celine glanced at the chained carnosaur. Genetic combination work of that kind was not easy. Within the United States it was also tightly controlled and monitored. If Gordy Rolfe had performed the gene mix himself, without licenses or oversight, he was already in violation of a score of statutes. Celine could remember no recent applications for similar experiments.

But why not go offshore, to any of a dozen Golden Ring labs that would happily do the work and deliver the results?

Because a crippled, wizened man enjoyed playing God? That she could believe. But she suspected a stronger motive. This underground stronghold was where Gordy Rolfe had been raised. It was his home, his fortress, his sanctuary. He wanted a guarantee that he could never be made to leave, for any reason.

"How much land are we talking about?"

"A circle of four miles, centered on the schoolhouse. There are no occupied houses, and I have checked ownership. Every landowner has already agreed to sell. The Argos Group is ready to make final purchase."

"I assume you realize that you can't be outside U.S. jurisdiction unless you are counted as a foreign territory. That's difficult to arrange legally."

"Difficult, but it happens all the time."

"Between countries, not individuals."

"I don't want you telling me how hard it is. I'm telling you how it has to be. You get me the land, you get more and better rolfes. Otherwise, forget it."

An independent country, completely surrounded by a single other country. There were precedents. Lesotho. Vatican City. More recently, Basque and Kurdistan. The area that Rolfe was demanding was tiny, but the political problems would be immense. Even the Indian nations on U.S. territory were subject to most U.S. laws. Celine began a mental count of the different Cabinet-level departments involved: State, Commerce, Interior, Agriculture, Defense, Transportation. After six she gave up. Congress would have to agree, and that might be the biggest hurdle. If it could be done at all, it would probably take years.

"I don't know. The best I can promise you is that I'll try. But it won't happen overnight." There was the understatement of the century. "Nothing in government happens fast."

"One reason I'd never work there."

"We need the rolfes at once."

"Then you're lucky I'm not the government. I'm willing to deliver. And I'm willing to wait for your part."

Celine stared at him in amazement. "Are you implying that you'll make the rolfes available?"

"Sounds like it, don't you think?" Rolfe lifted himself laboriously from the arm of the chair and wandered away behind the desk. "You do your bit," he said over his shoulder, "and I'll arrange a first shipment for three days from now. One other thing, though. These rolfes will have new circuits in them, still unprotected by patents. You tell your people to keep their hands off. No opening up. No examination of the entrails."

"I see no difficulty with that."

"Then we're all settled."

"You don't want something in writing from me?"

"Saying what?" He was lifting a cage from the stack, picking it up as though it was almost too heavy for him. Why didn't he tell the rolfes to lift it?

He went on, "Suppose you did give me a piece of paper. What could you say? 'I, Celine Tanaka, promise to do my best to get for Gordy Rolfe the land that he wants.' That's not worth shit in a court of law. You know it. But it's all you can offer."

"I will do my best."

"And I'm accepting that you will. So everything's fine."

Celine doubted that. Everything had been too easy. What had she missed? Rolfe went on, as though the discussion of rolfes and land rights was over and done with, "While you're here I want to show you something. See what I've got?"

The communications center was buzzing again to indicate an incoming call. He continued to ignore it. He turned a knob on the top of the cage and the slits on its front widened. Celine saw white whiskers and a pink questing nose.

"It's—a rat." She felt ridiculous. "Isn't it?"

"Sort of. Actually, it's a hundred and twenty rats." He lifted the cage with a great effort and carried it toward the leashed carnosaur. He paused out of reach, lowered the cage, and carefully pushed it forward. The scaly head dipped to peer in through the slits and the creature snuffled noisily.

Gordy Rolfe nodded approvingly. "The rats haven't been fed for a long time. Neither has the minirex. Rats are one of his favorite foods. If he could get at them, they'd be doomed. Small mammal against big dinosaur. A one-pounder against a ninety-pound meat-eater. You'd think the mammal would have no chance. Agreed?"

Celine said nothing. If Gordy Rolfe was losing his sanity, he might have any unspeakable thing in mind.

"No opinion?" Rolfe asked. "Well, let's find out."

"Whatever it is, I don't want to see it," Celine said loudly.

Rolfe took no notice. He touched a series of buttons on a device clipped to the belt of his jumpsuit. The green restraining muzzle on the carnosaur clicked open and fell to the ground. The animal leaned back on its thick haunches and opened its mouth wide. The tongue appeared—a gleaming leathery strip of black with a delicate forked end. Inch-long white teeth stood out against the mottled red-and-black background of the roof of the mouth.

Celine resisted the urge to back away. The carnosaur was still safely held by the thick chain. But it was strong. When it lowered its head and butted at the front of the cage, the solid frame dented.

"He really wants those rats," Rolfe said happily. "He can smell them, and he knows they're his dinner. You'd be a candidate for dinner, too, if he could get at you."

His fingers were again at the controller on his belt. There was a whirring of an electric motor and the front of the cage lifted. A single gray rat darted out and paused, a front paw raised. Before it could move, the minisaur swooped. It rose with the rat impaled on its long teeth, squeaking and wriggling in agony. Blood ran down the blunt jaw. The minisaur's head snapped back sharply. The rat was tossed in the air, caught, and swallowed in a single gulp.

"You might expect the rest of the rats to huddle in the cage," Rolfe said cheerily. He moved a little closer to Celine. "Or maybe you think they ought to come out and try to run away. That seems like the smart thing to do. The minirex is so much bigger and stronger than they are, it outmasses all of them put together. Worse than that, their teeth can't penetrate the armored scales. And the minirex can only reach to the limit of its chain. What would you do, Madam President, if you were the rats? Would you run away?"

Celine was too fascinated and horrified to answer. There was a moment of utter stillness, then the rats emerged all at once from the cage and moved across the floor like a gray tide. Rather than fleeing from the minisaur they were heading straight at it.

The saurian took a step back, so that the chain did not hamper its movements. The great head dipped and came up with two rats between its jaws. The minisaur growled, crunched, and swallowed. By that time the wave of rats had reached the taloned feet. They swarmed up the powerful tail and thick legs, heading for the belly and the head.

The carnosaur gave a deep, coughing roar. It flailed its tail violently from side to side, hurling a dozen rats away in all directions. A couple hit the wall and dropped maimed or unconscious, but the rest landed, turned, and at once headed back. By that time another score of rats had climbed as far as the softer wrinkled leather of the neck and were clinging there with teeth and claws. A shake of the head dislodged many, but half a dozen held on tenaciously. The short, withered arms of the carnosaur reached up to claw most of them away.

But not all. A rat at the back of the scaled neck was able to hold on through another shake of the head, climb higher, and claw its way forward until it reached an eye. It tried to sink its teeth into the eyelid, but it was batted away at the last moment by a forearm. Rats lay strewn on all sides, limbs and backs broken.

The carnosaur roared its blood lust and defiance, and ducked low to grab and swallow a crippled rat.

"Too soon for a victory feast, my friend," Rolfe said softly. "They're coming again. Watch out now."

Another rat had bitten into the softer hide below the chin and held on through all the shaking of head and body. When the carnosaur raised its head to roar again, the rat scampered up the side of the head, plunged its fangs into a ridge of scaly tissue above the eye, and clawed at the delicate surface of the left eye with its forepaws.

The carnosaur reached up and knocked the rat clear, but its left eye was bloody. At the same time another tormentor had found the right eye. It bit ferociously into the eyelid, hung with its weight supported by its fangs, and scrabbled with taloned paws at the eye itself. It too was brushed away by a forearm, but another bleeding wound was left behind.

Meanwhile, a horde of rats had climbed the legs and converged on the softest part of the belly. They hung there, tearing at the leathery skin and at the area of the hidden genitals.

The carnosaur could not see them or catch them easily with its short forearms. They tore and chewed, opening a three-inch tear in the skin that widened with every bite. In agony, the carnosaur crouched low on its hind legs and shook like a dog emerging from water.

It was less effective than before. The rats were learning. When the shaking began they gave up any attempt to deepen the wound and waited, clinging with fangs and claws. As soon as the shaking stopped they went back to work. Any thrown clear that could still move ran back and began another ascent of the living mountain. Their goal was the soft belly and neck, but they bit as they climbed, stripping off scales and gnawing at the skin beneath.

The carnosaur collapsed, flat onto its chest. Most of the rats were quick enough to dash clear, but an unlucky half-dozen were squashed beneath the leathery body and the hard floor.

"Not a great move," Rolfe said softly. "I wouldn't have done that if I were you. Get up, or you've lost."

The rats were much quicker than their opponent. While the minisaur still struggled to roll over so that its powerful tail and legs could lift it upright, the rats attacked again. Thirty of them went for the mouth and belly and genitals. A dozen others took advantage of the change in the carnosaur's position and tackled the head, ripping at the eyelids and at the exposed surface of the eyes themselves.

The carnosaur at last reared upright, but it was damaged. It possessed plenty of energy and defiance, but now it gave up any attempt to eat the rats. It tried only to dislodge them from its body and trample them beneath its powerful feet. Blood and aqueous humor was oozing from the torn eyes. More blood ran freely from a severed vein low on the belly, where the wall of the abdomen had been broached. A gray bulge of intestine was visible. The rats tugged at that with their fangs, pulling it farther, tearing pieces off and swallowing them.

Celine stared in horror. "They're eating it *alive*."

"Yeah. What did you expect them to do? Kill it, cook it, and wait for steak sauce?" Rolfe was edging close, as close as he could without coming within striking range of the carnosaur. The animal had begun a low growl of anguish.

Celine's feelings about the minisaur changed from fear to pity. "Shoot it. You must have some way to kill it quickly." She wished she had brought a gun herself—every one of her security detail carried weapons, she could have borrowed one easily. "You can't let it suffer like that."

"What do you want me to do?" Rolfe was smiling. "Go in and strangle it, the sort of mercy killing you offer to somebody being burned at the stake? You can try that if you want to. I won't. I hate to work with my hands." He held up his blackened fingers.

"Then shoot it. This is horrible."

"I don't keep guns here." He was studying the carnosaur. "Anyway, it won't be long now. The small mammals always beat the dinosaurs."

Eyeless and partly eviscerated, with bleeding wounds all around the neck and mouth, the beast still stood upright, but it was terribly wounded. As Celine watched, a rat wriggled out from a gaping hole in the belly. The rodent was smeared all over with blood and carried an eight-inch length of greasy intestine in its mouth. It dropped to the floor and hurried away.

"Even if you don't have a gun, there must be a way to kill it." Celine stared around, looking for anything that might serve as a knife, a club, a spear.

The floor of the chamber close to the carnosaur was a nightmare of blood and guts and dying rats. She dared not go too near. The blinded beast was sinking forward, unsteady on its legs. The uninjured rats knew. Now that the fight was over they stood at a safe distance, quietly waiting. The animal was still dangerous. The jaws, covered with a froth of saliva, snapped at imaginary enemies. The powerful tail thrashed the floor, flattening any rat too injured to crawl clear. Celine got the message: Pity it, but do not go near it.

Bizarrely, the little cleaning machines were already busy, removing the bodies of dead rats and wiping up blood and slime and fragments of entrails. The machines could be damaged by minisaur jaws, but a swipe of the tail simply knocked them a few yards away. They started right back.

Gordy Rolfe's gray eyes were bright behind the eyeglasses. If he heard Celine's words, they had no effect.

She surveyed the rest of the chamber. *Weapons.* Anything could be a weapon. She hurried across the room to the workbench. Most of the tools were too light or too short. She wanted something heavy and long enough to be used at a distance.

The biggest object on the bench was a huge pair of cutting shears designed to clip sheet metal or bolts. She hefted the tool and decided it was too cumbersome. The second-best was a four-pound steel hammer with a long handle, flat on its main striking face but with a three-inch punch spike sticking out in the other direction.

Celine lifted it. One hand would be possible, but two hands were better. She walked back across the room, swinging the hammer up and over her head to get the balance.

Was she really going to do this, when she had already told herself that it would be total folly to go too near?

Quickly, or not at all. She moved forward. She was now within the carnosaur's reach if the animal lunged to the end of the chain. The head swung in her direction. It could not see her, but could it smell her?

Quickly. One shot was all you got.

She took another step forward. Hammer up, above her head. Down with the spike, into the carnosaur's skull, between and behind the ruined eyes—blood and evil-smelling spittle, spraying her face and hair and clothing—a desperate leap backward, away.

She was barely in time. The carnosaur, from intent or muscular reflex, plunged in her direction. It was halted by the chain.

The head and torso fell backward at the same time as the legs jerked forward. Celine saw taloned, three-toed feet flex just inches away from her belly as the body convulsed and the legs stretched to their full length. For a moment the carnosaur stood balanced on the thick tail, then it slowly collapsed.

As the final death spasm began, the scaled head turned again in Celine's direction. The hammer spike was still embedded there. She saw that in her terror she had hit hard enough to fracture and split the whole skull.

She saw that Gordy Rolfe was looking at her. He was laughing. "Hell of a whack. I wouldn't like you to get mad with me. But you've got a nerve, killing my minirex."

Celine wiped carnosaur gore and spittle from her eyes and lips. "That was monstrous and unnatural. I had to put the poor beast out of its misery."

"It would have died anyway in a few minutes. As for unnatural, you're completely wrong. What we saw is totally natural. That's how animals die in the wild. Once they get old or sick, something drags them down and eats them."

Gordy Rolfe was loving every minute. Celine knew it from the pleasure in his glittering eyes and the flush of color on his pallid cheeks. Suddenly, all she wanted to do was get away from him and back to the surface.

"You leaving?" Rolfe watched her intently as she turned toward the circular exit hatch.

Celine did not trust herself to speak. She nodded and kept moving.

"Well, I guess the fun's over, anyway." Rolfe reached for the controller at his waist. "One more bit of cleanup to do, then I'll see you on your way."

He pressed a sequence of keys. The room filled with high-pitched squeaks. Celine saw scores of rats, their gray skins sparking and smoking, contort into unnatural shapes and collapse to the floor.

"Can't have them running loose, can we? There's no saying where they'd get to after they'd eaten." Rolfe glanced at Celine. "Don't worry, I only disposed of the ones running free. The ones in the cages are fine. And the dead ones go to the habitat, so they won't be wasted."

He led the way down the spiral staircase. Celine followed, very slowly. She felt weak in the knees. Although she had wiped her face, the reek of carnosaur blood saturated her hair and clothing.

Gordy went with her to the elevators. "Don't forget our deal," he said. "I'll keep my end; a set of rolfes will be on the way to Sky City before the end of the week. By that time I expect to hear what you're doing about my land."

"I'll work on it." Celine forced the words out and pressed the elevator button. She could not wait for the doors to close and the car to ascend. She craved fresh air and sanity. When the slow-rising elevator at last opened on the highest level, she found Chesley Reiter and the rest of his group waiting. One look at her, and the chief of security grabbed her arm.

"It's all right, Ches, I'm fine." She gently freed herself. "None of this is my blood."

"But . . . Madam President?"

He was inviting an explanation. Celine was not ready to give one. She walked past them, through the schoolhouse and on into the open air. It seemed that she had been underground for many hours, and she expected to find it was night outside the building. Instead she walked out into the twilight gloom of an early evening downpour. The thunderstorm had come and gone, leaving in its place a steady rain.

Celine turned her face upward, welcoming the drops. It would be a long time before she felt clean again.

The armored car stood with the door open and the driver waiting. Celine nodded to him and climbed in without a word. Before the door closed she was reaching for the telcom unit to call Nick Lopez. He answered so quickly that she suspected he had been waiting by his own unit.

"Rolfe agreed," Celine said at once. "He'll start shipping more up by the end of the week."

"I can't believe it. How did you talk him into it?"

"I don't think I did. I think he has his own reasons for wanting to send rolfes to Sky City, but I can't begin to guess what they are. Nick, I've never had a meeting like that in my whole life. Gordy Rolfe is crazier than you can imagine."

"I told you he was losing it. What did he do? Start lecturing you on the superiority of small mammals?"

"More than that." Celine glanced around the armored vehicle. The rest of the security staff had piled in and the driver was waiting for instructions. "Back to the White House," she said. And, as the car began to roll forward, "Our friend gave me his idea of a practical demonstration."

"Meaning what? With Gordy, I hardly dare to consider the possibilities."

Celine hesitated. Should she tell Nick, when the security staff would be hanging on her every word? Well, why not. They had waited for hours in the rain, probably imagining that she was down there being lavishly entertained by the powerful head of the Argos Group. They might as well learn the truth.

"Did you know he raises dinosaurs down there?"

"He showed them to me. Dwarf varieties, hidden in the jungle around his habitat control room."

"Not always hidden." Celine described the minirex and its battle to the death with the cageful of rats. She omitted only her own role in delivering the coup de grâce to the carnosaur.

Nick Lopez listened without saying a word. The security staff in the car with Celine were equally silent. The vehicle was racing back toward Washington at its highest speed, and the only sound adding to Celine's voice was the soft hiss of fullerene tires over sodden roadway. Recalling the final moments with the carnosaur, she again became aware of the smell of blood and saliva permeating her hair and clothes.

"We just have to hope that he's sane on other matters," she concluded. "Either the rolfes will appear in a few days for shipping up, or they won't."

"How did he sound when you left?"

"Cheerful. Manic. As though we'd been partying together."

"Then I think this might be a good time for me to call him."

"You might not get through, Nick. He ignored calls when I was there."

"I don't think he'll ignore me. I have a special tie line. One other question before we sign off."

"Ask. But keep it short." Celine was swept by a dreadful wave of fatigue. She wanted to put her head back on the padded car seat and go to sleep.

"What's the rest of the story? I've never heard of Gordy Rolfe making a deal just for money. What else is he asking?"

"The land around the habitat, four miles in every direction, for as long as he's alive and half a century more. His own personal paradise." Celine laid her head back and closed her eyes. She could see the carnosaur, eyeless and half gutted, sinking into its death agony. "But you and I might call it hell."

# 22

It was a nightmare from Maddy's childhood. You woke slowly, in near-total darkness, knowing that you were not alone in the room. The thing—the shadowy form of the he-she-it—stood still and silent at the end of the bed. You lay frozen, too scared to move, too scared to scream.

At last you went back to sleep. In the morning you looked and looked, but you found no trace of the phantom.

It was happening now, and you were not a child. You were Maddy Wheatstone, a grown woman with no time for adolescent fantasies. You were no longer in the family home in Edmonton. You were—where?

Maddy struggled to full consciousness. Her eyes were wide open. This was not a dream. The shadow was still there. It loomed by her bedside, leaning over her, shaped like a man.

And she was—oh God, she was on Sky City, where the murderer of a dozen girls wandered free.

Maddy gasped, drew up her legs, and threw herself over the other side of the bed. She grabbed a boot, the only solid object she could find, and stabbed at the wall panel.

The light flashed on. It showed John Hyslop, mouth open and eyes squinted half shut against the glare, standing by the side of the bed.

"John!" Maddy's curiosity was as strong as her relief. "What are you doing in my bedroom in the middle of the night?"

"I'm sorry. I did knock before I came in, but you slept through it. I've been standing here wondering if I ought to wake you."

"For what?" She saw the clock. "It's three in the morning."

He was not just looking at her, he was *staring*. Maddy realized that she was wearing a shorter-than-usual nightgown. Well, that was all right. Let him know what he was missing.

"You did say . . ." he began. "I mean, you did tell me you'd like to see it."

"See what?" Maddy frowned, trying to shift gears.

"Whatever there is to see. When we get under way."

"You mean we're on the move?"

"Very soon. Everything is ready. The boosters fire at four."

"Then of course I want to see it. I'm sorry, John, I shouldn't have snapped at you. Thanks for waking me." She saw his weary eyes. "Have you had any sleep at all?"

"No. I'll sleep when I'm sure everything is all right."

"Don't do another Neirling boost. They're bad for you." Maddy heard the mothering tone in her voice, but it was too late to do anything about that. She went across to the small closet and pulled out pants and a sleeveless top. "I have to dress. You can stay if you like, but if it makes you feel uncomfortable, you should step outside."

Back on Earth she wouldn't have thought to mention it, but different privacy standards applied on Sky City.

"I'll stay." John's mumble could barely be heard.

"Fine." Maddy slipped off her nightgown and pulled on her clothes. She noticed that he kept his back turned the whole time. So much for her girlish charms. As she pulled on her boots she asked, "Where should I go for the best view?"

"Actually, for the first day or so there'll be nothing to see. Sky City will accelerate so slowly, only the observing instruments will tell you that we're leaving orbit."

"You mean I won't even know we've started boosting?"

"Oh, you'll know all right. I hope we don't know too well." John smiled at Maddy's perplexed look, his first smile since the light went on. "The acceleration will be very small, but to push the whole of Sky City we'll be applying thrust to just a dozen areas, and each one's only a couple of meters across."

"Can that be a problem?"

"We're hoping not. Our calculations say we'll be all right. But imagine that you had an enormous dish, and you supported it on a dozen tiny pins around the edge and nowhere else. You'd worry that if the dish were heavy enough, the pins would push right through it. We can't let the local boosters push so hard that they stress the Sky City structure locally beyond what it can stand."

"What happens if the stresses are too great?"

"Well, we'll be watching closely. We won't let it go so far that the plates buckle or the joints fail. But if we have to reduce the thrust, we'll have other problems. The acceleration would have to be smaller, and then all our other schedules for the new particle defense system would have to change."

"I see." Maddy did see—several things. She liked John's hand on her arm, guiding her along. And he was comfortable again, away from the world of naked ladies and back to his stresses and strains and Poisson's ratios and buckling coefficients. "Oh, I forgot. What about the new rolfes? Are they on their way from Earth?"

"Not yet. We're expecting the first ones any day now."

He did not mention that the arrival of the rolfes would remove Maddy's reason for remaining on Sky City. She had called Gordy Rolfe two days ago, prepared to offer logic of her own as to why she ought to remain. Gordy had beaten her to it with his first remark: "Hyslop isn't on the Aten asteroid project anymore."

"I know."

"But you stay there. I want you glued to him tighter than ever. Report to me on his every move."

Gordy had glared at her out of the screen. The scene around him looked like a junkyard, bits and pieces of equipment everywhere. He looked like a junkyard, too, food on his unshaven face and the front of the black jumpsuit, feverish bloodshot eyes and trembling hands.

"But what do I tell Bruno Colombo? I need a reason for staying on Sky City." She knew that Gordy was in the underground habitat, because she could see the circular wall and the dark green plants beyond it.

"Hell, d'you want me to do your job for you? Tell him anything you like. Sweet-talk Hyslop. Smile at him, show him your tits, open your legs, whatever."

"I'm not sure that sort of thing works with Hyslop." *It hasn't so far, and I have been sort of trying. But Gordy can't be trusted with that sort of detail.*

"Fine. It wouldn't work with me, either. Maybe he's the one who should be working for Argos instead of you." Gordy lifted the spindly metal shaft that he was holding in one greasy hand. "All right, here's what you do. You tell them you have to stay up there until all the new rolfes have arrived, just in case they don't work right and you have to fix them. That will give you at least ten days."

"If the rolfes don't work when they arrive, there's not much chance I'll be able to fix them. I'm no great expert when it comes to electronics."

"Tell me news. It won't matter. They'll work exactly as they're supposed to, and you won't have to fix a damn thing."

"How do you know they'll work?"

He snarled at her. Somehow he had managed to get graphite on his front teeth. They were streaked with black. "The rolfes will work perfectly, because I'm making the fucking things. Personally. Now are you happy? Get back to work. Follow Hyslop, watch what he does. Especially if he starts digging into inventory records and delivery schedules, anything that relates to Argos Group activities. If that happens, you call me at once. Anytime."

"Anytime?"

"You heard me. You work twenty-four hours a day, the way I do."

*And look the way you do?* But he was gone before Maddy could be tempted.

In any case, there was no way to track John Hyslop day and night. Nights could have been easy, but sexually he was the most timid man she had ever met. He found her attractive, she felt sure he did, based on the few occasions when they had both let down their guards. But he never made a move. She had gone as far as she could without grabbing him and dragging him into the bedroom. Was that what he needed? It was about all that was left.

He still had his hand on her arm, leading her. They were going "up" toward the central axis of Sky City, and the centrifugal force against which they climbed was steadily dropping.

"Where are you taking me? To the engineering information center?"

"No. There's an observation chamber outside the main body of the city, near the power-generating plant. You'll have the best view from there."

Maddy had learned the basic geometry and jargon of Sky City.

The structure was in orbit around the Earth and at the same time spun around its central axis. That axis always pointed to a fixed direction in space, out toward the cone end of the space shield and Alpha Centauri. The simulation chamber where she and John Hyslop had discovered Lucille DeNorville's mutilated body lay on the "front" side of the city, the side facing toward the shield. The power-generation plant sat on the "back" side, with the bulk of the city between them and the shield to provide better protection from the particle storm.

"We won't be able to see the shield, will we?"

"Part of it will be in your field of view, beyond the edges of the Sky City disk. But I doubt you'll actually be able to see it. It's too tenuous." They had reached the axis, and John was floating her along the broad air-filled tunnel extending beyond the bulk of Sky City in the direction of the power-generation plant. "Don't worry; the shield isn't where the action is. You'll see everything worth seeing from right here."

They had come to a fork in the passageway, a place where on one branch a flat hatch was set into the side of the tunnel. John released Maddy's arm as the hatch began to slide open.

"Won't we need suits?" Maddy had been warned, over and over. *Be careful. Just because you can open a door anywhere on Earth and find air on the other side doesn't mean you can do the same thing on Sky City.*

"They're available for emergencies. But today this whole segment is at pressure."

The hatch slid open. Beyond was the observation chamber, and Maddy could see that a few unsuited people were already there.

"Make yourself comfortable." John glanced at his watch. "Still a few minutes to go. Enjoy the show. The others can answer any questions."

"What about you? Aren't you staying?"

"I'd love to. But I'm on duty back inside." He hesitated, then gave Maddy's arm a gentle pat and stepped back through the hatch. "As a matter of fact, I'm the one who has to make the final decision on whether to move. Without me in the control chamber there'll be no show."

The hatch closed. He was gone. *Follow Hyslop all the time? Right, Gordy. Why don't you tell me how I'm supposed to do that?*

Maddy turned. The observation chamber formed a sphere about

twelve feet across. It was equipped with gimballed seats that could swing in any direction, and most of the wall consisted of large transparent ports. The chamber was so close to free fall that assignment of direction was a matter of convention. "Above" Maddy lay the ugly tangle of the power-generation facility. "Below" her the main body of Sky City obscured the stars and shield.

The people in the chamber had all glanced at Maddy when she appeared, but now they were again looking outward. She was surprised to find that she recognized every one of them. Closest to her were two of Sky City's engineering team. They must be "the others" that John had referred to: Lauren Stansfield, as ladylike and elegantly dressed as ever; beside her, Torrance Harbish, lank-haired and saturnine. They were clearly present for some official purpose, because they sat by an array of screens and monitoring devices. In front of the two engineers sat Wilmer Oldfield and Astarte Vjansander, their heads close. Finally, in front of them, hunched so that his chin rested on his chest, was Seth Parsigian. When Maddy moved forward to sit next to him he turned and glared.

She had done what he asked her to, wandering endlessly around the dark corridors and hidden byways of Sky City. With no apparent results, but that was not her fault.

"I thought you were going back to Earth," she said softly.

"Likewise." He gave her a quick glance. "An' we're both still here. I think they stuck all the Earthsiders out here so we can't get in the way when they goose the whole place. Look, sometime you and me gotta talk some more."

"What about?"

"Stuff. New information. But we can't do it here and now." He jerked his head backward. "Too many ears."

Maddy doubted that. Wilmer Oldfield and Astarte Vjansander were making enough noise to cover anything that Seth said.

They were arguing. Anyone sitting in front of them had no choice but to listen. Maybe *that* was why Seth was so annoyed.

"Stands ter reason," Astarte was saying. "Yer can calculate and theorize and speculate 'til your eyeballs pop, but you still won't *know* 'less you measure. We have to do it."

"Do you think anyone but us cares?" Wilmer hissed. "Look at it from their point of view. We say, you have to build a system to detect and deflect particle bundles."

"They do, too. Or they're dead."

"Of course they are. So they listen to us, and they buy what we say, and they change all their plans. What do you think they'll do if now we say, by the way, deflect some of them particle bundles but not all of 'em because we need some? You can try that if you want, but not me. You'll be lucky if they don't grab you and whale your fat black butt."

"Yer think you're the only one allowed ter do that, don't yer, you dirty old bugger? You're a fossil, Wilmer Oldfield. You're all mouth and beer gut. Yer stopped thinking twenty years ago, and you don't have the brains and nerve of a paralytic parrot."

"Better a paralytic parrot than a jumped-up outback madonna who thinks if she just wiggles her tits in Bruno Colombo's face she can talk him into anything."

"Not Bruno Colombo, you soft old ponce. I said *Nick Lopez*."

"Colombo, Lopez, makes no difference. For starters, look at the bloody energy problem—"

Maddy leaned over to Seth. "What's all that about?"

"Technical discussion." Seth stared gloomily out of the port, to where a sunlit Earth loomed thirty times the size of a full Moon. "Far as I can tell, she wants to slow down a few of the bundles and catch them. Then they'd be able to study 'em and find out what sort of structure the bundles have. He's telling her no one would ever agree. I'm with him. I want to get rid of particle bundles, not sit an' play with 'em."

The musical chime of a bell interrupted his final words. It came from an invisible address system. "Two minutes," said John Hyslop's voice. "Station One?"

There was a five-second silence, then an unfamiliar man's reply: "Station One ready."

"Confirmed. Station Two?"

"Station Two all set." Lauren Stansfield's voice came from directly behind Maddy, and a fraction of a second later the words were repeated from the address system.

"Confirmed. Station Three?"

As the count went on, Maddy wondered where the other stations were located. Some of them, from what John had said, must be at the points where the thrustors would fire; engineers there would be alert for buckling plates or failing seals. Lauren Stansfield and Torrance Harbish were doing the same thing, monitoring from their bird's-eye view on the extended central axis.

"All stations confirmed. Twenty seconds."

Maddy listened closely to John's voice. It was calm, but with an odd undercurrent of excitement. She thought, *That weirdo, he's enjoying this. If I were a failing component, I'd get more of his attention than I do now. Engineers!*

The soft chime of the bell was back, counting off the final seconds. Everyone in the observation chamber fell silent. All of them were looking in the same direction: out and down, to where the mirror-matter thrustors sat on Sky City's broad disk.

The countdown was over. Maddy followed their gaze and saw nothing. That was surely the site of one of the thrustors; John had pointed it out to her on the Sky City hologram only two days ago. So why wasn't it working?

She stared again, and realized it was. Not the gaudy orange flare of rockets that you became used to in launches to Earth orbit, but a thin, near-invisible line of blue plasma stabbing out from the thrustor. Unless you followed it from its source you would never know it was there.

Was that *it*? Was that frail, gossamer strand of light, with eleven more like it, supposed to hoist the million-ton bulk of Sky City a hundred thousand kilometers to the end of the shield? The idea seemed preposterous.

Maddy turned. Lauren Stansfield and Torrance Harbish were calmly working their equipment. John Hyslop's voice came again over the address system. "Station Seven, we're showing an anomaly."

"Correct." It was a man's voice, one that Maddy did not recognize. "We have structural give in the main support beam. There's no danger of overall failure, but it's throwing the line of thrust off by a couple of degrees. Do you want us to try to do something about it locally?"

"I don't think so. Just wait a moment." There was a pause of a few seconds, then John's voice again. "General rotation will average most of it out. If we have to, we'll compensate with a reduced thrust on the opposite side. Hold as you are."

"We're holding."

"Station Two? Do you see anything?"

Torrance Harbish said into his throat microphone, "We verify Station Seven off-line thrust. Everything else is nominal."

"Noted. You may switch to automatic recording."

Harbish said, "Changeover in process." And then, in a less formal tone, "Good show, John. We're wrapping up here. Expect us in the control room in about five minutes."

Two more minutes, and he and Lauren Stansfield had set the scopes to automatic mode and left. Wilmer Oldfield and Astarte Vjansander followed, still bickering. Maddy turned to Seth Parsigian. "You want to talk?"

"Not yet." His sallow face was thoughtful. "Got some stuff I have to do first. I'll come to your rooms when I'm ready to chit-chat."

"If you do come, don't do it late at night—I found out how much I hate that. And let me tell you how to reach my quarters."

"Don't need to; I already know. But I got a question for you. Have you been workin' on the Argos Group deliveries?"

"Not up here. I worked deliveries down on Earth, years ago."

"That's all right, then. See you." Seth slipped out of his seat and was gone.

Maddy was alone in the observation chamber. She could go back to her rooms and wait for Seth, but she lacked the will to do so. This was a better place for thinking, here with the great wheel of Sky City below her and the silent stars above.

There was plenty to think about. Far beyond Sky City, out beyond the shield and more than four light-years away, lay the source of the particle storm. Maddy was in no danger. In principle, particle bundles spit out by the Alpha Centauri supernova could hit Sky City right this very minute, and she would be protected by the bulk of the massive structure.

Each particle bundle averaged four trillion separate nuclei, but each bundle was still minute, its mass less than a billionth of a gram. Even so, each one packed enormous energy. Maddy had heard Astarte's casual comment a few days earlier. "Yeah, they're little, but yer don't want ter underestimate them. They're really smoking. Traveling close to a tenth of light speed—not really relativistic, but getting up there—and energy goes like the *square* of velocity. Every one of the little buggers packs as much of a wallop as a half-gram pellet traveling at a third of a kilometer of a second—that's the speed of a bullet as it comes out of the muzzle of a handgun. A particle bundle can do a lot more damage to human tissue than a bullet, too, because the particles in it are all charged. If the bundle comes apart inside you when it hits, that's still worse. We still don't know if that will happen or not."

Maddy was protected by Sky City, but Earth was not. She looked to her left, where the hazy globe hung in the heavens. She could see the moving day-night boundary of the terminator, but the planet itself seemed exactly the same size as before. She held up her hand and measured the width of Earth between thumb and first finger. The space city was leaving its orbit, but you would never know by looking. Acceleration was imperceptible. It would be days before Earth began to shrink in the sky.

And yet Maddy had the uneasy feeling that she was already infinitely far away. Out here she had been thrown into the company of people whose dreams and ambitions and daily lives were so far removed from her own that they seemed incomprehensible. Odder yet, listening to them had made her own ambitions just as hard to understand. For the first time since she was fifteen years old, Maddy was not consumed by the immediate pressures of the here and now. She had been provided with a fatal indulgence: time to think.

Did she *want* to be the head of the Argos Group? Would she take Gordy Rolfe's job, even if he (unlikely thought) went down on his knees and begged her?

A month ago, she had thought she had the best job in the world and Gordy was a genius. He was still a genius in electronics and robotics, but more and more he was also an obvious lunatic. She had spent the past nine years trying to get close to him, doing whatever pleased him, clawing her way up the Argos Group ladder so that she could be a lunatic, too.

Surely there had to be more to life than that.

Drearily Maddy lifted out of her chair and began the solitary trek back to her rooms. The four o'clock blues. They came as easily in space as back on Earth. A few hours of sleep would probably make a difference.

After that, sooner or later, would come the unsought meeting with Seth Parsigian. They had roamed Sky City together, with no result. What else did he want from her—and could she wriggle out of it?

Probably not. Maddy saw before her the rough-cut hair, the bullet head, and the wary brown eyes. It was a close call, but in his own way Seth perched as far up the tree of lunacy as Gordy Rolfe.

# 23

**From the private diary of Oliver Guest.**

I agreed to contact Seth Parsigian only in an emergency. There has been no emergency, and it is eight days since we last spoke to each other.

For all I know, Seth could be dead, although I would hate to be the one who sought to bring about that event. Seth is a man with a tenacious hold on life.

Where is he? Presumably he is still on Sky City, but I cannot even be sure of that. Occasionally I have donned the RV helmet, and been rewarded only with a view of the interior of his apartment. The jacket has obviously been left to hang on the wall. Wherever Seth is, and whatever he is doing, he feels no desire to share his experiences with me.

That is an attitude with which I sympathize. I am impatient for results on the Sky City murders, but were Seth to call me at this instant I would be able to report negligible progress in my thinking. I know the murderer, yet I cannot suggest a foolproof method of capture.

In truth, my thinking has been embarrassingly limited about the whole problem. My mind has been otherwise engaged. Although I can point to no one overriding concern, we have seen several distracting events.

The term *we* offers its own ambiguities. The meaning extends from the single elevated personage—"We are not amused"—to a family or local group, and thence the whole human race—"We are not alone."

My comment concerning recent distracting events does not refer to our race, or, more correctly, our species, although it might well have. One might assume that the collective human mind of Earth would at this time be concentrated on the single issue of its own possible demise. The great swarm of particles generated by the Alpha Centauri supernova advances steadily, and no human power can halt or slow it. The most recent reports point to the arrival of a devastating sleet from space sooner than expected, just a few weeks or months from now. A new way of protecting Earth will be implemented, Sky City is already on the move toward the end of the space shield, the timing of everything is touch and go, and we (the species) could be wiped out or find our civilization sent back millennia.

And so one looks around the world. Are people consumed by contemplation of cosmic catastrophe, obsessed by their own potential demise?

I scanned the news leads this morning. Look on these words, ye mighty, and despair.

### Scientists Prove Alpha Centauri Supernova Was "Hand of God"

According to Star Vjansander, sexy young Australian superphysicist, a superbeing created the 2026 supernova of Alpha Centauri. The superbeing is being carried here in a cloud of superparticles and will shortly reach Earth.

### Ghost of Lucille DeNorville Haunts Sky City

Psychic Marion Mentorian, in contact with the soul of the murder victim whose body was recently discovered, is asking funding from the wealthy DeNorville family to visit Space City and reveal the identity of the killer.

### Clones of Bill Gates, Queen Victoria, Announce Plans to Marry

"True love knows no boundaries of space or time," declares the smitten pair.

### Energy from Nothing, Electricity "Too Cheap to Meter"

Inventor Raoul Segura today revealed a new form of engine that draws its power directly from the cosmic consciousness. He promises an era of "endless plenty and universal wealth" as soon as final tests are completed and government backing is guaranteed.

### The Missing Money: Where Did It Go?

Officials of the Golden Ring consortium Fortune Today pronounce themselves baffled by vanished assets that apparently exceed the total net worth of the organization. They promise a full investigation and a worldwide search for missing financial executive Lloyd Persil.

In truth, we (the species we) can tolerate but a little reality. I wonder if we (the individual *we* that is I) can tolerate much more.

In the last eight days, Paula and Amity reached menarche, apparently simultaneously; Gloria announced her undying love for and intention to marry Michael O'Brien, a witless seventeen-year-old from Derrybeg; and Beth, Dawn, and Willa disappeared from the castle.

For Paula and Amity it was a natural and irreversible event. In the case of Gloria, I suspected that sanity would reassert itself in a month or two—she so surpasses her professed lifelong love in wit and intellect that it would be like marrying a monkey.

Therefore, the last must be first. I had to concentrate on Beth, Dawn, and Willa. It was not until midday that I realized the three ten-year-olds were not present at lunch. Missing a meal was, especially for Willa, an unprecedented event and one that immediately caused me concern.

For most people in the world, this was a problem with a simple and immediate solution. If I forwarded the girls' digital DNA records to GSARS, the Global Search-And-Rescue System would tune its network to those signatures and use the body resonance patterns to locate each missing person to within twenty feet.

There were, however, obvious problems. GSARS was integrated into GGDB, the General Global Data Base, and the complete DNA patterns of my darlings might already be stored there. What alarm bells would go off if the genome of a ten-year-old matched, nucleotide base by nucleotide base, the genome of a pubescent girl who had been murdered more than thirty years ago?

I dared not take that risk. After a hurried lunch the other girls fanned out across the countryside to begin the search. I stayed behind, filled with my own presentiments. Had I made a mistake? Should I have asked for help from GSARS?

The call, when it came, was as good and yet as bad as it could be.

"We found 'em. They're all right, but they've got stuck on the cliffs. We'll need a rope." It was Gloria, red hair darkened by rain and eyebrows beaded with droplets. "Come on. Be sure to put your coat on—it's pissing down out there."

I had never told the girls of my irrational fear of heights. They would expect my immediate presence and assistance. I donned coat and hat and left the castle by the scullery entrance on the seaward side. Otranto Castle is thick-walled and solid, and when I stepped from its sheltering bulk I realized for the first time the severity of the weather. A strong westerly was blowing, driving sheets of rain at me horizontally. As I walked west it was almost impossible to see where I was going.

That was, I suspect, the only thing that allowed me to walk as far as I did. I knew that ahead stood the three-hundred-foot headland with its sheer drop to the waters of the Atlantic. I told myself that it was not yet close; I had a long way to go before I got to the edge.

In certain areas, however, I lack the power of self-deception. I came to a point where, try as I might, I could not force my legs to carry me forward. I could hear the wind, howling as it breasted the cliff after its three-thousand-mile journey across the open Atlantic. I could smell brine and seaweed. I struggled to take another step, failed, and sank down on the sodden turf. It took a supreme effort even to look forward. I peered into the driving rain and saw my darlings, a tight cluster of them, perilously close to the edge of the precipice. They were perhaps two hundred yards away, and I could not discern what they were doing.

I stood up, resolved to take one more step, and again sank to the ground. My thoughts, like my legs, lost the power to move. An endless interval passed before I heard Bridget's voice.

"We got 'em," she said cheerfully. "Hauled 'em up one at a time on the rope. They'd been bird-nesting, the idiots. They ought to have had more sense in this weather."

I recalled the cluster of girls I had seen at work. "You all pulled? That's what I saw you doing?"

"All except Paula and Amity. They've started their period and they're having cramps." Bridget reached out. "Here, let me give you a hand. You came quite a long way."

She is perhaps the strongest of all my darlings. She reached out and hoisted me easily to my feet.

I felt a great weariness. "I'm sorry. You don't know this, but I have a real problem with heights."

She stared at me. "Of *course* we know you can't stand heights. We've all known that for years."

I was saved from a reply by the arrival of the other girls in a great chattering throng. Dawn, Willa, and Beth were loudly defensive, insisting that they could have easily climbed back up the cliff by themselves anytime they wanted to. The others complained about being dragged out into the rain to save a set of senseless dummies.

I walked along in the middle of them. No one spoke to me, and I spoke to no one. But I noticed that they all watched me closely until we were safely inside the castle.

"Hot drinks all round, I think," Paula said. And then to me, "You didn't call GSARS, did you?"

"I did not."

"Good. I bet they'd have made us all fill out their stupid reports. None of us wanted that. You go on into your study. One of us will bring your drink."

She was humoring me. She knew about GSARS, which I had not realized. Gloria had insisted that I put on my coat before I left the castle. Bridget had kindly told me that I had come "quite a long way" toward the cliff. Yes, they indeed knew of my terror of heights.

These were my darlings, sheltered from reality all of their short lives. I wondered, what else did they know?


It is late on the evening of the same day.

When the excitement of the rescue at last died down I felt infinitely weary. My brain felt as though it was simply ticking over, barely able to keep my vital functions in operation. I lay back in my favorite chair and thought about Beth, Dawn, and Willa, and of the Global Search-And-Rescue System that I had chosen not to use.

The modern search-and-rescue system is a direct descendant of one introduced almost a hundred years ago. In its original form, a constellation of satellites in low Earth orbit picked up signals sent out by stranded travelers or others in distress on land or sea. By analyzing frequency shifts and travel times, the location of the emitted signal could be determined and a rescue party dispatched. The old system was a passive one—the spacecraft flew overhead and listened for a signal.

Suppose, however, that the person in trouble could not send a distress signal because they lacked the necessary equipment, or because that equipment had been damaged. With the original system, such a person could not be located.

The modern version of search-and-rescue came into worldwide use twenty years before the supernova (it languished, not surprisingly, for ten years after Alpha C, when all low-orbit satellites ceased to operate). Rather than a passive system, requiring that a distress signal be sent out, today's is an active one. The satellites, sweeping around the Earth, send out tuned signals of their own. These are designed to stimulate a response from a human body—a *specific* human body. The return signal indicates the exact location of that body. It is no longer necessary to carry a transmitter in order to use the Global Search-and-Rescue System.

Suddenly I was wide awake. Argument by analogy can be dangerous, but it can also be fruitful. In our quest to catch the Sky City murderer, Seth and I had so far acted passively. We were the equivalent of the old search-and-rescue system. Like it, we could not succeed unless a signal was transmitted: The killer must initiate an unprompted action.

That was not about to happen. Our murderer did not need to kill again and would do nothing.

Passive procedure would not suffice. Like the modern search-and-rescue operation, we had to move to an active approach. We must generate a signal able to force a reaction. The murderer must be made to respond to a stimulus created by us.

I put on the RV helmet and called Seth Parsigian. At last I had something that could fairly be termed an emergency.

He was wearing the hidden earphone, and answered at once with, "This better be good, Doc. I've been digging into Sky City operations, lookin' for odd stuff that might point to the killer."

"Did you discover anything?"

"No." His voice seemed to have an added delay. Sky City was on the move outward from Earth. "But I'm finding somethin' else that's interestin' in the data records."

"Events relevant to the Sky City murders?"

"If they are, I don't see how."

"Then they can wait. I know of a way to flush our murderer out of hiding."

I described my thoughts on active versus passive procedures, and I made my proposal.

Seth was silent for a long time. I wished I could see his face, but apparently he was not in his room. I was offered the usual annoying view of an empty apartment. The RV jacket must be hanging in its usual position on the wall.

"You're makin' some awful big assumptions," he said at last. "Yeah, Doris Wu's body is still missing. But how do you know it was chucked out into space?"

"It's been over six months since she vanished."

"It was close to that for Lucille DeNorville, and she still turned up."

"I have explained why it was necessary for the murderer that Lucille's body not be permanently lost. That argument does not apply to Doris Wu. And remember where Doris disappeared: level hundred, at the Sky City perimeter. You yourself offered the suggestion that she had been murdered and dropped out into space. Dump her outside, you said, and centrifugal force would carry her out and away. And you commented that would be pretty risky if any evidence had been left on her."

"We got no reason to think it was."

"I doubt very much that the murderer was so careless. But we are operating here at the level of doubt and psychology, not proven fact. Suppose that you were the murderer. You feel somewhat secure, comfortable in the knowledge that months have passed without threat of discovery. Now comes the news: The body of one of your victims has been found out in space. All the others are accounted for, so this is the last possible source of danger to you. Would you not feel an intense urge to confirm that no physical evidence links you to that newly discovered body?"

"I would. But suppose I knew that Doris Wu's body wasn't in space? Suppose I knew that I'd done somethin' else with her—chopped her up, or burned her. Maybe I ate her."

"This situation is disgusting enough without your adding to it. If you, as murderer, know that Doris Wu is not in space, then you also know that the report of her discovery is bogus. My plan would fail."

"I think it will anyway. It sounds real dodgy to me."

"Feel free to offer an alternative."

"You got me there. All right, I guess we try it. But we need some help from people up here."

"That is your department, not mine."

"I know a way we might work it. But we can't do it yet. We hafta wait a few days 'til things settle down a bit on Sky City. Until we're out at the end of the shield nobody has time for anythin' but work."

"How long?"

"A couple of weeks. But we'll get bigger signal delays."

"That is inevitable and acceptable. Before we act we must discuss the fine details."

"Why not now?"

"Because I have yet to think the matter through. This may be our only chance to catch the murderer, and we cannot afford to act precipitately." I prepared to end the conversation, but I was struck by one more thought. "I am receiving a useless visual feed from your apartment. Why do you not wear the RV jacket?"

"For three reasons. First, if you're not sitting there with the helmet on, an' mostly you're not, there's no point in me sendin' back scenes of me doin' the grand tour of Sky City when nobody's watchin'. Second, it's damn hot inside that thing."

"It is also hot inside this helmet. And the third reason?"

He hesitated. "It's them godawful pansy colors. Pink 'n' purple— who chose 'em? I had four guys hittin' on me in the first two days."

He broke the connection prematurely, leaving me filled with *esprit d'escalier.* "It is not the jacket, Seth, it is merely your native charm that attracted them." Or "I'm sure they told you that the colors contrast beautifully with your eyes."

Yes, yes. Cheap wit, unworthy of me. Also, in the case of Seth, not without its dangers. I have commented already on his sense of self-preservation. To that let me add his air of latent violence. Far better Seth Parsigian as an ally than an adversary. I must never forget my own vulnerability.

I am sitting half asleep in my chair, gradually becoming comatose after a long day; but tomorrow's imagined news lead drifts through my mind:

### Sky City Killer Caught Thanks to
### Efforts of Determined Pair

Two men, Seth Parsigian and Oliver Guest, today captured the long-sought Sky City murderer. Seth Parsigian receives a large reward and the thanks of a grateful world. Serial killer and legendary ghoul Oliver Guest goes back tomorrow to continue his sentence of long-term judicial sleep.

# 24

On her previous meetings with Seth Parsigian, Maddy had found him totally focused. This evening he was morose and distracted. Although he was the one who had insisted on the get-together, he acted like a man who had other things on his mind.

Well, so had she. With every hour that passed, the value of her prized position as Vice President of the Argos Group faded in importance. Gordy Rolfe seemed less the inspired electronics designer and organizing genius behind a huge international corporation, and more the eccentric and unkempt taskmaster who expected work from his minions twenty-four hours a day.

Those minions apparently included Seth Parsigian. As Sky City wound its slow way out toward its new position, Maddy had made a dozen visits to the engineering information center. She was looking for John Hyslop, but he was never there. Maddy learned that he spent most of his time out at Cusp Station, where the new particle defense system was under construction. The person who *was* always there, night or day, was Seth. He could usually be found studying a screen displaying scheduled meetings of personnel, timetables for equipment procurement, and recent use of facilities in Sky City and on the shield. If he hoped to pull out of those bald statistics useful information relating to the Sky City murderer, then good luck to him. Maddy felt sure that over the past six months the records had been dissected infinitely finely by scores of investigators.

When Seth arrived in her room he had a strange expression on his face. Was he still mad because their Sky City wanderings had produced no useful result? He should know, as well as anyone, the golden rule of the Argos Group when it came to cooperation: Your own assignment came first. Someone else's success would not balance your failure. If he couldn't find what he wanted, that was his problem.

He said abruptly, "I think I'm gonna do you a favor. You say you were sent up here to keep an eye on John Hyslop, right?"

"That's correct." Maddy added to herself, *And a lousy job I'm making of it.*

"If that isn't why you're here, then you better watch it. You're leavin' tracks big enough to fall over."

"I have no idea what you're talking about."

"That's what you would say, no matter what. Listen hard, 'cause I'm only gonna say this once. When we got nowhere a-walkin' the halls up here, I had to find me a different tack. I set up shop in the information center. I looked at what people in Sky City was doin' at the time of each of the murders."

"I don't think you'll find the killer that way. Other people must have attempted the same thing."

"Yeah, I'm sure they did. But you see, now I have me an advantage. I know the name of the murderer." Seth watched Maddy's reaction. "I guess that's news to you."

"It certainly is. Who is it?"

"Mebbe I'll tell you who—in good time. But first you gotta help me some more. An' I'll help you. Tit for tat."

"Forget it. I've done enough for you."

He went on as though she had not spoken, "See, it's not enough to know a name. You still have to catch 'em."

"Seth, I'm going. I don't need to listen to nonsense."

"Me neither. So when your buddy John Hyslop came over to talk to me last week, I didn't much listen at first. Then me an' him got to talkin'. Want to know what we said?"

He was goading her, luring her with Hyslop's name. "Go on."

"He'd been catchin' up on things that happened while he was away, records and actions and materials, that sort of crap. An' I'd been skimmin' the data banks. He told me he'd noticed somethin' peculiar. I told him that I had, too. We compared notes. He told me he didn't have time to follow up on it, the new defense system was takin' every minute he had. But what he'd noticed involved the Argos Group, and I was with the Argos Group. So he said, maybe I could take a closer look at it."

*Why didn't John ask me?* Maddy said, "You're here for the

murders. Argos Group activities seem more like my line of experience than yours."

"That's what I thought, too. Why not you? Me, I'm not a chart-and-figures type. But I doubt Hyslop's hopin' to get into my pants, so that could make a difference."

"If he wants to get into mine, he's certainly taking his own sweet time."

"As a friend of mine who you'll never meet an' would never want to keeps tellin' me, you have to be patient. Fact is, Hyslop asked me because I was already there an' already diggin'. So I look at the stuff he's pulled out, compare it with mine, an' guess what? Some of the Argos Group records are awful strange. If I had to guess, I'd say there's fiddlin' going on that don't sound like violins."

"Cheating?"

"Records of deliveries that were never made. Double entries for shipments. Differences between stated quantities delivered and shop counts. I'd call that cheatin'."

"I have nothing to do with shipments."

"I hear you. But again, that's what you'd say if you did. And there's more: defective materials in vital places. If I didn't know better, I'd swear that some Argos Group actions were designed to slow shield development, 'stead of speedin' it up."

"What do you propose to do about this?"

"Me? I'll do nothin'. Like you said, it's not my job. I don't care if old Gordy is robbin' Bruno Colombo and his boys blind."

"So why are you telling me?"

"To let you know that if you are playin' games, you better stop. And why am I doin' that? Well, I said I was gonna do you a favor, an' you're wonderin' why. So I'll tell you. You can do me a favor, too. I got a job to do, an' I don't want it screwed up by a bunch of morons in green eyeshades countin' the spoons an' clutterin' up every room on Sky City. So, a word to the wise: If you're the one doin' it, stop right now. 'Til I'm done, that is. After that, it's all yours, I don't care what you do."

A decision sitting at the back of Maddy's brain jumped to the foreground. "I never had anything to do with shortchanging Sky City on deliveries, or ruining schedules. But even if I had, it's irrelevant. I'm leaving the Argos Group."

His attention had been wandering, as though the meeting had

served its purpose and was now ending. He jerked back to face Maddy. "You're gonna quit?"

"You've got ears. Yes."

Brown eyes bored into hers. "You serious? Yeah, I can see you are. Bet you don't do it, though. What's your problem? You think Gordy's ready to be taken to the funny farm?"

"He is, but it's more than that." And what was it? Maddy needed time to think. Seth's words had started a whole new chain of logic running in her head: about John Hyslop and his changing assignments, about her own role and the timing of events. Aware of her long silence, she added, "I'm not even sure I'll go back to Earth. Not for a while."

"Ah. So *that's* what it's about." Seth sniffed. "Well, good huntin', that's all I can say. If you want my advice, tone it down an' go slow. You're a bit of a high-powered sexpot for someone like him."

"For Gordy?"

"Don't play dumb with me, Maddy Wheatstone. I mean John Hyslop. Act dumb an' flutter your eyelashes if you like, but don't rush it." Seth stood up. "Leaving Argos, eh? Well, I think about doin' that myself now an' again. But I bet you back off when it comes right down to it. I've seen Gordy when people tell him they're leavin'."

Maddy grimaced. "So have I. Maybe I won't get up the nerve. But I'm going to find out. Unless you have something else to say, I'd like you to leave."

"You want to sleep?"

"No. I'm going to call Gordy and resign."

"Says you. I bet you don't go through with it. But if you do quit, I'd like to know what he says."

Maddy paused, the telcom unit in her hand. "Tell me the name of the murderer. Then maybe I'll let you know what Gordy says."

Seth Parsigian didn't know the name of the Sky City murderer, Maddy felt sure of that. He had spoken with total confidence, but anyone with such hot information would be knocking on the door of Sky City security within a minute.

She had spoken with total confidence, too, announcing that she was about to present her resignation to Gordy Rolfe. But with that call ready to go through, she was suddenly not so sure.

Was she seeing a pattern to events where there was none?

When John Hyslop was assigned to the Aten asteroid project, shield development had been behind schedule but catching up rapidly. Maddy felt certain that John deserved credit for that. With him gone, there would be new delays. Then the news came in that the particle storm would arrive much earlier than expected. John was instantly reassigned to work on the shield. And Gordy told Maddy to stick with him and watch what he did, even though there was no logical reason for her presence.

John was being used to control the pace of shield development; and Maddy, without her knowledge, was being used to control John. If all that were true, there was no doubt who was pulling the strings.

That was even more reason to quit her job. And yet . . .

The Argos Group had a high turnover. Gordy Rolfe must be used to it, but he behaved as if each loss was an act of personal betrayal. She had been with Gordy in The Flaunt six months ago and seen him stamping and cursing and throwing things. That was when a midlevel project manager who couldn't take the pressure stepped into thin air out of a fortieth-floor window. That was the one sure way out of the Argos Group unless Gordy fired you.

Maddy was in a far more senior position, and the last thing she wanted was to explain to Gordy Rolfe her reasons for leaving. He would tell her—perhaps rightly—that she had gone mad.

Maybe she had. But now, when all her confidence was gone, it was too late to back out. The call had gone through and Gordy was frowning at her from the screen. He was in the underground habitat. From the look of him he was wearing the same clothes as ten days ago. He also looked like a man who had not washed in the same period.

"What do you want?" Gordy didn't bother with social pleasantries. "Couldn't someone else handle this, whatever it is?"

*Do it at once; delay will make it harder.* "No, Gordy. No one else could handle this, because I work directly for you. I called to tell you that I'm resigning."

His expression changed from anger to cynical amusement. "Oh, yeah? The old squeeze. I'll buy it, just this once. Ten percent increase in salary, double your old bonus at the end of the year if you don't screw up, and I'll see what I can do about an interest in profit sharing. But that's it, Maddy—I don't want you back in six months, pushing for more."

"You don't understand. I'm not pushing for more money and benefits. I'm leaving the Argos Group."

"You're what?" His face showed genuine incomprehension.

*Oh God. Don't make me say it again.* "I'm leaving, Gordy. I quit. I'm resigning from the Argos Group."

There. Now he had the message. His face twisted with surprise and rage.

"Leaving? You can't leave."

"I can. I'll wrap up any unfinished work, and then I'm gone."

"You ungrateful bitch! I *made* you. When you joined Argos you were a snotty-nosed child. You were *nothing* until I shaped you."

"I resign. I'll put it in writing if you want it that way."

"You were nothing, and you'll be nothing again. I'll see to that. You faithless fucker, when I'm done you'll never work again. Anywhere! Let me tell you what you are, you worthless whore."

Maddy knew Gordy Rolfe; his rants were famous, and he was just getting started. He went on and she sat, frozen-faced, until she could take no more.

"I've listened to enough, Gordy. Now you listen to me."

He stopped in midsentence and stared at her in astonishment.

"I've given you nine good years, Gordy Rolfe. I've been a hardworking and faithful employee who put you and the Argos Group above everything else in existence. *Everything.* Nothing mattered as much as impressing you. But that's over now. I want life and friendship. I want love."

"Aha." His eyes glowed behind the big glasses. "I get it. You've found a man. That's all right. But sex don't last, Maddy. Take a long weekend. Fuck him until your eyeballs drop out on the pillow. Then get over him and go back to work."

"It's not about sex."

"You mean you're not fucking him *yet*. You've got it worse than I thought."

"It's about a lot more than sex. Gordy, I don't wish you harm—

that's more than you can say about yourself. And I'll prove it." Fear of what Gordy might do made her suddenly cautious. She would not tell him all her suspicions. "I know the Argos Group has been cheating on some of the Sky City contracts. I'll not give anyone else that information, but I don't want to get caught in the middle. And you had better stop what you're doing and straighten the record. Otherwise, you're sure to be caught."

He had been twitching and fidgeting while they spoke. Now he became perfectly still. "Can you prove that? Have you been digging into Sky City shipping records?"

"No."

"Then how do you know anything?"

"I know what I was told."

"So you don't really *know* anything at all. It's just hearsay. Who was it who gave you the information?"

Maddy was ready to say Seth Parsigian's name. Why not? Seth also was an Argos Group employee, reporting, like her, to Gordy. But she saw the expression in Rolfe's eyes. She had said far too much already.

"I can't tell you that."

"The man you've got the hots for. Did he tell you?"

"No! He has nothing to do with this."

"I think I believe you. But who told you, Maddy? I have to know. Who was it?"

For close to ten years she had complied with every order from Gordy Rolfe. She had even tried to anticipate his unspoken wishes. The urge to obey was strong. Rolfe's eyes seemed to grow, glaring at her from the screen.

Maddy closed her own eyes. "I'm not going to tell you. And I'm not going to talk about this anymore. I'll send you my official resignation. I appreciate what I've learned from you and everything you've done for me over the years. But it's goodbye."

She pressed the disconnect key. She did not want to look at that malevolent countenance, those hot, disturbing eyes. Gordy hadn't always been this way. For the past few months he had been approaching the edge, sliding away from the rational. If he were not so far away and so reclusive, he would be a perfect candidate for the Sky City killer.

The real question was, would Gordy accept her resignation? And if he did, would he try to harm her? Kill her?

Maddy comforted herself with the thought that she was a long way from Earth. Gordy Rolfe was king of The Flaunt and of his strange underworld habitat, but that was all. Surely, although the arm of Gordy Rolfe was long, it could not stretch as far as Sky City.

There was only one problem. If Gordy was interfering with shield development, that had to stop. At once. Maddy could not make that happen, but she knew a person who could. Someone who could also turn Maddy's vague suspicions into established fact.

Slowly, reluctantly, feeling like a traitor to the man who had for nine years been at the center of her life, Maddy placed the call to Celine Tanaka.

The beep of the telcom unit went on and on. Nick Lopez did not want to answer. It was the dedicated line, and the only person who could possibly be at the other end was Gordy Rolfe.

"Aren't you going to answer that?"

Nick sighed. The representative from the Maldives was young and beautiful and oh so innocent-looking. But not perhaps so innocent. The discussion of trade agreements between the islands and the World Protection Federation was proceeding smoothly, and the transcript would show only official business. But underneath, at the submerged level that made the beginning of any affair so delightful, ran a current of physical awareness and mutual attraction.

"Martin, I don't want to answer the call. It's a private, dedicated line, and if I pick it up I'll have to ask you to leave."

"That would be all right." A sideways glance from blue eyes with long, dark lashes. A tiny smile. The husky voice saying, "We have more to discuss, but we could do it later. Couldn't we?"

The opening gambit. Nick's move. "I have meetings all the rest of the afternoon. It would have to be this evening. Are you free?"

"I am not free." A knowing smile, a hint of even white teeth. "But perhaps I can make myself available."

"Then may I suggest dinner? And afterward, a walk on the new Ipanema beach? That will give us ample opportunities . . . to talk."

A grave nod. "I suspect that we will find much to discuss."

"Undoubtedly. At seven, then? My limousine will pick you up."

"I will be waiting."

The farewell, a thin hand grasping Nick's great brown paw for one split second longer than necessary. And Martin Oliveira was gone.

Nick raised his hand and sniffed the faint perfume that Martin's touch had left behind. Exciting. At the same time proper, subtle, and wholly civilized. If only all the world were so. Nick picked up the telcom unit.

"What the fuck are you playing at?" Gordy's voice rasped at once out of the set. "I knew you were in your goddamn office, your secretary told me. Why didn't you pick up?"

"Gordy, I was in my office because I had a meeting here. I had to get rid of the other person. This is supposed to be a private, dedicated line for the two of us. Do you want others listening?"

"I want action. When you hear what I have to say, so will you. Get ready to crap in your pants."

Nick listened to the rapid-fire summary of Gordy's conversation with Maddy Wheatstone. At the end of it he said, "I agree, it sounds bad. Will Wheatstone talk?"

"No. She's no dummy, and I've been grooming her for a top Argos Group position for nine years. Right now she has the hots for Hyslop, but deep down she knows that once she gets over him she'll want her old job back."

"You have more faith in that than I do."

"Because I'm smarter than you. Even if Maddy did talk, all she has is hearsay. Right now we have to worry about the source, the one who dug into the records."

"She refused to tell you who that was?"

"Of course she did. You fucking half-wit, why do you think I'm calling you?"

*Im*proper. *Un*subtle. Wholly *un*civilized. But accurate, since only a half-wit would ever have become involved with Gordy Rolfe.

"I have no idea who Maddy Wheatstone was referring to."

"But you can find out."

"How?"

"Call your stooge, Bozo Colombo. The person we need must

have been digging into the data bases that deal with Argos Group transactions. Unless Sky City is screwed up beyond belief, the retrieval systems will hold a record of every inquiry. Tell Colombo we need names, everybody who's been into the records in the past few weeks. Have his technical staff make a list."

"And do what with it? I've told you before, Bruno Colombo has his limits. So do I."

"You're spineless, Lopez. You're just as bad as your stooge." Rolfe's voice changed to become a broad imitation of Nick's deeper one. " 'Bruno Colombo has his limits. So do I.' " Rolfe's raspy tone became flat and expressionless. "Well, I don't. You get me the list. I'll take it from there."

"And do what?"

"Never you mind. All you have to do is sit on your ass in New Rio and keep your mouth closed. I assume you're at least capable of that."

"Suppose it's one of my people, Gordy?"

"Suppose it is?"

"I could buy them off. That would be easier than anything else."

"And be sure they stayed bought? We've had this conversation before. I say, let's go for a permanent solution. Remember, I told you it would have been easier to get rid of Hyslop, and you wouldn't let me?"

"But I was right. I said we might need Hyslop, and we did."

"No. *You* did. I didn't. I don't give a flying fuck if the space shield works, or if it turns out to be a space sieve and everybody on the surface of Earth fries. And I'm not interested in a discussion; I want action. Tell Bruno Colombo to get his ass in gear and send you that list. Soon."

"You're not thinking—" Nick found he was speaking into a dead line. He replaced the telcom set, more upset than he wanted to admit.

And more perplexed. You went through life in public office, laying claim to high morality when you knew quite well that at heart you were totally immoral. You were well acquainted with the majority of the seven deadly sins. Certainly pride, anger, and greed had their place in your life. You could claim a lifelong familiarity with and affection for lust.

And then, at an age when a man ought to know himself, you discovered that your immorality had its limits.

Gordy Rolfe was right. Compared with the overlord of the Argos Group, Nick Lopez was a spineless stooge unwilling to follow through on the consequences of his own actions. If it came to a shoot-out with Gordy, Nick had the terrible conviction that he would lose.

Well, you did your best. A man was only as wicked as a man could stand to be. Nick turned his thoughts to the coming evening with Martin Oliveira, and felt comforted.

# 25

John Hyslop surveyed the assembled group. If only they were mountaineers as well as engineers!

When you were climbing the highest peaks of Earth you had to make a lot of technical decisions: from which side and along which path you would attempt to scale the mountain; where you would establish base camp; how much time you allot to the adjustment of the climber's body to extreme altitude; how much equipment you would carry; and when and where you would use oxygen. Would you even use oxygen at all?

Important decisions. Each could be the difference between life and death. But none of them was the toughest and the most controversial.

That problem came on the final day of the ascent. You were close to the summit, you were weary, your body was so starved of oxygen that your brain was on autopilot and your feet felt like lead. You had come to within a thousand—maybe five hundred—feet of planting a flag at the top. Now you had to make the hardest call of all: Did you keep climbing the final ridge to the mountaintop that you seemed so clearly able to reach? Or, with the goal so visible and so tempting, did you recognize that a descent must follow an ascent? You had to decide, very quickly, if you had enough time and daylight and strength to continue to the top, and after that return to base.

The team leader made the call. If you decided that the wise choice was to retreat, you gave the word to turn around and expected a monstrous amount of grumbling when you got back to base camp. But the team respected your decision during the climb. There could be only one boss.

John was about to make a similarly tough decision. He examined the group one by one. They had the worn-down pallor of people who worked too hard and slept too little, but in mountain-climbing terms they were not on the final leg of the ascent. They had hardly reached base camp. Sky City was flying steadily on toward Cusp Station, but the journey was barely past its halfway point.

How was the group likely to react to the news that their efforts were useless?

Wilmer Oldfield and Star Vjansander were not engineers. They would presumably go along with John's judgment. The same was true of Seth Parsigian and Maddy Wheatstone. He caught her eye, received a dazzling smile in return, and looked away.

Will Davis would be all right, too. He was the one who had brought the word to John, and he would be ready with his own supporting arguments. Amanda Corrigan would not argue; she was obsessed with her own problems of computer access and use. Jessie Kahn was probably too junior to question him.

That left Lauren Stansfield and Torrance Harbish. Both sometimes had strong opinions, and both were unpredictable. You never knew what thoughts ran behind Lauren's amber eyes or Torrance's dark countenance.

Everyone was staring at John. It was time to take the plunge.

"I have news, and it's not good. We can't go ahead with the new particle defense scheme." That certainly had their attention. "Not, at least, the way we planned it. The problem lies in particle bundle detection. We intended to generate a low-intensity wide-angle field, so that each incoming bundle would interact with the field and generate a traveling EM wave of its own. We would pick up that signal and use it to calculate the bundle trajectory. Then we could deflect the bundle away from Earth with a direct and stronger beam.

"It sounds practical, even easy. But the first part won't work. We have no way to generate a field complete enough to allow us to track every bundle." John nodded at Will Davis. "Will did the calculations, and he'll be happy to go over them with you. It looks like maybe ten percent of the bundles will escape detection."

"Ten percent get through?" Jessie Kahn reacted at once. "What does that mean for Earth?"

"The most you can say is that it's better than a hundred percent.

But it will mean the immediate loss of the ionosphere, the later loss of the ozone layer, massive heat imbalance between the Northern and Southern Hemispheres—which means freak weather—and a radio communications blackout. It could be as bad as the original Alpha C effects in 2026, but of course we'll be a lot better prepared for it."

"How long do we have?" Lauren Stansfield was making notes in her usual tidy fashion. She was as gray-faced and weary as anyone, but somehow, even though John had called the meeting without warning, she was carefully dressed and wearing makeup.

"That's another bit of bad news. Another Sniffer was launched two weeks ago on a crash basis. It can't do detailed analysis, but it reports that the big slug of particle bundles will hit in twenty-six days."

"Then we must keep going." Torrance Harbish spoke with force and conviction. "Look at the alternative. The old shield won't work, we know that. Even if it's not going to be perfect, we must have the new defense system. We're wasting time. We should leave here and work harder than ever."

"I hear you, Torrance. But I'm going to demand some more of your time. I didn't call you together just to pass on bad news." John glanced at each person in turn. "There's another reason for this meeting. Every one of you has a first-rate intellect. I want the benefit of those. You're all tired, but I called us together because we need *ideas*."

"I don't know about the first-rate intellect bit." It was Will Davis. "You've already had my two cents' worth, boyo, but I'll say it again for the benefit of everyone. We charge ahead with the new defense, even though it won't be perfect. And we tell Earth to get ready for trouble."

Amanda Corrigan added, "More than trouble, Will—disaster. I've got my whole family down there. Look, this isn't my area of expertise, so maybe it's a dumb question. But why can't we beef up the strength of the low-intensity field?"

"Will?" John didn't want to talk; he wanted to listen.

Davis nodded and turned to Amanda Corrigan. "We could. But that's not the problem. The field isn't generated from a single point; it's done with a distributed array of tuned oscillators. Even when the oscillator phases are matched as well as possible, you get regions where the contributions from different sources reinforce each other, and others where they tend to cancel."

Amanda was frowning, more than ever like a puzzled teenager. John asked, "Do you get it?"

"I don't think so. I guess I'm dumb."

"No. You're just tired."

"That too. So what if the fields cancel in places?"

"Will?"

Davis nodded. "Think of it as a three-dimensional interference pattern. The particle bundles will be coming in at random, so some of them will slide through along paths where the field cancels. If they don't encounter enough field to generate a signal, we don't detect them. If we don't know they're there, we can't zap them with a stronger pulse and direct them away. So they make it all the way, and hit Earth."

"Increasing the strength of the low-intensity field won't solve the problem?"

"No. We'd still have dead spots."

"Can't you do something to *average* the field?" Jessie asked. "If you could make it more uniform, the low points would disappear."

Will Davis shrugged. "You can fiddle with the oscillator strengths. But it's like working with an air mattress. If you push it down in once place, it bulges up higher somewhere else."

"What about putting something out in space?" Jessie was young, but she could be dogged when she had an idea in her head. "Couldn't a superconducting mesh average the field?"

"It could." Davis raised his eyebrows. "Have to be twenty thousand kilometers across, mind you, and thirty thousand kilometers out beyond Cusp Station. We could make something like that—if we had a few years. How long did you say we have, John?"

"Twenty-six days before the main hit. But Amanda and Jessie have the right idea. Keep thinking."

Advice easier to give than to follow. In the long silence that followed, John glanced from one perplexed face to the next. He was asking his engineering team for a miracle.

The person who eventually spoke was not one of his team. Star Vjansander had been nudging Wilmer Oldfield, muttering to him, and blowing out her round cheeks. Now she frowned at Wilmer and said, "What was it that feller Colombo said in our first meeting out here, about Missus Hommit going ter see a mountain?"

It was blank stares all round, until Wilmer said mildly, "Not Ma Hommit, you softheaded git. Mahomet."

"Yeah, that one. I'm rotten with names. If the mountain wouldn't go to Mahomet, he'd have to go ter the mountain." She nodded to John, as though confirming something he had said. "So that's what yer have to do."

"Star, you're jumping so far ahead you're falling all over yourself. You always do." Wilmer turned to Will Davis. "How close to finished was the old shield?"

"Ninety percent plus. All the structure and stability was done, but we were still missing batches of sensors." Davis shook his head. "Seven years of my life in that bloody thing, and it's useless. Ah, well. Easy come, easy go."

"Don't give up on it." Wilmer went on, slowly and thoughtfully. "It's useless as a shield, but it's covered with a superconducting mesh. That's what was going to divert the particles when we thought they were coming in as single nuclei. The mesh isn't enough to deal with the bundles, they're too massive. But could it do what Jessie said, and average the detection field that we create?"

It was like the promise of reinforcements to a tired army. John saw the engineers straighten up in their seats. "Can it, Will?"

"It could, very easily. But the shield is in the wrong place. To average the detection field, the shield would have to move thirty thousand kilometers farther out. That's not impossible, but the structure is so fragile and so finely balanced that the operation would take a few months. We don't have months. We have just a few weeks."

"I know." Star was bobbing up and down in her chair. "I know. That's why I said what I did. Yer don't take the mountain ter what's-'is-name, you leave the mountain where it is."

"Shut up, Star. You'll give people headaches." Wilmer reached out and pushed her back into her seat. "Just keep quiet, and let me explain your idea."

"I've heard you explain things before. Yer'll bore 'em to death, you old fart."

Wilmer took no notice. He went on in his unhurried way, "She's bright, you see, but when she gets excited she gibbers like a monkey.

Here is the position, as I understand it. The old space shield is no use as a shield anymore, because it's far too fragile to divert the high-mass particle bundles. However, it would serve perfectly to average the low-intensity field that detects those bundles. Unfortunately, it is in the wrong place relative to Cusp Station, where you have installed the generators for high-energy pulses that *can* divert particle bundles away from Earth. To serve that purpose, the shield would have to be moved thirty thousand kilometers away from Cusp Station, in the direction of Alpha Centauri, since that is where the particle storm is coming from. However, the shield is so delicate that such movement would have to be done very slowly, at minuscule acceleration. It therefore appears that we have reached a solution too late. The particle storm will be here before the shield can be relocated.

"We would appear to be faced with an insoluble problem. That, however, is an illusion. The fragile shield cannot be moved in time. But why not, as Star suggests, invert the problem? We do not care about absolute position, we care only about *relative* position. Rather than moving the shield thirty thousand kilometers toward Alpha Centauri, Cusp Station must move thirty thousand kilometers *away* from Alpha Centauri—*closer to Earth.*" Wilmer turned to John. "One question remains, which I regard as an engineering detail: Is Cusp Station strong enough to withstand the necessary acceleration?"

"If a group of you physicists wanted to land on the surface of the Sun and do experiments, you'd say the design of the ship that takes you there and back was engineering details." John was cursing—at himself. He was sure that the rest of his team was feeling the same way. To miss an obvious possible solution, and have it pointed out by a pair of *physicists,* who sat with their heads in the clouds . . . He went on, "Cusp Station has to be strong enough. We fly it inward even if it falls apart on the way. And we must change the trajectory of this place, too, so Sky City finishes next to Cusp Station's new location and we can fast-link the computers. Amanda?"

"A few hours' calculation." She rolled her head from side to side, as though she was attempting the calculation mentally. "If thirty thousand is a good working number for the move toward Earth, I'll have you a flight profile for Cusp Station and a modified one for Sky City by this evening."

"Will?"

"Cusp Station was built rugged. I'll be out there anyway, installing the field loop generators. Say, one day to decide where the mirror-matter thrustors go, two days to attach. Three days from now we'll be ready to move."

"Torrance? How about Sky City?"

"We're running close to maximum stresses in some places already. What are you looking for?"

"Too soon to tell. Aim for a factor of two."

"Christ. We may fall apart."

"If this works, we'll have plenty of time for repairs. If not, we won't need 'em. Lauren, you know the interior structure of Sky City better than anyone. I rely on you to pick out the weakest spots and be ready to strengthen them." John glanced again around the group. He saw new energy on every face. "Anything else? I know there are a thousand details to be discussed and worked through, but I don't want to take the time of the whole group on every one."

Lauren Stansfield said, "A question that's not engineering. When do we tell other people about this?"

"As soon as anyone asks. Just don't waste time on long explanations. From the point of view of most people, nothing has changed. The old shield can't handle the particle bundles, we're building a new particle defense system, and it's touch and go. That's all still true—the job just became more difficult."

"No." Will Davis stood up. "An hour ago it was impossible. Now there's hope, so it must be easier. Good one, Star."

He left, and the others wandered out after him. Star Vjansander went reluctantly, saying, "It was my idea. I oughter stay and help."

"It was your idea." Wilmer shepherded her out. "And you ought to go. Anything you touch, you smash."

Finally it was just John and Maddy Wheatstone. She came right up to him. "You know I'm not a trained engineer. But I'll do anything I can to help."

John asked the question he had been putting off for over a week. "Don't you have to go back to Earth? I'm sure the Argos Group has other assignments for you now."

"I don't work for the Argos Group anymore. I quit."

"You resigned? Why?" He saw the tormented expression in her eyes. "I'm sorry, I know that's none of my business."

"It's all right. I resigned because of—personal reasons."

"I see." But he didn't.

She seemed wilted, as though someone had sucked all the life out of her, as she said, "If you don't mind, I don't want to talk about it now."

"I see." John had no idea what to do next. He was tired, worried, and his head buzzed with a million technical problems. There was no way on earth that Maddy Wheatstone could possibly solve any of them. The logical thing to do was to let her leave.

Then he stopped thinking and said, "If you're not going back to Earth right away, would you have dinner with me?" He counted his racing pulse through a long and awful pause, then added, "I didn't mean tonight; I'm sure you have other plans. Anytime. I'm free anytime."

She stood a foot away from him, breathing heavily. At last she said, "You're not free ever. Not until the particle storm has been and gone."

"I'll make time. When?"

"Tonight's as good as any. Where?"

"I'll pick you up at your rooms."

"You know where that is?"

"Yes, I know. Remember?"

"I do. When I saw you standing there in the middle of the night it scared me half to death." Maddy smiled—at last. "I'll do better this time; I won't be scared. Let's eat early. All right?"

She stared at him, waiting, while he did and said nothing. At last she turned and left.

John collapsed back into his chair. His thoughts skipped all over the place. The old shield was no good. The new defense system did not exist. Earth was in terrible danger. The next few weeks were going to be filled with enormous amounts of labor and dreadful risks. And he was doing—what?

He wasn't quite sure, but whatever it was, he suspected that he had chosen the worst moment in history to do it.


Maddy left the engineering center with her mind in turmoil. They had been alone together, John showed real interest in her, and even then she had not been able to tell him what the Argos Group was doing on Sky City. She couldn't make sense of her own feelings. She hated what Gordy Rolfe had said to her, but he had taught her everything she knew about business. Gordy was the reason that she was here. He was also a crook and a lunatic. And if the Argos Group was delivering inferior products and sabotaging shield development, nothing could be more important than that.

Celine Tanaka, when Maddy finally got through to her, had been skeptical. "*Slowing* shield development? And delivering defective materials? That's quite an accusation, against your own employer."

"I don't work for the Argos Group anymore."

"Ah. I see."

Maddy knew what Celine must be thinking. "Look, it's not that I'm vindictive and trying to get back at Gordy Rolfe. This is really happening."

"You have proof? And others will back you up?"

"Not real proof."

It sounded weak, and it was. After an uncomfortably long silence, Celine said, "I'll look into this. But I have to move carefully. You're making a very serious charge."

"I know."

"Until I get back to you, don't say another word to anyone."

That order from Celine Tanaka was the hardest part. Maddy had wanted to tell John everything that she knew. But what *did* she know? Gordy himself had told her that it was all hearsay.

Was she helping to save Earth from destruction, or was she utterly deluded? There seemed nothing in between.

Maddy slowed her steps as she approached the elevator shaft leading down toward the perimeter. Should she go back?

The decision was made for her. There, waiting by the elevator, was one source of her problems. But for him she wouldn't be agonizing over her actions.

Seth Parsigian nodded. "Got a second?"

"If it's Argos business, I don't." Maddy needed to say it to somebody who understood, even if it was only to the unshaven thug lounging in front of her. "I'm out of there. I did it. I called Gordy and resigned."

Dark eyebrows rose high on the smooth forehead. "Whoo.

That's what I call livin' dangerous. I wondered if you'd carry through. I guess it helps that you're out here where he can't get at you. What did he say?"

"Nothing much. Called me an ungrateful bitch, a faithless fucker, and a worthless whore. Told me I'd never work again, anywhere. He took it real well."

"I'd say. What'd you tell him?"

Maddy hesitated. She had mentioned the Argos Group's fleecing of Sky City, but she had been careful not to use Seth's name or to quote his assertion of deliberate shield delays. "I kept pretty quiet. When Gordy's on a rant he doesn't leave you much space."

"Too true. Makes you wonder why we work for him. Or did, in your case. He's gettin' worse. Maybe I oughter be outa there, too." He was eyeing her, making some decision of his own. "Look, this is nothin' to do with Argos Group business. Yesterday I told you I knew who the Sky City murderer was. You didn't believe me, did you?"

"Of course I didn't. If you knew, you'd tell security."

"Suppose you were dead sure who it was, but you didn't have hard evidence. Nothin' enough to stand up legally. What would you do then?"

"I suppose I'd try to get evidence."

"You really want to catch the killer?"

"What sort of question is that? Of course I do."

"Would you ask other people to help you if you knew who did it?"

"I might."

"Well, so might I. I really do know the name of the murderer. But there's no hard evidence, so catchin' the killer ain't simple. There's a way that might work, only I'll need help."

"I already told you, I'll not go wandering around Sky City with you again."

"It's nothin' like that. I want you to do just one thing, an' for you it will be easy. I want you to arrange a meetin', just me, you, and lover-boy John. But before that meeting you gotta make him swear, to you personally, that he won't say nothin' to anybody else until the killer's under arrest."

"He'll not agree to that. Why should he?"

"For me, he wouldn't. Otherwise I'd ask him. You, it's different. He'd let you flay him and use his naked hide for seat covers."

"That is gross and disgusting. Also nonsense."

"You don't see him lookin' at you. He thinks the sun shines outa—well, never mind. If I'm wrong, you got nothin' to lose by tryin'." He was staring at her with an odd intensity. "Will you talk to him?"

"I will not. Why should I? I don't owe you. And I don't work for Gordy anymore, so I don't owe Argos."

"You don't owe me an' Gordy, all right. But mebbe you owe somebody else."

Seth stared at Maddy in silence until she turned away. She said softly, "I don't owe anybody."

"Mebbe you do. Could be you owe twelve teenagers."

Maddy looked again into Seth's brown eyes. He was conning her, she just knew it. It made no difference. She had lost the argument.

He said, "Listen to me. I'm gonna break one of my own rules. I'm gonna tell you before I know you're aboard."

For the next ten minutes he spoke and she said not a word. At the end of it, he asked, "Well?"

She had a perfect opportunity to ask John; she could do it when they were having dinner. A perfect opportunity to talk about a perfectly awful subject.

Would she do it? Why should she do it, when the evening offered the first-ever chance for a private and intimate meal with John?

The forlorn corpse of Lucille DeNorville, abandoned and floating in limbo, drifted slowly forward from the back of her mind.

She nodded. "I will. I'll ask him tonight."

Why didn't life ever go the way it was supposed to?

# 26

**From the private diary of Oliver Guest.**

When I suggested to Seth Parsigian a way in which we might catch our murderer, I realized that I was exposing him to a slightly increased risk. He would find it necessary to enlist the support of at least one other person on Sky City in order to carry out my plan, and that person, wittingly or unwittingly, might in turn permit the killer to discover our intentions.

I informed Seth of this when he told me of his conversation with Maddy Wheatstone. He shrugged and said, "Don't sweat it, Doc. It's a one-in-a-million long shot."

"Perhaps it is. So is the chance of being struck by lightning; but lightning does strike. I urge extreme caution. Lock your door, watch where you walk. You are dealing with an individual of great cunning and cold malevolence."

He said, "Ah, workin' with you ain't so bad. But I'll be careful."

On that low note, our conversation ended.

There is a well-documented and curious medical condition in which one person, apparently healthy, suffers another's symptoms. Husbands experience morning sickness, a mother develops sympathetic croup when her baby has it, a sister has trouble breathing during a brother's attack of asthma.

This phenomenon can be described as the ultimate form of synesthesia, the situation in which a sensation in one area arises from a stimulus applied to another. Normally, the two parties are intimately related: husband/wife, mother/child, brother/sister.

Seth Parsigian and I are, I hope and trust, not related within ten degrees of consanguinity. I reject utterly any suggestion that we are intimate or even close. We lack common interests, temperament, habits, or background. Some other explanation is demanded for the following events.


Sweet are the uses of insomnia.

It was well after midnight when Seth and I finished our call. It was logical that I would seek "care-charmer sleep, son of the sable night." I was weary, and it was late. After a noisy evening of revolt against programmed instruction followed by prolonged giggling, my darlings were finally in their beds and dreaming the dreams of the innocent. Otranto Castle stood silent.

Before I turned on the security system I opened the door for a moment and stood on the threshold. A cool, gentle drizzle touched my upturned face. Has there ever been a year, in all of history, with more rain? According to the global weather service, only during the initial onslaught of the Alpha Centauri supernova.

After five minutes I went inside. It is difficult to imagine anywhere on Earth darker, calmer, and more silent than the deserted western coast of Ireland on a night of dense cloud and no wind. It is a perfect setting for sleep.

Having said that, I am obliged to note that sleep would not come. For me she has been at the best of times an elusive and fickle mistress. After half an hour I rose from my bed, went to my study, and donned the RV helmet. This was done not as an invasion of Seth's privacy, but to assure myself that he was, as he had promised, being careful.

The RV jacket on its hanger on the wall offered me a ghostly view of Seth's bedroom. He lay on his back, covered by a light sheet and hardly touching the bed. On level eight, where his quarters were located, the centrifugal field was no more than a twentieth of Earth's gravity. Apparently the low-gee environment suited him, because he was sound asleep and snoring softly. I could just see the bedroom door at the extreme right-hand edge of my field of view. It was ajar.

So much for Seth's ideas of cautious behavior. He presumably still wore the earpiece. I could rouse him and again urge him to be careful; but was there any hope that I would be more successful this time? I thought not. It was synesthesia in its most irritating form. Seth, in the presence of possible danger, slept soundly. I, safe in Otranto Castle, felt the worry and uneasiness that should be his.

In irritation, I changed the setting of the RV helmet to accept only local inputs. Let Seth worry about his own safety. Out of sight, out of mind.

But not, it seemed, in this case. As the scene shifted to show my study, the nameless apprehension within me grew rather than subsided. Still wearing the helmet, I walked back to my bedroom, lay down, and returned to the Sky City setting. Seth's room again appeared before me. Nothing was happening. I stared at that nothing.

I was about to say "stared mindlessly," but that is not quite true. Late at night the body enters a new phase of its circadian rhythm and the mind plays strange tricks. Into my head drifted a story, one that each of my darlings had enjoyed as an infant: Jack the giant-killer. Brave young Jack ascended the magic beanstalk and found himself in the alien landscape known as Sky City. He entered the giant's castle. *Fee, fi, fo, fum.* With the assistance of the giant's wife, Jack escaped with—what? A goose that laid golden eggs; a speaking harp that warned the giant. A magic mirror? I was not sure. Magic looms large in children's stories. Snow White's evil queen had her mirror, too. "Mirror, mirror, on the wall, who is . . ." The killer's face, smiling and smug, stared out at me in place of my own reflection.

*Jacket, jacket, on the wall;* watching the sleeping Seth.

The stories blurred, conflated, ran together. Henri Poincaré was a fortunate genius. My own collision of late-night thoughts offered no new insight. The sleep that had so far eluded me was almost here. I was ready to close my eyes, but before I removed the helmet I must take one more look at Seth. Through the eyes of the RV jacket I saw the killer leaning over him. A silver blade slashed across Seth's throat. Bright arterial blood spurted across the room.

I blinked. Reality returned. The fancy vanished. The RV jacket showed Seth, still snoring, safe in his quiet bedroom.

I mocked my own fears, told myself not to be a fool. I should relax and go to sleep. As my eyes began to close I caught a flicker of movement on the far right of my field of view. The door of Seth's apartment was opening, slowly and silently. I looked for someone entering the dimly lit bedroom. I saw nothing, nothing at all. But I cried, "Seth! Look out!"

Look out for what? The only thing to see was the opening door. It seemed forever before Seth moved—the signal delay as Sky City moved farther out was having its effect. But finally he reacted. He must sleep like a cat, one eye open and alert for danger. As I called again he moved, not to either side, but straight up from the bed in a single spasm of effort. In the low-gravity environment of Sky City he rose all the way to the ceiling, still covered by the bedsheet.

Seth shared another of a cat's gifts. At the ceiling he twisted in midair until he was facing down toward the floor. He began to drop back, slowly because of the weak field. At last I could see something else in the room. A thin snakelike object reared up from the floor. The long, segmented neck rose to a round head that gleamed red in the weak light.

Seth was falling free, with no way to change his place of landing. The snake was moving to where he would come down directly on top of it.

I called out, "Don't land there! It's waiting for you." Useless advice, since he could change his fall in neither speed nor direction. And unnecessary advice. Seth held in his hands the bedsheet. He dropped it so that it landed on and enveloped the rearing snake.

The sheet convulsed and jerked from side to side. Seth was still falling, but he turned in midair so that he would land feet first. He kicked at the top of the heaving mass beneath him and used that momentum to carry him sideways across the room. He hit the wall headfirst above a chest of drawers, grabbed something from on top of it, and rolled away to the left.

The snake had wriggled its way free of the sheet. I saw its head lift again, turning and questing. Seth pointed what he was holding toward the snake. There was a flash of green light, and the head and long neck vanished. The room filled with smoke. Seth took a step forward, reached down, and whipped the sheet clear. Again I could see nothing. With the head gone, the rest of the intruder was too low to the ground to be in my field of view.

"I think that's the main job done," Seth said calmly. "But just in case, I think we'd be better off without them legs." He pointed the gun downward and I saw eight separate flashes of green light.

"And now let's have a look at you." He reached down, picked something up, and deposited it on the bed.

It was perhaps a meter long. I saw blunt stumps, four on each side, where the legs had been, and the remaining stub of the severed snake neck.

"A cleaning machine," I said.

"Nah." Seth shook his head. He glanced across to where the RV jacket hung on the wall. "Nice work, Doc. I coulda been dead meat without the warnin'."

"*Could* have been?"

"I was only half asleep. I mighta been, all right."

"You think perhaps that it did not intend you harm?"

"You kiddin'? Take a look." He walked a couple of paces and picked something from the floor. He held it toward the RV jacket for my inspection. "Construction laser, lot more powerful than the one I got. Good thing I fired first, or I'd've been Parsigian Cajun-style, charred on the outside and well done on the inside."

I am not unacquainted with death, but blood, carnage, and general messiness have never been a part of my own *modus operandi.* Everything here had happened so fast that I was only now beginning to react, with a fluttering pulse and a certain difficulty in breathing. I stared at the gun and at the mutilated object on the bed.

"If that is not a cleaning machine . . ."

I ran out of breath before I could complete my question, but Seth took my meaning. He went to the side of the bed, lifted the object by the stubby neck, and turned it over for my inspection.

"See this?" He pointed to a series of marks on the underside. "Series and model number, too high-level for a cleaning machine. It's a general-purpose rolfe. If you look here on the side, you'll see the place where it can plug in for instruction transfers. Hm. I guess this one's too high-powered for me, too, 'cause I never saw this model number before. Must be one of the new ones, fresh up from Earth."

"You are sure that it was programmed to attack you?"

Seth was still bending over the rolfe. He raised his head. "Not attack. Kill. That laser wasn't brought along to give me a nice all-over tan. You oughta be sure of that, if anyone is. You were the one, way back when, who asked if a cleanin' machine could be made to kill. You were the one, just tonight, who told me to watch out for my ass an' hat 'cause I might be in danger. Why were you watchin' me, anyway?"

"I was worried that the Sky City murderer might learn what we are doing and try to kill you to prevent it. The idea of sending a rolfe for that purpose never occurred to me."

"Me neither. An' I don't think that's what's goin' on." Seth sat down on his bed next to the machine. "This ain't from our buddy the killer. This is somethin' else."

"If not the murderer, then who?"

"I'm not sure. But I got ideas. An' don't worry, I'll find out." He nodded toward the remains of the machine. "Stumpy Joe there is blind an' can't go a-walkin' no more, but the brain oughta be intact. I'm gonna brang that thing to engineering, bust it open, an' squeeze the sucker dry. Then we'll find out where it got its instruction set."

"And after that?"

"Depends what I find. But don't be surprised if you catch me havin' a few words with Maddy Wheatstone." He stood up. "D'you see much action here in the next few days?"

"We cannot proceed with my plan until Sky City and Cusp Station are in their final locations. For what we have in mind, our timing and the killer's psychological condition will both be crucial. I would prefer to act at the height of the particle storm. Why do you ask?"

"Just thinkin' ahead." Seth picked up the battered rolfe. "If I get the answers I'm suspectin' out of this thing, I might have to make a little trip. But don't worry, I'll be back in plenty of time for your fun an' games."

He walked out, leaving me to stare at the empty room. I removed the RV helmet, took it back to my study, and stared at the wall clock in disbelief. Everything, from that first flicker of movement at Seth's door to this moment, had occupied almost no time at all. Five minutes ago I had drifted between fairy stories and the strange no-man's-land of impending sleep. Now I was totally wired, nerves jangling at the close escape from death.

I told myself this was *Seth's* escape, not mine. I was not, and never had been, in the slightest danger. And Seth felt certain that the Sky City killer was in no way involved.

Curiously, I found I believed him. The murderer had done nothing, because the murderer *needed* to do nothing. We had no evidence. The killer's safest course of action was continued total inaction.

Why, then, do I believe that Seth and I have a chance of success? Because human beings find it difficult to act on facts alone. We are plagued by overactive imaginations. And of the things that human beings are called upon to do, doing nothing can be the most difficult act of all.

# 27

John Hyslop scanned the table of values. If an anomaly was present, he couldn't see it. "Are you sure?"

Amanda Corrigan nodded. Shy in a group, she was perfectly self-confident one-on-one. "It's there. Hard to tell from the table of numbers, but when it's graphed it jumps right out at you. See for yourself."

She flashed up a different display, this one a curve of particle number against time. It showed a lopsided Gaussian distribution, the smooth mountain of the bell curve rising rapidly and then falling back to zero. On the left side of the mountain a secondary peak jutted up as a steep little hill.

John studied it. "Not much to look at."

"It's not, in terms of the maximum particle flux. Less than one percent."

"But more than enough to cause trouble. Where did this curve come from?"

"Data from the Sniffer that we launched two weeks ago."

"As a crash priority. What are the chances that something on board isn't working right?"

"Poor. The Sniffer passed every test we threw at it."

"Then we'd better start worrying about the earlier Sniffers. They were designed to catch this sort of thing, and they missed it."

"Not really." Amanda did more fast work at the pad. "Here's what the other Sniffers gave us, the way it was presented for visual analysis."

John rubbed his eyes. The new curve he was looking at showed a single mountain with no bordering foothills. Maybe he was getting old. He had drunk wine with dinner, but that wasn't it. After midnight he couldn't keep up with Amanda's speed and adolescent energy. She might be twenty-six, but she was like a fourteen-year-old in more than outward appearance.

"No peaks that I can see."

"Right. No peaks."

"Amanda, a peak in particle numbers can't pop up from nowhere. It represents a physical entity."

"It didn't come from nowhere. The Sniffers are working correctly—all of them. What you are seeing is a combination of the physical limitations of the earlier instruments and the way we handle their data. I'll show you."

More dancing fingerwork from Amanda, and another display flashed into view.

"These are raw counts from one of the old Sniffers. The older models measure only what they find right in front of them, and they make readings every two seconds. That sounds like frequent sampling, but the relative speed of the particles and the Sniffers means we have only one sample every fifty thousand kilometers. I think of the data as a count of the number of particles at each cross section of a long, thin tube stretching from Earth toward Alpha Centauri. The particles come in bunches and clusters, so the counts have high statistical variation. Lots of hash in the data, hard to analyze. The peak I just showed you is present in the counts, but it's really hard to see because of the noise in the signal. Now I apply a low-pass filter to the input, and there's the resulting profile. Nice and smooth, but no peak. We see the major increases and decreases. The minor blip disappears."

"In other words, we averaged away part of the signal." John leaned back. "Guess the name of the genius who said he couldn't read the raw hash, and told you to smooth it out."

"I wasn't about to mention that if you didn't." Amanda was smiling.

"I'd rather you didn't mention it at all. Colombo will have my scalp if he ever finds out." John tried to sound worried, but he was smiling, too. This was his arena, his natural playing field. Here he was the best, with the self-confidence that eluded him when it came to personal affairs.

He went back to the first display with its innocent little side peak. "So this is the real thing—no smoothing."

"You've got it. The new Sniffer detects and counts particle bundles over a cross-sectional area a hundred times as big as the old Sniffers could handle. We don't need averaging to get rid of statistical variations. There's something else peculiar in the counts from the new Sniffer, but I'd rather not talk about that until I know what I'm doing."

"Keep me posted. There's still one key piece of information missing in what we have so far." John highlighted the companion peak. "About this. I need to know *when*. It's going to hit sooner than the main pulse, but how long do we have? A day, a week?"

Amanda breathed out, explosively. "I'm sorry. The scale is shown along the abscissa, but it doesn't include the origin. We don't have much time. The particle bundles from the minor pulse will hit their maximum count forty-eight hours from now. Then the count will fall away and by sixty hours it will be back to normal."

"But maybe we won't be."

When things went wrong you could curse; when things went *really* wrong you didn't have time for that luxury. John, as a matter of habit, called a flow chart onto the display. It was more for Amanda's sake than his own, because he already had a good idea of what it would reveal.

"Here's the master schedule." He moved the cursor. "And this vertical line at fifteen days shows what we hope will be happening when the big pulse hits. But we're more interested in what happens here." He introduced another vertical line on the display. "That's forty-eight hours from now. As you see, we have no defense system in operation—old or new. We have to take that as a given, and see what everyone will be doing. I show you on Cusp Station, setting up the high-speed computer links with Sky City. Will Davis and his team are there, too, installing the pulse field generator. Cusp isn't shielded well enough; you'll all have to fly back and sit out the particle storm on Sky City. Torrance Harbish and Rico Ruggiero have a team outside, fine-tuning the balance of forces to hang Cusp Station and Sky City at the correct distance from Earth. They'll have to come inside. The people we have to worry about most are Nordstrom's group, out on the old shield. They're modifying the superconducting circuits so they work with the low-intensity detection field. They can't stay out there, even for a pulse this size. It's at least a ten-hour flight to safety. I want you to pass the word to Nordstrom at once."

"But what about Earth?" Amanda scanned the flow chart and saw only in-space activities. "What will people do there?"

"Dig. Hide below the surface, or stay under water. The new defense isn't ready, and the old shield won't stop the particle bundles. People down on Earth should be all right. Lots of fireworks for about twelve hours, but this pulse packs less than a hundredth of the energy of the main one. I'm a lot more worried about things out here."

"I thought Sky City had ample shielding."

"For individual particles, yes, but I'm not sure about particle bundles. Maybe they'll be stopped, maybe some of them will pass through Sky City like it's not there. I'm expecting a few to get through no matter what we do; statistically that's inevitable. But too many of those and our field generators and computers will stop working. Problem is, I don't know how many is too many. I'll ask Lauren to try another calculation—she's the least busy of the group."

John glanced at the clock. "Two o'clock. She's going to have a fit. Bruno Colombo, too. I'll have to wake him up."

"Hmph." Amanda made a face. "Good luck with that one. I wouldn't dare."

"Bruno will have to make worse calls than any of mine. He's got to wake Nick Lopez and Urbain Tosca, and tell them that the WPF and the UN have two days to organize the whole planet."

"What about me? I'll call Nordstrom, and I'll work on the other anomaly I mentioned. What else can I do to help?"

John studied Amanda's unlined face. "Not tired?"

"Fresh as a daisy."

"Then go and wake up Star Vjansander. She's been pestering me for weeks to let some bundles through the defense system so she can capture and study them. Tell her that her wish was just granted. By the time this peak has been and gone, we'll have more than enough bundles."

"Should I wake her right now?"

"Might as well. Everyone else is going to be up; why not Star? Oh, and Amanda."

She was already standing up to leave the information center. She turned. "Yes?"

"Tell Star that no matter how pleased she is with all this, she'd better not show it."

"Or else?"

"Or else she's going to find that everyone in Sky City engineering is too busy to make a capture-and-contain device for particle bundles."

"Isn't it easy? The bundles are all charged. You just slow them and contain them with electromagnetic fields. Star must know how."

"She undoubtedly does. But knowing how and making it happen are two different things. Star is no engineer."

Amanda nodded. "Wilmer Oldfield says that Star can't make coffee without breaking the jug." She grinned at John. "You'll probably kill me for saying so, but I'm sort of enjoying this. It's interesting and it's *exciting*."

"I'm glad you think so. But while this first pulse may be a small one compared with the main hit, people are going to die. Remember the old curse: May you live in interesting times."

As she hurried out John stared again at the display of the particle counts, with its innocuous-looking little side peak. That blip looked like nothing, but it derived from the huge stellar energies of a whole exploding star. He had told the truth to Amanda: People were undoubtedly going to die, if not here then down on Earth.

And yet Amanda was right, too. John felt worry, he felt nervousness, he even felt fear. But underneath everything, deep down, the excitement of the challenge was growing.

They were weeks away from the peak. They had not yet reached the first of the foothills. The hardest times surely lay ahead. But there, visible in the distance, loomed the mountain.


Maddy's dinner with John Hyslop had been a great success. A success, that is, if you didn't mind being with a man apparently impervious to any form of romantic suggestion. They had talked, with the ease of old friends, about everything on Earth and off it. They had compared Gordy Rolfe and Bruno Colombo as bosses, they had laughed, and they had lingered. He had agreed, instantly, to meet with her and Seth Parsigian the next day, without even asking her the subject—score one for Seth. And then, at the end of the evening, he had escorted her to her rooms, kissed her on the cheek with a chasteness and formality you might expect from a legal guardian, and left. He told her he had to work.

Surprisingly, after that Maddy had slept comfortably and easily. Apparently that made her a Sky City oddity, since the next morning every other person at breakfast claimed to have been up most of the night, making preparations for the "blip storm," an unexpected particle squall only a couple of days away. No one else had managed more than a couple of hours in bed. John Hyslop, according to Star Vjansander, had slept not at all.

Maddy and Seth were on John's schedule for ten o'clock in the morning. Last night it had seemed an excellent choice, an hour when John should be fully awake but not yet weighed down with the problems of the day. Now you could hardly pick a worse time. If he had been up all night, John would be too exhausted or too overwhelmed with work even to listen. And Seth Parsigian—the louse who had talked Maddy into the meeting with John Hyslop in the first place—would not even be present.

The voice message had been waiting for her after breakfast. "Hey. I gotta little problem to take care of down on Earth. I'm not sure how long I'll be gone, 'cause flights to an' from Sky City are gonna be tight as hell 'til the blip storm excitement dies down. You go ahead and handle John Hyslop. Tell him anythin', but make him say yes."

Didn't Seth realize that the same particle storm that could maroon him down on Earth would probably ruin all their chances of a meeting with John? The whole inside of the space city thrummed with energy and activity. For the first time in many months, worries about the Sky City murders had been pushed into the background.

Maddy went first to the plant engineering test facility, the meeting place that John had suggested. It was no surprise to find that he was not there. She sent a message over the Sky City general telcom channel. Ten minutes later she still had no reply.

Where was he? In one corner of plant engineering Maddy found Jessie Kahn and a slew of new attendant rolfes. A distracted Jessie, dictating rolfe assignments that yesterday would have been far above her level of seniority, waved a vague hand at Maddy. "Try the generating plant—they're going loony there because the bundles interfere with the control circuits, and that might shut everything down. Or the engineering information center; John was there most of the night. Or Bruno Colombo's office—I know a major flap was going on there. Maybe even Cusp Station. That has to be battened down before the storm hits. He could be there."

Jessie's tone said more than her words. *Go anywhere, Maddy Wheatstone, but get the hell out of my hair.*

Maddy went to the power-generation facility, on the axis beyond the main body of Sky City. Panic, yes, but no sign of John Hyslop. No one seemed to be expecting him. The engineering information center was deserted except for Torrance Harbish, who provided even less than Jessie Kahn: a gloomy shake of the head and a "Could be anywhere." At Bruno Colombo's outer office, guardian-of-the-inner-sanctum Goldy Jensen greeted Maddy with a snarl like a rabid wolf and a curt "Of course he's not here. And he's not on Cusp Station."

"Then where is he?"

"How should I know? Am I John Hyslop's keeper?"

*Not John Hyslop's, lady; Bruno Colombo's.* Maddy politely thanked Goldy and retreated.

Where? Maddy felt increasingly useless. Her wanderings through Sky City had made one thing evident: The space facility was in total turmoil. People were trying to cram weeks of labor into days, and it wasn't working. They didn't have a moment to spare.

It was already ten-forty. The time for the meeting with John had come and gone; still he had not answered her telcom message. Was there a place where he would be sure to go at some time in the next twenty-four hours?

Well, even if John were on a Neirling boost, he would crash by late tonight. And no matter where he passed out, he would be trundled back to his own quarters to sleep it off.

Maddy knew where John lived—a good thing Seth wasn't here,

or she'd have received his knowing wink. She ascended twenty levels, moved halfway around the cylinder of the city, and arrived at John's apartment. She tried the door, and it was not locked.

Her glance both ways along the curved corridor seemed ridiculous—maybe she had no right to enter, but after all she was not planning to steal anything. She only wanted to leave a message.

She slipped inside and gently closed the door. Once in, she stared around with curiosity. This was the place, in her imagination, they had returned to last night. The living room was small, decorated much the way she would have imagined it: simple but comfortable furniture; a dozen nonprofessional color photographs on the walls, with John against a background of vast suspension bridges; a 3-D hologram of Sky City's interior structure; and, a little more surprising, half a dozen of Escher's gravity-defying lithographs and wood engravings. She recognized "Relativity," "Waterfall," "Ascending and Descending," and "Other World," but the strange lithograph "Print Gallery," with its bizarre curved cityscape whose geometry somehow suggested the interior of Sky City itself, was new to her.

The bedroom was on the right. Maddy went into it, telling herself that John's bed was the one place he was sure to find a message when he came home. The room was much too functional for her taste, and noticeably short on furniture. Bed, dresser, closet, a door that presumably led through to the bathroom—there was not even a comfortable chair. Maddy perched on the small bedside table. She was all set to write a note when her eye caught another detail. The dresser was bare except for a single picture.

It was a portrait of Maddy, as she appeared in one of the Argos Group's rare promotional materials. She was smiling out of the frame in well-groomed and confident splendor, assuring the world that no job was too difficult or complex for the management skills of Maddy Wheatstone. The spoken blurb, as Maddy remembered it, said much the same thing.

The brochure was almost a year old. John must have found it somewhere in the records of Sky City, and cut out and framed the picture. That knowledge, much more than anything she was doing, made Maddy feel like an absolute intruder.

She stood up. Forget the note; she would find some other way to reach John. She headed for the bedroom door, and at that moment heard a sound behind her.

She gasped and the skin of her forearms prickled into goose bumps. Someone else was in the apartment. She could hear them, just a few feet away.

She swung around and saw nothing. Imagination? No. The bathroom. The door was open a few inches.

Maddy tiptoed that way and peered through the crack. She saw John, sitting on a radiator cover and slumped back in the angle of the walls. He was naked, his eyes were closed, and his hair was tousled and damp. A towel lay on the floor in front of him. It looked as if he had taken a shower and fallen asleep in the middle of drying himself. No surprise, if he had been up all night.

The right thing to do was tiptoe away. John would never know that she had been here. But he was sitting in an unstable position. If he fell forward in his sleep, a sharp corner of the sink was waiting for his head.

Make a noise to wake him up, then run?

Stupid. That was even more likely to make him fall over.

Maddy opened the door all the way. In the quarter-gee field it was easy to place one arm under his legs and the other behind his back and lift him clear of the radiator cover. Harder was the move through the narrow door, but she managed it without banging on either side. She carried him over to the bed and gently laid him down. He was on top of the covers, but it was not cold.

Time to leave.

Maddy moved to the foot of the bed and stood there, staring down at him. He had spoken of mountain climbing in his youth, and now that he was unclothed she could see the corded tendons of his legs and arms. His skin was fair and unnaturally pale—or maybe, for someone who lived on Sky City, it was naturally pale. Direct sunlight out here was a killer, rich in the hard ultraviolet radiation that never made it through the Earth's atmosphere to the surface.

But John was overworked, too. It was not ultraviolet, or its absence, that had placed the dark smudges below his eyes. Maddy moved her glance back along his body. She was startled to see that those eyes were no longer closed. John was staring—not at her, but straight up at the ceiling.

Was he still asleep, with his eyes open? Maddy backed away, through into the living room.

Time to leave. This time, *definitely*. She could hear sounds from the bedroom.

Again she hesitated. She was here; John was here. When would there be another chance of a meeting? Not until the present crisis was over, and maybe not for a long time afterward.

She went quietly across to the outer door and opened it. She knocked and called, "Anyone here? May I come in?"

How bogus could you get? But he was answering, "I'm through here. Just a minute."

It was more like twenty seconds before he appeared in slacks and a short-sleeved shirt. His hair still fell damp over his forehead, and he was barefoot.

"We were supposed to have a meeting this morning." Maddy tried to look him in the eye, and failed. "You weren't where I thought you would be. So I tried here. I guess you forgot we had a meeting."

"No." He smiled at her. "I'd never forget a meeting with you."

Something about him had changed. Maddy had an idea what. As long as the crisis lasted he would be the focus for all the engineering work on Sky City, and he drew power from that. Just as she felt more and more useless, he was increasingly in control.

He went on, "I came here because I'd been up all night. I wanted to look my best when I met you, and I thought a shower and a change of clothes would do the trick. It did the trick, all right. The last thing I remember is sitting down in the bathroom to dry myself off. Then I was on my bed, staring at the ceiling. You know all about the particle burst?"

"The blip storm? That's what they're calling it. Yes, nobody's talking of anything else."

"Then you know I don't have much time to talk. What's on your mind?"

Did he realize who had moved him from the bathroom? Had he seen her standing at the foot of the bed, inspecting him?

No time to worry about that. John had his shoes on, and he was already leading them out of his quarters.

Maddy said, "It's about the Sky City murders. That's what I wanted to talk to you about."

That stopped him. The corners of his mouth turned down, and he looked ten years older. "What about them?"

"Seth Parsigian and I know who did it. But we don't have hard evidence, so we need to set up a trap. It would work like this."

Maddy kept the story short and simple. At the end John seemed older than ever.

"You don't believe me?" she asked.

"The hell of it is, I do. But I hardly have a spare moment, and it's going to get worse. I can't see any way to help."

"We don't need help. We just want you to make an announcement."

"What about Doris Wu's family? They'll want details."

"They'll not hear of it. Only a few people will. Before word spreads, we'll have the murderer."

He hesitated. For the first time, Maddy thought she had a chance.

"When do you want me to announce it?"

"Not now. And not during the blip storm—we're not ready. The best time will be when the main wave hits."

"Maddy, that's the worst possible time. Everything and everyone will be stressed to their limit. This place will be in chaos."

"Chaos is what the murderer will rely on." They were approaching the open doors of the information center, and Maddy's last opportunity for a private discussion. She took John's arm, so that he had to turn and face her. "We'll probably only have one chance—ever. The evidence just isn't there. Will you do it?"

He nodded. "When I first heard about the murders I was upset because I could do nothing. Now maybe I can. Just tell me when. All right?"

Maddy wanted to shout, *Yes!* She also wanted to hug him. She had no time for either, because the entrance to the information center was suddenly full of people. At the front were Amanda Corrigan and Wilmer Oldfield. Behind them, crowding forward, were Star Vjansander and Lauren Stansfield and two data analysts whose names Maddy didn't remember.

Star and both data analysts all began to speak at once. But it was Wilmer's voice, calm and slow and serious, that continued and cut through the rest.

"Amanda found another anomaly in the Sniffer data. If Star's right in her interpretation, everything just got a lot more interesting. You need to hear about this."

# 28

As soon as John was settled in front of the displays, Wilmer Oldfield turned to Amanda Corrigan. "Ready to begin? It's your discovery."

"But I had no idea *what* I'd found." Amanda wriggled in embarrassment and looked at the audience. Seven people, including Maddy hovering at the back. That was too many for Amanda's comfort. She turned back to Wilmer Oldfield. "You explained it to me. Can't you talk about it?"

"I'll do the first bit, then we'll see." Wilmer moved to the display control panel and glanced at John. "Ask questions anytime, because I don't know the best place to start. Let's go with the first Sniffers we sent out, and what they measured. They were high-acceleration probes with low-cross-section instruments." He moved the pen across the control pad, and a thin, wobbly line with a distinct curve appeared on the display.

Wilmer stared at it with disgust. "These bloody gadgets. Isn't there a board someplace that I can draw on?"

"Behind you." Lauren Stansfield stepped over to a wall and opened two small doors to reveal a white board. Maddy noticed that Lauren alone, of all the people in the room, was wearing custom-made clothing. The pin on her left breast glowed with the varying colors of a fire opal. Expensive—even if no one else in the room but Maddy knew it.

"Write with this," Lauren went on. "Erase with this pad—a touch is enough, the pen is electronic."

"Right." Wilmer drew a small circle. "Here we are. And here's Alpha C." Another small circle. "And here's the path of a Sniffer."

He drew a wavering line between the two stellar systems. To Maddy's eye it was no better than his effort at the control panel, but Wilmer nodded at it in satisfaction.

"Good enough. Now let's look at the particles flung out by the Alpha C supernova. If you didn't know any better, you'd expect them to spread out pretty much equally in all directions. Spheres, like this, expanding in time."

He drew a set of rough circles, each centered on the point that depicted Alpha Centauri.

"If that's what was happening, the particle density would go down as the inverse square of the distance from the supernova, as the surface area they pass through goes *up*. Then the number of particles that a Sniffer measured would be less for the Sniffers that were launched later, simply because they meet the particle flux farther from Alpha C.

"But we know that the particles and radiation didn't come out equally in all directions—the gamma pulse proved that twenty-seven years ago. Instead, a shell of gases around the supernova bottled up everything inside. That shell expanded and thinned, until finally it was weak enough to rupture. Then everything—gamma rays and particles—could squirt out from inside in one particular direction. Like this."

Wilmer erased the set of spheres and replaced them with a narrow cone, its point on Alpha Centauri and its axis running toward the solar system.

"Think of it like a searchlight beam. No matter how tightly focused the beam is, as you go farther away from the searchlight the circle of light that it throws gets bigger, and the brightness of the light in that circle becomes less. With lasers, the spread can be very small, so sometimes it looks like the beam's not spreading at all. Sort of like this."

He replaced the cone by a long, narrow cylinder, running between Alpha Centauri and Sol.

"That looks like the worst case imaginable." Wilmer laid down the marker. "For it to happen, the particles thrown out by Alpha C would have to come straight at Sol, with no beam spreading at all. Looked impossible, so we didn't worry about that case. The most reasonable situation seemed like the second one, the particles lying in a narrow cone that gradually widened as they went farther from Alpha C. And that's exactly what the first Sniffers found. Sniffer-B met the particle wave farther away from the supernova, and the particle counts that it measured were less than for Sniffer-A.

The density was falling like the inverse square of the distance. No worries.

"Then we get the latest Sniffer data. It meets the particle wave much closer to Sol and farther from Alpha C, and it's also a different instrument design. Not easy to compare results. But your gal did it." He nodded toward Amanda Corrigan, who blushed like an eight-year-old. "First thing she finds is bad news. We have the blip storm on the way real soonish, and we're no way ready for it. You've all been working to batten down before it gets here. But Amanda noticed something else about the blip measurements. They didn't match the blip that she could pull out of the *old* Sniffer data, once she knew to look for it. The most recent Sniffer data was taken farther from Alpha C, close to us. The particle counts in the blip should have been lower than in the old data—the inverse square falloff—or, at the very worst, no bigger. But the data don't show that. They show the number of counts per unit volume *increasing* as the storm gets closer to the solar system. And that seemed flat impossible."

Wilmer picked up the marker again and stepped to the board. "Star and me happened to be around, so Amanda came to us. The only thing we could think of was the obvious one. The particle beam pattern isn't doing any of the things I drew. It's doing *this.*"

He drew two wobbly curved arcs from Alpha Centauri toward the Sun, making a form like a very long and thin cucumber. "The particle beam spreads until it gets to *here.*" He marked a point roughly halfway between the two stellar systems. "Then it begins to converge again as it approaches Sol."

Wilmer placed the marker carefully back on its holder and went to sit down. No one spoke until John asked, "Converges? Converges how much?"

"Not my department." Wilmer turned to Amanda Corrigan. "How much?"

"I don't know. We don't have enough data points yet to make a good extrapolation."

"We need an answer, even without data. Wilmer? Can theory help?"

"I can only go back to what Star has been saying all this past month. Alpha C didn't just blow up and randomly squirt radiation and particles this way. It was *made* to explode. The gamma pulse and the particle beam were *made* to aim right for us. If you'll accept those as working assumptions, plus a few other things, then we can calculate an answer."

"*Made* to happen?" One of the data analysts spoke—*Raymond,* thought Maddy. *No, Raoul.* "You mean somebody out there decided to make a supernova, just so they could wipe out humans? You're saying aliens exploded Alpha Centauri?"

Wilmer frowned. "You have expanded on Star's hypothesis. She did not say that, and I am saying only that we are involved in an event inconsistent with the standard theories of stellar evolution."

"But if it's *not* that, and aliens—"

John interrupted. "We'll worry about alternative theories later. You say that you've done a calculation and have an answer?"

"Star has." Wilmer nodded to his young protégé, who was bouncing excitedly on the edge of her seat. "Go on, girl. Tell 'em, before you burst."

"Yer have ter make some more assumptions before yer can get an answer." Star hopped up and went to the board. "Like, symmetry about the midpoint, and a parametric form for the strong-force modification that we assume holds the particle bundles together. But given that, and assuming that everything else goes linearly, the best guesstimate I can make says we get hit with everything emerging from a solid angle of one two-hundredth of a steradian of Alpha C. That's instead of everything coming from mebbe one three-thousandth, if we had a spreading cone."

"Translation?" said Lauren Stansfield. "I can't think in those units."

"The blip storm that arrives tomorrow will be about fifteen times as severe as we thought," Wilmer said. "It's not a blip anymore."

"A factor of fifteen. That's bad, but not totally disastrous." Lauren Stansfield was examining a sheet of notes. "Sky City will survive. From what Will says, the shield won't be totally destroyed. Earth will be worse off."

"Maybe." John had been watching Wilmer Oldfield's face. "That's not the whole story. Is it?"

"Looks like not. The convergence we're talking about applies to the whole particle flux, not just the small peak. Assuming Star's numbers hold up—we'll have a better test of that when the latest Sniffer hits the wave front—then everything scales by the same factor. The maximum particle density will be up by a factor of fifteen. Same factor for the energy that hits Earth."

"Fifteen." John was already moving to the message console. "I assume the direction the particles comes from doesn't change."

Wilmer shrugged. "Tiny bit. Not enough to notice—the beam convergence factor is less than one in a thousand. It's the energy delivered that we have to worry about. Without convergence, we predicted a maximum energy per square meter hitting the top of Earth's atmosphere at about three thousand watts per square meter. That compares with about fifteen hundred watts per square meter coming from the Sun as radiation. Now we're saying the energy from the particle storm will peak at more like forty-five thousand watts per square meter."

"Thirty times as much as the Sun?" John was opening simultaneous circuits to Bruno Colombo, Nick Lopez, and Urbain Tosca. Let Bruno be as mad as he liked over the breach of regular protocol.

"Thirty times as much *energy* as the Sun," Wilmer corrected. "But it'll be coming in a very different form. Instead of light you have charged particle bundles. We'll have strong forward scattering, tons of ionization, and God knows what secondary effects."

"One worry at a time." The lines were opening, and John could hear startled voices at the other end. Direct messages from the Sky City engineering information center were without precedent. "I ought to have known that something like this was going to happen—the work on the shield and the field generators has been going too smoothly."

Maddy, ignored at the back of the room, wondered if she had misunderstood everything. She had followed few of the exchanges, except Raoul's suggestion that the whole Alpha Centauri supernova had been intentional and created by aliens. But regardless of explanations, weren't they saying that in less than two days Earth would be hit by a particle storm thirty times as bad as anyone had expected? And if that was the case, why was everyone so calm?

She knew the answer. No wailing, no moaning about the imminent end of the world—because everyone with her was either an engineer or a physicist.

Maddy looked around, inspecting the others one by one. You didn't have to go all the way to Alpha Centauri to find aliens. There was a roomful of them right here.

# 29

Alpha Centauri lies at sixty degrees south on the celestial sphere. The preliminary particle storm—call it a blip if you like, but no longer dismiss it as insignificant—would hit Earth from that direction, with the zero hour of peak maximum occurring at three-fifteen local time. Every prediction from Celine Tanaka's science advisor, Benedict Mertok, said that Washington, at thirty-nine degrees north, should be affected only in minor ways.

And yet . . .

Mertok was confident and knowledgeable and polished, the very model of a modern senior advisor, but the person whose opinion Celine really trusted was Wilmer Oldfield. She placed a call to Wilmer on Sky City early in the morning. She had to radiate public optimism, but she needed to know the worst.

"Know for sure? Can't tell you that. Might as well be betting on a horse race." Wilmer was sitting at a Sky City communications unit and steadily consuming the huge breakfast of a man without a care in the world. At Celine's question he touched his hand to the bald spot on top of his head. "Star and me have a theory, you're right about that, but it's not a *tested* theory. We need new Sniffer data. We'll be able to give you a better answer in a few days."

"Wilmer, a few days is no good." Celine had drunk lots of coffee and barely nibbled at dry toast. How could anyone eat the way he did so early in the morning? "We've got a psychic calling all the media, telling people that the world is going to end at three-fifteen this afternoon. The Fist of God will strike, and Earth will split open like a melon dropped from a tenth-floor window."

"He's an idiot. You can quote me on that."

"It's a woman. So this won't be the end of the world. But what will happen? I have all emergency services on standby alert. I have a national broadcast this afternoon. I have fourteen planeloads of people asking permission, right now, to take off and fly south."

"Fly *south*? What for?"

"God knows. I guess for the fun of it. They're thrill seekers who see themselves as daredevils, on the way to Tierra del Fuego for a big whoop-de-doo storm party. I'm in a tricky position. On one hand, I'm supposed to make sure there's no panic, and to do that I have to minimize talk of danger. On the other hand, I don't want even lunatics to head south if they're likely to kill themselves. I need to know what to tell them, and everybody else. That's why I called you. I wasn't just being sociable."

"I can see that." His face was serious, the heavy brow furrowed in thought. "Celine, me and Star can't tell you what's going to happen today, and we shouldn't be telling you what to do. But let me say this for starters: Every single thing we've ever assumed about the Alpha Centauri supernova turned out later to be wrong."

He paused, for so long that Celine in her caffeine high wriggled in impatience. She wanted instant answers. Except that thirty years of experience had taught her that Wilmer wouldn't be hurried.

"We talk as though we know a lot about supernovas," he continued at last. "We don't. They are extremely rare events. You have only one or two a century in a typical galaxy, and most of them take place so far away that they give us little information. Did you know that there hasn't been a naked-eye supernova since the invention of the telescope? That's four and a half centuries. When scientists tell you we understand supernovas, they mean something very specific and very limited. What we should say is that we have been able, through computer models, to show how certain kinds of stars and stellar systems can produce the enormous energy release that characterizes a supernova. That *doesn't* mean no other type of star can possibly explode, or that some other supernova-creating mechanism can't exist. The limits we assign to Nature sometimes define our own lack of imagination.

"Alpha C is a great example. Before 2026, every astrophysicist—including me—would have told you it couldn't happen. Wrong type of binary system, no dwarf component, no supermassive star. But it happened. After that, no one predicted the gamma pulse would come along and wipe out all our microcircuits. It did. After the gamma pulse, we still didn't learn. The fact that the burst was aimed directly at the solar system was dismissed as an 'accident of geometry.' "

"But *you* predicted the particle storm," Celine objected. "Twenty-seven years ago, you told me it would happen."

"I did. That was in the pre-supernova theories. And based on those theories we started to build the space shield. Then we were surprised again by an observational result, that the particles come grouped in trillion-component lumps instead of singly. The old shield was useless at stopping bundles. So we had to come up quick with a new shield idea. This one still assumed what everyone 'knew,' that the strength of the particle storm would weaken over distance as it traveled farther away from the supernova. Now we find that the beam is *converging* as it approaches Sol. That means greater particle densities, and the new shield will be inadequate. I don't know what Ben Mertok and the others are telling you, but if everybody's track record—including mine—is anything to go by, *whatever* you are being told is going to prove wrong."

"Marvelous. Wilmer, you can sit back and say you have no idea what will happen. I'm not allowed that luxury. I have to say *something* to the media this afternoon, whether I turn out to be right, wrong, or ridiculous. You sound as though you haven't even been thinking about that."

"I have. I'll bet good money that we'll see surprises this afternoon—only I can't say what. Otherwise they wouldn't be surprises. But I doubt they'll be too awful. And today's not what I've been thinking about most. Today might be messy, in ways I can't begin to suggest, but I'm sure we'll pull through. Our concern has to be with three weeks from now."

"Three weeks?" Celine wasn't sure she wanted to know. "Three weeks, when the main storm hits. You're worried about more surprises?"

"I don't need more surprises to make me worry. The things we already think we know are enough for that. Did you see the figures for peak energy input when the big storm arrives? *That's* going to be the Fist of God."

"The only summary I've seen is based on your and Star's calculations. You said that the energy hitting us will be thirty times as much as we thought before. But the maximum impact will last only a few days, and thirty doesn't sound too bad. I figure we can live through that."

"You don't mean *figure*. You mean you *hope*." Wilmer turned to Star, seated next to him and so far silent. "You tell her."

Star nodded amiably at Celine. She was holding a shiny metal canister about the size of a beer can. "See what he does? Puts me on ter give you the bad news. No worries, you think. But I got new data, and things don't look good. D'yer know what cooperative phenomena are?"

"Assume I don't. Tell me."

"It's when a lot of little things hook up together, ter produce effects yer wouldn't expect from one of them. This here"—she held up the metal cylinder—"has a few thousand particle bundles in it. We collected 'em over the past day or two during the first slow rise in particle flux. Caught 'em in flight, slowed 'em down in a synchrotron, held 'em in using an electromagnetic field once they were down to thermal velocities. They're fascinating little buggers. For starters, they're stable as hell. We put individual bundles in the middle of a fusion plasma with an effective temperature of fifteen million degrees, and they hold together. When you get a lot of bundles, they exhibit a group attractive force—opposite ter what you'd expect, 'cause they're all positively charged. That makes 'em converge as they travel through open space, an' they're doing it now. The only thing they can't stand is neutral atoms—which is what they'll find when they hit Earth. They lose their charge and fall apart. Trouble is, they don't go quiet. A disintegrating bundle gives off loads of energy."

"How much is a load?"

"About twenty times their free-space kinetic energy. I used ter say that each bundle hits as hard as a small bullet. Now I'd say it's like an *explosive* bullet."

"Not thirty times as much energy as we thought, but six hundred?"

"Yerss. An' there's an outside chance of worse news. D'you know what homeostasis is?"

"I used to, before I rotted my brain with politics." Celine thought for a moment. "It's a feedback effect, one that gives a system the tendency to return to its original state when it's perturbed away from it."

"Yer got it. An' Earth's one big homeostatic system. Dump in more energy, and when you stop doing that the temperatures and pressures and all the biosphere tend ter go back ter the original states. That's how come the Sun could increase its energy output thirty percent over the past couple of billion years, like it did, but surface temperatures hardly shifted in all that time.

"But there's limits. Hit Earth hard enough and quick enough, an' homeostasis could fail. Yer might go to a steady state all right, but mebbe it's not the one you started from. An' that's the way it looks to me sometimes, when I run the numbers for the big particle storm."

"You mean Earth will be different forever after the main storm. Can you tell me how different?"

"Nah. I can't tell, and nobody else can neither. We're probably all right, but yer got some scary possibil'ties. One run I looked at has end-point oxygen at three percent—all right for plants, mebbe, but a bugger for animals. Another has global end-point temperature at forty-two Celsius. Blood heat for humans is thirty-seven Celsius. We'd all be goners."

Celine looked at Wilmer. "That sounds like the end of the world to me. But you said it wouldn't happen."

"I said it wouldn't happen *today*. We'll come through today just fine. I'm talking weeks from now, and it's all still speculation and theory. We might be wrong again. In fact, based on recent past experience, we will be. Victims of our theories, we are, like everybody else. Me and Star have some even newer ideas based on the bundles she caught, but it's too soon to talk about them."

"So what will happen today? What do I tell people?"

"If it were me, I'd follow what Ben Mertok said to do. You tell everybody that we'll be all right. I think we will be, and there's no point saying different. But I'd make damn sure there's no planes in the air or space launches scheduled between three and four o'clock. And I'd freeze ground transportation. People talk about zero hour coming at three-fifteen as though that's a single moment of time, but the blip has width. We'll be at fifty percent particle flux seven minutes before we hit peak maximum."

Celine nodded. She heard Wilmer, but already her mind was running ahead to another problem. What should the public know, and when? "About this possible change away from planetary homeostasis. I know science is an open field, and scientists hate any suggestion of secrecy. But could you avoid telling anyone else about Earth's becoming uninhabitable?"

Wilmer and Star looked at each other. "It's only a possibility," Wilmer said weakly.

*Scientific scruples.* "We don't even want a *possibility,* Wilmer. Not until we can decide on policy."

Star was shaking her head. "Yer don't get it, mam." Her wide mouth turned down. "We can't not talk ter nobody—because we already done it."

"Damnation. Who?"

"John Hyslop, an' Maddy Wheatstone."

"What did they say?"

"They asked us not ter tell anybody. Same as you did. But we have."

"That's all right." Politics was the art of the practical. "If they know, they know. It sounds as though they won't talk about it. Anyone else?"

"No, mam."

"Good. Then please keep it like that. Let's survive today, then we'll worry about tomorrow. Maybe by then you'll have a new theory." *One that doesn't sound so hopeless.*

"Maybe we will." Wilmer raised his cup and took a long, satisfied swallow. "I doubt if we'll think much more about theories today. It's going to be too interesting, just watching what happens. And if Mertok or anybody tells you they *know* what things will be like at three this afternoon, tell 'em they're full of it."

So much for breakfast reassurance. *It's not the end of the world today—we still have weeks to go.* Whatever she did, she was not going to say *that* to the American people.

*Don't look up. Behave normally. Smile.* Celine stood on the back lawn of the White House, very aware that in a couple of minutes she would be on national and international television. Three-oh-six in the afternoon, local time. A slightly overcast day of late summer, broken clouds a change after the year's near-interminable rains. Temperature, eighty-six degrees. Low humidity. Light breeze from the northwest. *Time to zero hour: nine minutes.*

The urge to look up, even when you supposedly knew better, was close to irresistible.

Celine vowed she wouldn't do that during the broadcast, but in the same moment she caught a flicker of movement out of the corner of her eye. She cursed under her breath. A media skycar was cruising north, about three hundred feet above the Mall. So much for day-long warnings to be on the surface—or better still, beneath it—when zero hour arrived.

"Tell security to get those idiots down," she snarled into her mike—and hoped that it was not yet connected to the network.

In spite of their assurances that nothing disastrous would happen in this part of the world, her staff had urged Celine to make her broadcast from one of the deep basement levels. She had refused. When all citizens could not hide away, she said, then she should not. She did not admit to a certain insatiable curiosity. Her decision meant the staff could not hide away, either. She could see Benedict Mertok eyeing her reproachfully, beyond the range of the cameras.

"Twenty seconds," said a voice in her ear. "Counting down . . ."

Celine could follow the digital readout on the left-hand camera. Three-oh-eight. On cue, she smiled into the cameras. "My fellow Americans. You do not need me to tell you that these are difficult times. In just a few minutes, a rain of high-energy particles generated by the Alpha Centauri supernova will strike our world. Fortunately for this country, the main effects will be felt far from here, in a remote area of the southern Indian Ocean."

She planned to talk right up to and through zero hour, her voice and image making it clear that this was a crisis survived, although at some possible cost.

"We are taking every possible precaution. Our scientific experts suggest that there could be another electrical surge, like the one that destroyed all Earth's microcircuits twenty-seven years ago. This time we are prepared. All vital communications have a microwave and fiber-optic backup. Emergency personnel are in place at every population center in every state. We have ample supplies of food and water and reserve power. All ground transportation is halted until the storm is over. All aircraft flights have been suspended until we give an all-clear."

*But I allowed fourteen planes full of nutcases to fly to Tierra del Fuego. I couldn't stop them and still tell people that things are fine and everything is under control.*

Three-eleven.

The storm was well over fifty percent intensity, moving fast toward its maximum. Far to the south, bundles of high-energy charged particles were smashing into the upper atmosphere, stripping electrons from neutral atoms of nitrogen and oxygen. The bundles moved so fast that they were hardly slowed by each impact, but according to Star it was an open question when the collisions would fragment the bundles into individual nuclei. No one could do more than guess the strength of the bundle binding forces in the presence of numerous free electrons. In any event, most of the bundles and their daughter particles would make it all the way down to the surface, each one accompanied by a flood of secondary particles and shortwave radiation.

Three-twelve.

Celine glanced quickly south. The Sun was peeping through high, broken clouds. Was it her imagination, or did the day seem a little dimmer?

"Although the new space shield was unfortunately not ready to deal with this first event, I have good news concerning the bigger storm that will strike us three weeks from now. Progress on our space facilities has been faster than expected, and I am told that the new shield will reach operational test status within ten days. The shield will be fully tested well before the next particle storm, ready and waiting to divert the danger. Not all particle bundles can be handled like this, but our own preparations continue, on the surface and beneath it. I have every confidence that we will deal successfully with the effects of any bundles that evade the shield."

The truth, but not the whole truth? How much truth was too much for the general population? You didn't want widespread panic and talk of Armageddon. What *was* the truth? Mertok and the other science advisors this morning hadn't agreed at all with

Wilmer and Star. Yes, Mertok said, more particle bundles would indeed get through the shield than originally expected. But the bulk of them would be deflected, and Earth would easily survive whatever was not. And any talk of runaway changes to a new steady-state Earth unrecognizably different from today's was nonsense.

Whom did you believe? She had heard from more than a dozen "experts." The trouble was, Wilmer had a terrible habit of being right.

Celine could read the clock while still looking straight into the camera. Three-fifteen. Zero hour.

*Keep talking. From now on it's an easy roll.*

"As for today's events, even as I speak the particle storm hitting the Southern Hemisphere has passed its peak. I feel sure that most of you, like me, have been completely unaware of its presence, and in another hour this first storm will be over and done with. We can go on with our normal everyday affairs and begin to prepare for the next challenge."

In the split second that it took to speak the word *challenge* the world suddenly became darker—much darker. Celine could no longer tell herself that the gloom was nothing more than the movement of the Sun behind a passing cloud.

In spite of herself, she looked away from the cameras and up into the afternoon sky. It was like no sky that she had ever seen. On the background of pale blue overcast ran hundreds of parallel dark streaks, so regular that they might have been drawn with a straight edge. They were everywhere, crossing the face of the Sun itself, dimming its brilliance and turning its warm circle into a ruled grating. As she watched, a new set of lines appeared, gridding the sky from north to south with another pattern of fine dark contrails. Afternoon had vanished. The White House lawn sat in the eerie half dark of a total solar eclipse.

There were cuss words that you could think but not say on a national broadcast. Celine breathed deeply and said, "Here in Washington we are experiencing an unusual atmospheric effect. It is presumably due to the particle storm. It will probably not last more than a few minutes, but I recommend that we all move indoors until this is over."

She forced a smile, turned, and walked steadily toward the stone path leading to the White House. When she was safely off camera she ripped away her cordless lapel mike, dropped it to the floor, and stamped it flat.

"Mertok! What the fuck is going on here?"

"It's all right, Madam President." He was hurrying to her side. "When the particle bundles hit the upper atmosphere they strip off free electrons. They follow Earth's magnetic lines of force, and they move fast. We knew this would happen. But there's some sort of group phenomenon that produces visible lines, and we didn't expect that. It is undoubtedly related to the size of the charged particle bundles. But I think that people have nothing to worry about."

"Nothing to worry about? I'm supposed to tell people they have nothing to worry about—when the Sun is going out in the goddamned sky? Mertok, when *should* I tell people to worry?"

"Madam President." He flapped a well-manicured hand toward the heavens. "See for yourself. It is already starting to fade."

Celine looked up. He was right. The lines were less pronounced. But the sky behind the dark streaks was no longer blue. It shimmered pink and gold and pale mauve. The sun was brighter, and had a greenish tinge.

She glared at Mertok—his face was an unnatural greenish yellow. "And this?"

"Electrical discharge effects from free electrons. Like an aurora, but much more powerful—that's why we can see it even in daylight, although of course the Sun is dimmed, too." He was staring up, not looking at Celine at all. "How very interesting. I wonder how long it will last."

Celine glared at him. He didn't notice. Of course he didn't notice. She had never realized it before, because Ben Mertok wore a veneer of political sophistication. But when you came right down to it, he and Wilmer and Star and the rest of the science advisors were the same under the skin.

They were all crazy. Show them a new scientific phenomenon, and the fact that the world might be ending became of minor importance.

Celine gestured to the crew to bring her a new microphone. She must continue her broadcast, reassuring anyone who had not run for cover that things were rapidly returning to normal.

Saying what?

*Yes, sure, the world may be going to end. But we don't want to talk about that, because it's weeks away. And if Maddy Wheatstone is right, some people on Earth have been trying to make things* worse, *rather than better, by screwing up shield development. But for now things are just peachy. Why don't we all go home and relax?*

# 30

The Southern Hemisphere, as predicted, took the brunt of the particle storm. But Star Vjansander alone had warned of the extent of the damage, amplified by the extreme stability of the particle bundles.

Reports from smart sensors scattered over land and sea, and from survey teams returning to the surface from their underground hideouts in Australia and Antarctica, gave a first estimate of conditions south of the equator. Ninety-nine percent of the incident flux had burned its way right through the atmosphere and tunneled deep below the surface, still moving at close to a tenth of light speed. It was preceded by a blue flood of Cerenkov radiation. Ground and water impacts caused the violent disintegration of ten percent of the bundles, but the rest remained intact and hit the surface as intensely charged nodules. These became electrically neutral in a few hours, exploding violently to individual atoms as ambient electrons dissipated their positive charge.

The effects on plant and animal life were immediate and devastating. Each bundle was minute, but it contained the energy of a bullet from a supervelocity rifle. The high positive charge greatly increased the interaction cross section with living tissue. The result of a single impact was a clean cylindrical hole four to six millimeters across, seared at the edges and surrounded by extended tissue damage like a radiation burn.

The arriving bundles peppered the surface with a mean separation distance of four meters. Survival of individuals became a matter of luck and statistics. Most populations of pelagic fish were little affected, protected by many meters of water depth. One pod of humpback whales had apparently dived at the right time and remained intact; another, only a few kilometers away, had suffered twenty percent losses. On the Antarctic ice cap, a survey team found a close-packed colony of emperor penguins quietly nursing their eggs in the polar winter; but one bird in forty was dead or badly wounded. Diving skuas fought over and dismembered the dying.

Humans, warned and well prepared, had done rather well. The only casualties were the result of ignorance or folly. The highest percentage of losses came among the nine hundred and seventy thrill seekers who had headed south to Tierra del Fuego for the "big blip party." The fourteen aircraft that took them there would no longer fly. Five hundred and ten survivors were waiting to be picked up and brought home, considerably chastened.

They were the exceptions. The general mood of the country and the world was upbeat. Even the southern countries, hardest hit, shared the euphoria. *We survived this one, we'll survive the big storm as well.*

Not everyone, however, was pleased that the planet had got off so lightly. Gordy Rolfe's best plans for Argos Group activities had been based on casualty counts in the tens to hundreds of millions, or at the very least a few million. Opportunities were always greatest in times of chaos.

He had followed the progress of the particle storm, moment by moment, from an observation post in a shallow shelter only a hundred meters from the northern edge of his Virginia estate. Of course, Argos Group equipment and staff were in place all around the globe, and they had reported to Gordy in real time. He rubbed his hands in satisfaction as the lands of southern Africa and Australia suffered their deadly sleet from heaven, more destructive than expected. He smiled when the Sun above his hideaway darkened in the sky and the broadcast from Washington was interrupted. But he frowned when Celine Tanaka returned, to announce that U.S. damage seemed to be minimal and the country would soon return to normal.

The best news was the rumor, reported to come from Washington but strongly denied there, that the particle storm due in three weeks would be vastly more fierce, energetic, and dangerous than anyone had expected. If a man couldn't get mileage from that, he didn't deserve to be in business.

Gordy, cheered by the thought, decided that nothing much more was going to happen today. It was late afternoon, and although it would soon be dawn on the other side of the world it was also the Southern Hemisphere's winter. Any reports could wait a few hours, until the short Antarctic day was over.

The sky was probably back to normal, too, but it might be worth taking a look at it. Gordy rode the one-man lift to the surface and looked around him. It seemed a disappointingly normal August evening, the Sun big and red and all set to dip below the horizon. He sauntered back toward the old schoolhouse. If nothing else, he could look forward to a pleasant evening deep within his private sanctum.

The elevator taking him down the thousand-foot drop creaked and groaned more than usual. It was probably time for some rolfe maintenance. Gordy's mind was on that as he left the elevator and ascended the tight spiral staircase of gray metal. If there was anything odd about the stairs or the locked hatch at the top, he certainly didn't notice. His home seemed just as he had left it, the door leading through to the green jungle habitat locked tight.

He started toward the study and workshop, the nerve center of the Argos Group underground headquarters, and suddenly halted. When he left, three rolfes had sat on the workbench in various stages of dismemberment. Now a fourth was beside them, an ugly truncated shape lacking head or legs.

By the time he turned it was too late. He glimpsed a moving shape, took one breath of sweet-smelling vapor, and then he saw nothing.

When he awoke he had no sense of lost time or unconsciousness, but he was lolling in a chair specially built to match the contours of his deformed back and shoulders. Six feet away, sitting on the workbench and watching him closely, was Seth Parsigian.

Seth nodded at him. "You weren't here, squire, so I made myself at home. Are you comfortable?"

"I would be more so if I were not tied up like this." Gordy gave an experimental tug at the tape that held him. It was far too strong to break. If he had a knife, he could cut it easily, but the useful tools were over at the workbench, where Seth was sitting. "Come on, Seth. This is ridiculous. Free me."

"You don't bother to ask why you're tied up. You're not cussing at me Gordy-style. I like that. Shows you got an efficient mind, know what's goin' on." Seth reached out and picked up the headless rolfe. "I though you might want to have this back."

"Why? Why would I want that one?" Rolfe was making a quick but covert survey of the room. The door to the jungle habitat was partway open. Everything else seemed normal. While Seth followed his look he again tested the tape that held him. There was a little give to it.

"I wouldn't bother doin' that while I'm here," Seth said. He ignored Gordy's question about the rolfe. "I don't mind you tryin' to get loose. I'd do the same. But if you look like you're winnin', I'll just have to tie you up again."

"I'm not trying to get loose. And I would like that rolfe back, but not for a while. It's one of the new models, isn't it, on lease to Sky City? It should be up there."

"Yeah. So should I. But actually, I'm not sure this one's gonna work anymore." Seth turned the rolfe over, revealing the gaping body cavity. "I pretty much had to turn its brain to mush to get at the hidden instruction set. But I found it. Why'd you try to kill me, Gordy? Wasn't I doin' the job you wanted me to?"

"You were. Plus a few things I didn't ask for."

"You mean findin' out about the Sky City game?" Seth grinned. "Ah, that was nothin'. You know me, I'm naturally nosy. Part of the reason you hired me. An' that's a lousy reason to try to kill me. Wouldn't it have been easier to buy me?"

"Of course it would." Rolfe sat up straighter in the chair. "Seth, you ought to know me better than that. If I'd wanted to dispose of you, there are more certain ways. I didn't expect that rolfe to kill you."

"Sure as hell looked that way to me. What did you expect?"

"Exactly what happened. That you would disable it."

"Yeah? Hm. S'pose it disabled *me*?"

"Then you wouldn't be the man I thought you were—the man you said you were when I hired you. Think of it as a little test, Seth. One that you passed with flying colors."

"That right? A test, eh?" Seth casually tossed the rolfe to one side, and it fell to the hard floor with a clang and clatter of metal. "Test for what?"

"For a more senior place in the Argos Group. I want you as my right-hand man." Rolfe leaned forward, as far as the tapes on his forearms and ankles would permit. His eyes burned with energy. "You may wonder why I would propose such a change at this particular time. I will tell you. A few days ago I had a great disappointment. Someone for whom I had planned a great future in this organization turned out to be less than I had hoped."

"Don't be coy. Maddy Wheatstone up an' quit on you. Right?"

"That is correct. She was a woman in whom I had invested much of my time and the group's resources, a woman who was being groomed for the top. Without warning or reason, she resigned."

"Oh, she had a reason. Sort of. She got swoony about her assignment."

"John Hyslop. I know that. But then I should blame myself even more, for a major error of judgment. Only a few weeks ago I was boasting of Maddy's dedication to the Argos Group and of her inner strength. I ought not to have done that. Such talk is hubris, an invitation to the gods to prove me wrong. And they did."

"Seems you oughta have been knockin' *her* off, not me."

"To what end? She has proved to be a weak reed. And I did not intend you to die."

"You said that before. But you programmed one of the new rolfes on the way to Sky City with a deadly bit of code, tuned just for me."

"Expecting, exactly as proved to be the case, that you would be able to look after yourself."

"Even so. Pretty hostile act toward an employee. Am I bein' dumb, or is it unreasonable to expect me to thank you for the chance at promotion?"

Rolfe shrugged, as much as he could with his constraints. "Are you looking for an apology? I will not offer one. You are here. You are unharmed. We are talking of future opportunities. You have no cause for complaint."

"Yeah. But you know, Gordy, you always talk formal when you're thinkin' hard. An' you're bein' formal now. So I better be thinkin', too. Can you gimme a minute?"

"Do I have a choice?"

"Guess not." Seth eased himself off the workbench and wandered around the chamber, examining communications equipment and controls. He spent a long time at the door to the habitat, apparently studying its design. Finally he wandered back.

"Seems like it ought to be tit for tat. You say you weren't tryin' to kill me. You were just playing a little game, testin' me out to see if I'm as smart as I'm s'posed to be. All right. But what about *you*? Are you as smart as *you're* supposed to be? If not, then *I'm* the one bein' cheated. If I had to pass a little test, you oughta do the same."

"Obviously I cannot be expected to agree with you. At the same time, I cannot deny the validity of your logic."

"Couldn't have put it better myself. So here's what we do." Seth pointed to the wall and the green jungle beyond. "I took a look out there earlier, and it's full of nasties. Mebbe they're all your sweethearts, but for me it's like Grandma: What big teeth you got."

"You are referring to the minisaurs."

"If that's what you call 'em. They didn't look much mini to me. They were quiet durin' the day, so I assume they're night feeders. I don't know how strong they are, but I'd guess plenty. If that door was open a few hours from now, an' they felt peckish, a man would have lotsa trouble keepin' 'em out."

"The door to the jungle habitat is always locked at night."

"That don't surprise me none. But tonight it won't be. I'm gonna smash the mechanical lock, an' fix the electronic one so it don't work, either. That door will stay open. Then I'm gonna bollix your communications equipment so you can't call for help from outside. I'm gonna take away anything that looks like it might be a weapon. An' I guess I'll take away the rolfes, too, even though they look busted. Then I'll leave by the hatch in the middle there, an' lock it from below so you can't get out that way." Seth came to Rolfe's side and examined the tapes. "Tight, but not too tight. My bet is you'll be free an hour after I'm gone. Then you can look for another way out, or find a way to stop the nasties gettin' at you while you work on the hatch, or anythin' else you feel like. How you spend your time is up to you. Think of this as your own little test—a lot easier than the one you gave me."

"You can't do this, Seth. It would take days to open the hatch from this side when it's locked below. I designed it that way. You would be leaving me to certain death."

"Would I? There's food here, there's water, there's tools. You're a smart man, a genius with electronic equipment." Seth returned to perch on the workbench and scrutinize Gordy Rolfe. He shook his head. "But I'm missin' somethin'. You're not sweatin', an' you're not screamin'."

"I refuse to scream and shout. I am not a coward."

"I believe that. I guess I didn't expect you would. But you should be thinkin' an' arguin' an' tryin' to talk me out of it, an' you're not doin' that, either. You got some hidden card, haven't you?"

"How could I have a hidden card? You've blocked the exits, you say you'll destroy my communications equipment, you'll leave me without weapons. Seth, you can't do this. You've seen the minisaurs. Any one of them can tear a human apart—and they hunt in teams."

"Save your breath, Gordy. I still say you got somethin' up your sleeve, though I can't guess what. But I'm not gonna complain. I had somethin' goin' for me that *you* didn't know about when your tin buddy come in to clobber me. So I figure we'll be even-steven."

Seth again stood up. "No more chitchat. I got work to do, an' I don't want to be here all night. Neither do you. While I'm busy, think how you'll get outa that tape."

He picked up two of the rolfes and tossed them toward the open hatch. They clattered away down the spiral staircase. "I'll wrap you a teeny bit more before I leave, so by the time you're free I'll be long gone. When you get outa here—assuming you do—call me. We can talk about my great future in the Argos Group."

First Gordy tried his teeth. Two minutes of chewing and tugging told him that would not work. The tape had a tough fiber substrate, and it called for something much sharper than human incisors.

His padded chair was not on casters, but by jerking backward and forward he could make the legs slide an inch or two each time along the smooth floor.

The workbench would be useless. Seth's definition of a weapon was a liberal one, and every saw, chisel, screwdriver, and knife edge had vanished down the spiral stair. Gordy humped his way slowly toward the kitchen. By the time he reached it, the overhead lights were dimming in concert with approaching dusk, far above the habitat. In an increasing gloom Gordy painfully turned the chair so that he could reach sideways with his right hand and pull open a kitchen drawer. No knives were left there, but he saw a vegetable scraper.

The scraper was at the back of the drawer, too far away for him to reach it. He pulled the drawer out as far as he could, then pushed it sharply in again. When he eased the drawer open, the scraper had jerked a couple of inches closer to the front.

Four more openings and rapid closings, and he had it. The scraper was an open-ended metal box, with metal corrugations of different roughness on each of the four sides. Gordy turned it by the handle on one end, very slowly and carefully. He had to work one-handed, and if he dropped it, there was no way to pick it up.

The side of roughest texture was the most promising. It was covered with a grid of sharp-sided holes, each about a centimeter across. The edges of the holes would cut into the binding tape—if only he could find a way to apply them. He measured distances by eye. If he held the scraper in his right hand, it would not reach across far enough to work on the tape that bound his left forearm to the chair.

That left few options. Gordy leaned down and took the handle of the scraper in his mouth. By moving his head he could pass its sharp edges over the tape on his right hand, but he could not get enough downward force to do useful cutting. He pushed the scraper down between his bound forearm and the kitchen counter, and used the limited sideways movement available to his arm to create the pressure he needed. When he raised his head, the sharp edges of the scraper cut into the tape. They also cut his arm. It was a painful quarter hour, pausing often to rest his jaw and neck, before the first strands broke. By that time drops of blood were dripping to the kitchen floor. It was also darker—too dim to see anything beyond the wall leading to the habitat.

Fifteen more minutes, and he had enough freedom of movement to reach a tape end with his fingers. Right hand, then left hand. With both hands loose, his legs took no more than another minute.

Too many things to do, and all at once. He scuttled across the dark chamber to the open door leading to the habitat. He pushed it closed. He couldn't lock it, but he could make a barricade. Work-bench, chairs, bed, kitchen drawers, small refrigerator, useless communications terminal, old bicycle—they all went against the door. It would take substantial force to move them.

He hurried to the middle of the chamber and gave the floor hatch one quick shake. His comment to Seth, that it would take days to open when it was locked from the other side, was completely accurate. Seth had left no loophole there. The hatch, by careful design, would not move a millimeter.

Gordy ran back across the chamber. He had piled every loose object in the room in front of the habitat door, with one exception. Now he knelt down by the ancient radio, the one that he joked had been used by Noah for ship-to-shore communication. He took hold of the set, with its carved walnut cabinet, black Bakelite knobs, and speaker cover of woven brown fabric. A hard tug, and the entire front face came free. Nestled inside, hidden among the antique tubes and condensers, was a box of dull gray plastic about four inches long.

He carefully lifted the set out and pressed an indented black circle on its side. A row of tiny red lights began to glow on one end. At the same moment a noise came from the door leading to the habitat. Something was pushing against the other side. Pushing gently, tentatively. Gordy heard a snuffle, the sniff of large nostrils testing the air.

His hands were no longer bleeding, but in his hurry he had not bothered to wash them or bind them. There must be drops of blood scattered in many places across the chamber floor.

Gordy retreated to the far side of the room, clutching the gray plastic box to his thin chest. It was time—past time—to play his hidden hole card.


Nick Lopez had chosen to remain in New Rio during the blip storm, but he had taken the sensible precaution of observing it from a suite of rooms two thousand feet belowground. Unlike Gordy Rolfe, however, he had no real taste for subterranean life. As soon as it was safe to do so he headed back to the surface and went to the headquarters building of the World Protection Federation.

Today, that name seemed a mockery. The tall pyramid of glass and white limestone had not been able to protect even itself. It stood, apparently intact, in another of this year's endless series of driving rainstorms, but as Nick approached he saw millions of small black pockmarks marring the clear lines of walls and roof.

He went inside and felt water dripping onto his head. He looked up. The particle bundles had slanted in from the south and east, creating holes all through the solid stone walls. He looked down. Apparently the good news was that the particle clusters had still possessed ample energy to penetrate the floor. Instead of pooling there, the rainwater was quietly making its way down to lower levels.

How many levels? Nick didn't know, but suddenly two thousand feet no longer felt like such a safe depth. He walked across the wet floor, through the great open plaza with its now-riddled marble mosaics, and on past the inner atrium to the escalators. Those were working—an impressively rapid repair job. Uniformed men and women appeared from nowhere, watching for his reaction. He nodded approvingly to everyone he passed, adding a personal comment to most of them. "I said we'd see it through, Miguel, and we did." "Nice work, Flora, I see you kept things going while I was gone." "Don't worry about the water, Josie"—this to a woman ineffectively dabbing at the floor with a sodden mop—"it will dry out as soon as the rain stops."

His private office was a disaster. *No, a mess. Save* disaster *for when you really need it.* Wet floor, wet walls, wet desktop. Someone had tried to dry the chair seats, but water was still dripping in from above. Nick sat down. His pants seat would dry out, too, as soon as the rain stopped. He called for a readout of waiting messages and mentally assigned them as they appeared to his three standard categories: ignore, assign, answer.

There was one surprise: Celine Tanaka was on her way here, to this building. She had flown low-orbital from Washington, on her way to Tierra del Fuego. Nick noted who was down there: the remnants of fourteen planeloads of American lunatics who had flown in for the particle storm. He automatically thought media opportunity. Celine would be shown talking with the survivors, and she would make some points relevant to her own agenda. Politics was alive and well.

But why was she stopping *here,* in New Rio? This was far off the great-circle route from Washington to Tierra del Fuego. If it was a question of suitable facilities, a low-orbital landing-and-takeoff facility existed at Punta Arenas, spitting distance across the strait from Celine's destination.

The red handset on his desk began to blink. Nick glared at it. The dedicated private line. Its buzz was loud and insistent. Damn Gordy Rolfe, he always thought his business was more important than anyone else's. Nick called down to make sure that Celine would be brought to him the moment she arrived, then picked up the set. Infuriatingly, at the very moment he placed it to his ear the connection went dead.

He could try to call back—but now his main line was active. "Yes?"

"President Tanaka is on the way up to see you."

"Good. Bring her right in." He had no idea what she wanted, but he liked Celine. She was one of the world's few rational people.

Whereas Gordy Rolfe definitely wasn't. Gordy Rolfe was an arrogant, obsessive little shit.

Gordy could wait.


The habitat lighting mimicked surface conditions, a thousand feet above. Now it was night. Gordy could turn on artificial lights anytime he chose, but for the moment he held that in reserve. Sudden brightness *might* scare away nocturnal hunters, but it was a big might for minisaurs who had caught a whiff of blood. Just as likely, it would attract interest.

Waiting on a call that no one answered was agony, and after thirty seconds Gordy gave up. He would try Nick later, but meanwhile time was too precious to waste. He recalled, with no satisfaction at all, that he was the one who had insisted that neither man have recording devices attached to the private line. To receive Gordy's call, Nick Lopez had to be in his office. He was, most of the time. But where the devil was he now?

Gordy replaced his hard shoes with soft-soled slippers. He crept across the floor in just enough light to follow the outlines of large objects. It was minutes since he had last heard the snuffling at the barricaded door. That had accompanied a scraping sound, the noise of a pile of furniture and kitchen fixtures shifting on the smooth floor. The minisaur had an advantage. The floor of the chamber was smooth, while anything on the other side had the purchase offered by the soft ground of the habitat.

He waited to make sure that the animal had gone away before he ventured close to the door. What he saw wasn't too bad. In the room's unnatural silence, the improvised barricade had sounded like it was collapsing or being pushed clear out of the way. In fact it had moved no more than an inch.

He eased everything back into position. As he was wedging a tilted chair against the handle of the refrigerator door he was struck by another thought. Could he hide *inside* the refrigerator?

But if he would fit in there, how long could he stay before he suffocated? And how would he know when it was safe to come out?

Not a good choice: death by suffocation, or death as a minisaur's dinner. But not a choice that he needed to make. He fully expected to be rescued.

All the same, Gordy opened the door of the refrigerator and confirmed that, small as he was, he could not fit inside. He went back to wedging the chair in place. As he did so, he heard new movement beyond the wall. He could smell a musky body odor, mingled with the stench of bad meat.

He sat down, braced himself with his back against the refrigerator, and took out the gray handset. He told himself that he had plenty of time. The minisaurs had learned to be cautious when dealing with humans. They would not attack until they were sure of the situation. Even so, Gordy felt a huge impatience as he waited for the row of red lights to indicate a call going through to its distant destination.


"And what can I do to help you?"

It was so like Celine's own technique for cutting through visitors' small talk that she couldn't help smiling at Nick Lopez.

"I'm not here for favors, Nick. Actually, I'm going to do you one—a doubtful one, and when you hear about it you may decide it isn't a favor at all."

The change in the world between the Washington takeoff and

the New Rio landing was striking. The first particle wave had arrived, swelled to a peak, and as swiftly subsided to its steady background level. After the gridded sky and beautiful aurora, Washington had become calm and sunny. Here, just a couple of hours later, torrential rain gurgled away from the surface through endless thousands of little black pits that riddled the landscape. Roads, metal covers, the sides of buildings, concrete sidewalks, bare soil—nothing was exempt. The dark pockmarks were everywhere. The room she sat in had a leaky ceiling and a leaky floor, water streaming in and out through openings not much bigger than pinholes. The only unchanged element was Nick Lopez himself. Tall and broad, with water dripping steadily onto his gray pompadour and down his cheeks, he sat on a wet chair as relaxed as if today's particle storm had never happened.

He listened carefully to Celine's words and said, "A favor? Then you're ahead of the pack already. I'm not used to favors. Everybody else who comes to the WPF wants something from me."

"I want something, too. I want you to keep a secret."

"That's a big something. Remember the standard political assumption: anything you say, anywhere and to anybody, is likely to become public knowledge."

"I know. I can't ask you to keep what I tell you totally to yourself, because you may need to act. But I'd like you to use extreme caution in deciding who is told."

Celine summarized her morning conversation with Wilmer Oldfield and Star Vjansander. At the end of it, Lopez was not smiling.

"You believe them?" he said. "Of course you do, or you wouldn't be here. But they may be wrong. They even told you they may be wrong. But I agree with you, this has to be handled very carefully. Who else knows? Or rather, who else do you *know* knows?"

"Wilmer. Star. John Hyslop and Maddy Wheatstone, up on Sky City. Me. And now you. Of course, it will spread."

"Of course it will. There's no such thing as a secret. What plans have you made?"

"None. What plans can you make to deal with the end of the world?"

"If this homeostasis thing is right, nothing." Nick flicked water droplets away from his bushy eyebrows. "Hiding a mile deep or ten miles deep won't do a bit of good if the planet has no oxygen, or if temperatures go up a hundred degrees. I think we stay with the original party line: We're in for a storm bigger than anything we expected, but Earth will come through it and finally return to normal. We plan for that."

"That's exactly what I decided. But I wanted another expert opinion."

"With something like this, there are no experts."

"I take that as approval. There's one other thing I want to mention. It won't affect anything now, but it could make a difference in the long run—if there is a long run. I've had a disturbing warning about the Argos Group activities on Sky City."

Celine described her conversation with Maddy Wheatstone. Nick listened closely, his face expressionless.

"Does she have proof?" he said when Celine finished.

"Apparently not. Nor do I. This hasn't exactly been my top priority."

"So what do you propose to do?"

"For the moment, nothing. Unless you disagree?"

"No. I don't disagree. It can wait." Nick glanced in annoyance at the red handset on the near corner of his desk. It had begun to buzz, loudly and insistently. "Damn that thing."

"Answer it, Nick, if you have to. I'm the one who's intruding."

He hesitated. "It's a private line. Would you . . . ?"

"Of course. I'll wait outside. Take your time."

Nick waited until she was gone and the door was closed before he picked up the handset. "Yes?"

"Where the hell have you been?" The voice at the other end was rasping and breathless.

"Working. I don't know how it is with you, Gordy, but we've had a particle storm and a major crisis down here."

"Yeah, yeah. The hell with that. Listen. I need help."

"Tonight?"

"Right this minute. I'm down in my underground headquarters, and I can't get out."

"How did that happen?"

"It's not relevant. I don't have time for chitchat. The point is, the hatch is locked on the other side and the door to the habitat is open."

"Can't you go out that way?"

"Are you crazy? Listen to the 'saurs."

Gordy stopped speaking. In the silence that followed at the other end of the line, Nick picked up guttural grunts and snorting.

"I hear them. What do you want me to do? I'm down in New Rio."

"I know. But you have people in Washington. How long does it take to get here from there by high-speed airdrop?"

"Half an hour. Maybe less. But you have people in Washington. Why don't you call your own people directly?"

"Can't. My communications are out and this is the only working line. Listen, soon as we finish talking, you get hold of one of your people. Send him here. Tell him how to get in through the schoolhouse. He comes down in the elevator, opens the hatch from below, and lets me out. You got that?"

"Yes. But it will take me a while to contact somebody, and they'll have to find a plane. That could be another hour."

"Shouldn't be a problem. The 'saurs are cautious. They're scared of coming into this chamber; I taught them that the hard way. I figure I can hold out five, maybe six hours. But don't rely on it. Get somebody out here at once."

"I'll do it. Sit tight, Gordy."

"*At once,* I said. Don't fuck up. I'll call you in half an hour to make sure everything's set."

"Right." Nick waited for the line to go dead, then slowly replaced the handset. He sat silent for half a minute, beads of water trickling unheeded down his forehead. At last he roused himself, stood up, and went to open the door.

Celine was waiting outside, leaning against the wall. "More problems?"

He shook his head. "I don't think so. Maybe one problem less. That was Gordy Rolfe on the line."

"Offering any help that he can give, I assume?"

He smiled at Celine's tone. "I see you know our Gordy. You're right, he wasn't offering help."

"Where is he?"

"At his northern headquarters—the underground one in Virginia."

"That place. I haven't forgiven you for talking me into going there."

"It's not that bad. And you were there before, when it was the stronghold of the Legion of Argos."

"It's worse now." Celine grimaced. "Horrible. I told you what he did when I went to see him, that fight to the death between a carnosaur and a group of rats. I feel sure he arranged it just for me."

"I don't think so." Nick led them back into the office and waited for Celine to sit down. "It's part of this general fixation Gordy has about dinosaurs and mammals."

"The superiority of mammals." Celine noticed that water was no longer dripping onto her head. She looked up. The ceiling was covered with suspended droplets, but few were falling. Outside, the rain must finally have ended. Flights would be resuming. "I know Gordy Rolfe's theory. He told me mammals always win. They beat dinosaurs."

"Get it right. *Small* mammals win, not big ones." Nick grinned at her. "I'm pretty big, so of course he made a special point of putting it that way to me."

"What did Gordy want this time? Oh, I'm sorry, I shouldn't ask. It was a private call."

"That's all right. It was nothing new. He wanted to yak on about his experiments on the survival of small mammals. Seems he's conducting one at this very moment."

"It sounds revolting. I'm sorry I asked."

"And I'm sorry he interrupted us." Nick stood up. "Look, I know you're in a hurry, but you and I need to discuss how we'll handle the next three weeks. There are going to be leaks—there always are—and I wouldn't be surprised if a few days from now everybody knows. Would you have any objection to my flying down to Tierra del Fuego with you, so we can talk?"

"No objection at all. I'd welcome your company. But don't you have things that need doing here?"

"It's a whole new ballgame now." Nick was staring at the red handset, but he seemed to be listening to something far away.

Finally Celine repeated, "Don't you? Don't you have things that need doing?"

He was with her again. He shook his head. "Sorry. I was just remembering something. The last time I spoke with Gordy he was furious with me."

"He's probably over it by now."

"Yes. If not now, soon." Lopez reached out a hand to Celine. "Come on. I'm ready. Let's get out of here before we have another nuisance call."

# 31

**From the private diary of Oliver Guest.**

Every human, I suggest, is a victim of this aberration: At the same time as we assert our common humanity, we seek evidence to show that we are different from, and superior to, our fellows.

I was drawn to this conclusion in examining an earlier statement I made, delivered from the Olympian heights of impartiality to which we so often aspire. Thus I find, in my own diary and in my own hand, the following: "Human beings find it difficult to act on facts alone. We are plagued by overactive imaginations. And of the things that human beings are called upon to do, doing nothing can be the most difficult act of all."

I was not, of course, referring to myself. Perish the thought. I would be above such frailties. Now, however, my words returned to haunt me. *"Doing nothing can be the most difficult act of all."*

It had been my conclusion that the best time to catch the Sky City murderer would be at the height of the particle storm, when everyone, including the killer, would be distracted by events. It did not occur to me that such a decision had a corollary: Until the storm arrived, it was necessary that Seth and I take no action relevant to capture.

A principle easy to state, but oh so difficult to observe. As the particle storm continued its steady march toward the solar system and the Sky City defense system prepared for the final onslaught, I found myself in an agony—a chafing, a ferment, a convulsion—of enforced inactivity.

I had nothing to do. My preparation of the deep shelters had long since been completed. My darlings had been thoroughly briefed and knew exactly what each would do on the day of the particle storm. Seth was employed in his own inscrutable pursuits, on Earth and off it. And I? I suspect that I became intolerable, since my darlings tiptoed around Otranto Castle and minimized their interactions with me.

The days crept by. At last they turned into weeks. And finally, after an interval so apparently protracted that within it mountain ranges rose and continents were subducted, the weeks also passed and I rose one autumnal morning to discover that today was the day. *The* day. The day when the particle storm would strike. The day when Seth and I would also strike and, with a modicum of luck, bring to justice the Sky City murderer. The day, after endless eons of subjective time, for a final confluence of significant events.

Seth is a man able to handle major hardship with considerable fortitude. He is, however, less tolerant of small irritations.

Witness today.

The next few hours would bring danger and possible death. Beyond that, scant days hence, stood the prospect of universal destruction. So what were, in this time of final crisis, Seth's concerns? His complaint—his only complaint—revolved around the RV jacket. "Makes me feel stupid," he grumbled. "Lookatit. Them colors."

I could have pointed out that the previous occupant of the apartment he occupied on Sky City had favored walls in shades of mauve and pale orange. Instead I said, "As you well know, looking at your jacket is for me impossible, unless you choose to stand in front of a mirror. However, if today's outcome is satisfactory, you will never need to wear it again."

"Yeah. 'Bout time. But I'm not goin' near no mirror so you can sit there laughin' at me."

His ranking of concerns might be, as that final comment suggested, in some part posturing. But perhaps not all, since I felt a curious sympathy of outlook. My own worry lay not with the fate of the world and its varied billions. It centered on the personal safety and long-term future of my darlings. As the particle storm moved to its crescendo, they would retreat to the deep sanctuary below Otranto Castle.

And they would return, a day or a week later, to—what?

That was my question. Talk to me not of global escape from devastation and planetary blight. Rather, guarantee the survival of a small part of western Ireland, where my darlings and a few others could comfortably survive, and I would ask for nothing more.

It occurs to me that such an attitude may be prerequisite to the continuation of our species. Nature admits no welfare programs, and although we may die in multitudes we must struggle for survival one by one.

And so, as word spread of a curious and possibly fatal convergence of the particle storm on the solar system, the news media eschewed discussion of universal death in favor of personal survival schemes.

Many plans featured that old standby, prayer. Its historical record of effectiveness apparently discouraged few people, although I, regrettably, am among the skeptics. All the churches were full. It is not clear to me exactly what prayers were being offered by their occupants. A temporary suspension, perhaps, of the laws of physics? The art galleries and theaters also reported record crowds. If religion is an opiate, art is an anodyne.

Some other notions seemed equally unlikely to succeed. An American group, the Trust In Government coalition, displayed matching ignorance of biology and geology by intensifying their frenzied efforts on Project Way Down, the continuation of a wide-bore mine deep in the Anadarko Basin. The natural geothermal temperature gradient would make human life impossible at their projected twenty-mile end depth, without help from Alpha C, but—sublimely indifferent to both logic and cost—the TIG coalition dug and dug. They would have done well to remember the tragical history of Dr. Faustus: "*Then will I headlong run into the Earth. Earth gape. Oh, no, it will not harbor me.*"

More radical was the scheme, conceived in haste and executed at panic speed, of a European group, Earth Will Provide (*La Terre Suffira*). Its three hundred members, all among the world's richest individuals, had rightly concluded that if Earth's surface provided some protection, then the whole of Earth should offer more.

They had ascended to high orbit three days ago. There they would hover on their mirror-matter engines at Alpha Centauri's antipodean point, two thousand kilometers above the surface, while Earth turned below them and the particle storm attained its maximum. The vast bulk of the planet would shield them until the storm blew past. When all was over they would return.

It was tempting to ask, return to what?

A logical mind might offer two alternatives. Either they would find a world that had survived the particle storm, in which case their flight was unnecessary; or they would return to a dying planet, where the old definition of wealth had lost its meaning and their own quietus, unhindered by privilege, could not be long delayed.

But who am I to mock the dreams and prayers of others? Their hope, like mine, is that the prevailing scientific view lacks validity. God knows, humans have been wrong often enough. We may be wrong again.

Meanwhile, business continues, though it is difficult to justify the customary added phrase "as usual." Seth and I prepare ourselves, mentally and physically, for a meeting with a murderer. That encounter, unlike Earth's rendezvous with the particle storm, will be decided by human actions alone.

# 32

The geometry had been set in place six days ago and fine-tuned every hour. The hollow tip of the conical shield pointed its arrow toward Alpha Centauri and maintained a fixed distance of half a light-second from Earth. Cusp Station hovered thirty thousand kilometers behind, precisely on the axis of the cone. Sky City in turn was locked in position one kilometer behind Cusp Station, whose newly installed field generators bathed the shield in a low-intensity glow mediated and diffused by the shield's fine network of superconducting fibers.

Each particle bundle impinging on the shield would generate a burst of radiation, whose direction and signal frequency shift contained enough information for a precise trajectory to be computed. But to be useful, the calculation—like every other action—had to be made *fast*. Within seconds of hitting the shield, a free-flying particle bundle would reach Earth. Before then the detection data must be received on Sky City, necessary calculations completed, a loop field generated and sent on an interception trajectory, and the particle bundle caught and diverted safely away.

It was all possible—just. Maddy had watched the first tests, when the flux of particle bundles was still limited to a few thousand arrivals per second. Before the human eye could detect anything at all, each bundle was intercepted, netted, and curved away to miss Earth by thousands of kilometers. After a few hundred successful encounters, the conversation in the engineering control center became casual and upbeat. What no one mentioned—what Maddy wondered if most people knew—was the projected change in the situation as the storm approached its height. If the convergence of the beam was as strong as expected and the maximum arrival rate of particle bundles came even close to the projected value, the field generators would be unable to produce enough loop fields to handle the entire flood. At that point some of the bundles would begin to get through. Cusp Station and Sky City would have to be preferentially protected, since if their systems failed all defenses would be lost. But the consequence of that would be weaker protection at the edges of the shield, and thus of the parts of Earth that lay behind them.

One thing was certain: The team on Sky City would know the worst before very long. The flux counters had begun their final climb. Storm maximum would occur in less than three hours, and long before that the defense system would be tested to the limit.

Maddy stared around the room, with its score of working engineers and data analysts. She wondered again: How far had the word spread of Wilmer Oldfield and Star Vjansander's worst-case prediction? Did they all know?

She herself had told no one—but news, especially bad news, leaked out no matter how you tried to contain it. Yet she had seen no small groups closely-knit in conversation, and she had overheard not a dropped word.

On the other hand, she *knew* that John had heard Wilmer's worst-case assessment—she had been with him at the time. And he now showed no hint of interest in anything beyond the task at hand. In fact, she was beginning to wonder if he had forgotten to make a promised announcement on a quite different subject. In the circumstances, that would be more than reasonable. A dozen murders must seem like nothing in the face of billions of deaths.

But John had not forgotten. When he finally spoke he was terse, almost casual. He addressed the room at large, his gaze intent on the displays. "We're at zero minus two hours forty-one minutes, and are approaching one-tenth flux maximum. By the way, the particle storm seems to have produced an unexpected result. Because of it, they've found Doris Wu's body."

He seemed ready to leave it at that, leaning over the control panel and monitoring the final countdown, but Will Davis whistled loud through his front teeth and said, "You can't stop there, boyo. Where, and how?"

"One of the last up-leg shuttles to Sky City. A million-to-one chance. If we hadn't moved to our present position, the body might never have been found. The shuttle passed within forty meters, and a passenger made visual contact. They took her body on board and brought it here. It's sitting in Cargo Bay Fourteen."

Maddy was standing inconspicuously at the back. She said under her breath, *Go on, go on.* But John seemed intent on the controls.

"Did they find anything that might tell who killed her?" Torrance Harbish asked. Engineers from all around the center, their tasks for the moment ignored, looked up or moved closer.

"I don't know," John said. "I doubt it. Until this is all over, the security staff must have other things on their mind." He looked up. "And so do we. Lauren, do you have those capture rates? Wilmer Oldfield is panting for them."

"Right here. Shall I transmit?"

"Waste of time. Wilmer won't look at the feed. Do you have time to take it to him?"

"I'll find time. Where is he?"

"At the back of the water buffer. He and Star want to compare the bundles they get now with what they caught during the blip storm."

"I hope the results they're getting make more sense than mine do," Amanda Corrigan said. She had three separate displays running in front of her. "We have a set of quickie Sniffers a few light-days out, and they're showing a stronger storm convergence toward Sol than we've ever seen. But the counts I'm making locally fail to confirm. Both sets of data can't be right. Take a look. Where are the bundles?"

The first display was a simple two-axis graph. The horizontal axis showed distance from Sol in astronomical units. The vertical axis was estimated beam area. As the storm approached the solar system, the area decreased dramatically. The Alpha C storm was homing in on the solar system.

The second display was a table of total beam area versus predicted particle count per second at Sky City. The third display was another graph, with time as the horizontal axis and particle count as vertical axis. Both predicted and observed counts were shown. The predicted count rose rapidly at the time of maximum flux, and fell away as fast beyond it; the observed count went only up to the present time, but at the moment it was close to constant over time and looked nothing like the predicted peak.

John Hyslop gave the curves and tables in front of Amanda a cursory glance. "I've no time to look at them now. Get them to Wilmer and Star, let them figure it out. Matching predictions and observations isn't our business. Our job is to deal with whatever arrives."

He caught Maddy's eye. She wondered if he could possibly be as calm as he looked. She surveyed the whole information center, with people constantly hurrying in and out, and found everyone busy and preoccupied. But she saw no sign of nervousness. The only nervous one was Maddy herself—maybe because she had too little to do.

She waited a few more moments, then quietly slipped out of the room. She was no help here, an engineering nonentity surrounded by the pick of the solar system's engineers. But somewhere on Sky City there must be someone who needed assistance. If it was not true now, it would be when the storm arrived.

# 33

When the storm hit Earth, regardless of intensity and duration, one thing seemed sure: The sky would seethe with electromagnetic energy, and during the final few minutes all forms of radio communication might be lost.

*Temporarily* lost? Celine had posed that question to Benedict Mertok. He shrugged and gave a less-than-useful reply: "Madam President, we need to define temporary. Nothing lasts forever."

But some things seemed to. Pressure on a President to hide away from every form of danger was one of them. Celine had refused all suggestions that she retreat to a deep underground refuge.

"Didn't you tell me that there is no chance of direct bundle impact this far north?" It was early morning on what she secretly thought of as doomsday, and she was sitting in her specially designed padded chair in the Oval Office.

Ben Mertok frowned. "Well, yes, I did . . ."

"Then that's good enough for me. I'll wait out the particle storm right here. You can go now."

"I think maybe I should—"

"I said you can go now, Ben. I need privacy."

It was wrong to take even a mild pleasure in Mertok's discomfort. But at times like this pleasures were few and far between, and you took them wherever you found them. As soon as she was alone Celine tilted her chair back and stared up at the ceiling. She had displays all around her, hooked up through ground-based fiber-optic feeds to every country on the planet, but the one link she wanted might be blacked out. The front line of battle was nowhere on Earth; it was up on Sky City and Cusp Station. Already the view of the shield seemed grainy, and the speckling of random points of light that she saw might be transmission noise, nothing to do with the detection of particle bundles. On the other hand, there was a good chance it was all her imagination, and the image of the shield looked exactly as usual.

"The Honorable Nicholas Lopez is on line eight," said the calm voice of the autocom. Celine sighed and returned her chair to its upright position.

"Nick? Where are you?"

"At the airfield in New Rio. Waiting for takeoff."

Celine glanced at the clock. Two and a quarter hours to flux maximum. "You're cutting it fine."

"Not from choice. The space defense can't stop a hundred percent of the bundles, and a few are already getting through. At our longitude they are coming in close to horizontal, but they're still coming in. Nothing like the way they will be in another couple of hours, but we already lost a suborbital to an unlucky hit on the flight control box. This is the last flight out, then everybody who's left here heads for the deep shelters."

"I thought that was your plan."

"I thought so, too." The visual feed finally kicked in, and Nick's face appeared on the display. He was smiling ruefully and smoothing his gray hair back with one hand. "The trouble is, the shelters have only energy-sensor contact with the surface. When it comes right down to it, I'm too curious to know what's going on."

"You remember what curiosity killed."

"I know. I comfort myself with the thought that only the good die young. But I expected you'd be in the underground Washington refuge. What's your excuse?"

"I'm here because it's second-best. What I really wish is that I were *up there*." Celine pointed her thumb toward the ceiling.

"On Sky City? Then go. You remember what Saul Steinmetz said? Sometimes when you're President, you have to do something that nobody else in the whole damn country could get away with, just to prove that you can."

"It's too late. We have an embargo on outgoing spacecraft until the storm is over—issued on my instructions."

"A good decision, I think. We've just lifted off. Take a look from the plane here, and remember it's only just starting."

Nick's face on the screen was replaced by a close-up view over the great bay at New Rio. The overall landscape was peaceful, but the nearby waters showed widely spaced spurts of foam disturbing the calm surface. An occasional sun glint came from the silver-white bellies of dead fish.

Celine glanced at the other displays scattered around her office. An unfamiliar one caught her attention. She stared for a few seconds, then said, "Don't waste time sightseeing, Nick. Get out of there and head north. At once."

"What's wrong?"

"I'm not sure, but I'd like to show you something. Can you accept visual feeds?"

"For the moment. The radio link is supposed to get noisy, but we're cleaning it up pretty well using high signal redundancy."

"This is a fiber-optic lead that the ID says is coming from Kerguelen Island, fifty degrees south in the Indian Ocean."

"I know Kerguelen. I've even been served Kerguelen land cabbage at a French embassy dinner. Famous, and supposed to be nutritious; but it tastes disgusting."

"Well, you're ahead of me—I've hardly heard of the place. But at the moment the particle storm is hitting there from almost directly overhead. A reporter suite is planted near the summit of a peak called Mount Crozier, about a thousand meters up. The mobiles can go anywhere, but the main imager looks down and across the Morbihan Gulf to a peninsula on the other side. We're getting a high-data-rate feed via landline and submarine cable, and the reporter is mixing mobile high-resolution and fixed low-resolution sequences. Tell me what you make of these."

The first image came from the fixed imager. On the island, halfway around the world from Celine, it was already close to dusk and the illumination was poor. The scene showed the surface of the shallow gulf alive with white jets of steam. Now and then a deeper eruption brought a spouting geyser meters high into the air. The bodies of a diversity of sea creatures rolled and floated half submerged in the turbulent waters. Seals? Penguins? Black-backed sharks? Killer whales? Identification would have to wait for pictures from the mobile reporters.

Beyond the gulf, the peninsula looked to be on fire. Not just the dark green scrubby bushes, but the fat round bodies of cabbagelike plants and even the windswept ground itself flamed and sparked and quivered in angry dots of red and orange.

Nick watched in silence for a while, then said, "Pretty impressive, and we still have a long way to go before maximum flux. Believe it or not, this was anticipated. It was even requested."

"Not by me, it wasn't. How do you mean, *requested*?"

"All the U.S. is north of the Tropic of Cancer, so you're shielded by Earth's mass from direct bundle impact. The Southern Hemisphere isn't so lucky. The more advance information that we have about effects, the better. A consortium of countries near and below the equator asked Sky City to run a control experiment on Kerguelen Island. Particle bundles with trajectories that terminate in and around Kerguelen are not being diverted at all. They smack right on in. Every scientist with ground-based data feeds is getting a look at what could happen to a full hemisphere of an unprotected Earth. It's tough on the local wildlife and the vegetation, but the population of Kerguelen has been completely evacuated."

"Nick . . . I don't think so." Celine had been staring at an image from one of the mobiles. The flying imager was zooming steadily in toward a starfish splash of yellow that stood out against the somber beach of the peninsula. Soon she could make out arms and legs and the dark blob of a helmeted head sticking out of the bright jacket. It was the body of a man lying facedown.

"Damnation. That's a Media Guild logo on his back." Lopez sounded more angry than concerned.

"What did he think he was doing?" Celine wanted a close-up of the man's head, but she was not getting it. "The mobiles can go anywhere that the reporter tells them. Isn't the reporter smart enough to know what's worth imaging, or ask for studio guidance when it's not sure?"

"Of course it is. Celine, you're looking at human stupidity and arrogance. The reporter can handle the job; it was *designed* for it. But I've seen this over and over. No matter what the event—hurricane, riot, particle storm, tsunami, earthquake, volcano, you name it—and no matter how much you warn people, some idiot will decide he can ride it out and get a news exclusive by recognizing something that 'only a human can tell is important.' I bet this one's a freelance. He heard through the wires that Kerguelen had been picked out for special attention, and he went there deliberately."

Now that Nick had made the identification, Celine could recognize the small black video unit that sat a couple of feet away from the man's outstretched right hand.

She asked, more to say something than because she cared to know the answer, "How do you think he died?"

As she spoke the body's left arm jerked to one side, giving her the momentary impression that the man was still alive. Then she saw the puff of smoke close to the shoulder.

"He died like *that,*" Lopez said. "See, another one just hit him."

Celine glanced at the data table accompanying the Kerguelen display. "It's surprising that he would be hit twice. The particle bundles on Kerguelen are arriving at a rate of three per minute per hundred square meters, and they're coming down close to vertical. An upright human provides a target less than half a square meter in area. You'd expect to be able to stand outside for an hour before you'd get hit. And he was hit *twice,* counting that last one."

"We don't know how long he stood around taking pictures. But let's say he was unlucky as well as stupid."

"*Extremely* stupid. See, he's wearing a hard hat—heaven knows what he thought that would do for him. The particle bundles are whipping in there at thirty thousand kilometers a second."

There was a five-second silence before Nick said, "Maybe none of us is too smart in situations like this. I should have known better, but I told my staff to put on hard hats until they could head for the deep shelters. And now you've got me wondering about the cross-sectional area of this suborbital, and the particle rate over the Caribbean."

It sounded like a rhetorical question, but Celine happened to be able to answer it. "Once you're north of Venezuela, you'll be safe if you keep below a couple of hundred kilometers altitude. Your path puts you behind Earth relative to Alpha C."

"Safe." Lopez laughed, but Celine would bet that he was not smiling. He went on, "I like that word, *safe.* Is anybody safe? Is the particle beam still converging?"

"Faster than ever, according to Sniffer reports."

"Then we better hope that our smart boys and girls on Sky City know what they're doing. Otherwise, we might as well all be on Kerguelen Island and finish up like *him*."

Lopez and Celine fell silent. The sea boiled and the land burned, while drifting black smoke intermittently hid the forlorn yellow-clad figure on the beach. The bodies of marine animals of all sizes darkened the lifeless shore of the gulf. Mobiles, most of them no bigger than a cicada, flew over and under the water, seeking targets. Their small size provided some immunity from particle bundle impact.

*But you can't shrink a human down to cicada size,* Celine thought. *And humans are what this is all about. Am I looking at my own future on that screen, and the future of everybody on Earth? Will only the machines be left as observers in another month or two? Come on, Nature. Let's get this over with—one way or another.*

In front of her, the Kerguelen Island data showed the bundles arriving more and more frequently. After a fifty-year journey through interstellar space, the particle storm from Alpha Centauri was ready to show its power.

# 34

Maddy had heard the official Sky City line: When the storm hit, you would be better off here than anywhere else on Earth or off it. The defense system would concentrate on protecting Sky City, Cusp Station, and the field generators, even if it was effective nowhere else. You should be especially safe if you stayed near the rear face of the disk, the one that pointed away from Alpha Centauri. The city was a hundred and ninety meters thick. Every centimeter of that thickness would help to slow or stop the flying particle bundles.

Maddy had listened to all that and been unpersuaded. She was not a specialist on the effects of high-speed particle bundles, but she knew a lot about human nature. You tried not to worry people by telling them things they could do nothing about. Sky City might be safe, or it might prove very unsafe. Now, as she left the information center and wandered toward the rear face, she was starting to tilt toward the second opinion.

She could see the marks left by the bundles that had made it through the defense system. The wall seals, designed to protect the city from micrometeorite impacts, had no trouble closing the holes. However, the seal marks sat not only in the forward walls of chambers. For every one of them, another matching mark could be found in the rear. The particle bundles could not be stopped by a wall. They came into a chamber, crossed it, and went right out the other side.

Her idea was confirmed as she approached the rear face of Sky City. There were no fewer holes here than in the information chamber, close to the front. What there were—because people had come to the rear-facing chambers, seeking safety—were more casualties.

The first one that Maddy saw was an old man with an injury to his right hand. The particle bundle had drilled a neat hole through his palm, removing flesh and bone with surgical precision. There was no blood, and you might easily have missed the wound if the man were not holding his hand out in front of him. He was suffering the triple effects of shock, painkillers, and sedatives. He sat on the floor, arm extended, jaw sagging, tears trickling down his cheeks. Whoever had provided the painkillers had moved on, leaving the man alone.

Maddy went over to where he leaned against the wall. "Are you all right?"

Stupid question. Of course he wasn't all right. He stared at her and mumbled something.

"What? Say that again."

Maddy bent close. She heard his faint words: "I came to Sky City because it's easy on your heart."

"Do you feel dizzy? Are you in pain?"

"Extend your life for fifty years, they told me. Safer than the telomod treatment, they said. No danger of cancer. I flew up to Sky City because my heart wasn't good."

"Is someone coming back for you?"

"Look what they did to me."

It was no good. She wasn't getting through. Maddy raised the old man to his feet, and he offered no resistance.

"Come on."

Taking most of his slight weight, she led him on a spiral course downhill toward the city perimeter, until she came to an open area filled with people. It had been converted to a makeshift emergency room.

Maddy set the old man on one of the beds and placed his wounded hand where it could easily be seen. As she was straightening up, a woman in a pink housecoat approached.

"You can't leave him here." The woman was perfectly made up and wore expensive jewelry, but she had suffered her own narrow escape. She had a swath cut through her red hair, a cylindrical furrow that missed her scalp by a fraction of an inch. "These are private quarters. We have no space for strangers."

Maddy said mildly, "If you can explain that to him, I'm sure he'll leave."

"This is disgraceful. We paid for the best location on Sky City, and we were promised safety and security. And do we have it? We do not."

"I'm sure that Sky City is the best possible place to be." Sometimes the official line had its uses. "The defense system will protect us better than anywhere else."

"That's not good enough. Do you see what happened to my hair? That particle thing might easily have hit me. I am going to file a formal complaint with Bruno Colombo."

"I think you ought to do that. I doubt if he's busy." Maddy turned before the woman could reply. She went on her way, heading toward the rear face.

She thought, *You might easily imagine, spending time with John Hyslop and his group, that everyone on Sky City is supercompetent and superdedicated. But even here you can find stupidity and selfishness.* She recalled Gordy Rolfe's words when he first hired her for the Argos Group: "You might say, well, if people weren't so dumb, we'd have no reason to exist, but I like to think of it differently. Sure, we take money from stupid people. But we also give service. We *protect* them from doing something even dumber with their money." Someone with Maddy's skills would make a living on Sky City with no difficulty.

*If, that is, you and Sky City and Earth survive.* Maddy looked at her watch. Forty-seven minutes to the storm peak. How much of the chaos around her was the fault of Gordy Rolfe and the Argos Group, delivering defective materials to Sky City? If she lived, she was going to find out.

A sharp *ping* sounded, and Maddy saw a streak of blue light just a couple of feet in front of her face; another particle bundle through the defenses. All the evidence suggested that she was no safer here than up near the front of Sky City with John Hyslop. So why wasn't she with John, where she most wanted to be?

Not hurrying, Maddy began her return to the engineering information center.

# 35

**From the private diary of Oliver Guest.**

The RV jacket worn by Seth Parsigian was less than totally satisfying. It provided clear visual and auditory signals, but for me, attuned as I am to olfactory and tactile stimuli, Sky City remained no more than a hollow shadow of reality. Attempts to draw supplementary information from Seth proved a waste of time.

"Smells of *what*?" I said.

"I dunno." Seth paused in the empty corridor and sniffed loudly. "I told you, it stinks like something's been burnin'. Feathers, mebbe?"

"Feathers! You're up in space, and you smell burning feathers?"

"Well, you were the one who asked. Don't worry; it's usually that way on this level."

We were approaching Cargo Bay Fourteen. Clearly, Seth knew the area well, while to me much of the region was *terra incognita*. I was aware of his distaste for wearing the RV jacket, so it was no surprise to learn that some of his Sky City roaming with Maddy Wheatstone had been done without my vicarious participation.

At the entrance to the cargo bay, Seth paused.

"Where do you want it?"

*It* referred to the bundle, swathed in white cloth, that he carried under one arm. Even from as close as a few feet away it bore a plausible resemblance to the body of a human.

I paused before I answered. We had been forced to settle for whatever John Hyslop could make available, and this air-filled cargo bay, up in the low-gravity region close to the central axis, was larger than I had anticipated. In addition to a chamber big enough to house an entire shuttle, the sides of the cylindrical void were honeycombed with separate storage cupboards and racks. At the end farthest from where Seth floated with his burden, a web of guys and thin ropes provided convenient attachment points for larger items. The walls of the chamber were painted a mustard yellow, which glistened stickily in the spotlight that Seth shone on them.

I regarded the whole cargo bay with distaste. It was not an appropriate resting place for a murdered girl. On the other hand, it would surely never be one. "Suppose that Doris Wu's body really had been found and brought here by a shuttle," I said. "Where would it have been placed?"

"In one of the cupboards, mebbe?" Seth moved forward and opened one. "Like this."

"No." I could see inside, and the RV jacket's enhanced optics gave me a clearer view than Seth. "It's dusty. No one would risk contamination before security had done their inspection for evidence, and that won't happen until the particle storm is over."

"Then it has to be put somewhere over there." Seth turned, so that I again had a view of the far end of the chamber. "Looks like the cleaning machines work the main chamber, but not the cupboards. Hang it on one of the support points, an' it won't be disturbed."

"Then let us proceed." In spite of the fact that at least an hour would elapse before anything could be expected to happen, I was filled with a disquieting sense of urgency. Patience has its limits. This promised to be the culmination of more than a month of frustrating inaction, and I could hardly wait.

Seth carefully suspended the cloth-wrapped figure between two of the web nodes, then moved back to admire his work. "That do?"

"It will be fine." I wanted to head at once into hiding, but now it was Seth who displayed the caution and attention to detail that should have been mine.

"Hold on a minute," he said. "Better make sure you can see it easy from every way in."

He was right, of course. I restrained my impatience as he went slowly and carefully to each entry point of the cargo bay, moved outside, and then came in again. We agreed, the white figure would catch the eye at once no matter where a person chose to enter the chamber.

"So now let us make sure we are not equally visible," I said. "I suggest the storage cupboard over on the extreme right, where the light is dim."

"In a minute." Seth pulled a high-intensity beam weapon from his belt and subjected it to a thorough, and to my eye excessively lengthy, inspection.

"I thought we agreed that we do not anticipate violence," I said.

"Mebbe we did, an' mebbe you don't." Seth completed the leisurely review to his own satisfaction before slipping the weapon back into its holder. "I been shot at too many times to take the chance. It ain't your ass on the line if things go bad. If it don't work out right, you'll be laughin' an' scratchin' back in Ireland with your feet up, while I'm up here pullin' arrows out of my tuckus."

It was compelling and undeniable logic. I waited quietly while Seth, muttering complaints, established himself within the storage cupboard. Then it was my turn to object.

"If I am to play any useful part at all in this proceeding," I said, "it is essential that I see what is happening. My entire view of Sky City is at the moment limited to the two square feet of storage locker visible from the RV jacket."

"It has to be like that if you want me stuffed inside this cupboard."

"Then let me make an alternative suggestion. Whatever happens next will take place within this chamber. Remove the jacket and hang it in the darkest corner. I will be able to see, and I can offer my comments to you through your earpiece."

"I thought you wanted me hidden out of the way ASAP." But Seth climbed out of the cupboard, irritatingly slowly, and removed the jacket. For a few seconds my view was a collage of rotating snapshots of parts of the cargo bay, overlain on the ghostly background of my own study in Otranto Castle. When it steadied I could see the whole chamber spread out before me. Seth, ten meters away, was sauntering back to his hideout in the cupboard. I noticed that in addition to the beam weapon he had an older projectile weapon in a rear holster. The folly of using high-speed bullets in an environment where momentum transfer was a major question and vacuum lay outside most walls was beyond dispute. On the other hand, as Seth had so succinctly pointed out, my ass was not on the line. The danger was all his.

Finally we were in position, and probably an hour early. Now there was nothing we could do but wait. And speculate.

What would happen here in the cargo bay? What would happen in the rest of Sky City as the particle bundles flooded in from space with ever-increasing numbers? And what would happen down on Earth, where my corporeal body resided?

Cargo Bay Fourteen was almost empty, but as the minutes slipped by it was far from silent. First there was an eerie creaking from the walls, evidence that some part of the structure of Sky City was under unusual stress. Then I heard a loud *ping* a few yards away, followed by a hissing sound that quickly faded. At the extreme edge of the RV jacket's field of view I saw the hole left by the particle bundle. There had to be another one somewhere at the other side of the chamber. I searched carefully, and at maximum magnification I thought I could just make out a dark dot on the far wall.

"Looks like a few are gettin' through," Seth said calmly.

"Yes. I gather that is inevitable. Do you want to be in a suit?" Six of the dark spacesuits hung on an open rack midway between Seth and the RV jacket.

"Not worth it. The sealers can handle anythin' small. Anythin' big comes along, a suit won't be no help." He paused, then added, " 'Course, it won't be too good if this place gets fulla little holes from the small stuff."

There we have a typical Parsigian understatement. If Sky City were riddled by particle bundles, it would mean that the defensive system had failed. Seth, and eventually the whole of Earth, would probably die.

I waited and listened, gradually relaxing as no more noises of bundle impact sounded through the chamber. However, before I could be in any sense at ease, something else snapped me to full attention.

It came not via the RV helmet, but from within Otranto Castle. Not far from where I was sitting I heard a girl cry out.

I stood up at once and switched the helmet to local viewing. It was early afternoon, and sunny, and my study sprang into view in full color. I indulged in one rapid glance out of the window—no sign of any particle storm effects—then ran toward the kitchen.

As I suspected, a girl—no, three girls, Katherine, Charity, and Victoria—were there. Two of the tall kitchen cupboards stood open, heavy doors of dark oak thrown wide. The girls were rooting around inside. The cry that I had heard, I now realized, was Charity's high-pitched and poorly suppressed snort of laughter.

I was in my stocking feet, and I made no sound even on the hard floor of gray slate. The girls remained unaware of my presence until I cried, "What the devil do you think you are doing?" They turned, and I went on, "I told you, the Alpha Centauri particle storm reaches its peak today. And you all promised that you would remain in the deepest cellars until I told you it was safe to come out. Why didn't you keep your word?"

"We did." Little Victoria, smallest of all my darlings, looked up at me with blue eyes filled with guilt. I saw that she was clutching an armful of jars and boxes. "We just came up for a minute. We were going straight back."

"Why did you come up at all?" But I had already guessed the answer.

"For these," Katherine said. She, like Victoria and Charity, was carrying a load of provisions. She held them out toward me. "We're having a storm party. But there was nothing good to eat and drink."

"Get back down there." I turned away. "I don't want anyone else up here, for any reason at all, until I come down and tell you that the storm is over."

It is not clear to me whether the insouciance of youth will be the doom of humanity or its salvation. I prefer to think the latter, but I have my doubts. I made my way back to the study, returning the helmet to remote viewing as I did so.

"Wanna tell me what all *that* was about?" Seth asked, and I realized that in my haste I had not switched the sound to local mode. He had heard every word that I said.

"It was nothing. Merely the girls organizing a party. What has been happening there?"

"Not a thing. Wish they'd organize a party for me; this place is as boring as it gets."

Perhaps. But I heard a soft hissing, steadily becoming fainter.

I said, "There has been another particle bundle penetration."

"Well, yeah, we did have that. But you'd hardly call it much of a party."

As Seth was speaking, his voice, already low, dropped to a whisper. He put a finger to his lips and pulled back farther into the shadow of the cupboard.

"What is it?" Speaking at this volume I was sure that only he could hear me.

"We got visitors. Better be ready."

There was a sound of footsteps from beyond the other end of the chamber. A second later a gray-clad figure zoomed into the room, used the web of ropes to change direction, and just as rapidly shot away through an exit on the opposite side. It was a man. He passed within ten feet of the shrouded white figure and did not seem even to notice it.

"Tech services, in a hurry," Seth said. "Using the cargo hold as a shortcut. Must be trouble someplace close."

"Not, one hopes, too close." It had seemed like a splendid idea, arranging our trap at a time when everyone on Sky City would be desperately busy with his or her own duties; unless, of course, the focus of those duties happened by accident to lie in the very place where the trap was set, and we became inundated with visitors. On such chance events, I suspect, rests many a man's reputation for cunning or folly.

The cargo bay again became quiet except for the unnerving groan of walls and supports and the occasional *crack* and *hiss* of a particle bundle. I switched briefly from remote viewing in order to catch a glimpse of local conditions at Otranto Castle. The sky outside the castle was darker now. The clock on my study indicated that the peak of the particle storm lay only forty minutes in the future. If anything were to happen, on Earth or in Cargo Bay Fourteen, this was surely the time.

I returned to Sky City and realized at once that the situation had changed. In the few moments of my absence a dark-clad figure had appeared at one of the entrances to the cargo bay. It stood there, silent and immobile, apparently examining every detail of the interior of the chamber. The face was shadowed and in half profile, and I could make out no features. Finally the figure moved forward and upward, heading for the white shroud suspended from the rope nets.

"Now, Seth," I whispered. "This is it."

He nodded. I saw him ease the beam weapon from his belt, and then he was gliding across the room toward the newcomer. He uttered no sound, but as he turned to glance at me I could read his lips. They mouthed, "Party time."

# 36

The water supply tanks of Sky City sat on the forward face of the great disk, turned now to point directly toward Alpha Centauri. Their value to the space city had always been incalculable, but in advance planning for the particle storm they promised extra value. In principle, their multiple billions of gallons provided protection to whatever lay behind them. In practice, like many other notions involving the Alpha Centauri supernova, the idea had been ruined by the discovery that the particles arrived as dense and massive bundles of huge penetrating power.

Star Vjansander sat cross-legged on the floor of a room behind the water tank that had been converted to a makeshift lab. Wilmer stood beside her. She shook her head in irritation. The floor of the room already had a small puddle near the wall. Now another bundle had evaded the snaring loops of the defensive shield, zipped effortlessly through the twenty-meter layer of the water tank, and created a neat hole in the bulkhead midway between Star and Wilmer. Before the hole could seal itself, a jet of water squirted through from the tank and splashed Star's cheek and neck.

"Garr." She rubbed at her face with a grimy hand, and glanced at the wall where the hole was quietly closing. "That didn't miss by much, did it? Thirty centimeters one way or the other, yer'd have been needing either a new partner or a new pecker."

She did not sound too distressed by their close shave. It was Wilmer, sitting on a chair a couple of feet away, who seemed more upset. He scowled down at Star and said, "I'm beginning to think I *need* a new partner. You seen these figures?"

" 'Course I have. I'm the one got 'em off Lauren an' give 'em ter yer."

"I mean, *really* seen them—tried to analyze them? Bruno Colombo must be tearing the hair off his head, wondering what to tell Earth."

"I don't care if he's pulling hair off his arse; he's all mouth and trousers. How d'yer expect me ter know what the figgers mean? I've been doin' convergence calculations the last two days, an' these are observed counts." Star took the sheet from Wilmer anyway, and ran her eye down the column. "Nobody but me an' you will think this *is* a problem. Colombo will love these numbers. They show the particle counts are way below what we calculate."

"I know. And how does that make me and you look?"

"I dunno."

"Well, I do. Like a couple of daft buggers, that's what. We predicted the form of the convergence, and every Sniffer reading confirms that we got it right. The pencil of the beam is *narrowing* as it approaches the solar system. On the strength of that we went to Celine Tanaka and told her it was all over, Earth was in deep shit. Now the counts don't agree. An' they *have* to be right, they come from observation. Data rules."

"So maybe we don't get wiped out after all. Yer a hard man ter please, Wilmer Oldfield." Star bounced up in one easy movement and pulled her shorts away from her damp rump. She handed him the data sheet. "Here. All yours. Me, I'm going aft to see what's happening with Hyslop and his crowd. You might as well do the same. We need a better idea, an' we don't have one."

"Right. I'll be there." Wilmer stared at the sheet he was holding. He started to stand up, stood motionless for a long time, and at last plopped back onto the chair. After a few moments his hand went up to the pink patch on top of his head. He started rubbing.

# 37

Night had vanished two hours ago. Now it seemed to be returning. The office was darker, with interior lights turned off and most of the illumination provided by the display screens.

Celine glanced at each of them. Everything coming in by radio feed showed a blur of electronic noise added to the video signal. Contact with Nick Lopez had been lost, though he should now be well north of the equator and safely landed. Fiber-optic links with the Southern Hemisphere revealed a world empty of human life. People had fled north, or moved to deep shelters. Plants and animals were not so lucky. The landscapes of South America, southern Africa, and Australia were strewn with dead creatures large and small, and the smoking remnants of trees and shrubs cast a purple-gray haze over everything.

Most of the mobile observation units still functioned, but their pictures jerked and twitched and veered as though the guidance signals from the main reporters were not quite working. As Celine watched, the screen showing a feed from McMurdo Sound collapsed to a kaleidoscope of random colors. An Antarctic reporter had taken a direct hit. After a twenty-second delay, a substitute circuit closer to the South Pole cut in with images of bare rocks and steaming, desolate ice cliffs.

She went to the window and stared southeast toward the Sun. She was in the supposedly "safe" Northern Hemisphere. But the gold circle of Sol was dimming, minute by minute, overlaid by a grid of dark lines. They were wider and more numerous than during the previous storm, and as Celine watched the Sun faded steadily in a cloud-free sky. Soon it became a ghostly gray cutout against a black background.

As the Sun dimmed to extinction, the first lightning bolt split the sky. It ran not between Earth and heaven, but cut a jagged path across the overhead blackness from east to west. The flash was so bright that Celine flinched away from the window. She automatically counted, waiting for thunder that never came, and at last realized that she was observing something in the highest reaches of the atmosphere, eighty to a hundred kilometers above her head. Before that realization, a second and a third bolt had streaked across her field of view.

As the lightning continued, the aurora began. Faint at first, it strengthened gradually to intense yellow-green streamers of light. The background of the sky turned ice blue and salmon pink. In that false dawn, plant leaves became dark purple and human skin took on the unpleasant green of the undead.

Celine glanced at her watch. Twenty-eight minutes to flux maximum. She turned to face her desk and said, "What's the situation on Sky City?"

"We still have good contact." Vice President Auden Travis's reply came at once. He and the Cabinet were, following Celine's orders, in the deep shelters. Celine had insisted that the President must stay in the White House, providing an example to the country by rejecting protection unavailable to most of the people. But the nation had to function after the particle storm, no matter what happened to her, so others must go below. Auden Travis had agreed—reluctantly. Celine was sure that he understood the real motive, which was her desire to see what happened firsthand. But he had gone, and he was undoubtedly monitoring everything that happened in her office. If the VP saw anything dangerous, Celine suspected that security staff would appear to drag her below, her orders notwithstanding.

"The amount of electronic activity in the atmosphere is incredible," the Vice President went on. "We're handling it all right, with tightly focused beams and repeat patterns with high redundancy. If it doesn't get worse than this, we'll keep transmission right through storm maximum. On the other hand, twenty minutes from now we may get nothing but gibberish."

"How are the space defenses performing?"

"Working at full capacity."

Travis said no more. It sounded like good news, but Celine knew better. If the defenses were at full capacity and the storm had yet to reach its maximum, then in the next half hour something had to give. What that something would be was quite clear, and it had been agreed to ahead of time. The first priority of Sky City and Cusp Station was to preserve—in order—the integrity of the particle detection system, the computational facilities, and the generators for loop field interceptors. Without them, there was no defense system at all. To keep those units functioning, the number of particle bundles hitting the immediate neighborhood of Sky City had to be as low as possible.

There was, of course, an inevitable but unspoken implication: If the number of bundles exceeded the capacity of the defenses to handle them, then other portions of the defenses, those farther from the axis of the cone of the shield, must suffer more collisions. The damage that caused would decrease their effectiveness. In turn, a steadily larger fraction of the storm would strike Earth.

It seemed as though Sky City was getting the better part of the deal, but their advantage would be only temporary. The space city could not survive for long without supplies from Earth.

Celine returned to the window. The sky was all fire. In the minute or two while her attention had wandered, the yellow streamers had turned solid, dimming the lightning itself with flaming lances of light along precise north-south lines. It hurt her eyes to look at them. She turned, and the afterimage of gold bars burned on her retinas. Her office was brighter than noon on a summer's day, yet it seemed dim.

Celine glanced again at her watch. She had to blink water from her eyes several times before she could make out its face.

Twenty-five minutes to go.

The optimist in her said, *Only twenty-odd minutes, a third of an hour, and Earth and I are still alive.*

The pessimist said, *Yes, we are; but for how long?*

# 38

The climber picked his way with carefully selected hand- and footholds up a sheer face of naked rock; the foot soldier marched forward with pike at the ready toward a waiting enemy; the captain wrestled with the steering wheel of his ship, fighting to keep the bow into the wind while the tempest raged; the hunter tracked a wounded tiger through the deep forest.

John Hyslop, in his youthful imagination, had been all of them. Fed on stories of old adventures, he had fought and conquered a hundred dangers. The difference between early fantasies and today's reality was simple: Then, his own actions had defined the line between success and failure. Now, as danger came closer, nothing that he did would make any difference.

The terms of engagement had been decided days and weeks ago. The defenses were the best that humans could make. They were working as well as could be expected, given the haste in creating them and the crude modifications to the old design. Now it was John's fate to take on the role of spectator, waiting to learn who and what might survive.

But even a spectator can be in danger. John jerked away as, two meters to his left, a particle bundle blasted into and through the information center. He heard the now-familiar staccato *ping* and saw a blue flash of Cerenkov radiation. He glanced around to make sure that no one had been hurt, and returned his attention to the displays.

*Working as well as could be expected.* That did not mean perfect. Close to one percent of the particle bundles were eluding the field loops. It wasn't supposed to happen. Someday—if all went well, and certainly not today—he would find out what had gone wrong. For the moment, he had to accept that there were going to be casualties, on Sky City as well as back on Earth. Or the other way round: *On Earth, as it is in heaven.* No one, so far, had been hurt in the information center, but urgent announcements had called for medical assistance on the perimeter levels of Sky City.

The perimeter levels. The exclusive levels, the expensive levels. Particle bundles drew no distinction between rich and poor, and there was no secondary form of protection that a wealthy man might buy. Once a bundle was past the defensive line, nothing could stop it.

John was aware that the information center was filling up. He saw that Maddy was here. He had watched her leave at the first onset of the storm, but he had not noticed her return. She gave him a thousand-watt smile and came closer. Will Davis and Rico Ruggiero had drifted back into the room and were hovering over by one of the main displays. If you were not involved in emergency services, looking after people who were hit, or making repairs to damaged equipment, there was little to do but watch and wait.

He noted the pulse rate of the field generators. It had reached a maximum value, and neither prayer nor tinkering could increase the frequency of the pulses.

He did not propose to advertise the fact that the defense system was at its limit, so that now too few loop pulses were being generated to provide complete protection. The defense system automatically allocated as many loop fields as were needed to ensure an acceptably low number of bundles at the detectors and field generators. That zone of relative safety covered Cusp Station and Sky City and extended a few kilometers beyond their edges. Within the zone the hit rate was constant at about one bundle per minute per ten square meters. Outside the zone, the number of bundles getting through was rising. The monitors said it was already far beyond anything seen during the blip storm. Earth must be taking a hammering, although there was no direct proof of that. Uplink and downlink communication was proceeding more or less as usual, even though the particle flux rate would go through the roof in another twenty minutes.

The *ping* of an arriving bundle sounded again through the information center. John glanced to his left. One of the data technicians, a middle-aged woman sitting in front at a control desk in front of

Will Davis and Rico Ruggiero, had been hit. She was staring down at her own midriff, where a neat round hole had been punched to the right of her navel. She said, in a wondering voice, "Son of a bitch. Will you look at that? It got me!" Then she crumpled to the floor of the information center without another word.

John watched long enough to be sure that she was carried away for treatment. The position of the particle bundle indicated that it had passed through one lobe of her liver and perhaps the ascending colon. Neither wound would be fatal, but she might be the first of many.

He turned his attention back to the displays. It had been Amanda Corrigan's idea to color-code the data on the number of bundles getting through the defenses versus their position on the surface of the space shield. Blue meant a safe zone—as much as anywhere could be safe, given the certainty of random penetration whenever a loop field failed to do its job. Red was the danger area, behind which Earth would be hardest hit. Amanda had probably never expected to see it this way, but the whole shield, viewed end-on, had become a rainbow of light. It ranged from the blue-violet bull's-eye of the cone end beyond Cusp Station and Sky City, out to an angry orange ring close to the outward edge of the shield. In those regions, the protection offered to Earth was negligible. Even beyond that was an annular zone of dull red where there was no protection at all. Particle bundles in that region would hit the planet's atmosphere, but not the planet itself. The surface would be affected only by secondary particles and radiation.

He swiveled his chair to take in activities in the information center. Every chair at every desk and panel was occupied, as it should be. The problem was, no one had anything useful to do. Even if the field generators failed to function, it would be impossible to reach and repair them before the particle wave hit its crest. Everyone, John himself included, had become no more than a spectator.

He knew that was true, but not everyone did. Young trainees like Jilly Wong and Al Morcelli thought that the senior engineers of Sky City were like gods, able to fix anything. Their eyes were on him now, waiting for him and the seniors to perform miracles.

John stood up. "All right." He forced himself to speak louder than usual. This was the sort of thing he hated doing. "You've done a great job, but now it's time to think of your own safety. This information center is close to the forward face of Sky City. It's much safer at the rear face, where the bulk of the city shields us from the particle bundles. I'd like everyone to go there now. I'll join you after I've taken care of a few details here."

He saw Will Davis's lopsided smile. The other engineer's eyes signaled to John, *That's a crock of shit, boyo, and you know it. The particle bundles whip right through Sky City like it's a paper bag. But I know what you're doing.*

Aloud, Will called in his best sergeant-major's voice, "All right, everybody. You heard what the boss said. Another half hour, and we'll all be home free. So let's go sit it out in some safe place."

It took a few seconds, but after a final glance at John and at the screens the others in the information center stood up and began to file out.

Finally there remained only John, Will, and Maddy. Will gave John another glance and said to Maddy, "It's a lot safer—"

"I know what it's like near the rear face, Will. I've been there, trying to help injured people. It's no safer than here. The bundles have easily enough energy to pass right through Sky City."

"Aye, well, if you know that—"

"But it would be good if you and John would go back there. Your presence will give people reassurance."

John said simply, "I can't. I must stay with the information center. We're still trying to get signals through to Earth."

"You, then, Will. You should go. I can stay with John."

"But . . ." Will Davis frowned. "Maddy, this makes no sense. *I'm* the one who should stay."

"Why? To show us you're brave? We already know that. And it's no more dangerous here than it is with the others near the rear face. I know. I've been there."

Davis looked to John Hyslop, who nodded. "Take off if you like, Will. There's nothing for you to do here—nothing for anybody to do but watch. If things go wrong, you'll know it as soon as I do."

"That's one way to put it. All right, I'll go and cheer up the trainees."

"Why just them?" Maddy asked.

"Because I can't cheer up the other engineers. They know too much."

He turned and wandered out of the information center. John decided that Will might not be the man to comfort anybody. He certainly hadn't gone out of his way to reassure Maddy.

As Will was leaving he passed Star Vjansander coming in. John, ignoring the displays for a moment, asked her, "Any new ideas?"

"Not a sausage." Star sat down by his side. "Except me and Wilmer think maybe our old ideas are wrong. I suppose yer might call it progress."

"I'd like something more definite than that."

"Well, wait a few minutes an' yer'll likely get it." Star gazed at the displays. "Only seventeen minutes ter flux peak. Then we'll *really* have data."

She waited a few moments and added, "We'll have it. But I'm not saying we'll like what we get."

# 39

**From the private diary of Oliver Guest.**

When all else in the universe has been explained, the mystery of the human mind will remain. I am far from the first to make this observation. However, for this particular moment it possesses a special relevance.

Consider. Humanity was suffering its greatest threat ever. I, and my darlings, might not survive to see another sunrise. In the longer term, life itself might become impossible on the lands and in the oceans of Earth.

And what, at this time of crisis, occupied my mind? Three things: Was I right? Would my plan work? Were we about to apprehend the Sky City murderer?

To this should be added a fourth factor affecting all of the first three: No matter what Seth did on Sky City, I might be unable to observe it. In an unpardonable display of stupidity, I had overlooked the possibility of decreased telecommunication capability between Earth and Sky City. As the particle storm grew to its height, the images received at Otranto Castle faded and dimmed. Although I saw a flickering image of a dark-clad figure moving along one of the guy ropes, closing in on the white shroud, the picture quality was inferior and the angle was wrong for me to see the face. Seth, clear of his hiding place, glided forward with his beam weapon held at the ready.

He made no sound that I could hear. The other was facing the wrong direction to see him. Nonetheless, when he was still ten meters away the newcomer turned from the shrouded figure and looked directly toward Seth.

At last I had a view of the face. It was Lauren Stansfield.

I felt a thrill of immense satisfaction. No matter how powerful a theory might be and no matter how supported by collateral evidence, when verification comes through observation it is a special moment.

"No need to look inside the bandages, Lauren," Seth said quietly. "You didn't leave any evidence there. We checked."

Lauren Stansfield remained totally still. I could see her shocked face. Even now, at this time of ultimate crisis, she wore dark eyeliner and careful makeup. Her clothes were elegant and well cut to show off her figure.

Finally she said, "What do you mean, I didn't leave evidence on the body?" Apparently she didn't realize that the figure was a dummy. "I didn't kill Doris Wu. What possible reason could I have for killing Doris Wu? I didn't even know her."

Seth and I had agreed in advance on our approach. We had to hit her with so many facts, or what she thought were facts, that she would assume a watertight case against her.

"I agree, you didn't know Doris Wu," Seth said. "I thought for a while you might be part of some big conspiracy, a group killing for some fancy motive. But it wasn't that. It was all you. A solo effort. What reason could you have for killin' Doris Wu, if you didn't even know her? Why, the same reason you had for murderin' Myra Skelton an' Tanya Bishop an' all the rest of 'em. Except for Lucille DeNorville, I mean. She was the one you were really after. The rest, and the fake sexual attacks, they were all smoke screens."

"Why would I want to kill Lucille—" But Lauren Stansfield paused and swallowed.

"Because of who you are," Seth said calmly. "Or rather, because of who you believe you *deserve* to be."

"I don't know what you mean." Lauren turned her head and stared haughtily away from Seth. "And I don't need to talk to you at all."

"Ah. What is it, *Princess* Lauren? Don't like communing with the peasants?"

I saw the swift head movement and the flash of her eyes. "My family was royalty when yours was still—"

Seth nodded. "Nobodies? Indeed we were. It wasn't the money, was it? Though that would be nice, given the way you dress beyond your income. But it's never been about money. It's about bloodlines, and privilege, and position. If there hadn't been a late second marriage in the DeNorville family two generations ago, everything that Lucille DeNorville stood to inherit—title and property and money and family estate—would have been yours."

Lauren was silent. I saw the look of distilled hatred on her face, but you cannot convict based on a facial expression. We had to have much more.

Seth knew it. He went on, "You're related to Lucille, of course. Not that close, otherwise you'd never have needed to work on Sky City. But it's no good sayin' that even with her out of the way you don't inherit, because there's others in line before you. That's true enough, but they're old, all three of 'em. If they died in the next few years, nobody would think it odd that they went sooner rather than later. You killed twelve teenage girls, all to get your hands on Lucille's title and inheritance. After that, a few old-timers on Earth would be easy meat."

She was smart, and she was tough. Her first couple of remarks had been slightly wrong as responses of an innocent party. Now she said, "You're crazy. I had nothing to do with killing anyone. The Sky City murders were committed by a man."

"That's what we were supposed to believe. An' everybody did, for a long time. But if we'd been thinkin' logical, we'd have asked some basic questions. After the first death or two, how could a man wander around alone with nobody askin' him what he was doing? I tried that, an' I'll tell you, it can't be done. But you were in charge of Sky City's life-support systems, you could go anywhere with a good reason. And nobody would notice a woman, except maybe to tell her to take care about bein' alone. An' after the first deaths, what girl would let herself get in a situation where she was alone with a man she didn't know well? Nobody would. But a woman, if she offered to provide a girl with a safe escort, an' said there was safety in numbers, no problem. How many did you kill, Lauren, when they were off guard because they thought you were there to protect them?"

Lauren stood her ground. When I zoomed in under maximum magnification I could see her eyes, thinking, calculating. Finally she shook her head and said, "I don't know what you're talking about. I don't know how somebody did the murders, but I'm not a security officer and it's not my job. I only know that I had nothing to do with it."

It was my worst fear. All that she needed to do was sit tight and deny everything. She could insist that she had wandered into the chamber with Doris Wu's body by accident, or because she simply had been curious, or because some component of the life-support systems merited her attention.

"Ask her why she came here, Seth," I said softly. "Make her talk."

He did not betray, by the slightest look or gesture, that he had heard my suggestions in his earpiece. But he said, "Lauren, you'll have to do better than that. We got you, an' we got plenty of other evidence, so you might as well admit it. Julia Vansittart was killed at a time when the outside detection system on Sky City was down for maintenance. The murderer—you—had to be in a position to arrange that, or at least to know about it. And Lucille DeNorville's body had to be found. Otherwise questions would have been raised when you came to inherit. People would have asked, was she really, provably dead?"

Lauren Stansfield stood still and said nothing.

Seth went on, "And why would you come in here, lookin' at Doris Wu's body, if you weren't afraid you might have left somethin' on it?"

"I was taking a shortcut, on my way to see if the particle storm was doing any damage to the city's air systems."

She had her composure back. I noticed, for the first time, that she was carrying a weapon. A beam device, much the same as Seth's, sat inconspicuously in a belt holster close to her right hand.

"Seth," I said urgently. "She's armed. If she were innocent, there'd be no possible reason for her to be armed. Ask her why she's carrying a gun if she's doing her usual work."

Again, his actions did not indicate that he had heard my remarks. This time he also ignored my suggested question. I wondered if my words were getting through—the image was beginning to break up. Then he said, "Lauren, we could stand around here and talk all day. But there's no point to it, so let's get this over with. I'm arresting you."

"You can't arrest me." On that point I was inclined to agree with Lauren Stansfield. If she simply sat tight, we lacked hard evidence. She went on, "And you're not security. You haven't been long on Sky City. I don't even think you are working with security."

"Quite right. I'm not security. I don't live on Sky City. I'm a bounty hunter, and you know the reward for catchin' the Sky City killer. I got more than enough evidence to ice you down for a long time. Come on, let's go."

Bounty hunter! What was the man gibbering about? He was no bounty hunter. But that was not what made me gasp. What Seth did next was something I would not have believed had I not witnessed it. He stuck the beam weapon that he was holding into his belt and casually began to turn away from Lauren.

Before I could do more than cry, "Look out!," she had her own weapon out and was pointing it at Seth. I saw a blue-green flare, and at the same moment heard a loud double crack. The weapon flew out of Lauren's hand. She spun around and fell backward onto the web of ropes.

Seth waited a few moments, then began to approach her slowly and carefully. He held his old projectile weapon in his left hand, and when he was a few feet away from Lauren he blew into the barrel and returned it to its rear holster. As he lifted her I could see why the weapon was now unnecessary. Her delicate nose had been ruined by a bullet that entered just above the nostrils and continued until it hit and destroyed the base of her brain. She had another wound in her chest.

"I guess that does it," Seth said. "Over-the-shoulder shots. Pretty nice, eh?"

"You shouldn't have put your gun away when you did," I said. "She almost killed you."

"Not a chance." He leaned easily against the web of ropes—but I noticed that a patch of hair on top of his head was charred. "I wanted her to fire at me."

"Why?"

"Because otherwise she'd have got away with everythin'."

"We had evidence. Not strong evidence, admittedly, but if we had—"

"Doc, pardon me for interruptin'. You're a genius, an' I'd never have made it to first base on this case without you. But now you're on my territory. I want to ask a sorta personal question. When they tried you, did you have a defense lawyer?"

"Of course I did. The state insisted on it. Not a very good lawyer, I thought."

"Well, I'm tellin' you, Lauren Stansfield would have had a *very* good lawyer. The best that money can buy. She's third in line to a superfortune, and she'd be royalty as well. The top scumbags in the business would have lined up to take her case on a contingency basis. An' with the miserable evidence we had, she'd have walked."

"But to put your weapon away like that, knowing that she was a multiple murderer . . ."

"I had to. She didn't know we had lousy evidence, but I did. That's why I told her I was a bounty hunter, goin' after the reward for the Sky City murderer."

"Which you're not."

" 'Course I'm not. But if she believed that, then I was halfway there. Bounty hunters operate lotsa different ways, but you can bet on a couple of things: They don't want *nobody* beatin' 'em to it, and they don't want to share a reward. So she thought, 'Hey, he won't have told anybody what evidence he has. If I take him out and get rid of the body, I'm home free.' "

"But you put your gun away—you turned your back on her."

"I put one gun away. I took the other one out as I turned. See, she had to take a shot at me. That way, I got a reason for firin' at *her*. If she hadn't tried to get me, I'd be the one facin' charges. As it is, with her tryin' to put me out of action, plus your evidence pointin' to her as the murderer, we're in good shape. 'Specially with her not here to argue."

"You *wanted* to kill her," I said.

"Let's say I didn't much like her. I don't care for people who look down on me. But I only kill people who try to kill me." He came across to where the RV jacket still hung on the wall, and put it over his arm. My view of Sky City became even worse, random and distorted as well as horribly noisy. "Anyway, Doc, you know what she did, an' you know why. Are you tellin' me you think she should have got away alive an' free an' rich? Should she have been a queen?"

"I think that Earth—and the rest of the universe—is much better off without Lauren Stansfield."

"So what's to talk about? We're agreed." Seth, carrying the RV jacket over his arm and making me feel rather like a ventriloquist's dummy, started to stroll out of Cargo Bay Fourteen. "I'm headin' forward. It's time to find out if there's goin' to be anyplace to *be* better off without Lauren Stansfield."

"I will leave that to you," I said. "I'm losing the picture, and I must attend to matters here. Call me later."

"Have to be after storm peak. Even with redundancy we lose signal, up and down, a few minutes from now."

"That's all right. Make it a video link—if you can get one."

"Hard to come by today. Might have to call you tomorrow—if there is one."

There was a final grainy swirl of color, and Seth was gone. I yanked the RV helmet off my head. For the past few minutes the contribution of the local scene to what I saw had steadily faded. Now I knew why. Before I donned the helmet, flaming streamers of light had filled the heavens outside the castle. Where had they gone? Peering through the shutters, I saw nothing. Earth was descending to hell, Milton's hell, I thought. "Not light, but darkness visible" and "Hide me from the heavy wrath of God."

I had switched poets in midstream—in midsentence—but that is one of the problems facing those of us of a morbid or fanciful disposition. We overdramatize. Fortunately, there is a cure. I left my study and headed for the elevator that led to the deep cellars.

The elevator does not go all the way, and the final descent is made down a long flight of stairs. Even before I reached the first step I could hear the screams and shouts of laughter. The storm party was going well.

I continued down, to fulfill the role of stern parent and to read the riot act. The putative end of the world deserved to be taken more seriously.

# 40

The Sky City communication systems provided minute-by-minute news to outlets on every level. So why was the engineering information center again full of people, after John Hyslop had told everyone to go away? He hadn't objected when Maddy had stayed at his side, but she hoped that she was a special case. He had even smiled at her, the John Hyslop equivalent of a passionate embrace. His only condition for her presence, implied by attitude rather than words, was that she not interfere with his work. He was struggling to maintain an open communication channel with Earth.

But what were all the others doing here?

Maddy had her own answer: People would risk anything, even death, to see the action firsthand. She glanced around the room.

Star Vjansander had stayed, too—rather to Maddy's annoyance. Maddy liked being alone with John, even when he was too preoccupied to notice her. Star's hair was wet and she was unusually quiet, sprawled prone on the floor with her short skirt riding almost to her waist and her chin cupped in her hands. Maddy looked for Wilmer Oldfield and did not see him. That was odd. The two went everywhere together.

Will Davis had returned and stood close to John. Most of the other senior engineers had come back, too, filling the vacant desk seats. Amanda Corrigan was obviously scared, biting her nails and staring at nothing. Torrance Harbish played a different role, totally calm and pretending to be more interested in his fellow engineers than in the displays. But Maddy saw the white, strained look around his mouth.

Seth drifted in last, nondescript and inconspicuous, with the usual rolled-up bundle of clothing under his arm. He caught Maddy's eye and nodded.

Meaning what? Maddy knew of the trap. But where was Lauren Stansfield? Had she been taken into custody? She raised her eyebrows at Seth. He just grinned.

A gasp and a murmur from the other people in the room brought her attention to the displays. The biggest one had suddenly changed, switching from the outward views of space and the defense system to an image of Earth. The big scope on the rear face of Sky City was in use, and it showed the whole of the Southern Hemisphere. With winter there, the pole ought to be dark. Instead, the great ice shield of Antarctica glowed an electric blue. The surrounding oceans were obscured by clouds of white steam and vapor as far north as the tip of South America. Every sunlit land area, from Tierra del Fuego to as far north as Panama, was hazy and indistinct, ground details lost behind a continent-wide pall of black smoke.

A faint and unidentifiable man's voice sounded from the audio channel. "We make it five minutes to maximum flux, and I hope to hell that's right because we're taking quite a beating here. Our monitors show a Southern Hemisphere temperature rise of thirty-eight Celsius, and still climbing. Sky City, can you hear me? Are you able to confirm that number with bolometric readings and thermal IR?"

John began speaking into a microphone. Maddy, close as she was, could not hear his reply, but the display suddenly changed. The image still outlined the continents and oceans of Earth, but the colors on the globe were different. She had no idea how to interpret that until Will Davis said, "Thermal map, radiance corrected for emissivity and differenced from yesterday's numbers. We're looking at big temperature increases down there."

His remark was intended for the young technician next to him, not Maddy, but she examined the display with new understanding. The particle storm was scorching a wide swath on the turning Earth. Although the hottest region corresponded to latitude sixty degrees south, directly below Alpha C, there were changes all the way down to the South Pole and north to beyond the equator. Thirty-eight degrees Celsius. The difference between a cold winter's day and a hot summer's one. And that was an *average* increase. If the particle bundles didn't kill the plants and animals in the red zone, heat would. Thank God it was the Southern Hemisphere, where there was less land area. The southern oceans formed a huge heat reservoir and would not easily be warmed beyond the surface.

She looked at the countdown below the display. Four minutes to storm peak. After that the particle bundles would still be coming but the number of hits should start to diminish. Maybe her sense of time was distorted. The number of bundles bursting through the information center didn't seem to have increased during the past quarter hour. If anything, it seemed a shade less.

She was ready to dismiss that as her own wishful thinking when a new voice came from the speaker. This time it was a woman, barely making sense above the static. "I don't know how you're doing it, or exactly what you're doing up there, but keep it up. We're hanging in. If it doesn't get worse than this, there's a chance we'll make it all the way."

Will Davis said, softly enough so that only the people nearest to him could hear, "What the hell *are* we doing, John? We were at the limit of the defense system when I left, and that was half an hour ago. I thought that by now Sky City would be a sieve and Earth would be beyond contact."

"So did I." John Hyslop stood up and turned to where Star Vjansander lay on the floor in a near-obscene sprawl of bare limbs. "What's going on, Star? We made our estimates based on the numbers that you and Wilmer gave us. How come they're so far off?"

"Yer got me." She stared up at him and rolled her chocolate-dark eyes. "Wilmer and me got no more idea than you do. He said yer'd be on ter us as a couple of silly buggers soon as yer saw the counts was wrong. But I calc'lated the convergence right, I swear it. The beam's narrowing in; no other way ter read the Sniffer data. But we're not seeing near enough particle bundles."

"You mean enough to match your blessed theory," Will Davis said. He had turned away from John Hyslop to face Star. "For me, there's more than enough—"

Maddy heard the sharp sound of a particle bundle ripping its way through metal. Will paused and gave an odd grunting cough. Maddy, standing behind him, saw the hole appear in his back just above his waist. At the same time the big display on the front wall went dark.

"Will's hit!" she cried, and a moment later realized there was more. John had been between Will and the forward wall. The particle bundle had entered the information center, passed through John's body, through Will, and gone on its way. Will was on his feet, standing and swaying and clutching at his middle. But John was falling.

Maddy lunged forward and was able to catch him and lower him to the floor. She looked in terror for the wound. Will was a good deal taller, and John had been looking down toward Star Vjansander. If it was his head or spinal column—

It was his neck. The bundle had entered right rear and exited left center-front, by the Adam's apple. Spinal cord intact. No spout of blood from jugular or carotid; with any luck no major blood vessels had been cut. Nerve damage they'd fix later. Breathing, hard but fairly normal. The windpipe must be intact.

Or was it? His eyes were open, staring up at Maddy. He seemed to be trying to speak, but no words came out. Vocal cords affected? The bundle had missed the Adam's apple itself, but it was close. There might be other damage.

"John!"

Nothing but harsh breathing. Eyes trying to talk to her.

Maddy glanced up. "A doctor—we need a doctor!"

"Call's gone out." A burly engineer crouched beside her. "Don't mess with him if you don't know what you're doing."

Did she? One course, thirteen years ago. His head was on the hard floor. She slipped her right hand underneath, providing support, raising his head as little as possible. She felt wetness on her hand and looked down. John's fall had opened his wound and he was bleeding at the back of the neck. Didn't seem too bad, a little pool on the floor. So long as he was breathing and remained conscious . . .

Where was the doctor?

Maddy looked up again. Will Davis was still standing, his hands held on his belly three inches to the right of his navel. If the vigor of his cursing was anything to go by, his wound was not life-threatening.

Where was the damned doctor?

The big-screen display was back in operation. Two minutes to storm maximum. The view was no longer of Earth. Now the imaging sensors showed the defense system at work as it was seen from the front of Cusp Station. The whole of the shield scintillated with tiny flashing points, too many and too briefly lit to count. The incoming particle bundles were detected crossing the shield. Sky City received the information and computed trajectories. The field generators threw their electromagnetic nooses out at light speed. What Maddy saw was the field loop as the field caught and diverted the particle bundle away from the shield. When Maddy said it that way, John had insisted on correcting her. Maddy was actually seeing the radiation that the charged particle emitted when it was accelerated.

Engineers. Logic, accuracy, precision. No room for emotion. Would he die without emotion, cool and calm?

*No!*

She turned back to John, wondering what she could say. "Just two more minutes, and we'll be over the worst."

She was appalled at her own words. Intended to reassure him, sure, but what did the particle storm matter if he was dying?

His lips were moving. She bent low, her right ear to his mouth.

"Don't go to Earth." It was a thread of sound, a whisper so faint that it was as much imagined as heard. "Stay here."

She jerked up and stared down into his face. It was white and drained. His eyes were wide. His lips still moved, soundlessly.

Again she bent over him. Blood from the pool on the floor was soaking her knees.

"Stay here." Fainter yet. "With me. Forever. Will you?" And then, puzzled, "Why we alive? Maddy? Why not all dead? Maddy . . ."

His eyes began to close. She straightened up. "John—" Before she could say more a pair of hands grabbed her and lifted.

"Out of the way." It was a huge woman in a nurse's outfit, the front of it filthy with blood. She picked Maddy up like a baby, set her down three feet away, and turned at once to John.

*No! I have to talk to him.* But the words came out, "Is he dying?"

"Of course he isn't dying." The nurse was already staunching the wound at the back of John Hyslop's neck. "He's one of the lucky ones. But he can't stand to have you pestering him, so either go away or keep quiet. And if you don't have anything better to do, take his legs."

Maddy found herself lifting John onto a stretcher. His eyes had closed. Ten seconds more and he was being carried out. She started to follow.

"Not you!" The nurse glared at her. "Not now. I told you, he's going to be all right. There'll be plenty of time to see him later. Say, three hours from now. And here. You're a mess. Use this."

She and the other stretcher bearer left the information center. Will Davis, rejecting offers of assistance, walked out after her. He was still cursing. Maddy stood alone, wiping her bloodied hands and knees with the rag that the nurse had thrust at her.

She stared around her. The countdown showed one minute *past* storm peak. While she had been busy with John, zero hour had come and gone. All the displays were alive. The battleground of the shield still flared and glittered, Earth still flamed and smoked and seethed. But minute by minute, the intensity of the attack would decrease. Two hours from now, if she lived to see it, Sky City, Cusp Station, and Earth would begin to calm. They could all begin the long road back.

She heard a loud and distorted voice over the communication channel. "Sky City? We are still holding on, and we show count rates starting down. Can you confirm?"

Bruno Colombo appeared from nowhere. He took John's chair, grabbed the microphone, and spoke into it.

Maddy couldn't tell what he said, because everyone in the information center was suddenly talking. She picked her way through the chaos to where Star Vjansander still lay on the floor, her hands cupping her plump cheeks. She was thoughtful, ignoring everyone.

It was John's question, but Maddy had to ask it. When she saw him later, she wanted to have an answer. Two answers—but one she already had.

"Star, the storm didn't get as bad as you said it would. Not nearly as bad. What happened?"

Star raised her head and stared vacantly at Maddy. "Uh?"

"What happened? How come we're alive, and Earth's alive? We should all be dead."

"I dunno." Star slowly stood up, with nothing like her usual fluid grace. "I been wondering, too. We were way off. An' I don't know why." She stared all around the information center. "Where's Wilmer?"

"I don't know. He hasn't been here since the storm buildup began."

"Well, I got ter find him. Me an' him have ter rattle our skullcases. We got data coming out of our ears. But now we hafta do the brain work."

She wandered off. After a few moments Maddy left the room, too. Rather than following Star, she walked along the corridor that spiraled out toward the perimeter of Sky City. The occasional *ping* still sounded as particle bundles evaded the defenses and blasted through everything they met, rattling overstressed metal. But there were fewer of them. The defense system had smart components, and efficiency had increased all through the particle storm. There was still danger, and would be for another few hours, but the worst was over.

In any case, that was not where Maddy's thoughts were concentrated as she traversed deserted corridors and escalators and moved toward the higher-priced levels. By every logic, she should have been thinking of John's narrow escape from death. In fact, she was seeing Sky City with new eyes.

This place was in need of a thorough overhaul. It had been run like an offshoot of an engineering lab for too long, but now there were eighty thousand people here, men and women and lots of children. It needed to be made to feel like a real city. She could do that. And who would her competition be? Bruno Colombo? Goldy Jensen? She could eat them.

If she wanted to. Maybe she didn't. Maybe she was ready for a completely different kind of life, not just a Sky City continuation of the sort of work she had done in the Argos Group. Wasn't that the life she had decided to leave, just a few weeks ago? Gordy Rolfe, with his rages and his ego and his suspected sabotage of shield development, felt a million miles and a thousand years away. She would find out—someday—if her warning to Celine Tanaka had been necessary and heeded. But that could wait.

Maddy wandered on, looking, wondering, making an evaluation. Deciding if this level of effective gravity was more comfortable than that. Assessing appearance. Balancing cost against comfort. Putting a value on convenience. Picking the nicest area.

Just what you did with anyplace when you realized that you were going to live there.

# 41

"Why isn't everyone dead?"

Six hours had produced a dramatic change. The communication channels between Earth and Sky City were again free of noise. Celine Tanaka was looking at Bruno Colombo, and his image was perfectly clear and solid. Forget the signal delay, and you would think he was sitting just next door.

She had expected to be talking only to Bruno Colombo, but a dozen other people were packed in with him. She should have predicted that. The Oval Office was just as full. In both places, everyone crowded in who could justify a presence.

Plus, perhaps, a few who couldn't. Celine wondered about Maddy Wheatstone, standing next to a pale and bandaged John Hyslop. Perhaps the particle storm had led Goldy Jensen to relax her iron grip on access to Bruno's office, and a few extras had slipped by her.

Celine went on, "Not that we're complaining, mind you. It's nice to be alive, those of us that are, and know that Earth can start on the road to recovery. It's going to be a long and hard road, we realize that, but it's a shock being here at all, after you've sat for weeks preparing for the worst."

"Yes, indeed." Bruno Colombo was nodding a mile a minute. "Madam President, we are as delighted as you are that the damage and casualties on Earth are less than anticipated. We, of course, have had our own injuries." An extra nod went in John Hyslop's direction. "We also suffered tragic loss of life. However, this should also be a time for thanksgiving, if not for actual celebration. We have seen, if not a miracle, at least a supreme achievement. I would like to take this opportunity to congratulate and to thank publicly every individual on Sky City, all of whose exceptional efforts permitted the damage inflicted on Earth to be far less than was originally feared, and every one of whom—"

"We share your gratitude, Director Colombo." Celine could see the others on Sky City wriggling with impatience or embarrassment. Bruno Colombo had a rare talent for blather, and he was barely getting started. "I would welcome an opportunity to discuss that with you in more detail—on some other occasion. For the moment, however, we have a practical question: We survived, but *why?* What, if you like, went *right?* I thought the storm was predicted to be far more than the defense system could handle. We came to the limit, but the defenses held. How were they able to do that?"

Bruno Colombo looked across at John Hyslop. "I think that our chief engineer, despite his severe injuries, is the person best equipped to handle that question."

*If the poor beggar can talk,* Celine thought, *what with that choker bandage round his neck, and the blood on it. But he looks cheerful enough.*

"No thanks to me." John Hyslop's voice was a throaty whisper. "I was as surprised as anybody. Star knows what's been going on, though. Star? Wake up. I'm talking to you."

"Me? Ooh! Sorry." Star seemed startled, but she grinned at Celine. "How are yer, mam? Still got Calvin Coolidge's seat down there, have yer?"

"It hasn't been used by anyone since you," Celine said gravely.

Star cackled. "Don't wonder, if they know what he did in it. Dirty old beast! Whadyer want to know, mam? I wasn't list'ning too close."

"Why weren't we all killed by the particle storm? You're supposed to be the expert. And *don't* say that if we had all been killed, we wouldn't be here to talk about it."

"Never thought of that." Star blinked. "Anyway, I'm not the expert. I was the dummy on this one, just as bad as the rest of yer."

Celine heard Nick Lopez snigger behind her. "But you understand it, Star. Can't you explain it?"

"No, mam. I mean, I could explain. But Wilmer oughter do it. He was the one figgered it out, so it's like his, not mine."

"But he's not there."

"No, mam, because he's here. Hey, Wilmer. Tell 'em."

Celine groaned as Wilmer appeared in the field of view. It was always nice to see a former colleague, not to mention a long-ago lover, but she had tons of work to do before the day ended. She had been hoping for a quick explanation and a rapid advance to other topics.

"We got most of it right." Wilmer wasn't being defensive; he didn't think in those terms. He simply wanted to be accurate. "I mean, we got most of it right *eventually*. But not on the first shot.

"Star gave us a good theory as to how Alpha C could go supernova. We knew the particle beam was heading in our direction, and it didn't seem that could have happened by accident. And when we had the Sniffer data we realized that the particles didn't travel separately, they were tied together in big bundles of a few trillion each. Soon as we had a chance to grab some, Star could start to play around with 'em. Their behavior turned out to be peculiar."

"Funny little buggers," Star added. "Put a bundle in some place at a humongous temperature, it don't give a damn. Sits there, totally comfortable. Surround it with cool matter and lots of slow-moving free electrons, though, an' it's buggered. It falls apart."

"When we knew that," Wilmer went on, "we still didn't see how it helped us to guard against them. We went ahead with a redesigned defense to divert particle bundles, but we didn't seem any closer to real understanding. We didn't know what was going on with the Alpha Centauri supernova, or why it happened."

He paused and looked thoughtful.

"And we still don't know why it happened," Nick Lopez said softly behind Celine. "And at this rate we never will. Tell him to get a move on."

Celine knew better. She sat and waited, and at last Wilmer went on. "Then we got newer Sniffer data, and knew we were really in trouble. The particle beam wasn't just coming our way, it was *converging*, homing in on us. That's when me and Star decided we—meaning humans—were really up shit creek. The way the beam was narrowing as it approached the solar system, we'd be hit with a whole load of particles, far more than we'd ever expected. Far more than the new defense system could cope with. Far too much for Earth to stand, or for Sky City."

Nick Lopez, behind Celine, muttered, "So we all died."

Celine said patiently, "But it *wasn't* too much for Earth, or for Sky City. We're still here. How did that happen?"

"Because me and Star, we took two correct facts, added an assumption, and drew a false conclusion." Wilmer shook his head woefully. "Not Star's fault, mine. I ought to be old enough to know better. Let's do the facts. First fact: The Alpha Centauri supernova didn't just happen. It was *made* to happen."

"Something hardly anybody in the world believes," Celine said.

"True. But that doesn't make it any less a fact. And it's not what caused our problem. Second fact: The particle beam was converging. The number of bundles per unit volume was *increasing* instead of decreasing as the beam came closer, and the devastation it could cause was that much greater. And now the assumption: Human beings are important."

Everyone in the Oval Office jerked to attention. Celine said, "I hope *that's* not what you mean by a false assumption. If so, you won't find anybody here in the Oval Office who agrees with you."

"Then I'm glad I'm not in the Oval Office." Wilmer held up his hand. "Don't get starchy on me; I'm going to explain. I had this thought when I was by myself and the particle storm was sluicing through Sky City. I thought, if I had the science and the technology to make a supernova happen, would I waste a whole star system just to wipe out a lot of silly buggers like me? Of course I wouldn't. I've heard all the talk, that something tuned in on our radio signals over the past century and a half and decided to do away with us. I can't buy that. I mean, the media programs are bad, but they're not *that* bad.

"Once you decide the human race isn't important enough to be worth killing, you stop saying, 'Something's out to get me,' and you draw a different conclusion. Not the wrong conclusion, the one that me and Star made, that the particle beam was converging on Earth. The right conclusion: Whatever made the supernova and the particle beam hasn't the slightest interest in Earth. The beam was converging *on Sol*. The Sun was the target, and the only target. And what saved us—what made the difference between total extinction and a near miss—is Earth's *distance* from the Sun. We're alive because all but a tiny fraction of the particle bundles went to their intended destination: Sol. The convergence worked almost all the time. We got the failures, the misses."

Celine said, a moment before her brain caught up with her tongue, "You mean the particle bundles were designed to destroy the Sun?"

"Of course they weren't." Wilmer stared at her in amazement. "Destroy the Sun? That's barmy. Star, got that bottle with you? Show it off there, would you?"

Star rummaged in the bag hung over her shoulder and pulled out a glossy metal canister about eight inches long. She held it up so that everyone could get a view of it and said, "Ta-daa!"

"Particle bundles." Wilmer took it from her. "In here. Quite stable, they're kept away from ordinary matter using electromagnetic field suspension. Harmless. Harmless here, and on the Sun. They wouldn't destroy it. Why would they want to, when they live inside stars?"

Bruno Colombo said, "You talk as though the things in there are alive!"

It was his turn to receive Wilmer's withering stare.

"Well, I don't know. Maybe they are, maybe they're not. Depends how you define *alive*. Me and Star, we've been wrong too often and too recently to stick our necks out. But let's say we feel sure that the Alpha Centauri supernova was designed to spread these particle bundles to other stars. We don't know how they're aimed, or what they do when they get there. But I'd make a case for saying anything that propagates itself in an intentional way qualifies to be thought of as alive."

"And sentient?" Bruno Colombo was out to restore his good name. "If they are, and they are able to produce a supernova, think what we might learn from them."

"I wouldn't count on it." Wilmer peered at the bottle. "The bundles in here would be more like spores, or seeds. How much high-tech information would you get from a human sperm? I don't think it'd produce the theory of relativity, or tell you how to send an expedition to Mars. And if one of these little beggars *could* tell us anything, I don't know if I'd trust it. They're a star form, we're a planet form. We might not have much in common."

Nick Lopez, behind Celine, said suddenly, "How long do we have, Wilmer?"

Celine turned to face him. "How long for what?"

"How long before the bundles develop to whatever they finally become, and do whatever they do? If they're like seeds, eventually they'll turn into something that produces more seeds. How long before they change the Sun, or decide it's breeding time and they need another supernova?"

"No worries. Stellar processes are slo-o-o-w—a star like Sol can spend ten billion years and more on the main sequence."

"It can. But does it have to? Remember, there was no way that Alpha Centauri could go supernova—until it did."

"He's right, Wilmer." Star moved forward to peer at Nick Lopez with new interest. "I thought it the first time I met yer. Yer got a weird mind, mister. I like that."

"And in fact we know very little about supernovas and how they work," Wilmer added. "Maybe they proceed from star to star like a chain of firecrackers, one every ten million years. We've not been watching for long enough. In a whole galaxy you get only one or two supernovas a century, and mostly so far away we don't learn much. Did you know we haven't had a naked-eye supernova since—"

"Thank you, Wilmer, I've heard that before." Celine cut him off. "No more speeches today. The wounded have to be looked after, the dead buried, Earth and the institutions of Earth rebuilt, and Sky City moved back to its old position. And then we must set new goals for humans, including everything we had before the supernova came along, and more."

She thought, *That sounded an awful lot like a speech. It must be catching.*

"And while we're doing all that," Nick Lopez said quietly, "there's one other thing that we'll be doing."

The others paused expectantly. Not Celine. When you were a world-class worrier, you didn't have to be told what else you needed to be nervous about. "I know. From now on we'll have a new hobby—maybe we should say a new religion."

"Maybe we should say, more like an old religion."

"Whatever you call it, one thing's for sure. We'll all be watching the Sun."

# 42

## EPILOG
### From the private diary of Oliver Guest.

At Otranto Castle a wind from the south-southwest should be a warm zephyr, bringing the lotus ease of the lazy tropical ocean whence it came. But not this time. The wind had blown as a force-five gale for six days and nights, a fury that carried in its dark heart sleet and hail and the sour, bitter stench of cindered lands and dead seas. The castle, windows shuttered, crouched down and endured this blast, as it had stood and withstood for more than two and a half centuries.

Soon after dawn on the sixth morning, I opened the heavy oak door of the main entrance and stepped outside. The wind was strong as ever and rain sheeted at me sideways, but there was a freshness in the air and a clarity to the sunrise. It was possible to believe, for the first time since the onset of the particle storm, that Earth had a future.

In that moment of spiritual rebirth, the castle Alert blurted in to steal joy from the morning. *Warning,* it shouted in my ear. *Possible intruder sighted to the southwest. Human evaluation requested.*

I sighed and went inside. Under high magnification I studied the solitary walker. He was enveloped in waterproof clothing that flapped like dark wings in the gusts, and he maintained a wide and wise separation between himself and the edge of the cliffs. This time, however, I had no doubt as to his identity. For more than a week I had been waiting and wondering; not if, but when.

I opened the door and held it as he approached. He hurried into the dark hallway as though the wind bore him across the threshold unassisted.

"A nasty morning," I said.

"You might say." Seth grinned at me as he stripped off his overcoat and leggings. "But we've both seen worse."

His clothing had been inadequate protection. His hair and shirt were soaked. I led him through to the far end of the kitchen, where towels hung drying on a line and a gallon pot simmered on the blackened stove.

He took a towel and rubbed at his hair until it was a drier but more tangled mess, then went over and sniffed the pot. At my nod he filled a bowl and carried it to the long wooden table.

"Beans?" he asked.

"With ham hocks," I said. "From the gentleman who pays the rent."

"Huh?"

"It's an old Irish joke. It means a pig."

Those were our first words after the initial greeting, and they were not inspiring. After that neither seemed inclined to speak again. The silence continued until Seth had emptied the bowl and refused more with a shake of the head. Finally he said, "You were expecting me."

"It was my preference." I led the way to the study, and we sat down in front of the peat fire. "Otherwise I would have ultimately been obliged to seek you."

"Yeah." He removed his boots and held his stockinged feet close to the red peat coals until the soles began to steam. At that point he moved back a couple of feet, accepted my offer of whiskey, stared into the low flames, and said, "We got unfinished business. It'd be nice to say, go back to the way it was before any of this started. But we can't. You know that I know."

"And vice versa. I know about you. More, perhaps, than anyone else in the world. Even in these troubled times, the curious demise of Gordy Rolfe was widely reported."

"Yeah. There's rumors that he was part of some big conspiracy, robbin' Sky City blind, an' his business partners knocked him off so he couldn't talk. But some people talked conspiracy with the Sky City murders, an' we know how that turned out. Me, I think nobody's goin' to find anything more. Old Gordy made hidin' what he knew an' did into an art form."

"I will not dispute the conspiracy theory. However, I suspect that you and I alone are aware of your intention to visit Gordy Rolfe on the day before he died."

"Ah, but did I go there? I vote for natural causes, Doc, comin' as a result of unnatural experiments. You heard what the media said about poor old Gordy. 'Hoist with his own petard,' if you want to put it fancy. They found one of his boots, an' that was all. Nobody's lookin' for me as a killer. Can't say quite the same for you."

"Are you threatening me?"

"Wouldn't dream of it."

"Or thinking to blackmail me?"

"Never."

He glanced toward the door behind me and frowned. I turned and saw four faces peering in a vertical line around the jamb: Paula, Bridget, Beth, and Trixie. They had been in the cellar earlier, but they must have seen the Alert flashing or heard the outer door.

"This meeting does not call for your presence," I said sharply.

That would probably have been enough had not Seth made the mistake of adding condescendingly, "Run along, kiddies. You heard your dad."

Paula frowned, and Bridget flushed and opened her mouth as though about to speak. Before she could do so, Paula dragged her out of sight. A moment later the other two faces vanished.

Seth waited to make sure they had gone, then went on. "Take it easy, Doc. I'm just sayin' we need to have some sort of negotiation or truce, an' it's nice to know where each of us is startin' from. Seems to me you're startin' off vulnerable. Not because of you; you're fire-proof." He gestured toward the door. "Because of them."

"If you imply that through the existence of those girls I have, in the words of Francis Bacon, given hostages to fortune, then I am obliged to agree with you. However, you know my history. The addition of one more victim to the roster for the sake of security would not, if discovered, change my sentence at all were I ever to be recaptured."

"One more victim. Are you threatenin' me, Doc?"

"I would not dream of it."

"Or tryin' to blackmail me?"

"Never."

Seth grinned. Far from being intimidated, he seemed amused. "So we both know where we stand. Question is, what do we do?"

"If you are referring to the reward for the apprehension of the Sky City murderer, I neither need nor want it."

"That's good. I need it, an' I want it, 'cause with Gordy gone I don't have a job. But the reward ain't the problem. How do we work the *other* stuff?"

I had no immediate answer. Regrettably, he was right. I was far more vulnerable than he. Eighteen young girls are not easy to hide. With them to protect and nurture, I would need a permanent and safe base of operations for many more years. A single male like Seth, on the other hand, could vanish with ease or wander the world as he chose.

Should I seek to kill him *now*, this very minute, while he sat drinking my whiskey? He was undeniably accessible, but I felt a reluctance even to consider that prospect. I ascribed it to a worry that my darlings might somehow become aware of such a bloody deed. There was also, of course, a more practical consideration: Seth Parsigian's whole history proved that he was no easy man to kill.

Before I could decide on action or inaction, another complication reared its head. My darlings appeared again; not, this time, in the form of the previous four. All eighteen came trooping into the study and stood in an orderly line, oldest to youngest, along the wall opposite the fireplace.

"Paula." In spite of her short stature I addressed her as the most senior and the usual ringleader. "I told you once to go away. What do you think you are doing here?"

When Paula spoke it was not to me but to Seth. "We wanted to meet you," she said in her deep, husky voice. "And we wanted you to meet us. We thought it was important."

This time he did not try to dismiss her. He studied the girls, carefully and one by one, his tawny eyes moving steadily along the line. "Important how?" he said. "We never met. You don't know me."

"You came to our home on one previous occasion. You are Seth Parsigian."

Seth jerked around sharply in my direction. His face was more surprised than I had ever seen it. I shook my head. "Not from me, Seth. I swear on my nonexistent soul, that did not come from me."

He turned angrily back to Paula. "So you know who I am. Clever girl. Do you also know who—"

He caught himself, but she had followed his eyes.

"Who he is? Yes. He is our father, Kevin Baxter. Not our biological father, of course. But he raised us, and so far as we are concerned he is our true and only father."

Seth looked at me, but he did not speak. My eyes told him that he was on very dangerous ground. To protect my darlings, I would do anything. But Paula was not finished.

She added, "He is our father. And he is also Dr. Oliver Guest, who in the year 2021 was sentenced to six centuries of judicial sleep for the murder of fifteen teenage girls. That number was later, through his own confession, increased to eighteen."

If Seth was surprised by that announcement, I was stunned. I made a faint sound in my throat. I think I was trying to offer a denial, stupid as that sounds, but no words came out.

"And," said Paula, "we know who we are." She took a step forward out of the line. "I am Paula Baxter. I was once Paula Searle. I was raised in Norfolk and in the Atlanta Scantlingtown. I never knew my father, but my mother was a druggie and a whore, and I was mostly a nuisance to her until I became old enough to go on the game."

While I gaped—how did she know any of that? There was to my knowledge no written record—she stepped quietly back in line and made a little hand gesture. Amity, standing next to her, moved forward.

"I am Amity Baxter. I was once Amity Carlisle. I was born in San Antonio. My mother was only fourteen, so I was sent to El Paso to live with an aunt and uncle whom I had never met. She beat me most days and when I was ten years old he raped me. I ran away when I was eleven. I lived along the transport strips. Money was short, but I always knew I could get some from older men if I did the right things to them."

Amity, my magical, innocent Amity who insisted that she believed in fairies and danced with joy when she saw a rainbow. Not even I knew all of what she had said. But she was back in line, and Rose was stepping forward.

"I am Rose Baxter. I was once Rosa Gonzales. I was born in Coral Gables. When I was little we had plenty of money, but my father was ruined in the economic collapse after the Turnabout riots, and he killed himself. Mother had to work, and so she left me home alone . . ."

I knew what was coming, the slow descent and degradation until she sat hopeless by the roadside and I drove past. But Seth did not. It was news to him, the whole tawdry parade, from Paula's beginning until little Victoria had had her turn. The cavalcade of events that they offered was appalling and bizarre, yet I was oddly proud of them. Each of my darlings spoke so clearly, so confidently, and so calmly.

Finally Paula again stepped forward.

"As you see, Mr. Parsigian, we do indeed know who you are. We also know who our father is, and who we are. It took a great deal of research, and lots of time. But we did it."

He shot me an accusing glance. "You son of a bitch. You smartened 'em. You never told me that."

"Minimally. They were intelligent already, every one."

Paula went on, as though Seth and I had said not a word. "Mr. Parsigian, each of us may seem to you to be helpless and naive. Perhaps we are, considered singly. But a person who seeks to harm any one of us—including our father—will face not just one of the Baxter family. He will have to defend himself against our combined resources. I hope I make myself clear."

Seth again said, "Son of a bitch." This time it was addressed to nobody. His eyes went once more along the line. "Son of a bitch."

"Actually, that's not much of an answer, Seth," I said.

"Never intended as one." His eyes were alight. He was looking not at me but at the serried rank of my darlings, and I believe that in his own way he was enjoying himself. "Young ladies, permit me to assure you of just one thing, and I will leave it at that." His manner, for Seth, became curiously formal. "I do harm only to those who seek to harm me. Dr. Oliver Guest, or if you prefer it, Mr. Kevin Baxter, will never be troubled by the authorities because of any information revealed to them by me, unless he first seeks to do me injury. I rely upon all of you to make sure that the latter event does not occur. Is that good enough to satisfy?"

He turned his head toward me, but he was watching them from the corner of his eye. "Not only that, with you ladies backing him I wouldn't dare try anythin'. Me an' him have needed each other real bad in the past. The way the world goes, chances are we'll need each other again."

"Girls," I said, "it is time for my guest and me to enjoy a drink in peace. So if you would not mind . . ."

My darlings all looked to Paula, who after a moment's hesitation nodded. They began to troop out.

"Manners!" I called. They halted and chorused, "Nice to meet you, Mr. Parsigian."

"Nice to meet you too, ladies." Seth watched almost all of them leave before he turned back to the low table. He picked up the decanter and did not see Victoria stick her tongue out at him. I would reprimand her later for that unconscionable rudeness.

Seth poured, as usual disdaining water, and hovered the decanter over a second glass. He raised an eyebrow at me.

"I think so," I said. "It is not yet nine o'clock in the morning, but this surely must count as a special occasion."

"One in a lifetime—let's hope." Seth poured again and handed me the glass. "Don't know quite when we'll next meet. But I bet we do. The world is gettin' stranger all the time. *When shall we three meet again, in thunder, lightning, or in rain?*"

"There's only two of us, and you claim to lack all forms of classical erudition. Don't spoil your image, Seth. This is the second time in ten minutes that you have quoted Shakespeare."

"I'll watch out for that." He raised his glass. "Good luck."

"Good luck. May the wind be always at your back."

We clinked glasses. Seth drained his whiskey in a single gulp. He glanced at the door from which my darlings had departed. "Don't take me wrong, Doc, if I say I think that in a year or two you're gonna *need* luck."

"We all need fortune to smile on us. Another drink?"

"Not for me. If you don't mind, I oughta be going—before the weather turns bad."

I could hear the gale, trumpeting like a herd of elephants around the chimneys and false gables of the castle roof. Hail lashed at the shutters. I said gravely, "It would perhaps be wise to do so."

Seth donned his boots and outer garments and I walked him to the door. In the shadow of the main entrance we stood together for a few moments without speaking. Then he nodded and headed south. The wind was not at his back. It was in his face. He bent low against a howling storm that ripped at his clothes. I watched, foolishly, until the pelting sleet had soaked me.

When I went back inside, Paula was anxiously waiting. She said, "Did we do wrong?"

"You did wonderfully. Every one of you." I put my arm around her, wetting her blouse. "But I have a question."

"What?" She sounded worried.

"Do you have any more surprises in store for me?"

She smiled, and in that mobile mouth I saw far across the years to the dimpled face of Paula Searle, holding in triumph her treasured alley-taw blood-orange marble. "We wouldn't do anything like that, Father," she said. "We're too fond of you."

I nodded and returned to my study. Tomorrow the girls would again be their usual selves, squabbling, conniving, demanding; impetuous, imperious, and inconsistent. Today, however, I refused to see them as anything less than perfect.

Although Seth was not there to provide justification, I poured myself another drink.

God knows, I did not deserve it. But, obscurely, I felt that I and my darlings and perhaps the whole world had earned it.

## About the Author

Charles Sheffield's most recent works are the novels *Tomorrow and Tomorrow, Aftermath,* and *The Cyborg from Earth,* the story collection *The Complete McAndrew,* and the nonfiction volume *The Borderlands of Science.* He is a winner of the Nebula, Hugo, and John W. Campbell Memorial Awards.